THE SAGA OF THE ARIAX
The complete saga

Part One

1: BIRDS IN ARCENDAK — Section **1**

2: IN THE GRIP OF FROST — Section **191**

3: RAID ON IRO — Section **361**

4: DEATH FROM THE PAST — Section **561**

Part Two

5: ICE IN THE TOMBS — Section **1**

6: EGRATAR FALLS — Section **221**

7: SURVIVAL OF THE ARIAX — Section **431**

THE SAGA OF THE ARIAX

1: BIRDS IN ARCENDAK
2: IN THE GRIP OF FROST
3: RAID ON IRO
4: DEATH FROM THE PAST
5: ICE IN THE TOMBS
6: EGRATAR FALLS
7: SURVIVAL OF THE ARIAX

The Saga of the Ariax © August 2007

Birds in Arcendak © February / March 2008
In the Grip of Frost © April / May 2008
Raid on Iro © July / August 2008
Death From the Past © August / September 2008
Ice in the Tombs © October / November 2008
Egratar Falls © February / March 2009
Survival of the Ariax © July / August 2009

This edition © July 2017

Typeset in Arial 10
Cover and illustrations by the author

Any similarities to any persons living or dead…means you're probably fictional. Although I did know a chap called The Vzler once.

All rights reserved. No part of this publication may be reproduced, stored in a retrieval system, or transmitted in any form or by any means, electronic, mechanical, photocopy, recording or otherwise, without prior permission of Kevin Downing. Nor can it be circulated in any form of binding or cover other than that in which it is published and without similar condition including this condition being imposed on a subsequent purchaser.

Author's note

This edition collects together all seven books in The Saga of the Ariax in one volume for the very first time. The numbering begins again from book 5 as the books were originally separated into two volumes.

Rules of the game

The Saga of the Ariax is a little different to ordinary books: YOU are the main character! You should begin reading each book at the section indicated in the contents, but rather than read every section in order, you will be given choices to make and told where to turn to and read on from. If the worst happens and the adventure ends in failure you will need to start again from the beginning and learn from your mistakes!

At some points in the story, an event could be down to chance, in which case you will be instructed to roll an ordinary six sided die to see what happens.

Some situations require an immediate decision. The text will say *react on instinct* and this means that you should choose where to turn to next very quickly as in reality you would not have time to ponder the options!

You may be given codewords (in capital letters) to note down. These secretly keep track of some of the things that have happened and you may be asked if you have a particular codeword later on. All instructions for these are given in the text. Sometimes codewords are good; sometimes less so. Also be sure to keep an accurate list of any objects you find along the way and decide to take with you. No codewords, objects or any other bonuses or penalties *ever* carry over from one book to another (except feats; see below).

You may try an adventure several times and find death seemingly lurking at every turn! But there is one true way through each book, and the right choices mean facing little risk to succeed. Persevere, discover (and stay away from) the many danger areas and search for the clues you need to eventually meet your goal!

Quick start

To fully immerse yourself in the Saga of the Ariax, you should read the background and recent events sections below. But if you just want to get on with the game as soon as possible, read this quick summary instead.

In this story you are Xanarel, one of a tribe of birdmen called the Ariax from the land of Arian. You are twenty years old and therefore just about to undertake your coming of age trial: to find a herb called Orphus Latix in the Forest of Arcendak. You are led to the forest along with your friends Rical, Darfak and Snyblo by an elder Ariax called the Vzler.

Now turn to **1** to begin…

Optional rule: Feats

In The Saga if the Ariax, whenever you roll the die, it is generally desirable to roll as high as possible. Your character, Xanarel, is destined for great things. Therefore **once** in each book, if you roll low, you can regard this as one of Xanarel's exceptional feats and instead turn to the section indicated as if you had rolled a 6. Any modifiers the text gives you (such as to add or subtract 1) are then applied. You should decide to use a feat *before* turning the page! The exception is if you are asked to roll for an odd or even number, this is a random roll and you may not use a feat.

Unused feats may be carried over to subsequent books.

Background

There's nothing better than the feel of the fresh mountain air on your face as you swoop down to land at the cave entrance to your home. For you are not human; your name is Xanarel, one of the legendary birdmen (known as the Ariax) from the secluded, snow-covered land of Arian in northern Faltak.

Like all Ariax you are humanoid; tall and powerfully built with great feathered wings extending along your arms and protruding from your elbows. You have sharp eyesight and can see clearly even in darkness. Ariax have a peculiar life span, in that while you are fully grown and just coming of age at twenty years old, one hundred and fifty years is a common age to live to.

Throughout your young life, you have been taught the ways of the Ariax. You can fly as easily as walk and know how to survive and hunt in the wild mountainous region in which you live. You are a dangerous fighter on the ground or in the air with your sharp talons and beak. But your race prides itself on a collective and individual sense of justice and honour, even towards your enemies. It is almost unheard of for Ariax to come to blows with each other.

Your tribe (of around three hundred Ariax) make their homes in caves cut high into three steep mountain faces that can only be reached by flight. The land of Arian is a vast mountainous region dotted with arctic forests. There are legends of strange lands of men beyond the mountains but these are of little interest to your race.

For reasons unknown, female Ariax are very rare, maybe one in a hundred. Currently, there are only two living female Ariax. Females are all born flightless, frail and blind, living out a sheltered existence deep within the mountains. Of course they are nonetheless highly revered as the continuing survival of the tribe depends on their egg production!

The head of the tribe is called the Talotrix. He dwells in the only structure built outside of the mountains: The Tower of Egratar, which rises majestically from the highest peak like a curved talon reaching skywards. The current Talotrix, Astraphet, has ruled wisely for longer than you have lived.

Once an Ariax becomes a fully-fledged adult member of the tribe, they are expected to follow one of two career paths, known as the flight of the talon or the flight of the feather. The flight of the talon, overseen by an aged birdman known only as the Vzler, involves all physical work such as hunting, reconnaissance and keeping order. The flight of the feather covers duties such as healing, food preparation and looking after the female and fledgling Ariax. In overall charge of the flight of the feather is a senior birdman named Arguttax. Arguttax and the Vzler are second only to Astraphet in importance in the tribe.

The only other intelligent race known to live in Arian are the hated Scarfells, the barbarian men of the mountains. Famed for their power, cruelty and ferocity, Scarfell adults all stand over six feet tall, broader and more muscular than an Ariax. In battle they are fearless, wielding immense battle-axes and wearing the furs of beasts they have personally killed over their armour. The Scarfells live in the vast mountain city of Musk (many miles to the west) and have a long standing enmity with the Ariax, having arrived in these mountains hundreds of years ago and claimed them as their own. The Scarfells are unable to attack your home as they cannot fly; your tribe in turn dare not assault the impregnable fortress that is Musk. Therefore the two races co-exist in Arian, each wishing rid of the other but unable to do anything about it.

THE SAGA OF THE ARIAX: 1
BIRDS IN ARCENDAK

Recent events

You walk apprehensively down a tunnel underneath the Tower of Egratar, the morning sun behind you becoming more and more distant with every step. You are following your three closest friends Rical, Snyblo and Darfak, each also twenty years old, on your way to the annual 'coming of age' trial known as the Fygrinnd.

The Fygrinnd is shrouded in mystery. You know that all male Ariax take this test when they reach twenty years of age and all are sworn to secrecy. You will be given a dangerous task and must not return home without fulfilling it. If you did, you would be made an outcast and expelled from the tribe!

Of course you've speculated at length as to what it may involve but now at last you are about to learn the truth and face the challenge yourself. As you walk, you flex your wings nervously, remembering that there have been many who have not returned…

The four of you are following the Vzler, one of the most senior Ariax. Although old and grey-feathered he carries immense presence and authority. His calm, dignified manner masks a sharp intellect and undoubted power. You see an ugly scar across his back where no feathers grow and wonder how he got it.

The Vzler soon reaches a large cavern containing a low ring of benches carved out of rock. It is a place you have heard about but never been to: the Iriox Ring, one of the meeting places of the elder Ariax. You are motioned to sit down and share an excited sideways glance with Rical.

"Later today," explains the Vzler, "you will come with me to the Forest of Arcendak in the mountains. It is an inhospitable region, and so dense with trees that flying is often impossible. You will enter alone. Your task is to find and bring back a certain plant that grows only in the Forest of Arcendak." He takes a clump of dark green leaves from a wooden box on the floor behind him as he speaks. "This is Orphus Latix," he explains, "All you need to do to pass the Fygrinnd and enter the ranks of the adult Ariax is return to the Tower of Egratar with a handful. Do *not* return empty taloned."

You furrow your brow. Sounds straightforward enough! You take the opportunity to study the plant in front of you, as do the others. Snyblo mutters under his breath that this will be a breeze, a comment the Vzler either does not hear or chooses to ignore!

"Be wary, young ones," warns the Vzler. "Arcendak is no safe place. Many strange and dangerous things call it home. As you know, not all return from the Fygrinnd. Make for the centre of the forest as quickly as possible. This is where you will find the Orphus Latix."

You look at each of your friends nervously. You get the funny feeling that this will be far more of a challenge than it first seems…

Now turn to **1** to begin…

1

You fly for an hour and a half or so due west, following the Vzler once more. As you learnt before leaving, the Forest of Arcendak lies not far from the Scarfell city of Musk. The mountainous landscape sweeps beneath you like a vast white sheet, in stark contrast with the deep blue sky. The noonday sun beats down, casting only the smallest of shadows.

You are each to be dropped off at different locations around the edge of the forest to prevent you from working together. You take your bearings and memorise a few landmarks on the way so that you can find your way back to the Tower of Egratar.

Snyblo is first to go in and you bid him a solemn farewell. Then you are following the line of trees south and westwards until the Vzler lands before a large blackened fir tree.

"Xanarel, this is your entrance to the forest," he says and indicates a narrow path with his outstretched hand. "Good luck."

With a nervous smile, you nod to Rical and Darfak and enter the Forest of Arcendak heading due north.

The gloom descends on you immediately. The arctic pines are close about you and you are forced to pick your root and branch strewn paths carefully. This feels even more enclosed than being underground in the mountains! The air is musty and heavy and although there is an eerie silence most of the time, it is occasionally broken by far off animal sounds, many of which you do not even recognise!

Then, after ten minutes or so of getting used to the unpleasant atmosphere, you hear a noise much nearer. The roaring sound of more than one animal - maybe a wolf or a bear you think – is to your left, not far away from the path. If you want to investigate this commotion, turn to **110**. To ignore it and hurry on, turn to **50**.

2

You flap your wings powerfully but the plant attempts to constrict even more fiercely. Roll the die. If you roll 4 or less, turn to **99**. If you roll 5 or 6, turn to **45**.

3

Whatever you try to pacify the dwarf seems hopeless. He can understand nothing that you say and even as you back away with arms outstretched in peace he advances with his axe raised. You decide that you are going to have to fight your way out and curse your decision to be inquisitive in the first place! If you want to run at him and try to barge him out of the way, turn to **82**. To stand and strike with your talons, turn to **131**.

4

You arrive at the standing stone which stretches high into the air above you. You stand atop the mound enjoying the strong shafts of midday sunlight that stab down through the forest canopy. Sadly, the gap above you is not wide enough to fly through, but it is a glimpse of the sky nonetheless.

You can make neither head nor tail of the carved writing on the stone and soon give up trying. Although three well-worn paths lead down the slopes of the hill, you take your bearings from the sun and decide to take the northward trail towards the centre of Arcendak.

You plunge back into the thick forest. The ground is hard and cracked underfoot and the path winds this way and that before terminating at a larger, east-west path. Will you go west, which seems the easier, downhill direction? (Turn to **39**) Or will you go steeply uphill and to the east? (Turn to **149**)

5

You fly as high as you can but that which you feared the most happens. You glance down and watch in horror as the hideous arms surge upwards towards you and grab you with brutal strength. You cannot break free and are pulled into the murky depths, from which you are never seen or heard of again...

6

Quickly you back off and stare in disbelief at the horror before you. It is easily the most repulsive sight you have ever witnessed!

The creature is shaped like a massive, bloated toad, easily double your height and at least that wide! Its black, warty skin glistens with some sort of slime that drips disgustingly down its flanks. And the smell! You see Erim retch beside you and Vashta hold his cloak up to his nose. The toad-thing's red eyes regard you all malevolently as it slowly advances, gripping the rocky ground with cracked yellow claws.

Vashta is first to take action. He holds up his staff and begins muttering the words of a spell. You do not know whether the toad is intelligent or reacting instinctively, but it looms over the wizard and deals him a sickening blow. Vashta slumps to the ground, unmoving!

Erim pulls out his spear to defend himself, crying out in a trembling voice as Vashta is dispatched. His shout recalls you to your senses and you must act! Will you stand shoulder to shoulder with Erim and face the beast head on? (Turn to **134**) You could signal for Erim to make his way to one side of it while you go the other, resulting in a split but two pronged attack? (Turn to **55**) Or will you fly up to the lower branches of the trees and try to make your way round to the rear of the creature? (Turn to **128**)

7

Respectfully, you pick your path carefully through the glade, leaving its unexpected tranquillity undisturbed. Turn to **149**.

8

You grab and throw on instinct and a strange creature indeed you have been attacked by! It is humanoid but only waist height to you. Its brown-skinned body is covered in hair or fur, encrusted with frost. It has devious, beady eyes and looks at you with hostility, seemingly unafraid of you despite your size.

He is not alone: a small spear flies at you but you see it coming and avoid it easily. Will you flee back the way you came? (Turn to **75**) Or drive through the few of the creatures who bar the way onwards and try to escape that way? (Turn to **93**)

9

You stumble along the trail. Note down the codeword ROOT. You see another clearing ahead of you and you are half way across it when you hear a soft breathing sound. Turning, you see the sleeping form of a huge frost bear, nestled in between the roots of a tree! You decide not to hang around! But would it be best to creep forwards slowly and carefully (turn to **47**) or run for it? (Turn to **144**)

10

Bravely you leap forwards, but pitched against an enraged, adult frost bear, there is little hope. You manage a few good blows but soon succumb to the power and savagery of your adversary. No Ariax has ever gone toe to toe with an adult frost bear in mortal combat and lived and you are not destined to be the first…

11

You slide back the clasp on the box and open it cautiously. Inside you see a few leaves belonging to some sort of plant. But it is not Orphus Latix! This plant is lighter in colour and has leaves with a jagged edge.

Erim looks over your shoulder eagerly and is keen to taste the leaf despite the fact that Vashta does not recognize it ("Even with my herb knowledge!" he informs you) and advises you to throw it away. If you want to take a bite yourself first, turn to **108**. If you'd rather follow Vashta's advice and throw it into the undergrowth, turn to **73**.

12

Working with real urgency and trying not to breathe (as somehow the smell is even worse close up) you brace yourself and put a huge effort into moving the logs. They begin to shift…but the exertion becomes too much and you let them go again. You feel the huge toad-thing begin to turn to investigate what you are doing. If you want to persevere and try again, in spite of the danger, turn to **146**. If you'd rather slash out at the back of the thing while it is still unprotected, turn to **187**. To dodge to the side and rejoin Erim, turn to **125**.

13

Not willing to risk your life any further at this stage, you cut a hurried dash out of the clearing and back onto the original path. Turn to **50**.

14

Deciding nothing is to be gained by dying at this stage, you flee back down the path. If you have the codeword LOG, turn to **177**. If you do not have this codeword, turn to **69**.

15

Pulling back the drape and ducking your head, you enter what appears to be a storeroom of some kind. Crude shelves have been hacked out of the rock wall and these are crammed with jars, bottles and root-vegetables. A few joints of meat hang from hooks on the opposite wall. If you decide to help yourself to some of this food, turn to **119**. If you've seen enough and want to leave the cave, turn to **178**. If, before you do, you'd like to explore that high up tunnel (if you haven't already), turn to **58**.

16

You just have time to act. *React on instinct*. Will you flee back the way you came? (Turn to **75**) Or drive through the few of the creatures who bar the way onwards and try to escape that way? (Turn to **93**)

17

You don't stay to wonder about the eerie log circle any more and discover that the path leading onwards is climbing higher and higher, almost in steps. If you have either the codeword SILVER or FUR, turn to **189**. Otherwise, turn to **109**.

18

You launch yourself savagely forwards and cut down the leading wolf with three swift strikes. Erim accounts for another with his spear and Vashta weaves more magic with his staff. But the sheer weight of numbers begins to tell as more wolves join the fray. Vashta falls beneath a flurry of teeth and claws and you soon follow, torn to shreds on the rocky forest floor…

19

You have not really had room to even flex your wings in your journey so far and this is trickier than it looks. Roll the die. If you roll a 4 or more, you manage it safely (turn to **38**). If you roll 3 or less however, turn to **123**.

20

Suddenly, in the blackness of the hole, you see something moving: moving towards you, fast! *React on instinct*. If you move away immediately, turn to **111**. If you stay hovering where you are to look, turn to **182**.

21

Fortune favours the dwarf defending his home: he brings up his axe which slices deep into your side. You reel back in agony against the cave wall. Off balance and off guard, you do not even see the death blow coming.

22

The blows rain in; the dead bodies of at least four spiders thud to the ground around you. The rest fall back before your ferocious attack, scuttling back to the shadow and safety of the trees. You wipe your bloodstained talons on a tuft of frozen grass before continuing in a northwards direction. Turn to **71**

23

Your mighty leg muscles push through the mire. To your dismay, you realize that this is just making things worse; you are rapidly sinking! Your wings are thick with mud and there is still a way to go to safety. You desperately try to keep calm in the face of death but the Arcendak swamp has you up to the neck and slowly but surely claims another victim…

24

The poison seeps through your pores and rapidly enters your nervous system. Within seconds you are sprawling in agony on the ground with your vision blurring and your insides on fire. Fortunately you black out and death comes swiftly…

25

A moment later, something else catches your attention from the opposite side, from the trees! Another snake darts towards you and you desperately try to fend off its attack. Roll the die. If you roll a 3 or more it surges past you on to the path, turn to **80**. If you roll a 1 or 2 however, turn to **129**.

26

It is easy going on this downhill track. The ground here is loose and stony and the trees slightly thinner. Then up ahead you see something unusual blocking the path.

A barrier of maybe thirty thin logs has been constructed by thrusting them across between the trees and wedging them in the branches on either side. There is a crudely-daubed wooden sign nailed to the front, though it is in a language unfamiliar to you. Keep out, perhaps? You could easily pull the logs away and proceed (turn to **112**). You could climb over them but leave the barrier intact (turn to **136**). Or you could leave the area well alone and turn back (turn to **63**).

27

What was in that sack? You leap over the intervening bushes and find that you can just about forge a path through the undergrowth well enough to keep the owl in sight. He swoops between branches and boughs with incredible agility and you are so intent on avoiding injury yourself that you do not notice that you have stumbled into a clearing inhabited by two frost bears until it is too late! One is sleeping behind you...but the other is very much awake and barring your way! If you have the codeword BEAR, turn to **113**. If you do not have this codeword, turn to **10**.

28

You plunge into a steep dive, but the rooks match this and bank to meet you! Roll the die. If you roll a 1, 2 or 3, turn to **155**. If you roll 4 or more, turn to **77**.

29

Grasping the initiative, you use your speed and skill to outmanoeuvre the mole-like beast. You soon have the upper hand, using the creature's bulk against it. Suffering from many wounds, it roars in pain and decides to retreat and live to fight again another day. You let it go, guessing that it was only defending its home from what it thought was a dangerous intruder.

You continue on and discover that the path leading onwards is climbing higher and higher, almost in steps. Turn to **109**.

30

The bottle slaps into the rubbery folds of skin around the toad-thing's mouth and bounces onto the ground. In its next step the beast squashes it into the mud and it is lost to view. What will you do now? Will you attack a nearby leg? (Turn to **61**) Or swoop up and attack it from the air? (Turn to **164**)

31

It is not a pretty sight; the wolves make short work of the bears. They begin to feast, but a fearsome roar from behind them makes them stop and they turn to behold the enraged form of a fully-grown frost bear charging headlong through the undergrowth to the attack!

You can only admire the speed, ferocity and sheer power of the creature as it engages the murderous wolves and begins to tear into them! If you want to wait and see what happens next, turn to **92**. If you'd rather get away immediately, turn to **13**.

32

You have not gone much further through another very dense part of Arcendak when you come under attack from the forest itself! Thick vine-like branches are wrapping themselves around your leg and waist in a hostile manner! How will you rid yourself of this new menace? *React on instinct*. Will you:

    Slash at them with your talons?   Turn to **160**
    Try to go airborne and break free?   Turn to **2**
    Or try to pull them off gently?   Turn to **105**

33

You carry on following the course of the rock face. Soon it is enveloped by the forest once more and the oppressive gloom returns.

You suddenly get the strangest feeling of being watched. Will you hurry onwards quickly? (Turn to **167**) Or stop and look around to see if there is anything there? (Turn to **137**)

34

It feels good to be able to stretch your wings and take to the air properly once more! Note down the codeword BEAK and turn to **168**.

35

All seems hopeless. Who in all of Arian could you expect to hear you? But moments later, miraculously, two figures emerge from the undergrowth, chattering to each other in an unfamiliar language, and one throws a rope out to you!

Your two rescuers are strange looking indeed! They are a head shorter than you and are wearing travelling clothes and cloaks, but they have no beak, wings or talons! You guess they must be humans; men from the far off southern lands that you have heard about. They cannot be Scarfells - they are far too feeble looking for that!

The man who holds the rope looks the younger of the two and has a backpack and spear strapped to his back. He calls to the older, bearded man in crumpled purple robes, who comes across to help. Gradually you are pulled free of the bog.

As you lie recovering on solid ground once more, the bearded man picks up the staff he had dropped to help you and begins muttering, apparently to you, in more words you cannot understand. Meanwhile, his companion coils up the rope and stores it in his pack.

"Well feathered one, it is fortunate indeed that *we* happened to be passing!" exclaims the bearded man and you are relieved to hear him talking in your own language! "And am I right to think that you are one of the legendary birdmen of The Great Northern Wastes?"

You sit up and confirm that this seems indeed to be the case, though you would call yourself Xanarel, one of the Ariax from the land of Arian. You ask in turn who they are.

"My name is Vashta and this is my servant Erim," replies the bearded man, leaning now on his staff. "We have travelled hundreds of miles from the city of Iro in the distant south-east, following the line of the Rune Mountains north and facing hardship and danger in good measure along the way!"

"My master is a powerful wizard and he discovered ancient scrolls that told of..." begins Erim, but Vashta chuckles and cuts him off with a wave of his hand.

"Now, now, never mind boring this poor fellow with that!" he says and holds out a hand to pull you to your feet. If you are carrying a small green bottle, turn to **121**. If not, Vashta continues: "We go this way!" and indicates the northward route that you yourself must take. He seems to be offering for you to share the journey with them. If you would like to travel with these men, turn to **150**. If you'd rather let them go on ahead and follow after, turn to **186**.

36

Always ready to meet a challenge head on, you grip the earth with your taloned feet and stand ready. But the horror bearing down on you is easily the most repulsive sight you have ever witnessed!

The creature is shaped like a massive, bloated toad, easily double your height and at least as wide! Its black, warty skin glistens with some sort of slime that drips disgustingly down its flanks. And the smell! You stare straight into the toad-thing's malevolent red eyes as its vast bulk bears down upon you, squeezing the air from your lungs. Your slashing talons appear to be having little effect and despite their valiant efforts, this time there is nothing Vashta and Erim can do to save you...

37

A plan's a plan you decide and in goes a second rock. This time, you get your result. With a roar from somewhere beneath the surface, the arms appear, flailing angrily at thin air and spraying the disgusting pool-water all around. Finding nothing, they eventually slide back beneath the filthy surface and you pick this moment to make your flight across. Roll the die. If you roll a 1, turn to **5**. If you roll a 2 or more, turn to **66**.

38

Gladly leaving the webs behind, you notice the path beginning to slope uphill again. You soon come to another path leading away from the main one. This path heads generally eastwards, where you can see that it meets a cliff face stretching upwards on the left hand side as it follows it round. To go this way, turn to **94**. To continue northwards on the main path, turn to **147**.

39

You soon come into a particularly thick patch of trees. After a short battle through the branches (which seem determined to bar your way) you come unexpectedly to a great cliff face stretching up in front of you. The sky is still almost completely blocked out by the imposing overhanging trees at the top, as you have become accustomed to.

You are able to fly up it easily enough but about halfway up you notice a series of roughly circular holes punched into the cliff face, each about the same width as your forearm. Mysteriously, wooden logs have been hammered in to each hole. If you want to try to pull out one of the logs and investigate, turn to **81**. If you'd rather leave them alone and rejoin the path at the summit, turn to **142**.

40

You stoop and carefully pick up the bag. As soon as it sees it, the owl takes off and swoops towards you, claws extended! You duck out of the way but catch your foot on a tree root and fall backwards! The owl screeches angrily and snatches the bag from your hand, then glides away and disappears into the trees. If you want to chase after the owl, turn to **27**. If you want to ignore it and continue on your journey, turn to **167**.

41

You wheel and bank through the air, enjoying the momentary feeling of freedom before reminding yourself of your quest and re-entering the forest.

You are not far down the new path when you feel something on your wings. Looking about, you see a multitude of sticky webs being thrown down from above and further up you can see a host of giant spiders, each the size of your head! If you have the codeword SILVER, turn to **126**. Otherwise, how will you free yourself from this assault? Will you:

Slash at the webs with your talons?	Turn to **173**
Try to fly at the spiders and attack them?	Turn to **107**
Or grab the webs and try to pull the spiders down from their position in the trees above?	Turn to **95**

42

Vashta seems pleased to have his potion back. Roll the die; if you roll an even number, turn to **133**. Otherwise, Vashta says: "We go this way!" and indicates the northward route that you yourself must take. He seems to be offering for you to share the journey with them. If you would like to travel with these men, turn to **150**. If you'd rather let them go on ahead and follow after, turn to **186**.

43

Luckily it flaps just wide of you, giving you a chance to act. You decide that a frontal attack is too dangerous. Instead, will you signal for Erim to make his way to one side of the toad-thing while you go the other? (Turn to **55**) Or will you fly up into the lower branches of the trees and make your way round to the rear of the creature? (Turn to **128**)

44

You feel a sudden stabbing pain in your foot and look down in horror to see that you have trodden on a wooden stake, hidden in the undergrowth. The stake has been coated with a deadly poison, prepared from flowers being grown in a second glade not far away. Minutes later a slow paralysis begins to creep up your leg. It spreads throughout your entire body until all you can do is slump down against a tree and wait for death to take you...

45

It's working! Within a minute you are completely plant free and hurry away from the area, shaking your head in disbelief. The Vzler wasn't lying when he called Arcendak an inhospitable region!

You proceed warily in case there are more plants like that. Soon you come to another fork in the path. If you have the codeword ROOT, turn to **51**. Otherwise you can see nothing much to help you make up your mind; both paths look the same to you. Will you go left? (Turn to **101**) Or right? (Turn to **71**)

46

It feels good to be able to stretch your wings properly for the first time since entering this claustrophobic forest! You follow the ravine westwards and soon see a rickety looking bridge spanning the gap above you. You fly up to check it out and find a forest path leading north. If you want to try this path, turn to **41**. If you'd like to fly for a bit longer and carry on west, turn to **168**.

47

You hold your breath and keep one eye on the sleeping predator. Then you see another frost bear coming towards you, blocking the path you planned to take! *React on instinct.* Will you run away, past the first (still sleeping) bear? (Turn to **132**) Or attack this second bear, hoping to force your way past? (Turn to **10**)

48

You scoop up a blob of the slime and hold it to your beak. It does not smell particularly bad. Unfortunately though, this is the drool of a particularly unpleasant and highly poisonous creature. The poison seeps through your pores and rapidly enters your nervous system. Within seconds you are sprawling in agony on the ground, your vision blurring and your insides on fire. Fortunately you black out and death follows swiftly…

49

You pull out Erim's spear and thrust it back into the dying monster with all your might. Bile and slime sprays out from the wound, landing in thick splodges over your legs. Unfortunately, it is the same substance that coated its tongue and made it so deadly! If you have the codeword BITE, turn to **170**. If not, turn to **24**.

50

The path takes you deeper into Arcendak. Despite it being an arctic forest, the temperature is warmer than you are used to as you are sheltered from the chill winds of Arian. You round a corner and find the path abruptly ends in a fork. Neither pathway looks particularly inviting!

Then you notice something: has that branch been carved to look like a finger pointing to the right-hand path, or is it just a strange natural occurrence? If you want to follow the finger and go on the uphill path to the right, turn to **98**. If you'd rather take the left-hand path, which slopes more downhill, turn to **26**.

51

As you are considering your decision, you notice a clump of white fur caught on a branch a little way down the left hand path. You take a closer look and recognise it as frost bear fur! A bit further on you discover claw marks in the earth too. Deciding that you'd rather not run into another of these beasts, you take the right hand path instead. Turn to **71**.

52

The dwarf proves to be no match for you in single combat! You take a couple of minor injuries but eventually deal him a blow that sends him reeling backwards against the wall. Before he can recover, you take the chance to rush for the entrance of the cave. You catch your breath a little farther down the path and are relieved to find that the dwarf has not followed. Turn to **33**.

53

It feels good to be able to stretch your wings and take to the air properly once more! You swoop and glide, enjoying the freedom of the ravine. Eventually the rocky walls converge into an impassable wall. Up above, you find thick forest once more but also a pathway leading from the cliff edge. North is the direction you want to go, so you follow it, back in Arcendak's clutches once more. Turn to **138**.

54

The undergrowth is thick and unyielding here, but you may be able to beat a path through. Roll the die. If you roll an odd number, turn to **156**. If you roll an even number, turn to **115**.

55

Erim gets your idea immediately and makes his way to the creature's far side. You edge round carefully, wary of the toad-thing's immense bulk and power. It notices what is happening and unfortunately for you whips out its huge, slimy tongue in your direction! Roll the die. If you roll a 3 or less, turn to **140**. If you roll a 4 or more, turn to **67**.

56

You stoop and pluck one of the flowers from the ground. Holding it to your nostrils, you enjoy a sweet smelling aroma. Roll the die. If you roll a 1 or 2, turn to **104**. If you roll a 3 or more nothing else happens and eventually you press on, turn to **149**.

57

Deciding nothing is to be gained by dying at this stage, you flee back down the path. As you do, a well aimed spear lodges itself painfully in the small of your back! You manage to keep on your feet and continue running, but the injury will hamper your movement until it heals. For the rest of the adventure you must subtract 1 from every die roll you make (unless the text asks whether you have rolled an odd or even number).

If you have the codeword LOG, turn to **177**. If you do not have this codeword, turn to **69**.

58

You clamber up the rock and peer in. The tunnel goes back a surprisingly long way and is nearly high enough for you to stand up in. If you'd like to follow this tunnel, turn to **143**. If you've seen enough and want to leave the cave, turn to **178**. If, before you do, you'd like to explore behind the fur drape (if you haven't already), turn to **15**.

59

Your raking talons buy the lives of several of the surprised spiders, but more scuttle to the attack. They begin to drop onto you from above and you feel a sharp stabbing pain on your back: one has sunk its fangs into you! A shooting pain runs immediately down your right hand side and you drop to your knees. The spiders of Arcendak are highly venomous and you black out. The spiders see to it that you never recover consciousness…

60

You are sinking fast and try desperately to beat your powerful, but now mud-encrusted wings. This proves futile; it merely saps your strength even more. You desperately try to keep calm in the face of death, but the Arcendak swamp claims another victim…

61

The flabby, sticky hind leg is an easier (if no less horrible) option for attack. The beast roars a hideous, burping, gurgling roar of pain, and kicks out with surprising speed and force. It takes you completely by surprise and your body slams into the tree behind. You are stunned momentarily and the toad-thing's attention is unfortunately focused on you now. Erim drives his spear into its side in an attempt to distract it, but it is too late to save you from the full force of the beast's jaws…

62

This proves an astute decision. Something catches your attention from the trees and another snake darts towards you! You are easily able to avoid it though and it slides into one of the holes on the ground, presumably after its natural prey. You hurry onwards, glad to leave the snakes' territory to them! Turn to **80**.

63

You have not yet reached the fork with the finger-pointing branch when you notice a smaller path leading off to the east. You did not notice it on the way as it is overhung with branches. If you'd like to try this way, turn to **147**. To continue to the fork and follow the finger this time, turn to **98**.

64

You feel a breeze up ahead and rush towards it, sensing more pleasant air. Your beak drops open in amazement at what you find.

You stand on the brink of a huge chasm, a great tear in the ground. It stretches as far as the eye can see to your left, but ends in an impassable wall of rock in the distance to your right. Looking up, you see that the trees grow so tall and bent in this place that they still blot out the rays of the sun almost entirely! Hundreds of feet below you runs a dark, gloomy river. Your keen eyesight picks up the forest path again on the far side of the chasm.

Flying across won't be a problem. If you want to do this, turn to **138**. However, it occurs to you that you could fly westwards instead inside the chasm itself. If you want to do this, turn to **46**.

65

You find yourself surrounded by two snarling, bloodthirsty frost bears! If you want to take the fight to them, turn to **10**. If you'd rather leap into the trees and somehow avoid them (even though they are nearly as tall as the lower branches), turn to **179**.

66

To your relief, the arms do not appear again. You touch down on the other side and stride on determinedly without looking back. Turn to **102**.

67

Fortunately you just manage to keep out of the way of the tongue. If you have the codeword DROP, turn to **181**. If you do not have this codeword, you decide to take to work your way around to the rear of the beast. Turn to **128**.

68

Choosing a suitable bough, you are soon making short work of the fragile webs. As you do, many of the silky strands become streaked in your feathers, creating a shimmering effect. You brush at them to get the majority off. Record the codeword SILVER and turn to **38**.

69

As you approach the log barricade, you suddenly realise that this resembles a dead end. You scramble up as fast as you can but this is enough of a delay for the little creatures to catch you up. You are bombarded with thrown weapons and as you reach the very top of the logs they begin to swarm over you from all sides. You can do nothing against their weight of numbers and you fall, brought down by many blows.

70

With stunning speed, you take the dwarf completely by surprise. He is knocked from his feet and tumbles to the cave floor. You hurdle over his body and are out of the cave before he can swing his axe in anger! You take off down the northward path you had been following before. Turn to **33**.

71

By now, you must be deep within the forest. The place gets no less uncomfortable with time and once more you wonder if you're even close to finding the Orphus Latix glade and beginning the journey out again!

Up ahead, you see a large, greyish pool, extending into the gloom under the trees in both directions. Your path leads right into it and out the other side. Above the pool, the trees give you just enough clearance to be able to fly over. This is good news: it smells far too foul to even consider wading!

You watch a bat flapping lazily across from tree to tree. Suddenly, the eerie silence is rudely disturbed as two huge, warty brown arms surge upwards out of the water, swipe through the air and grab the unfortunate bat which is pulled screeching to its doom beneath the surface! Then the arms are gone.

The ripples stream smoothly outwards and lap gently at the water's edge before disappearing. It is as if the bat had never even existed.

Now how are you going to get across? If you want to trust that the arms won't return and fly across, keeping as high as you can, turn to **169**. If you want to try to draw the arms to one side of the pool by throwing in a rock, then fly across to the other side, turn to **127**. If you want to turn back and force a path through the undergrowth to avoid crossing the pool, turn to **54**.

72

Sure that you can out-fly a group of mere *birds*, you scramble and surge upwards. The chasm-rooks follow you up, but you are able to beat them to the top and hurry into the forest once more on a northerly path. If you have the codeword BEAK, turn to **138**. If you do not have this codeword, turn to **32**.

73

Vashta leads the way onwards, you follow and Erim brings up the rear. Roll the die. If you roll an odd number, turn to **175**. If you roll an even number, turn to **97**.

74

You pick up a handy branch that looks big enough to trouble the wolves, then you wade in, dealing the first one a heavy clunk to the head and slashing out with your talons at the next. The wolves prepare to counter, but as they do, a terrifying roar sounds from behind you and you turn to see an adult frost bear crashing furiously through the undergrowth in defence of its cubs!

The wolves have seen enough and take off in haste! You'd better act too! *React on instinct*. If you want to flee as quickly as possible, turn to **13**. If you want to back away slowly, turn to **171**. If you want to discourage the bear from attacking you by throwing the branch at it, turn to **135**.

75

Knowing when the odds are stacked against you, you take to your heels and run. Roll the die. If you roll a 1 or 2, turn to **124**. If you roll a 3 or more, turn to **57**.

76

You tell Vashta that it tasted foul to you! "Well it wasn't full when I lost it!" he exclaims, "Let me guess – you found it in the forest river?" You nod.

Vashta seems fascinated by the discovery; Erim looks glum at the prospect of more stale food! Vashta pours a few drops onto a rock in front of an inquisitive lizard. The lizard licks up the drops…and seconds later rolls over onto its back, dead! "Intriguing…but it doesn't seem to have done *you* any harm, Xanarel…" wonders the old man, slipping the bottle into his pocket.

Vashta then indicates the northward route that you yourself must take, saying: "We go this way!" He seems to be offering for you to share the journey with them. If you would like to travel with these men, turn to **150**. If you'd rather let them go on ahead and follow after, turn to **186**.

77

The chasm-rooks prove no match for your aerial skill! You have the pace and leave them trailing in your wake. Chuckling to yourself (though perhaps unaware of the danger you could have been in) you fly up to the lip of the chasm and rejoin the forest path you discover. If you have the codeword BEAK, turn to **138**. If not, turn to **32**.

78

You climb a small hill and arrive in a little clearing with grisly decoration! Six wooden sticks have been driven into the ground, each supporting the rotting skull of a different creature! You recognise some of them as animal skulls, but others are very odd indeed!

You decide to hurry through the clearing before whoever has done this returns! Then you notice a battered wooden box lying on the ground, half covered by a bush. If you want to pick up the box and open it, turn to **184**. If you'd rather leave it and press on, turn to **109**.

79

The path is wide enough to walk three abreast and you do this, weary but still determined. Just minutes later Erim stops. "What was that noise? It sounded like growling…" he says.

You all turn round and discover that he was right. A pack of at least a dozen wolves is stealthily advancing from the undergrowth behind you! You ready yourself for battle, but the wolves, though snarling, do not immediately attack. Instead they circle round, trying to cut off your escape! "They are waiting for reinforcements!" cries Vashta. "As if this wasn't enough! We must make for the top of this crag, it's our only hope!"

If you agree and make for the cliff, turn to **122**. If you think you can fight it out, turn to **18**.

80

The track you are now on cuts straight through the forest. You then come across a smaller path leading off to your left. Peering down it, you see that it leads gently uphill to what looks like a standing stone. If you'd like to go this way, turn to **4**. If you'd rather continue in the direction you were heading, turn to **159**.

81

The log slides out quite easily. You drop it to the ground and peer in. Roll the die. If you roll a 1 or 2, turn to **182**. If you roll a 3 or 4, turn to **20**. If you roll a 5 or 6, turn to **130**.

82

You move with agility that befits your race but the dwarf bars your way in this enclosed space. Roll the die. If you roll a 1 or 2, turn to **21**. If you roll a 3 or more, turn to **70**.

83

You manage to cross the clearing without drawing the attention of the moths. You stand on the far side, brushing the dirt from your knees and wings, then turn your back on them and carry on northwards. Turn to **102**.

84

The leaves taste bitter and you cannot say that you feel any more nourished for having eaten them. A little disappointed, you discard the rest and press on with your quest. Note down the codeword BITE, and turn to **109**.

85

You dive sideways, but feel it thud into you as you fall. The slimy substance now on your body is not only disgusting; it is also highly poisonous! If you have the codeword BITE, turn to **158**. If not, turn to **24**.

86

You are as quick as a flash, and looking down, you see that you have dashed the brains out of a snake which had coiled itself around you. As you wonder if it was venomous, it occurs to you that there could be more. But did it come from above you or from the foliage at ground level? As you continue will you be particularly watchful of attack from the trees? (Turn to **62**) Or from the ground? (Turn to **141**)

87

The cool water is refreshing and it is nice to wash away some of the dirt of your journey so far. Half way across, you accidentally kick a smooth object lying on the river bed, which is lost in a cloud of silt and mud. If you want to reach down and find out what it was, turn to **148**. If you'd rather ignore it, wade the rest of the way and get back into the forest, turn to **32**.

88

Intrigued by this unnerving bird, you turn towards it and address it politely. It turns its head in your direction but does not appear to understand your words. Will you now pick up the bag? (Turn to **40**) Or ignore it and continue on your way? (Turn to **167**)

89

You fail to climb high enough; one of the bears raises itself on its back legs and digs its huge claws into your back! The shock causes you to lose your grip and fall. From a prone position, sprawling before the angry animals, there is no protection. They rapidly tear you to pieces.

90

Erim eagerly takes the box from you and slides back the clasp. Inside you see a few leaves of some sort of plant. But it is not Orphus Latix! This plant is lighter in colour and has leaves with a jagged edge.

Erim impulsively takes a bite out of one of the leaves. He makes a face at the taste and sticks out his tongue. "Well, I'm sure you're happy now?" asks Vashta, who does not recognise the plant, even with his 'extensive herb knowledge'.

Erim holds out the box to you, apparently suffering no ill effects. If you want to try some too, turn to **108**. If you decline, turn to **73**.

91

The stench is painful to bear as you swoop up onto the toad-thing's back. From here you begin to stab with your talons, but although you do indeed seem to be harming the creature, its hide is far tougher than it looks!

In fury, it rears up with a violent kick and you are thrown onto the slimy earth behind it. As you groggily try to rise, its back legs kick out and deal you a stunning blow to the head. You black out, never to regain consciousness…

92

Carnage ensues; the wolves are dispatched rapidly. The frost bear, its white coat bloody from the fight, turns sadly to the bodies of the babies. It picks them up in its teeth and slopes off into the trees. You feel sickened by the scene and hurry away. Turn to **50**

93

You take the little creatures by surprise and bowl several of them over as you push them roughly out of the way. Roll the die. If you roll a 1, turn to **124**. If you roll a 2 or 3, turn to **106**. If you roll a 4 or more, turn to **166**.

94

The path hugs the cliff face and it is strange to walk with a solid rock wall on one side and the menacing foliage still ever present on your right! From the few beams of sunlight that pierce the green canopy overhead you deduce that you are now heading roughly northwards again.

Then you stumble across a cave entrance. It is large enough to accommodate you, though you would need to stoop to enter. You hear nothing from within. If you want to investigate the cave, turn to **154**. If you'd rather continue along the path, turn to **33**.

95

You grab tightly and yank sharply to unbalance the spiders from their position of safety. Unfortunately, they begin to drop onto you and you feel a sharp stabbing pain on your back. One has sunk its fangs into you! A shooting pain runs immediately down your right hand side and you drop to your knees. The spiders of Arcendak are highly venomous and you black out. The spiders see to it that you do not recover consciousness…

96

You some come upon a clearing containing a log circle. But this place oozes the feeling of evil. The tree stump seats are blackened and charred and bones litter the floor. You also notice a thick, black slime trailing across some of the stumps and wonder where it can have come from. If you want to put your finger in the slime and smell it, turn to **48**. If you'd rather hurry out of this dark place, turn to **17**.

97

Without warning, a massive black...*thing* powers out of the bushes to your left. Before he can react, Vashta takes the brunt of the impact and his body is flung to the ground! You stare in disbelief at the horror before you. It is easily the most repulsive sight you have ever witnessed!

The creature is shaped like a massive, bloated toad, easily double your height and at least that wide! Its black, warty skin glistens with some sort of slime that drips disgustingly down its flanks. And the smell! You see Erim retch beside you, but he fights back the tears for his fallen master and draws his spear to defend himself.

His actions recall you to your senses: you must act! Will you stand shoulder to shoulder with Erim and face the beast head on? (Turn to **134**) You could signal for Erim to make his way to one side of it while you go the other, resulting in a split but two pronged attack? (Turn to **55**) Or will you fly up to the lower branches of the trees and try to make your way round to the rear of the creature? (Turn to **128**)

98

This path goes uphill for quite a way before levelling out again. It leads right through a large clearing surrounded by particularly tall fir trees. Stretched horizontally across the clearing at chest height are a mass of tangled webs. They must have been made by a giant spider (or spiders) though you can see no signs of life. How are you going to cross? Will you:

Fly over the webs (there is just enough room to try this)?	Turn to **19**
Crawl underneath them?	Turn to **152**
Or beat a path through them with a branch?	Turn to **68**

99

The plant has amazing strength; you are unable to break its monstrous grip. You continue to struggle, but eventually you tire and collapse. It drags your lifeless body into its lair in the undergrowth...

100

Eurgh! Just a few drops of the repulsive liquid has you on your knees, gladly washing your mouth out with river water! Note down the codeword DROP. When you finally rid yourself of the taste in your mouth, you are ready to continue. Note down the bottle if you choose to take it with you and turn to **32**.

101

You stumble along the trail. You see another clearing ahead of you and are half way across it when you hear a soft breathing sound. Turning, you see behind you the sleeping form of a huge frost bear, nestled in between the roots of a tree! You decide not to hang around, but would it be best to creep forwards slowly and carefully (turn to **47**) or run for it? (Turn to **144**)

102

You stop for a brief rest, hands on hips, and wonder how Rical, Snyblo and Darfak are faring. For a second you imagine that you hear the sound of fighting somewhere off in the distance, but then it is gone, replaced by the familiar quiet, oppressive atmosphere you have become used to.

You march on. Now you come to a narrow trail and have to constantly brush away overhanging branches. It becomes sludgy underfoot. It becomes *very* sludgy underfoot and you decide to turn back. But you can't! You have stumbled into a pool of quicksand and are sinking fast! You must act quickly! Will you:

Try to wade to the far side (you are more than half way across)?	Turn to **23**
Beat your wings and try to pull yourself up and out?	Turn to **139**
Stretch for a branch to pull yourself out with?	Turn to **180**
Or simply screech for help?	Turn to **35**

103

You hurry over to where Vashta fell. Erim is already with him, kneeling beside his master. "He is not dead!" he cries in joy and relief, tending a bloody wound on the old man's head.

You leave Erim to administer aid, knowing nothing of humans yourself! Vashta regains consciousness when Erim trickles a yellow liquid from a flask into his mouth.

"In all my days…" mumbles Vashta, gazing at the oozing form of the slain creature. "I have never seen the like! Yet you two prevailed! This is certainly a deed to be long remembered!" He gets shakily to his feet, leaning on his staff once more as his servant hands it to him.

"It was Xanarel who thought to use the verusaramorr!" says Erim. You in turn play up the brave young warrior's part in the victory, saying that you are glad to have been able to repay the debt you owed them!

You are all eager to continue as soon as possible, if anything simply to get away from the stench of the toad-thing! You decide to journey with the humans for the time being, at least until you have recovered your strength. After a brief rest and some welcome provisions from Erim's pack, the three of you take a northward path once more.

Ten minutes or so later, you come to the bottom of another mighty rock face, with a lip at the top. The path carries on with the cliff to its right, but Vashta observes that it looks like there is a way onwards up at the top. He seems interested to find out. If you want to fly up and lead the way, turn to **122**. If you want to recommend staying on the path, turn to **79**.

104

Very nice! You take another sniff. And another! Then your head starts to swim and coloured spots appear before your eyes! Though refreshing, the flower's scent is in fact mildly toxic. The next time you roll the die, you must subtract 2 from the result. Then the effect will have passed. Turn to **149**.

105

Gingerly you begin to uncurl one of the many tendrils of the plant, but it attempts to constrict even more fiercely! Roll the die. If you roll a 3 or less, turn to **99**. If you roll a 4 or more, turn to **45**.

106

You run like the wind, and suffer many minor injuries as you flee. Then a well-aimed spear lodges itself painfully in the small of your back! You manage to keep on your feet and continue running, but the injury will hamper your movement until it heals. For the rest of the adventure you must subtract 1 from every die roll you make (unless the text asks whether you have rolled an odd or even number).

The creatures do not pursue you any further. You curse them under your breath as you nurse your injuries.

The track you are now on cuts straight through the forest. You then come across a smaller path leading off to your left. Peering down it, you see that it leads gently uphill to what looks like a standing stone on a hill. If you'd like to go this way, turn to **4**. If you'd rather continue in the direction you were heading, turn to **39**.

107

Reckoning that this is not what the spiders expect, you take to the air with fury blazing in your eyes. Roll the die. If you roll a 1 or 2, turn to **59**. If you roll a 3 or more, turn to **22**.

108

The leaves taste bitter and you cannot say that you feel any more nourished for having eaten them! A little disappointed, you drop the box back in the bush and press on with the quest, following Vashta and Erim once more. Note down the codeword BITE, and turn to **73**.

109

You trudge on, thinking to yourself that the forest seems more and more unpleasant the further you go, if that is possible! Then you hear shouting from somewhere up ahead and a horrible smell assails your senses. You hurry towards it, intrigued.

Rounding a tree, you stare in disbelief at the horror unfolding in the clearing before you. It is easily the most repulsive sight you have ever witnessed!

You see Erim, standing with his back to you, spear drawn, facing up to a creature that looks like a massive, bloated toad. It is easily double your height and at least as wide! Its warty, black skin glistens with some sort of slime that drips disgustingly down its flanks. And the smell! You see Vashta's unmoving body on the ground to your right, dispatched already by the despicable beast!

You decide that you cannot leave Erim to his fate - he saved your life! But what will you do? Will you stand shoulder to shoulder with him and face the beast head on? (Turn to **134**) You could signal for Erim to make his way to one side of it while you go the other, resulting in a split but two pronged attack? (Turn to **55**) Or will you fly up to the lower branches of the trees and try to make your way round to the rear of the creature? (Turn to **128**)

110

You make your way down a little track and cautiously approach the clearing from which the noise is coming from. There you see two large wolves viciously attacking two juvenile frost bears! You have seen the like of these animals before on hunting trips in the mountains and know that this is a one sided fight: it's only a matter of time before the wolves slaughter the bear cubs. If you want to intervene and try to drive the wolves off, turn to **74**. If you want to watch what happens from your hiding place, turn to **31**. If you'd rather let things run their natural course and creep away, turn to **50**.

111

You push yourself away from the cliff face and hover in the trees. You are soon glad of your decision! A huge centipede-like beast with large pincers lunges out of the hole and snaps angrily at the air in front of you. Luckily it cannot quite reach you and shortly it gives up and slips back inside. You fly down to fetch the log and stopper up the hole again, wondering who had the sensible idea to do that in the first place! Then you ascend the cliff and plunge deeper into the forest. Turn to **142**.

112

This proves to be the work of just a few minutes and you have soon cleared the way. Note down the codeword LOG. A few minutes further up the path, you suddenly feel that something vaguely humanoid in shape (but not very big) has dropped onto your back! *React on instinct*. Will you grab this thing and throw it off you? (Turn to **8**) Or pause in case it is not attacking? (Turn to **172**)

113

Sweat breaks out on your brow: it's going to take something amazing to pull you through this one!

The frost bear that had been sleeping stretches out and snarls at you. Then its expression relaxes and it approaches you inquisitively. You back away, looking for somewhere to run, but no attack comes. The frost bear growls towards the other; then they turn and slink away into the forest! It dawns on you that this must be the very same bear whose cubs you fought to save from the wolves!

Feeling very lucky, you nevertheless decide not to follow the bears; you retrace your steps to the last junction and go the other way! Turn to **64**.

114

You just scramble high enough out of reach to be safe. Slowly you begin picking a path across the boughs of the trees and apart from a few scratches and minor cuts, you do so successfully. Leaving the bears behind, you cut across until you find yourself on another forest path. You take the northerly direction. If you have the codeword ROOT, turn to **64**. If you do not have this codeword, turn to **71**.

115

You pay with many small scratches and cuts, but persist and manage to force your way through to another pathway. You have avoided the pool, anyway! Turn to **138**

116

You take careful aim and release the bottle, which spins through the air towards its target. Roll the die. If you roll a 4 or less, turn to **30**. If you roll a 5 or more, turn to **164**.

117

You are in time to see a small snake that has coiled itself around you sink its fangs into your leg! You dash its brains out on a nearby rock but the damage has been done. The snake was venomous and sweat breaks out all over your forehead almost immediately. You try to stagger on but collapse against a tree. When consciousness does leave you, it is for the last time…

118

You glide through the air with barely a noise, wary of possible observation from either side of the river bank. Soon the tree-tunnel opens up and you find yourself near the bottom of a huge ravine! Looking up, you see that the trees grow so tall and bent in this place that they still blot out the suns rays almost entirely!

You swoop and dive, feeling the freedom in the air. You carry on until you see an impassable wall of rock in the distance. Note down the codeword BEAK, and turn to **168**.

119

You tuck into a joint of what looks and smells like yak meat and swig from a bottle of cool mountain-spring water. You turn to put the bottle back and are startled by the figure of a dwarf standing in the entrance of the cave!

He also looks surprised, but this look soon turns to anger and he draws a battle axe from where it was strapped to his back. If you want to try and talk to the dwarf, turn to **3**. If you want to escape by charging at him and trying to barge past, turn to **82**.

120

Your talons slice swiftly and furiously, buying the lives of the first few bold spiders. You then make the snap decision to try and force your way through the remaining webs to freedom before the spiders begin to drop onto you. This is successful and, wasting no more time, you run as fast as you can, not stopping until well out of the spider's territory! Turn to **71**.

121

As he pulls you up, Vashta notices the bottle that you still carry, almost forgotten, in your hand. "The verusaramorr!" he cries. "I thought I had lost it! You must have come on the same route through the forest as us! What luck!" You ask him what it is. Erim answers, "It's my master's best potion! Just a few drops on even stale or rotten food makes it taste delicious! Very useful on a long expedition like ours!" If you have the codeword DROP, turn to **76**.

Vashta is holding out his hand for you to return the bottle. If you want to give it to him, turn to **42**. If you'd rather keep it yourself, turn to **174**.

122

Despite their weary limbs, both Vashta and Erim seem to be decent climbers. You swoop upwards, but stay near to your wingless companions in case they should slip during their ascent. In fact, they reach the top with only one pause for a rest. Soon the three of you stand at the cliff top.

There is indeed a way onwards. You find yourself in a shallow dell with another dark, tunnel-like path leading away. This you follow for a few minutes until it opens up into a clearing differing from any other that you have seen in Arcendak. This clearing has no covering of trees overhead and you can see the early evening sky reddening above you!

The floor of the clearing is quite rocky and you notice that around two other sides is a sheer drop similar to the cliff you flew up to get here. It's like being on the summit of a small flattened mountain in the middle of the forest!

Most interestingly of all however are the plants that coat the rocky floor. You recognise at last what you have been searching for all this time: unmistakeably Orphus Latix! You fall on your knees and carefully uproot a healthy looking specimen.

When you turn back to the humans, you are surprised to see Vashta with a look of wonder on his face and you realise that this is what he had been seeking himself! Before him, Erim is cutting a few sprigs with the same care as you.

But you dismiss this co-incidence in the excitement of concluding your quest and the bonus that you can simply fly home without trekking back through the forest! No wonder the Fygrinnd candidates are sworn to secrecy: it would be simple to succeed by flying over the forest and spotting this clearing, if you knew of it!

Vashta holds out his hand to you in some sort of human tradition of farewell. You wish him and Erim a safe return journey before taking to the skies and leaving the menace of Arcendak well behind you. Turn to **190**

123

You would never normally misjudge these things, but an overhanging branch catches one of your wings and you lose control, crashing down through the glistening webs. Fortunately you are not hurt and your destructive behaviour does not draw the attention of any forest nasties! You hurry on anyway, brushing away the many silky strands that have become streaked in your feathers as you do. Note down the codeword SILVER and turn to **38**.

124

There are so many of them! You are bombarded with thrown weapons and as you stumble and fall, they begin to swarm over you. You can do nothing against their weight of numbers and sadly meet your end here, brought down by many blows.

125

Erim stands frozen in fear, eyes wide, holding his spear out to try and keep the terrifying creature at bay. The toad-thing plods slowly towards you. If you have the codeword DROP, turn to **181**. Otherwise, will you will you attack a nearby leg? (Turn to **61**) Or swoop up and attack it from the air? (Turn to **164**)

126

As quickly as they appeared the spiders are gone, scuttling back into the shadowy eaves of the forest. Slightly unnerved, you make your way onwards, wondering if they smelt the webs still stuck in your feathers from earlier and this is what caused them to leave you alone. Turn to **71**.

127

You choose a suitable lump of rock and fling it to the left hand side of the pool. It lands with a thick splosh, but nothing else happens: all is quiet once more. Note down the codeword CLAW. If you now want to fly across, turn to **169**. To throw another rock, turn to **37**.

128

You manage to gain the lower branches and steady yourself but you are still in danger. You clamber through the trees until you perch unsteadily above the rear of the monster. You notice for the first time that it is sat astride three large logs. From here, will you:

Leap down and attack from on its back?	Turn to **91**
Land behind it and slash it from the rear?	Turn to **187**
Or land behind the toad-thing and try to overbalance it using the logs as a sort of lever?	Turn to **12**

129

You sweep your arm through the air, but the snake somehow latches on and sinks its fangs into your flesh! In pain, you dispatch it with a nearby rock but the damage has been done: the snake was venomous, and sweat breaks out all over your forehead almost immediately. You stagger on and collapse against a tree. When consciousness leaves you, it is for the last time…

130

You are slightly disappointed to see nothing in the hole. If you want to forget it and fly up to the top of the cliff, turn to **142**. If you want to pull another log out, roll the die again. If you roll an odd number, turn to **182**. If you roll an even number, turn to **20**.

131

You bare your talons as the dwarf readies his axe. Roll the die. If you roll a 1 or 2, turn to **21**. If you roll a 3 or more, turn to **52**.

132

You turn to run, but the second bear throws back its head and roars, waking his sleeping mate! If you have the codeword BEAR, turn to **188**. Otherwise, turn to **65**.

133

Vashta takes the stopper out of the bottle and sniffs it. You tell him that it tasted foul to you! "Well it wasn't full when I lost it!" he exclaims, "Let me guess – you found it in the forest river?" You nod.

Vashta seems fascinated by the discovery; Erim looks glum at the prospect of more stale food! Vashta pours a few drops onto a rock in front of an inquisitive lizard. The lizard licks up the drops…and seconds later rolls over onto its back, dead! "Intriguing…but it doesn't seem to have done *you* any harm, Xanarel…" wonders the old man, slipping the bottle into his pocket. Note down the codeword DROP.

Vashta then indicates the northward route that you yourself must take, saying: "We go this way!" He seems to be offering for you to share the journey with them. If you would like to travel with these men, turn to **150**. If you'd rather let them go on ahead and follow after, turn to **186**.

134

"Stand firm Erim, together we can slay this thing!" you cry, trying to distract him from the demise of his master. He looks heartened by your words and clenches his spear tightly.

The toad-thing makes its move: the disgusting tongue snakes out towards you. You both instinctively try to dodge. Roll the die. If you roll a 3 or less, turn to **85**. If you roll a 4 or more, turn to **43**.

135

You fling the branch and it spins through the air, scoring a direct hit on the nose! The bear looks in your direction, then bares its teeth in anger as it spots you! Hackles up, it advances slowly, growling deep in its throat. Will you take the initiative and spring to the attack? (Turn to **10**) Or flee? (Turn to **13**)

136

This is easy enough and you feel that you have respected the owner of the barrier too! You are a few minutes further up the path when you suddenly become aware that something which feels vaguely humanoid in shape (but not very big) has dropped onto your back! *React on instinct.* Will you grab this thing and throw it off you? (Turn to **8**) Or pause in case it is not attacking? (Turn to **172**)

137

You scan the surrounding trees and find that your intuition was correct. A little way behind you, sitting motionless and silent on a branch is a huge owl! Underneath the owl's tree you notice the body of a dwarf lying slumped face down in a thicket, a canvas sack or bag in one outstretched hand. Surely nothing to do with the owl? Will you:

Try to retrieve the sack?	Turn to **40**
Call up a greeting to the owl?	Turn to **88**
Or ignore it and continue on your way?	Turn to **167**

138

Your pathway winds this way and that, sometimes very narrow, then all of a sudden opening up into a wide, corridor like space. You come to one such area and observe a bizarre but beautiful sight. The air is full of fat-bodied, multi-coloured moths, flapping lazily between the trees. You don't quite know what to make of this! If you want to avoid them, you'll have to crawl across the clearing (turn to **83**). If you'd rather walk straight through them, swiping them out of the way as you go, turn to **162**.

139

Your wings are powerful but not enough to overcome the suction of the quicksand! You realise that this is just wasting energy; you are now up to your waist! Will you try to wade out? (Turn to **23**) Stretch for a branch to pull yourself out with? (Turn to **163**) Or screech for help? (Turn to **35**)

140

You dive sideways, but feel it thud into you as you fall! The slimy substance now on you is not only disgusting, but also highly poisonous! If you have the codeword BITE, turn to **151**. If not, turn to **24**.

141

You keep your eyes low as you walk, particularly on those strange holes. Are they burrows? Then you see something moving inside one of them: a small, furry creature poking its nose out inquisitively. If you want to approach it slowly and quietly, turn to **165**. If it doesn't interest you, turn to **25**.

142

The forest at the top of the cliff is identical to that of the lower level: just as thick, just as dark, just as uninviting. But the path is on a gentle decline, and not as overgrown as some. A little further on you hear the sound of running water and find a forest river cutting across your path, about ten strides wide. It is quite clear and does not look deep. There is just enough height to allow flight here. Will you wade across? (Turn to **87**) Or fly across? (Turn to **153**)

143

You try walking while stooped at first, then change to crawling as it proves to be more comfortable. The tunnel goes on and on and shows no sign of stopping. Is it a short cut to another part of the forest? Eventually, it opens out into another small cave. It is empty, and only because you can see so well in the dark can you even see the cave entrance as it is covered with foliage, probably to hide it from the outside. You pull down the barricade and find yourself in a completely different part of the forest! Deciding it would take too long to go back, you take this new path instead. Turn to **32**.

144

You decide to make a hasty exit, keeping one eye on the sleeper. As you get to the edge of the clearing however, you come face to face with another adult frost bear, very much awake! It roars in anger, waking its mate! If you have the codeword BEAR, turn to **188** Otherwise, turn to **65**.

145

You scramble to your feet to combat the ponderous beast. Roll the die. If you roll a 1, turn to **185**. If you roll a 2 or more, turn to **29**.

146

You shout for Erim to help you, which he does. Together you heave up the logs but just as they begin to shift, the monster kicks out with extreme force, catching you in the midriff. You are smashed into a fir tree behind you, one wing broken with a sickening snap. But the pain does not last for long: the monster's other hind leg also kicks out at you, this time breaking your neck…

147

You are walking along a trail of hardened, flattened earth between banks of dried mud. At seemingly random intervals on both sides are holes, like small animal burrows. You are just wondering what may lie within when you feel something wrapping itself around your ankle! *React on instinct*. If you bash whatever it is against a nearby rock, turn to **86**. If you look down first, turn to **117**.

148

It turns out to be a small green bottleful of clear liquid. You pull out the stopper and sniff it; it smells slightly acidic. If you wish to taste the contents of the bottle, turn to **100**. Otherwise, you may choose to take the bottle with you (note it down) or throw it back where you found it. Either way, you have soon completed the crossing of the river. Turn to **32**.

149

The path eventually turns northwards and continues to rise steeply until you arrive at a surprising sight.

You stand on the brink of a huge chasm, a great tear in the ground. It stretches as far as the eye can see in both directions. Looking up, you see that the trees grow so tall and bent in this place that they still blot out the rays of the sun almost entirely! Hundreds of feet below you runs a dark, gloomy river. Your keen eyesight picks up the forest path again on the far side of the chasm, which is reached (by the regular traveller) by a rickety looking rope bridge, several planks of which are missing.

Flying across won't be a problem. If you want to do this, turn to **41**. However, it occurs to you that you could fly west or east instead, inside the chasm itself. If you want to do this and go west, turn to **34**. To fly east, turn to **53**.

150

The pair seem pleased to have you as their travelling companion. Your unfamiliar physique and mannerisms intrigue them. You of course, feel the same about them!

Vashta leads the way along this new trail, which abruptly forks about a fir tree. He decisively strikes up the right hand path. The three of you climb a small hill and arrive in a little clearing with grisly decoration! Six wooden sticks have been driven into the ground, each supporting the rotting skull of a different creature! You recognise some of them as animal skulls, but others are peculiar!

You decide to hurry through the clearing before whoever has done this returns! Then you notice a small wooden box lying on the ground, half covered by a bush. Erim sees it too, but you pick it up first. "Open it Xanarel!"

he urges. "It could be treasure!" If you want to open the box, turn to **11**. If you want to give it to Erim to open, turn to **90**.

151

Unbeknown to you, the leaves you ate earlier had strong powers of anti-venom, and it is only this that has saved you from death! You will not survive another dose however; remove the codeword BITE. If the text asks for this codeword again, you do not have it!

You cannot see Erim from where you are. If you have the codeword DROP, turn to **181**. If you do not have this codeword, you decide to take to work your way around to the rear of the beast. Turn to **128**.

152

You keep glancing upwards as you crawl in case the web-creators return, but you see no sign of arachnid activity. Relieved, you hurry out of the clearing. Turn to **38**.

153

It feels good to be able to stretch your wings and take to the air once more, even if it is for such a short flight! As you cross, you notice glancing east that there is a sort of tunnel of trees that extends quite a long way into the gloom. It occurs to you that you could fly this way and search for alternate routes. If you want to do this, turn to **118**. If you'd rather take the path leading off on the other side of the river, turn to **32**.

154

The cave is dry and warm, the legacy of a smouldering fire that you see in the centre of the main chamber. Whatever calls this home has made it reasonably comfortable with furs on the walls and a hand carved wooden stool.

You look around. To your left, you see a tunnel opening at about head height, reached by a simple climb up the rocky wall. On the opposite wall to this is what looks like an opening into another room, covered by a curtain of animal fur. There is nothing else of interest. If you want to investigate the tunnel, turn to **58**. To see what is behind the fur, turn to **15**. If you'd rather not be nosey and want to leave the cave, turn to **33**.

155

You plough headlong into the pack! The stiff beaks of dozens of the birds rake your body with surprising aggression as they swoop past! You suffer multiple wounds and spin momentarily out of control. The chasm-rooks bank and turn for another run, and this time they take you out of the air for good…

156

After suffering several minor cuts and scratches, you give up on this as a hopeless task. It looks like you will have to cross the pool after all! Note down the codeword TWIG.

Once back on the edge of the foul water, will you fly across keeping as high as you can? (Turn to **169**). Or will you try drawing the arms to one side of the pool by throwing in a rock, then fly across to the other side? (Turn to **127**).

157

You scramble to your feet and easily outdistance the ponderous creature. Back at the fir tree, you take the right hand path instead. Turn to **78**.

158

Unbeknown to you, the leaves you ate earlier had strong powers of anti-venom, and it is only this that has saved you from death! You will not survive another dose however; remove the codeword BITE. If the text asks for this codeword again, you do not have it!

Will you now signal for Erim to make his way to one side of it while you go the other for a two pronged attack? (Turn to **55**) Or will you fly up to the lower branches and try to make your way round behind the creature? (Turn to **128**)

159

You soon come to a most surprising oasis in the gloom of Arcendak: a glade carpeted with sweet smelling flowers of pink and purple! You stand observing the peacefulness, the buzzing of busy insects the only distraction from the harmony. If you want to pick some of the flowers and savour the scent, turn to **56**. If you decide to walk carefully through the flowers, turn to **7**. If you want to skirt the flowers by forging through the undergrowth at the side, turn to **176**.

160

Your sharp talons rake the plant, cutting deep into the wood and severing many smaller limbs. But rather than let you go, it attempts to constrict even more fiercely! Roll the die. If you roll a 1, turn to **99**. If you roll a 2 or more, turn to **45**.

161

Luck is on your side: the toad-thing is focusing on Erim and the tongue lashes out towards him. He manages to avoid it by leaping into a bush, but the attack has given you the opportunity to run forwards and hurl the bottle: a direct hit!

You know straight away that it has worked. The toad-thing's mouth lolls open and it emits a bellowing, gurgling roar of pain. Where it had been on the offensive, all energy seems to have seeped away and it just slumps onto the ground, lying defenceless. The tongue thrashes about in death within its bile filled throat. Its limbs flag and begin to droop to the ground.

With a sickening squelch, Erim's spear thuds into the side of the monster. If you want to press home the attack and make sure the thing is dead, turn to **49**. If you'd rather fall back, turn to **103**.

162

You decide that the moths pose no threat to you and screw up your eyes as you try to keep them from flapping in your face. The stupid creatures constantly bump into you though and when you finally get clear of them, you notice that your feathers are coated with some sort of sticky moth goo! Note down the codeword FUR, and turn to **102**.

163

With all the effort left in your exhausted body, you stretch desperately for the lowest branch you can reach. You just get fingertips to it…and it slips through! One last try…and the end of the branch snaps off in your hand! The quicksand begins to close about your head and you realise that your last chance of survival has gone…

164

The bottle disappears from view into the monstrous mouth of the toad-thing. You know straight away that it has worked. The creature's mouth lolls open and it emits a bellowing, gurgling roar of pain. Where it had been on the offensive, all energy seems to have seeped away and it just slumps onto the ground, lying defenceless. The tongue thrashes about in death within its bile filled throat. Its limbs flag and begin to droop to the ground.

With a sickening squelch, Erim's spear thuds into the side of the monster. If you want to press home the attack and make sure the thing is dead, turn to **49**. If you'd rather fall back, turn to **103**.

165

You try not to frighten the little creature, but it almost immediately flashes out of sight back down the hole. It was not you that alarmed it however, it was another of the snakes, slipping silently from the trees to strike! Seeing you in the way, it decides that you would provide an even tastier meal and sinks its fangs into your shoulder! You dispatch the snake with a nearby rock but the damage has been done. The bite was venomous and sweat breaks out all over your forehead almost immediately. You stagger on, collapsing against a tree. When consciousness leaves you, it is for the last time…

166

You run like the wind and although you suffer many minor injuries as you flee (including another small spear in your side) you are not badly hurt and the creatures do not pursue you. You curse them under your breath as you nurse your injuries.

The track you are now on cuts straight through the forest. You then come across a smaller path leading off to your right. Peering down it, you see that it leads gently uphill to what looks like a standing stone on a hill. If you'd like to go this way, turn to **4**. If you'd rather continue in the direction you were heading, turn to **39**.

167

This route looks little used judging by the amount of forest debris littering the path. You are watching out for sudden pitfalls so hardly notice the path splitting. Assessing both routes, the left hand path looks more rocky to you, but the right hand path more overgrown. To go left, turn to **64**. To go right, turn to **9**.

168

You become suddenly aware of danger. To your left, you see a large flock of black chasm-rooks taking off in formation. You have seen these birds before in the mountains of Arian and know them to be both fiercely territorial and aggressive in defence of their homes! What action will you take? Will you:

Swoop upwards?	Turn to **72**
Swoop downwards?	Turn to **28**
Or fly to meet them head on?	Turn to **183**

169

Will the terrible lurker in the water detect you? Roll the die, subtracting 1 from the roll if you have either of the codewords CLAW or TWIG. (If you have both, subtract 2 from the roll!) If you score 2 or less, turn to **5**. If you get a 3 or more, turn to **66**.

170

Unbeknown to you, the leaves you ate earlier had strong powers of anti-venom and it is only this that has saved you from death! You brush the slime from your feathers, unaware quite how fortunate you are! Turn to **103**.

171

Eager not to provoke the adult frost bear, you slowly edge away, maintaining eye contact. For a second you imagine that you see in its eyes that it recognises you were trying to save its cubs from the wolves. Either way, you manage to safely make your way back to the main path. Note down the codeword BEAR and turn to **50**.

172

You soon realise that it *is* attacking you! Small sharp fangs sink into your unprotected shoulder! You wrestle with your assailant and manage to throw it off. You have been attacked by a strange creature indeed! It is humanoid, but only waist height to you. Its brown skinned body is covered in hair or fur, encrusted with frost. It has devious, beady eyes and looks at you with hostility, seemingly unafraid of you despite your size.

Suddenly – a stabbing pain in your shoulder! Turning, you see that a horde of these creatures has emerged from the undergrowth to your left while you were fighting off the first! One of them threw a small spear like weapon and this is what struck you. It's an ambush! Roll the die. If you roll a 3 or less, turn to **124**. If you roll a 4 or more, turn to **16**.

173

The webs are quite easily shredded by your sharp talons, but it seems that this makes the spiders redouble their efforts. More and more sticky strands lance down towards you and the spiders scuttle down to the attack! Roll the die. If you roll a 4 or less, turn to **59**. If you roll a 5 or 6, turn to **120**.

174

Not fully trusting this strange wingless creature, you withdraw your hand. Vashta frowns and glares at you. "Very well," he says slowly, and you do not notice his hand slipping under his cloak. When it reappears it sweeps in a wide arc, scattering some sort of grey powder all over you as the wizard speaks a word of power.

You stagger forward and slash out at Vashta, but he easily avoids your clumsy attack. He has in fact only cast a sleeping spell over you, but the forest floor of Arcendak is not a safe place to lie unguarded! You are destined never to awake. Within half an hour, with the humans long gone, a hideous beast of the forest finds your defenceless body, and makes a feast of it...

175

Without warning, a massive black...*thing* powers out of the bushes to your left. *React on instinct*. Will you stand and slash out at whatever it is? (Turn to **36**) Or retreat before it? (Turn to **6**)

176

This is not easy; it is wise to stick to the forest paths. Roll the die. If you roll a 3 or more, you make it safely (turn to **149**). If you roll a 1 or 2 however, turn to **44**.

177

You breathe a sigh of relief as you come to the dismantled log barrier and leap over it easily. You stop to catch your breath when you realise that you can hear no more sounds of pursuit and surmise that the little creatures have given up the chase now you are out of their territory.

You are heading back the way you came, nearing the fork with the branch in the shape of a finger. Then you notice a little side path heading east that you had not noticed before. If you want to try his way, turn to **147**. If you'd rather stick to the main trail, you pass the finger branch, this time following its advice (turn to **98**).

178

Suddenly you hear the sound of footsteps and come face to face with the owner of the cave returning home: a burly looking dwarf!

He initially looks surprised, but this look soon turns to anger and he draws a battle axe from where it was strapped to his back. If you want to try and talk to the dwarf, turn to **3**. If you want to attack him, turn to **131**. If you want to try to escape by shoving him over then running past, turn to **70**.

179

Thus begins the most desperate scramble of your young life! Savage claws rake thin air behind you, missing by a fraction. Roll the die. If you roll a 4 or less, turn to **89**. If you roll a 5 or more, turn to **114**.

180

With all the effort you can muster, you stretch desperately for the lowest branch you can reach. You just get fingertips to it...and it slips through them! One more try...and the end of the branch snaps off in your hand! You realise that this is just wasting energy and you are now up to your waist! Will you try to wade out? (Turn to **23**) Beat your wings and try to pull yourself out? (Turn to **60**) Or screech for help? (Turn to **35**)

181

You glance at Vashta's fallen body nearby and suddenly remember the verusa...whatever-it-was and the effect it had on the unfortunate lizard. You rush to the fallen wizard and rapidly rifle through his pockets to find it. When you turn round you find that the toad-thing is a short distance away. You decide to aim for the creature's mouth. If you want to wait until it opens its mouth and throw the bottle from where you are, turn to **116**. To try and get closer first, turn to **161**.

182

You get a shock! A huge centipede-like beast with large pincers lunges out of the hole and snaps angrily in your face! Then, as you struggle to defend yourself from this creature, another slithers underneath the first and hurls itself onto your body! The weight of it brings you crashing to the ground and you soon find yourself struggling against both of them together!

Then the world begins to spin before your eyes. What is happening? The centipedes are emitting some sort of intoxicating fumes from their nostrils!

Hampered by blurred vision, you cannot properly defend yourself from their nipping pincers. Slowly they begin to get the upper hand and in your final thoughts you wonder why you had to pull out those logs in the first place…

183

Deciding the best form of defence is attack, you wheel yourself in the direction of the rooks. Roll the die. If you roll a 3 or less, turn to **155**. If you roll a 4 or more, turn to **77**.

184

You slide back the clasp on the box and open it cautiously. Inside you see a few leaves of some sort of plant. But it is not Orphus Latix! This plant is lighter in colour and has leaves with a jagged edge. It has no particular smell. Just at that moment your stomach rumbles, reminding you how hungry you are.

If you'd like to take a bite of the strange herb, turn to **84**. If you don't want to risk it and want to press on, turn to **109**.

185

You cannot take to the air due to the low branches in this area, but you duck and dive, striking the huge mole and moving away quickly. The mole is surprisingly agile however and very tough. It suddenly lunges at you with all its bulk and you stumble on part of the broken ground. The full weight of the creature comes crashing down on top of you, breaking several bones. The agony does not last long however; the creature's claws see to that…

186

You bid them farewell, thanking them once again for saving your life. A few minutes later you make your own way along the same northwards trail, which soon forks about a fir tree. Both ways look equally inviting (or uninviting you could say!) If you'd like to try the left hand path, turn to **96**. If you'd rather go right, turn to **78**.

187

You deal the toad-thing savage blows with your left and right hand talons but it takes great effort just to break the skin! It grunts rather than roars in pain and, almost ignoring you, begins to lumber towards Vashta's defenceless body. Erim shouts a battle cry and launches himself forwards. What will you do? Will you attack a nearby hind leg? (Turn to **61**) Or swoop up and attack the thing from the air? (Turn to **91**)

188

Sweat breaks out on your brow: it's going to take something amazing to pull you through this one!

The frost bear that had been sleeping stretches out and snarls at you. Then its expression relaxes and it approaches you inquisitively. You back away, looking for somewhere to run, but no attack comes. The frost bear growls towards the other; then they turn and slink away into the forest! It dawns on you that this must be the very same bear whose cubs you fought to save from the wolves!

Feeling very lucky, you nevertheless decide not to follow the bears; you retrace your steps to the last junction and go the other way! If you have the codeword ROOT, turn to **64**. If you do not have this codeword, turn to **71**.

189

Suddenly the ground begins to crack beneath your feet, knocking you off balance! You look up from your prone position and see two heavy-clawed feet break through the surface. Rock and soil showers over you as a huge, mole-shaped creature emerges from underground, nose twitching to sniff for your position! Do you want to get up and fight the mole? (Turn to **145**) Or flee this subterranean monster? (Turn to **157**)

190

Your thoughts turn to your friends: Rical, Darfak and Snyblo. You desperately hope to find them awaiting your return!

It is nearly dark when you glide in to land at the window of the uppermost room of the Tower of Egratar. An Ariax on duty hails you and takes your precious find from your hands. A small gathering waits inside, including the Vzler, who greets you with a warm smile.

You ask him about the others. "Well young Xanarel, you are the first to return!" says the Vzler. "But fear not," he adds, seeing your look of concern. "There is plenty of time yet. The night is young!"

Rical is next to return, before an hour has passed. You are first to spot him in the distance and greet your old friend jubilantly as he too hands over the Orphus Latix. Then you are comparing notes excitedly about the dangers that you overcame!

Darfak soon follows Rical, wounded in his side. He has made a makeshift bandage, but collapses soon after landing. The Orphus Latix drops from his hand to the stone floor: he too has passed the Fygrinnd!

The night hours tick by. You and Rical fly between the caves where Darfak is recovering and the Tower of Egratar awaiting Snyblo's return. Eventually, you are ushered to get some much needed sleep.

The morning brings mixed news. Darfak is conscious and well on the mend. But the three of you are muted in your celebration: the watch for Snyblo has been called off. A few Ariax scouts sweep the area between your home and Arcendak, but it looks as if the forest has claimed another victim.

You spend the day resting. When you see the Vzler, you ask him the significance of Orphus Latix, as you guess from Vashta's value of it that it is more than just a random choice. The Vzler smiles at your astuteness but tells you that you will have to bide your time before this knowledge is yours.

You have achieved your goal and your adult training may now begin. But danger will soon be upon you again in the next stage of your life, as chronicled in book 2 of The Saga of the Ariax, entitled:

IN THE GRIP OF FROST

THE SAGA OF THE ARIAX: 2
IN THE GRIP OF FROST

Recent events

Three weeks have passed since you successfully undertook the coming of age trial known as the Fygrinnd. Since then you have begun the flight of the talon with your best friend Rical (who also completed the Fygrinnd) under the guidance of the Vzler. Your other friend who survived this year's trial, Darfak, has chosen instead the flight of the feather.

Although the Vzler is in overall charge of the flight of the talon, most of your time has been spent in the skies of Arian with your new master, Nimax. Whilst both you and Rical have great respect for the Vzler, Nimax has hardly endeared himself to you so far. At only twenty years your senior, he is not one of the elder Ariax and he is a natural bully. For some unknown reason he instantly took a dislike to you. The feeling is mutual! Maybe he is jealous of the raw talent you have displayed so far, which far exceeds Rical's (though you'd never point this out to your friend, of course!)

One clear sunny morning, you and Rical report to Nimax as usual and he ushers you down to a rocky crevasse large enough for you all to stand in.

"Today is going to be *different*," says Nimax, with a devious glint in his eye. "It is three weeks into your training and customary at this stage for you to undertake a simple patrol mission to test out your skills." You glance at Rical and see that he too is suspicious of your mentor's use of the word 'simple'.

"Head in a north-westerly direction and report back on anything unusual," continues Nimax, "It pays to keep an eye out for Scarfell activity. Go as far as the Horned Mountain, an unmissable landmark about three hours away. To prove to me that you have been that far, report back the precise colour of the vegetation growing on its eastern slopes."

Without wishing you luck or offering further advice, Nimax turns and flies out of the crevasse. From his tone of voice you guess that this won't be as straightforward as he makes it sound…but what has he got in store for you?

Now turn to **191** to begin…

191

Rical leads the way to the supplies cave where you grab some food, talking excitedly all the way. You eat well, but decide not to take any food with you as you'll be back well before dark! Then you take to the skies, darting and swooping about, trying to outdo each other as usual! You fly in a carefree way so near to home; there is nothing in these skies that can trouble you! Eventually you point out that you are on a reconnaissance mission and that you had better keep a look out for unusual activity below.

"Xanarel!" calls Rical across to you. "I've been thinking about this. We could make today far more *interesting*. Let's face it, there's *nothing* going on out here, is there? How about going westwards a bit more and seeing if we can see Musk – not too close mind! Then we'll have something to report to Nimax, won't we! We can still go north after that and take a peek at his precious mountain!"

You consider this idea. A sense of adventure naturally runs through your veins and you've always wondered what the legendary city of the Scarfells looks like. But you have been told on numerous occasions that Musk is a far more dangerous place than you could guess and you don't know how big a detour this would be. You only know that Musk is roughly westwards.

If you want to go with Rical's suggestion and fly west, turn to **343**. If you'd rather stick to your instructions and continue north-west, turn to **238**.

192

The ogre either sees you move or lashes out anyway, because at the exact moment you attack, he swings out his club. It strikes you in the body with terrifying power, knocking you senseless to the wooden floor. Rical cannot stand up to the monster alone and you both provide fresh meat for him tonight...

193

You fly with great urgency and it does not take you long to catch up with the Scarfell force that you saw earlier. Frustratingly, you immediately notice that the body of the giant is nowhere to be seen and it is not exactly the kind of thing you can hide! But what have they done with the body and is the ring still on it, or did they notice it and take it? You curse the fact that their tracks were not clear enough to show up a detour.

You hover a safe distance behind them. The only way you can think of to find out is to question one of the Scarfells and when you see one of them lagging behind on a very slow yak, you decide that you've got to take this opportunity. You only hope that Vashta's spell covered the Scarfell's language too!

How do you plan to capture this Scarfell for questioning? You could fly down, grab him and fly him off for interrogation? (Turn to **239**) You could knock him from the yak and drag him behind a rock, which would be easier but carries more risk of being caught? (Turn to **356**) Or you could make a sound and let him see you, hoping to lure him over into an ambush? (Turn to **337**)

194

The cleft continues downwards another few hundred feet before your feet touch down on rock once more. The foul smell down here is incredibly strong and blue smoke curls lazily from a large cave opening. There is no sign of the giant. If you want to investigate the cave, turn to **334**. To fly back up and try the other cleft, turn to **240**.

195

You rush over and grab the massive axes. You can just about carry five of them. Peering under the back of the tent, you see that the coast is clear and slip underneath. Just in time! As you stealthily take to the skies with your loot, you see two Scarfells approaching from the other side and going into the supply tent!

You make it with difficulty to a dell on the nearest mountain slope where you hurriedly cover the axes with snow. They'll never find them up here, of that you are certain! Then you make your way back down to the Scarfell camp. Turn to **242**.

196

As your keen eyes observe your enemies from range, you become suddenly aware of two of them wandering over to the enclosure. You duck back and keep your head down, peering through a crack in the fence.

As you listen, you realise that the two men's conversation is less than honourable! "'Ee's got it on 'im, in *there*," grunts one, indicating the tent with the banner. "I couldn't get it!"

"Well tomorrow, we'll watch 'im close!" replies his co-conspirator. "'Ee's gotta stash it sometime! That ring's too big for 'im to wear on 'is fingers and too small for 'is wrist!" They both chuckle.

They've given you the clue you wanted. After they've gone, you stealthily make your way over to the lead tent. Turn to **219**.

197

You pull with force, but so does he! The axe comes loose in a shower of splinters and the Scarfell grins at you malevolently. If you have the codeword ASH, turn to **232**. If not, turn to **266**.

198

You lead the way into the gloomy depths, glad that you can see in the dark. At the bottom you hear sounds of life; but they are unnerving cackling sounds.

Without warning, there comes a sensation like rushing wind and the two of you are enveloped in a flurry of black wings, sharp claws and hideous screeching! Something takes hold of your arms and legs! You glance over to where Rical faces a similar struggle for his life and you see black-skinned, red-eyed harpies drag him helplessly away in a cacophony of screeching! Struggle as you might, there are too many of them and you share your friend's grisly fate…

199

You choose a second suitable looking rock and take aim. Roll the die, again subtracting 1 from the roll if you have the codeword SNOW. If you score a 4 or less, turn to **273**. If you get a total of 5 or more, turn to **344**.

200

Your talons rake the Scarfell's face, causing him to stagger backwards in pain. You have just seconds to act. *React on instinct*. If you want to fly away, turn to **257**. To press home your attack, turn to **335**.

201

You don't have to wait long for the right opportunity: a lone Scarfell warrior walks past your hiding place, helmet under his arm, ready to hit the sack. You rush up behind him. Roll the die. If you roll a 1, turn to **241**. If you roll a 2 or more, turn to **286**.

202

One step, a quick swipe of the arm and the candle tumbles to the ground. Roll the die. If you roll an odd number, turn to **287**. If you roll an even number, turn to **225**.

203

You fail to notice the nearby Scarfell archers who have taken up their bows. A volley of arrows arcs through the sky and two of them thud into your body and bring you tail-spinning down to the ground. Mercifully, you are finished off quickly by the bloodthirsty Scarfell pack.

204

Sadly, although the rock lands amid the travellers below it doesn't actually hit anything. The Scarfells look up and spot the two of you and several arrows accompany the angry shouting. You are too high to be troubled by them and wheel off, laughing to yourselves. Note down the codeword SNOW and turn to **295**.

205

Desire to get the ring back wins out. "Very well, feathered one," he growls, "You have until sunrise. But do not fail me or I will grind the bones of your companion!"

Rical gives you a grim nod and you vow to them both that you will *not* fail in this mission. Wasting no more time, you run to the cave mouth and swoop into the afternoon sky.

Fortunately, you have a good sense of direction and know roughly where to find the Scarfell tracks, which should still be visible. It would be easier to see tracks flying low, but you can cover a wider area and spot the Scarfells themselves if you flew higher up. If you want to fly low, turn to **256**. If you'd rather fly high, turn to **333**.

206

"You're going to show me exactly where!" you say, sternly. "I need to find that ring!" The man cries out in protest, but you grab him roughly by the shoulders and take off, glad that his weight is bearable. He soon stops struggling when you get high up! Though a hardened warrior, he is clearly not great with heights!

He directs you to a massive chasm that he indicated. You can just make out the Scarfell tracks leading up to it and the signs of something big being dragged to the edge and not away again. You swoop down into it and come to land on the first of the large ledges that jut out from the rocky wall, letting the Scarfell fall a few feet first! He scrabbles to his feet, glad to be on solid rock once more and you watch him assess his surroundings: he can see that the only way out is by flying.

"Look," he says, after careful thought. "Here's the thing. I didn't know you was going to grab me like that, and now we're *here*, on something like a fool's errand." You ask him to explain, wary of a trick.

"Y'see," he says, staring you directly in the eye, "We *did* find that ring, course we did! And our warlord took it. 'Ees back there! I jus' told *you* it were here to get rid of yer! So poke about all you want down here, but I can help you get it if you'd drop me back."

You consider this carefully. Scarfells are certainly not to be trusted and he is looking to escape from his current situation. But did he tell you a lie at first, or now? Surely one or other must be true and this new story does make sense…

If you choose to believe that the ring is back with the Scarfells and want to return to them (without the prisoner, of course!), turn to **322**. If you decide that it probably *is* here with the giant's body, or just want to check first, turn to **349**.

207

You reach the mouth of the giant's cave as night descends on Arian. There is nothing to be heard. If you want to call out to the giant from the cave entrance, turn to **270**. To be more stealthy and creep in (maybe you could find Rical?), turn to **323**.

208

You notice that as he fell, your adversary dropped the ring which falls to the floor with a soft tinkling sound. Note down the codeword GRUB. You attempt to press home your advantage but the warlord kicks out strongly with his legs, hitting you in the midriff. You stagger backwards and this gives him the chance to get to his feet once more.

If you have the codeword ASH, turn to **232**. If you don't have ASH but you do have HAFT, turn to **266**. If you have neither of these codewords, turn to **318**.

209

You leave the ramshackle hut behind you. After five more minutes of flight, you spot a sizeable set of tracks in the snow below and swoop down to investigate, Rical following. You judge that a party of at least two dozen has passed this way, on some sort of hoofed animals (probably yaks). From the deep furrows in the snow, they appear to have been dragging something heavy.

You find a few discarded items: a bulky glove here, a chewed bone there; nothing of interest. Both of you have long since jumped to the same conclusion: Scarfells! Rical wants to follow the tracks, which lead in the general direction of Musk, but says he won't if you think it too dangerous!

If you want to follow the Scarfell trail, turn to **272**. If you suggest following them the other way, to see where they have come from, turn to **233**. If you'd rather stay right away and continue north-west, turn to **295**.

210

Steeling your nerve, you run from your hiding place and launch yourself in a low swoop towards your target, wrapping your taloned hand around his lower face. Roll the die, subtracting 1 from the roll if you have the codeword SNOW. If you score a 3 or less, turn to **245**. If you get a total of 4 or more, turn to **301**.

211

The left hand cleft drops down another hundred feet or so. You see as you hover above that a river flows into this crevasse, filling it with murky looking water. You wonder out loud how deep it is and suggest dropping your prisoner in for him to find out!

The Scarfell ignores your attempt at humour and directs your attention to a large cave that you have passed. The river flows out of it and he thinks it more likely to find the body in there. If you want to enter the cave and follow the river, turn to **309**. Otherwise you could investigate the right hand cleft (turn to **280**).

212

You soon find the Scarfell trail again and with nightfall no more than an hour or so away you finally catch up with them. The Scarfells cannot reach Musk before dark and have set up camp overnight, which could be an ideal time to infiltrate their ranks and find the ring! If you want to rest and wait until dark before making your move, turn to **304**. If you want to make your raid as the few last Scarfells mill around in the sunset, turn to **350**.

213

Unfortunately, the disturbance you created earlier has increased the Scarfell activity in the camp and one eagle-eyed guard saw you entering the tent. Recognising immediately what you are, he bursts in and raises the alarm. Soon you are surrounded by foes; there will be no escape…

214

Shaking numerous bits and pieces from the top, you lift the table and confront the warlord with it. He raises his newly gained axe to strike. Note down the codeword HAFT (if you don't already have it). How will you use the table most effectively? Will you:

Throw it at him, then drop and try to sweep out his legs?	Turn to **312**
Throw it at him and follow up by	

grappling and trying to get the ring?	Turn to **353**
Or simply duel with him, using the table against his axe?	Turn to **254**

215

Suddenly, there is a deep, angry growl from outside. Rical had not been alert at his post and has been caught out! You both turn to see a huge mountain ogre framed in the doorway. He is dressed in furs and long straggly black hair tumbles down over his shoulders. He carries a massive wooden club: it looks as if he has uprooted a small tree!

As you both edge away, Rical gasps, "I have seen one of these before…in Arcendak!"

"And how did you defeat it?" you reply.

"Well…actually, he was attacked by a passing frost bear and I got away!"

"Very useful to us now!" you complain.

This time, there is no frost bear in sight. The ogre suddenly lurches forward to the attack! *React on instinct*. Will you:

Shout: "Go for his arms!"	Turn to **313**
Shout: "Go for his legs!"	Turn to **255**
Or throw a nearby chair at him?	Turn to **347**

216

What a feat! You pull up again at such an angle that the Scarfell has time to do no more than feel the air being sucked from his lungs! You quickly fly away before there is time to be spotted. Turn to **235**.

217

You walk alongside the river and follow its course down the slope. Around the corner it becomes narrower; walls of rock close in on both sides and you have to tread carefully to avoid falling in. Eventually the narrow causeway opens out again and you come to a shallow lake at the top of another waterfall. You look down, musing whether it would be worth searching about down there. If you want to do this, turn to **338**. If you'd rather go back and try the other way down, turn to **315**.

218

You eventually get the better of him and he falls face first into the lake, dead. You stand back, breathing heavily from the exertion of the fight: though he was unarmed, this is still your first Scarfell kill. Leaving the body in the water with the giant, you take to the air once more, mission unaccomplished. Turn to **257**.

219

You creep cautiously towards the tent, which has large wooden stakes holding it up at seemingly random points. Then you fling yourself to the ground behind some barrels as a Scarfell walks towards it. He peers in at the flap, but decides not to enter and strides away purposefully.

What will your next move be? Will you creep round to the far side and try to look underneath the edge of the tent? (Turn to **340**) Or make an incision in the side of the canvas with your sharp talons and peep in there? (Turn to **293**)

220

You throw the table violently at the lamp which smashes into pieces and goes out immediately. The Scarfell warlord bellows in rage as he is plunged into darkness. If you have the codeword GRUB, turn to **282**. If you do not have this codeword, turn to **299**.

221

You lead the descent and glide in to land on the edge of a fissure. You cannot see the bottom because of all the steam, which is unpleasant and smells somewhat unnatural to you.

While you are not looking, Rical leans over and drops a stone to see if he can tell how deep it is. Roll the die. If you roll a 1, turn to **267**. If you roll a 2 or more, turn to **244**.

222

You swoop down swiftly. The mysterious object is in fact the body of a Scarfell, face down and half covered in powdery snow that has blown over him. He appears to have suffered multiple axe wounds in the back, which suggest that he was murdered by a fellow Scarfell!

There is nothing of use on the body and as you take to the skies again you shake your head in disbelief. The nature of this race of men sickens you. Turn to **256**.

223

You wade as fast as you can through the water until you reach the giant's corpse. Both of his hands are submerged and you heave out the nearest one quickly. No ring. You splash round to the other side of the body, heart pounding, and lift out the second dripping arm.

You stare in disappointment at what you find! The left hand is lacking one finger, crudely hacked off! The Scarfell was telling the truth!

You turn angrily towards your prisoner, forgotten for the moment, and are just in time to see him launching himself at you! The fact that he is slowed down by the river gives you just enough time to *react on instinct*. As he springs at you, will you:

Fall backwards, roll and fling him off?	Turn to **321**
Slash out with your talons?	Turn to **246**
Or try to fly up and out of reach?	Turn to **345**

224

You wait impatiently, silently urging him to go, knowing that every minute is one that Rical must spend pondering his fate. After about twenty minutes (that feel like hours) he finally does stretch and yawn before wandering off to retire for the night! Turn to **329**.

225

The flame plays along a pile of discarded clothing on the floor and a thin curl of smoke snakes up as it catches alight! The Scarfell is standing nearby and stamps it out immediately, but this hands the advantage to you. If you are asked to roll the die in the next section you turn to, you may add 2 to the roll. How will you attack? You could:

Pick up the makeshift wooden table next to you and use it as a weapon?	Turn to **214**
Flap you wings frantically and drive him backwards?	Turn to **298**
Or drop to the floor and try to sweep his legs out from under him?	Turn to **341**

226

You step up to the lamp and knock it aggressively to the floor where it smashes into pieces and goes out immediately. The Scarfell warlord has gained his axe, but bellows in rage as he is plunged into darkness. If you have the codeword GRUB, turn to **282**. If you do not have this codeword, turn to **299**.

227

Your attack knocks the ogre off balance, but he swings out his club and catches you a glancing blow to the body. You reel backwards but luckily discover that both you and Rical are now on the side of the hut with the door.

"Run!" yells your companion and you follow his lead, still in pain from your wound. The ogre's angry bellowing rings in your ears as you fly safely above him. On a nearby mountaintop you pause to assess your injury.

Although not life threatening, it certainly hurts and will slow you down. For the rest of the adventure you must subtract 1 from every die roll you make (unless the text asks whether you have rolled an odd or even number).

Shaken but alive, you take off once more in a north-westerly direction. Turn to **209**.

228

You bravely spring to the attack but the giant brushes you off with a dismissive sweep of his hand. You are knocked to the ground like an insect, momentarily winded. He does not even appear to have felt your talons on his arm! If you want to try again, turn to **327**. If you judge that he is just too powerful and want to back off, turn to **262**.

229

Your luck is not in. As the terrifying creature flies overhead, it sees your prostrate form and streams of burning flame pour down on you. You are roasted in seconds.

230

Hoping the darkness will cover your approach, you rapidly steal up behind the guard. But he hears the crunch of your feet in the snow behind him at the last minute. Roll the die. If you roll a 3 or less, turn to **247**. If you roll a 4 or more, turn to **310**.

231

You secrete yourself at the edge of the tent and await your opportunity. The warlord continues blundering about, smashing up this and that before catching the side of the tent so furiously that he pulls out one of the supporting ropes! The whole tent begins to collapse and you take the opportunity to dive onto him from behind, trying to wrestle the ring from him while he cannot use his axe.

Strong arms seize your wings which protrude from the edges of the tent. You are dragged forcefully out by three Scarfell warriors and the warlord frees himself from the mass of collapsed canvas. You cannot break free from the vice like grip of your captors and you can expect no mercy…

232

Suddenly the tent flaps beside you are pulled back and several ugly Scarfell faces peer in, looks of astonishment on their faces. "Be gone!" roars the warlord, but from that moment you know that there is no escape. You hear the pounding of heavy boots outside in the snow as the men close in to witness their leader slaughter one of their hated foes…

233

Rical grudgingly agrees to this safer option. After ten minutes of following the tracks you come to a battleground. Blood has been spilt here and some of it Scarfell blood too; you count four dead bodies scattered about. Immense footprints lead into the site from the other direction. A giant?

There is nothing else to be found here. As time is getting on, Rical suggests continuing your original mission. You follow him into the skies of Arian once more. Turn to **295**.

234

"By *nightfall*, I said!" thunders the giant. Anger blazes in his eyes and you wisely judge that further argument would be futile. Note down the codeword MOON.

Rical gives you a grim nod and you vow to them both that you will *not* fail in this mission. Wasting no more time, you run to the cave mouth and swoop into the afternoon sky. Fortunately you have a good sense of direction and know roughly where to find the Scarfell tracks, which should still be visible. It would be easier to see them flying low, but might you spot something else if you flew higher up? If you want to fly low, turn to **256**. If you'd rather fly high, turn to **333**.

235

Safely hidden behind the shelter of a large rocky projection, you pin the Scarfell to the ground by the neck, one of his arms twisted beneath him. It takes all your strength to restrain the brutish barbarian!

"Where's the giant?" you demand, talons poised threateningly. His eyes widen from anger into surprise: he can understand your words! You are again silently thankful for Vashta's spell!

"Get off me, feathered scum!" he growls. "I know nothing of any *giant*!" He makes a sudden effort to break free but you are ready and force him back down again, repeating your question and telling him you know they killed a giant earlier today. This time he yields.

"Useless lump of flesh it were too!" splutters the Scarfell. "We threw it down a chasm a few miles back. But it's shown them who the real power is in these mountains…*our* mountains." He sneers up at you, hatred conquering fear.

"Why drag the body so far and then discard it?"

"Eh? *You* try draggin' something that big mile after mile! And attractin' carrion birds too. Dirty great fings. Anyway we see this chasm and it went before the warlord even knew!" he chortles to himself.

"And did you take anything from the body?" you ask, narrowing your eyes. "Tell me the truth and you may yet live…"

"Weren't nuffin worth takin'," grumbles your captive. "Why, what do you mean? What do you *want*?"

"A gold ring." You search for recognition on the Scarfell's face but see none. You resolve to check out the chasm - you'll soon find out if he's telling you the truth.

You can't murder a prisoner, even if he *is* a hated enemy, but you could fly him several miles away and let him make his own way back to Musk. To do this, turn to **285**. If you think it could be useful and worth the risk to take the Scarfell along with you, grabbing him and flying off before he can struggle, turn to **206**.

236

To your dismay, the majority of the yaks wheel round and thunder towards the tents! Soon the camp will be in uproar with Scarfells everywhere! Note down the codeword ASH. You wait a while for the commotion to die down a bit but are ever wary of the time. Will you now try to take a prisoner for questioning?

(Turn to **324**) Head for the stores and supplies tent? (Turn to **213**) Or the largest tent? (Turn to **276**)

237

You smash your legs into his and he stumbles momentarily before regaining his balance. Snarling viciously, the warlord drops on top of you, his thick, hairy forearm jammed into your throat. His immense strength is too much and he throttles the life out of you with his bare hands…

238

You fly for another half hour or so. Then Rical sees something and swoops down to take a look. You follow in his wake and land beside a large, dilapidated wooden shack in the middle of nowhere, roof covered by snow, built up against a cliff face. There is only one door and no sound from within.

"Let's look inside!" whispers Rical and he peers round the door. "Empty, as I thought!" he chirps. If you want to pull him back and point out that the hut must have an owner, who could return at any time, turn to **209**. If you wish to join him in investigating the hut, while keeping one eye out for the said owner, turn to **261**.

239

You take to the sky, flexing both your wings and your biceps. Then you ponder over how best to approach this. If you want to glide down as horizontally and silently as you can behind him, turn to **308**. If you want to dive down vertically; more difficult but less likely to be spotted, turn to **268**.

240

The left hand cleft drops down another hundred feet or so. You see as you hover above that a river runs into this crevasse, filling it with murky looking water. You wonder how deep it is.

Then you notice a large cave that you have passed on the way down. The river flows out of it. If you want to enter the cave and follow the river, turn to **302**. Otherwise you could investigate the right hand cleft, turn to **194**.

241

You pacify your prisoner and drag him behind a rock. Unfortunately, you were seen by a keen eyed Scarfell watching from afar. Recognising immediately what is going on, he comes to the aid of his kinsman. You don't even see him swing his axe…

242

You stumble on and look for a place to secrete yourself. You make for the nearby yak enclosure; there are no Scarfells nearby. Then an idea comes to you: if you let these animals out, they may stampede away leaving your enemies to walk home! If you want to try this, turn to **305**. If you'd rather move on and continue to search for clues as to the ring's whereabouts, turn to **196**.

243

Standing firm, the warlord throws out his great arms and tries to envelop the flailing feathery explosion before him. But this may leave him vulnerable. If you want to change tactic and try to sweep out his legs from under him, turn to **237**. If you want to press home your attack with your talons, turn to **277**.

244

You hold your breath, listening for any sign from below, but there is nothing. "Well, what do you think?" asks Rical. "Do we go down there?" He doesn't sound keen. If you want to investigate down the chasm, turn to **307**. If you'd prefer to leave well alone and continue your mountain journey, turn to **272**.

245

The Scarfell proves amazingly quick to react. Your grip is not secured and he manages to break it, pushing himself off his yak and crashing down on top of you in the snow. Although he does not call for help, he soon gets it anyway, two burly Scarfells running towards you. You attempt to break off, but the tables have been turned. You meet your end here on the slopes of Arian…

246

You fling both arms outwards, talons speeding towards their target. Roll the die. If you roll a 4 or less, turn to **269**. If you roll a 5 or more, turn to **200**.

247

You unfortunately discover exactly why the Scarfells are famed for their battle prowess. Despite having the initiative, you fail to strike a telling blow and the

Scarfell's iron constitution enables him to turn the tables on you and gradually wear you down. You fall in battle to your most hated of foes.

248

You roll underneath the edge of the tent and look cautiously about. A tall man is sleeping on a makeshift bed on the far side of the tent with his helm resting over his face. From his size and trappings, you guess him to be the Scarfell warlord in charge of this expedition! A huge axe rests against the table and an oil lamp hangs over the bed, in whose dim light you catch a glint of gold. You see the giant's ring being held on two of the sleeper's fingers, such is its size!

You feel unable to murder even such an enemy as this in their sleep, but Rical's fate rests on getting that ring! If you want to try and tie the warlord's hands (which rest on top of one another) together with a handy piece of rope, turn to **346**. If you simply want to try to snatch the ring, turn to **259**.

249

You glide in to land at the cave entrance, your heart in your mouth. Not wishing to be trapped in the giant's lair, you stand silhouetted against the moon and call out that you have the ring.

There is a grunting sound, followed by the heavy lumbering footsteps of the giant. He emerges from the gloom with a suspicious look on his face but when you hold up his treasure he recognises it at once, a mixture of joy and sadness in his eyes.

The giant reaches forwards with thick, stubby fingers but you pull it back quickly. "Where's Rical?" you demand, making your voice as bold as possible, though secretly afraid that he is already dead. The giant disappears once more.

When he returns you can see Rical stumbling along behind him, still tethered by the thick rope. The giant holds out his hand and you toss him the ring. To your relief, he lets his end of the rope go and you rush to support an exhausted and dispirited Rical.

"Let's get out of here Rical!" you exclaim, although you can see that the giant is lost in thoughts for his departed brother and no longer interested in a couple of Ariax. Rical has just enough strength to fly and the chill night air seems to revive him a little.

"I knew you'd come back for me!" he murmurs, a tear in his eye. "You truly are a champion among the Ariax, Xanarel!"

You fill him in on the outline of your adventures as the pair of you head for home, requesting that your gift of languages be kept just between you for now. Turn to **360**.

250

You grasp the top of the banner and try to jerk it from the hands of the rider. Unfortunately you find it attached by a thick leather strap and are forced to bank sharply. Note down the codeword SNOW and roll the die. If you roll a 1, turn to **203**. If you roll a 2 or 3, turn to **278**. If you roll a 4 or more, turn to **295**.

251

You choose a suitable rock, shake off the snow and take careful aim at the Scarfell's head. Roll the die, subtracting 1 from the roll if you have the codeword SNOW. If you score a 2 or less, turn to **273**. If you get a total of 3 or 4, turn to **320**. If you get a 5 or 6, turn to **344**.

252

You descend vertically, the Scarfell hanging beneath you like a pendulum. You land on a tall pinnacle of rock that separates two deep clefts. You cannot see to the bottom of either but blue smoke is drifting up from the one on the right. Will you investigate the left hand cleft? (Turn to **211**) Or the right hand one? (Turn to **280**)

253

You wait for an opportunity when you cannot see any watching Scarfells and slip silently around a few other tents to the supplies tent. If you have the codeword SNOW, turn to **292**. If you do not have this codeword, turn to **329**.

254

He sneers at your clumsy weapon, but it is even bigger than his axe and seems effective at keeping him at bay. Actually defeating him like this is another matter!

Suddenly he takes a big swing and you block with the table. The axe becomes embedded in the wood, giving you a moment to exploit this advantage. *React on instinct*. Will you pull hard and try and yank the axe from his grasp? (Turn to **197**) Throw the table towards him hoping to overbalance or disarm him? (Turn to **358**) Or drop down and sweep his legs from under him as he tries to free his weapon? (Turn to **288**)

255

You dive forwards and Rical throws his muscle in too to try and bring the fearsome ogre down. Roll the die. If you roll a 1 or 2, turn to **192**. If you roll a 3 or 4, turn to **227**. If you roll a 5 or 6, turn to **294**.

256

Very soon you see the Scarfell tracks, now partially covered by drifts of snow blown by the wind. They are still just about clear enough for you to deduce their direction. If you have the codeword YAK, turn to **193**. If not, turn to **284**.

257

You land on the mountain slopes a little way away from the ravine to pause and gather your thoughts. It looks as if you've just been wasting time here, something that you can ill afford to do!

Suddenly you hear a sound like a rushing wind and turn to see a massive flying creature emerging from the very chasm you have just explored!

It is shaped like a huge scaly snake, light blue-green in colour, with the head of a dragon and large, bat-like wings. You judge that it could wrap itself at least once around the thickest part of the Tower of Egratar! Smoke curls from its nostrils, and you shudder: it is one of the most ancient and fearsome beasts of Ariax legend: the Moogoll!

React on instinct. Will you drop face down onto the snow, unmoving? (Turn to **352**) Or rush about ten paces to your left and hide behind an outcrop of rock? (Turn to **328**)

258

You hear the heavy crunch of boot on snow and immediately abandon the idea of this tent. Scrambling to your feet, you run to avoid the approaching guard and hurry away, unseen. Turn to **242**.

259

You grab the ring, confident that you can be away before he even realises it's gone! But his grip is vice like and as you tug, he speaks calmly and menacingly. "Ah, so you've come back! But this time I have you!" He tips back his helm, evidently pretending to sleep in order to trap a greedy sub-ordinate, but a look of amazement spreads over his face when he sees you!

"What?" he snarls, the surprise soon turning to anger. *React on instinct*. Will you:

Slash his hand, hoping he will release the ring?	Turn to **330**
Knock the bedside candle over, aiming to start a fire or at least distract his attention?	Turn to **202**
Or grapple with him and try to take the ring?	Turn to **317**

260

You both go for the axe at the same time. But the warlord's biceps seem to be made of iron! You are viciously elbowed to the floor and then left to face the berserk fury of an axe-wielding maniac, one on one. The battle does not last much longer…

261

You follow Rical inside and begin to search round the hut. You keep glancing nervously through the door, so Rical volunteers to keep watch for a bit. The hut is sparsely furnished with little of value, but from the many bones littered about and general filth you deduce that the occupant would make a significant foe! Roll the die. If you roll an odd number, turn to **215**. If you roll an even number, turn to **336**.

262

The giant stands up to his full height, lifting Rical high in the air as if he was a feather. He looks at you both inquisitively from under bushy, frost-encrusted eyebrows. "Now then, what have we here?" he says slowly and carefully, yet in a voice that rumbles like thunder.

"We're Ariax," you reply, warily.

"Aah!" booms the giant. "Ariax is it? This is a day for trespassers it seems! Those cursed barbarian men…but we will be avenged…" He tails off and gazes into the distance with an expression of anger on his face.

"But the men you speak of are our hated enemies too! You can surely see we are not the same as them!" you protest.

At this point you notice an extremely confused expression on Rical's face. As the giant continues to stare into the distance he hisses at you: "Xanarel! Since when could you talk to giants?"

"What do you mean?" you ask.

"Well," says Rical. "It's like this. *He's not speaking our language!*"

Before you can respond, the giant bellows angrily and ignoring you but still clutching Rical, turns and heads up the mountain side.

"Wait!" you cry, seeing that Rical still cannot get his arm free. "Let him go!" You fly up in front of him, as close as you dare. "We can help you get revenge on the Scarfells!" you add desperately, without really knowing what you mean.

The giant stops. "Hmmm…" he murmurs. He begins striding on again, his mind taking its time to process its thoughts on the matter. Then he speaks again. "You could be of use to me…" Another long pause. "Earlier today, the infernal barbarians…*Scarfells* you called them, attacked my brother and I while we were walking home. There were many of them and they had bows as well as axes. I was forced back. My brother…was slain. They took him…" He pauses again, in sadness. You notice nasty looking wounds on his legs and lower body.

"But *he* can understand *me*!" you whisper to Rical as the giant seems uncommunicative once more.

"Giants can't speak the language of the Ariax!" replies Rical. "No-one can!" He turns to his captor to demonstrate. "Let me go, yak-breath!" But the giant reacts only as he would to a bird twittering. He clearly doesn't understand Rical's words.

Then it dawns on you. Whilst in the Forest of Arcendak you were aided by two humans named Vashta and Erim who you were able to talk to and understand! Vashta was a wizard, and he must have cast a spell which not only still affects you, but translates the language of giants as well!

The giant reaches the mouth of his cave. "You cannot bring back my brother," he says to you. "But I will let your friend go if you find his body and return to me the gold ring he wore. It has much value to me; it is identical to the one I bear." He shows you the ring on his finger; huge and dull through age. "I give you until nightfall."

As the giant ties Rical securely with thick rope in such a way that he cannot get to it with his beak or talons, you assess that rescue is not an option. You quickly tell Rical what the giant has said.

It is already afternoon. If you want to protest to the giant that you need more time, turn to **348**. If you want to accept this mission and get on with it, turn to **279**.

263

You manage to avoid his flailing arms and take to the sky. If you want to fly away, turn to **257**. To continue fighting the Scarfell, turn to **335**.

264

You soon find the Scarfell trail again and with nightfall no more than an hour or so away you finally catch up with them. The Scarfells cannot reach Musk before dark and have set up camp overnight, which could be an ideal time to infiltrate their ranks and find the ring! But time is running out. If you want to return to the giant's cave, tell him what you know and ask to be allowed until morning to complete your task, turn to **207**. If you want to make your raid on the camp immediately, turn to **350**.

265

Luckily the yaks do indeed stomp off in the direction of the mountains. A couple of nearby Scarfells notice and run to the supplies tent to fetch some equipment to help round them up, but otherwise not much attention is paid as the yak-pen is away from most of the tents. Will you now try to take a prisoner for questioning? (Turn to **324**) Or head for the tent with the banner? (Turn to **276**)

266

The warlord holds his axe ready, fixing you with an intimidating stare. He could have called for help long before now but is clearly supremely confident of victory. You circle warily and realise that he is trying to get you away from the entrance of the tent so that you cannot escape! Of course you have no intention of leaving without the ring!

Then an idea springs to mind. The candle has gone out and you are now nearing the bed, above which hangs the only remaining source of light in the tent: the oil lamp. You can see perfectly well in the dark of course…but as far as you know, Scarfells can't! Maybe the warlord's tactic of cutting off your escape route has given you the chance of an unlikely victory!

The lamp is only a few steps away now. If you want to lunge towards it and try to destroy it, turn to **291**. If you want to use the table to break it, turn to **220**.

267

Nothing happens immediately. But then, without warning, there comes a sound like rushing wind, and the two of you are enveloped in a flurry of black wings, sharp claws and hideous screeching! Something surges at you and takes hold of your arms and legs! You glance over to where Rical faces a similar struggle for his life and you see black-skinned, red-eyed harpies drag him helplessly away in a cacophony of screeching. Struggle as you might, there are too many of them and you share your friend's grisly fate…

268

You swoop high into the sky before banking, ready to scream down towards your quarry. Roll the die, subtracting 1 from the roll if you have the codeword SNOW. If you score a 2 or less, turn to **314**. If you get a total of 3 or more, turn to **216**.

269

The Scarfell manages to wrap his powerful arms around you and brings you down into the water with a mighty splash. You battle desperately to get back to your feet but he is incredibly strong. Slowly he gets the upper hand, twisting you and holding you under, seemingly ignoring the wounds you inflict on him. Eventually your oxygen starved body goes limp in the water.

270

Your screech echoes around the cavernous walls of the tunnel. You soon hear the giant lumbering up to meet you but you edge back warily and hold your hands up to show him that you do not have the ring.

"What's this?" asks the giant, furrowing his mighty brow.

You explain that you have located the ring but that you can get it only under cover of darkness. "Kill Rical now and you will have to get it back yourself!" you reason.

The giant looks grim. Finally he speaks. "Go!" he snarls. "I will grant you the time you request. But do *not* fail me…"

You thank him and fly off for the Scarfell camp immediately, relieved and determined. Remove the codeword MOON and turn to **304**.

271

You glide in to land at the cave entrance, heart thumping in your chest. There is no sign of the giant so you rush inside and follow the tunnel into a huge cavern, lit by blazing torches on the walls. You call out, but there is no reply.

Suddenly you see Rical lying on the floor in the corner. You rush over to him and discover the worst; he is dead. Tears spring into your eyes and anger burns in your heart.

Your entrance must have woken the giant, for he now stumbles into the cave, rubbing his eyes. In fury you spring forwards, talons slashing and wings beating. But you are no match for him. He flings out a great fist, which in your state of distress you do not see coming. Your body slams against the rocky wall and the giant deals you another bone-crunching blow with his club. He later discovers his brother's ring on your lifeless fingers…

272

The pair of you continue to cut rapidly through the skies, allowing the chill winds to carry you on in haste. Then you give a shout to Rical: "Look! Down there! Scarfells!"

You hover high up and get your first glimpse of your enemies from a safe distance. You can see forty or so Scarfells heading due west, mounted on the great shaggy mountain yaks that they breed for transport. An icy-blue war banner with gold trim flies proudly at the head of the party and much equipment is being dragged along including rolled up tents, indicating that they have been on a prolonged journey. They are still a significant way away from Musk. Note down the codeword YAK.

In their midst something else is being dragged along: the dead body of a giant! Presumably this is a trophy from a recent battle!

Despite the fact that your priority is to observe and report, Rical suggests giving them something to teach them to so brazenly march through Arian! If you agree, he suggests either flying over them and dropping a rock (turn to **283**) or swooping down and trying to snatch the war banner (turn to **300**). If instead you want to suggest following the Scarfells tracks to see what they were doing, turn to **233**. If you think you've seen enough and want to head off, turn to **295**.

273

Sensing something, the Scarfell turns his head split seconds before the rock hits him and manages to dodge out of the way. He sees you and angrily charges towards you, unarmed. You meet him head on but he unexpectedly throws his weight at you and takes you to the ground. As you scrabble about in the snow you hear the pounding feet of other Scarfells coming towards you, axes ready. Death is swift.

274

You feel nothing. When you look up, the Moogoll has gone. Mightily relieved, you brush the snow from your body before resuming your mission. If you have the codeword MOON, turn to **264**. Otherwise, turn to **212**.

275

You rush over and grab the bows. You can just about carry them all. Peering under the back of the tent, you see that the coast is clear and slip underneath. Just in time! As you stealthily take to the skies with your loot, you see two Scarfells approaching from the other side and entering the supply tent!

You make it with difficulty to a dell on the nearest mountain slope where you hurriedly cover the bows with snow. They'll never find them up here, of that you are certain! Note down the codeword RANGE. Then you make your way back down to the Scarfell camp. Turn to **242**.

276

You creep cautiously towards the tent. It has been crudely erected, with huge wooden stakes holding it up at seemingly random points. Then you fling yourself to the ground behind some barrels as a Scarfell walks towards it. He peers in at the flap, but decides not to enter and purposefully strides away.

You are unsure what to make of that, but know you cannot just stroll in! Will you sneak round to the far side and try to look underneath the edge of the tent? (Turn to **340**) Or make an incision in the side of the canvas with your sharp talons and peep in? (Turn to **311**)

277

You draw blood; the warlord breaks off his attack. If you have the codeword ASH, turn to **232**. If you do not have this codeword, turn to **318**.

278

You failed to notice the Scarfell archers standing about who had grabbed their bows as they came to investigate the disturbance. A volley of arrows arcs through the sky and one catches you in the leg. It is not life threatening, but certainly hurts and will slow you down. For the rest of the adventure you must subtract 1 from every die roll you make (unless the text asks whether you have rolled an odd or even number).

Shaken but alive, you take off once more into the mountains. Turn to **295**.

279

Rical gives you a grim nod and you vow to them both that you will *not* fail in this mission. Wasting no more time, you run to the cave mouth and swoop into the afternoon sky. Note down the codeword MOON.

Fortunately you have a good sense of direction and know roughly where to find the Scarfell tracks, which should still be visible. It would be easier to see them flying low, but might you spot something else if you flew higher up? If you want to fly low, turn to **256**. If you'd rather fly high, turn to **333**.

280

The cleft continues downwards another few hundred feet before the Scarfell's feet touch down onto rock below. You release him and hold your hand to your face; the foul smell down here is incredibly strong! The smoke curls lazily from a large cave opening. There is no sign of the giant. If you want to investigate the cave, turn to **334**. To fly back up and try the other cleft, turn to **211**.

281

You keep your head down and your eyes open as you flit from tent to tent. It is easy to take a torch without being seen and soon two tents are burning. From your hiding place you hear raised voices and see half a dozen Scarfells rushing about, packing snow on the flames to dampen them down. Note down the codeword ASH.

You wait a while as the commotion dies down a bit, but are ever wary of the time. Will you now try to take a prisoner for questioning? (Turn to **324**) Head for the supplies tent? (Turn to **213**) Or the tent with the banner? (Turn to **276**)

282

You spot the ring lying unguarded on the ground. Eying the furious warlord carefully, you are able to wait for an opportunity to snatch it up. You slip it over three of your own fingers, where it sits securely.

The warlord's taunts and angry shouts ring around the tent as you pull back the flap and make your escape up into the night sky. If you have the codeword RANGE, turn to **306**. If you do not have this codeword, turn to **203**.

283

"Excellent idea!" you cry, and with mischievous grins on your faces the two of you set about finding a suitable projectile. You find one: a rock which you can only just lift together!

You strain to heave it into the air and glide over the unsuspecting Scarfells below! Roll the die. If you roll a 3 or less, turn to **204**. If you get a 4 or more, turn to **319**.

284

You fly with great speed and it does not take you long to catch up with the Scarfell force. You hover high above them and get your first glimpse of the enemy from a safe distance. There are forty or so Scarfells mounted on the great shaggy mountain yaks that they breed for transport. You see an icy-blue war banner with gold trim flying proudly at the head of the party and much equipment being dragged along including rolled up tents, indicating that they have been on a prolonged journey.

To your dismay, you cannot see the body of the giant and it is not exactly the kind of thing you can hide! But what have they done with the body, and is the ring still on it, or did they notice it and take it? You curse the fact that their tracks were not clear enough to show up a detour.

The only way you can think of to find out is to question one of the Scarfells, and when you see one of them lagging behind on a very slow yak, you decide that you've got to take this opportunity. You only hope that Vashta's spell translates the Scarfell's language too!

How do you plan to capture this Scarfell for questioning? You could fly down, grab him and fly him off for interrogation? (Turn to **239**) You could knock him from the yak and drag him behind a rock, which would be easier but carries more risk of being caught? (Turn to **356**) Or you could make a sound and let him see you, hoping to lure him over into an ambush? (Turn to **337**)

285

You drop your captive off several miles out of the way. He picks himself up from the snowy ground and shakes his fist in anger as you spiral high up into the sky. There is no way he can return to his kinsmen before your mission is complete and you somehow doubt a search party will be sent out for him! Soon he is lost to view beneath you.

You arrive at the massive chasm that he indicated; here you can see the Scarfell tracks leading right up to it and the signs of something big being dragged right up to the edge. You swoop down into it and come to land on the first large ledge that juts out from the rocky wall.

You are on a large rocky plateau. A waterfall bursts from the rock nearby, running into a pool that becomes a river very soon afterwards. The river runs off into the distance downhill and round a bend in the cliff. You notice as you near the water and confirm as you cautiously dip a taloned toe in, that it is warm! How this is possible you do not know, but it explains why it is not frozen!

Over the edge of the plateau the ravine extends downwards as far as the eye can see. You can therefore see two options to search for the giant's corpse.

You could follow the river? (Turn to **217**) Or you could fly deeper into the chasm? (Turn to **315**)

286

You pacify your prisoner and haul him behind a rock. Déjà vu sets in as once more you find yourself staring into hate-filled Scarfell eyes! This time though there is even more need for urgency. You grab a fistful of snow and cover his mouth with that hand, causing him to splutter and choke.

"*Point* to where I can find the giant's ring and you will live," you whisper harshly. The man immediately juts out an arm and points a gloved finger in the direction of the tent with the banner.

The speed of his answer leads you to believe him. Not taking any chances however, you knock him unconscious and drag him behind a pile of nearby barrels. Turn to **219**.

287

Unfortunately it goes out as soon as it hits the floor! The warlord snorts through his nose and the momentary pause has given him time to pick up his axe, which looks a formidable weapon! Note down the codeword HAFT. What will you do now? You could:

Pick up the makeshift wooden table next to you and use it as a weapon?	Turn to **214**
Flap you wings frantically and drive him backwards?	Turn to **298**
Or drop to the floor and try to sweep his legs out from under him?	Turn to **341**

288

His legs are built like tree trunks but the power and speed of your attack catches him by surprise. He topples backwards and falls to the floor, temporarily vulnerable. If you have the codeword GRUB, turn to **331**. Otherwise roll the die, adding one to the score if you have the codeword HAFT. If you get a 4 or less, turn to **331**. If the total is 5 or more, turn to **208**.

289

Rical takes the lead and screeches into the darkness of the cave. Roll the die. If you roll a 1, 2 or 3, turn to **267**. If you roll a 4, 5 or 6, turn to **354**.

290

You explain all about the Scarfell war party that you saw earlier and try to be especially clear about the fact that they will be setting up camp overnight. This will be your chance to infiltrate and regain the ring without being seen. The giant considers this for a while, before desire to get his trinket back wins out. "Very well, feathered one," he growls, "You have until sunrise. But do not fail me or I will grind the bones of your companion!"

Rical gives you a grim nod and you vow to them both that you will *not* fail in this mission. Wasting no more time, you run to the cave mouth and swoop out into the afternoon sky.

Fortunately, you have a good sense of direction and know roughly where to find the Scarfell tracks, which should still be visible. It would be easier to see tracks flying low, but you can cover a wider area and spot the Scarfells themselves if you flew higher up. If you want to fly low, turn to **256**. If you'd rather fly high, turn to **333**.

291

You move with all the speed you can muster: you need to make this blow count! Roll the die. If you roll a 2 or less, turn to **325**. If you roll a 3 or more, turn to **342**.

292

You duck back suddenly: there is a guard! But he is standing with his back to your hiding place. If you want to wait around, hoping that he will leave, turn to **224**. To silently creep under the other side of the tent, turn to **357**.

293

The canvas yields easily and you soon have a handy spy hole. There is one occupant: a tall man on a makeshift bed on the far side of the tent, snoring lightly with his helm resting over his face. From his size and trappings you guess him to be the Scarfell warlord in charge of this expedition! A huge axe rests against the table and an oil lamp hangs over the bed, in whose dim light you catch a glint of gold. You see the giant's ring being held on two of the sleeper's fingers, such is its size!

Warily you roll under the side of the tent and stand up slowly in the candlelight inside. The man murmurs but does not move.

You feel unable to murder even such an enemy as this in their sleep, but Rical's fate rests on getting that ring! If you want to try and tie the warlord's hands (which rest on top of one another) together with a handy piece of rope, turn to **346**. If you simply want to try to snatch the ring, turn to **259**.

294

The attack takes the ogre by surprise and you manage to get between him and the door. Rical stumbles and you catch his arm, semi dragging him out into the cold once more. The ogre's angry bellowing rings in your ears as you fly safely above him. Shaken but alive, you take off once more in a north-westerly direction. Turn to **209**.

295

The sun shines directly overhead in the clear blue sky. You fly to a mountain crest that commands a breathtaking panoramic view of the slopes of Arian. Rical lands behind you and you discuss the day's discoveries so far.

Suddenly, Rical cries out in surprise and pain! Turning, your beak drops open in shock as you see him being lifted off the ground by a fur-clad snow-giant who you judge is easily four times your height! You cannot believe that you did not hear him approach!

If you want to attack the giant, despite his apparent strength, turn to **228**. If you do not wish to be so hasty and want to see what he does next, turn to **262**.

296

You walk alongside the river and follow its course down the slope, pushing the Scarfell in front of you. Around the corner it becomes narrower; walls of rock close in on both sides and you have to tread carefully to avoid falling in. Eventually the narrow causeway opens out again and you come to a shallow lake at the top of another waterfall. You muse whether it would be worth searching about down there. If you want to do this, turn to **355**. If you'd rather go back and try the other way down, turn to **252**.

297

You creep along on your knees behind a line of low rocks then scamper across to the edge of one of the outer tents. There you are fortunate to catch the whisperings of a conversation between two Scarfells who are talking quickly and urgently. You gather that they are plotting something; all is not well within the camp! Something is definitely said about the tent with the banner but then the men move off and you hear no more. If you want to investigate that particular tent now, turn to **219**. If you'd sooner explore the rest of the camp a bit more first, turn to **242**.

298

This takes the Scarfell by surprise and he takes an instinctive step back. If you have the codeword HAFT, turn to **325**. Otherwise, roll the die. If you roll a 4 or less, turn to **243**. If you get a 5 or more, turn to **351**.

299

Your heart thumps frantically in your chest; how can you get the ring from the berserk warlord, now stumbling round the tent, sweeping the air with his deadly axe? If you want to close in cautiously and try to wrestle away the axe, turn to **325**. If you'd rather stand back and hope for a different opportunity to present itself, turn to **231**.

300

You lead the way in steep descent. Just as you near them, Rical lets out a terrific battle cry that makes the Scarfells nearby look up. Roll the die. If you roll a 3 or less, turn to **332**. If you get a 4 or more, turn to **250**.

301

The Scarfell is taken completely by surprise and his eyes widen in amazement when he sees you. But you are too quick and manage to get him on the ground and muffle his face before he can cry out. You drag him away hastily before you are spotted. Turn to **235**.

302

Wading through muddy water in a tunnel of rock is not your idea of comfort but you do so all the same and soon find yourself out in the open air in a huge lake. And in the distance you can see, face down in the water, the eerily still body of the unfortunate giant you have been seeking!

You wade as fast as you can through the water until you reach the giant's corpse. Both of his hands are submerged and you heave out the nearest one quickly. No ring. You splash round to the other side of the giant, heart pounding, and lift out the second dripping arm.

You stare in disappointment at what you find! The left hand is lacking one finger, crudely hacked off! You let it drop into its watery grave once more and stare upwards in frustration. The Scarfell lied to you! Pausing only to remind yourself never to trust one again, you fly upwards, drips of water trailing below you. Turn to **257**.

303

You catch him just right and he plunges head first into the water with a loud splash. He scrambles to his feet cursing you, but you are already airborne, leaving him a lonely little speck in the depths below. Turn to **257**.

304

The moon casts a ghostly light over the panorama below you. You have taken up an observation position high up overlooking the camp.

You can see a ramshackle gathering of about twenty tents, lit by occasional flaming torches thrust into the snowy ground. A few Scarfells wander to and fro on various errands but it looks as though the camp is settling for the night. On the far side you make out a pen for the yaks, currently attended by a couple of guards.

You yawn; it has been a tiring day. You consider taking a nap and searching for the ring in the middle of the night, but decide against it in case you didn't awake until after sunrise. You are quite capable of staying out of sight of a few sleepy *humans*, anyway!

You wonder where you are most likely to find the ring and narrow down your options. The largest tent flies an icy-blue war banner with gold trim. To investigate this tent, turn to **219**. You saw a few of the Scarfells carrying provisions into and out of a second prominent tent and decide this must be a supplies tent. Could it also contain treasure? To see, turn to **253**. You could quite easily take one of the torches and cause havoc by setting something alight. Maybe this would be a useful distraction? To try this, turn to **281**. Otherwise, you could try to capture a prisoner for interrogation. To follow through on this idea, turn to **201**.

305

You unhook the wooden latch that holds the gate closed and drop it on the ground. Then you skirt the perimeter of the pen, poking and steering the great hairy beasts towards the opening. The nearest ones start to get the idea and soon the rest of the herd begins to follow! Roll the die. If you roll an odd number, turn to **236**. If you roll an even number, turn to **265**.

306

You soon leave the camp far behind you. You have struck a blow for the pride of the Ariax tonight and even now the warlord will be frantically trying to conceal the fact that a single birdman infiltrated the camp and stole his precious treasure!

You fly like the wind through the darkness to the giant's cave. Finally, you see it, a forbidding downturned mouth in the mountainside. If you have the codeword MOON, turn to **271**. If you do not have this codeword, turn to **249**.

307

You lead the way and the freshly enthused Rical follows. You land on a bulky outcrop of rock which protrudes from the cliff. A dark tunnel only just taller than you leads ominously into the rock-face. You look at your friend, but he shrugs indecisively.

If you suggest calling out down the tunnel and see what happens, turn to **289**. If you'd rather enter more stealthily, turn to **326**. To ignore the cave and fly deeper down the chasm, turn to **198**. Your only other option is to leave the ravine and carry on with your journey. To do this, turn to **272**.

308

The Scarfell hears nothing as you glide in. Before he can even exhale in exclamation, you hoist him up by his burly shoulders and are airborne once more. You quickly fly away before there is time to be spotted. Turn to **235**.

309

Wading through muddy water in a tunnel of rock is not your idea of comfort but you do so all the same and soon find yourself out in the open air in a huge lake. And in the distance you can see, face down in the water, the eerily still body of the unfortunate giant you have been seeking! Turn to **223**.

310

The guard turns but you strike him a hard blow to the back of the head. He crumples to the ground, fortunately with little sound. You creep into the tent.

The interior is spacious, lit by dim candlelight which has been left unattended. Crates of dried food lie half open and picked at. Leaning against them are numerous weapons: about a dozen heavy looking two-handed axes and half that number of longbows. Quivers of arrows are carelessly discarded beside them. To your disappointment, there is no sign of any treasure.

You are just about to leave when a thought occurs to you: you could take some of these weapons and hide them in the mountains. But would this make much indentation on your enemy's strength? If you want to steal the axes, turn to **195**. To take the bows, turn to **275**. Otherwise, there is little else to find in this tent. Will you next head towards the largest tent? (Turn to **219**) Or to the other side of the camp? (Turn to **242**). If neither of these appeals to you, you could follow up an earlier idea and start a fire to create a diversion? (Turn to **281**) Or capture a prisoner for interrogation? (Turn to **201**)

311

The canvas yields easily and you soon have a handy spy hole. But before you can use it, you hear what sounds like footsteps crunching through the snow nearby. You make the snap decision to hide in the tent. If you have the codeword ASH, turn to **213**. If you do not have this codeword, turn to **248**.

312

The table flies through the air. The warlord looks surprised, but parries it with his axe. You are already down and trying to knock him to the floor. Roll the die. If you roll a 1, turn to **237**. If you roll a 2 or more, turn to **288**.

313

You dive forwards and Rical throws his muscle in too to try and keep the fearsome ogre from striking. Roll the die. If you roll a 1, turn to **192**. If you roll a 2 or 3, turn to **227**. If you roll a 4, 5 or 6, turn to **294**.

314

You grasp your target by the shoulders and lurch upwards, but the manoeuvre proves a stretch too far. As you pull up, the Scarfell slips out of your hands! He reacts with the speed of a seasoned warrior, grabbing out at you. His grip is immensely strong! He propels himself from his mount and as the pair of you scrabble about in the snow, you hear the pounding feet of several other Scarfells coming towards you, axes ready. Death is swift.

315

You descend vertically. The smell you noticed is definitely getting stronger and the amount of smoke has increased. You land on a tall pinnacle of rock that separates two deep clefts. You cannot see to the bottom of either, and have a simple decision of whether to investigate the left hand cleft? (Turn to **240**) Or the right hand one? (Turn to **194**)

316

You don't have to wait long for the right opportunity: a lone Scarfell warrior walks past your hiding place, helmet under his arm, ready to hit the sack. You rush up behind him. Roll the die. If you roll a 3 or less, turn to **241**. If you roll a 4 or more, turn to **286**.

317

Before he can stand, you throw your weight onto his shoulders and try to twist his arm beneath him. But with a bellow that resounds around the tent, the warlord flexes his mighty biceps and hurls you to the ground! As you stand again, you see he now has his war-axe and stands facing you in a battle-stance. Note down the codeword HAFT. How will you attack? You could:

Pick up the makeshift wooden table next to you and use it as a weapon?	Turn to **214**
Flap you wings frantically and drive him backwards?	Turn to **298**
Or drop to the floor and try to sweep his legs out from under him?	Turn to **341**

318

The warlord fixes you with an intimidating stare. He could have called for help long before now but is clearly supremely confident of victory. You circle warily and realise that not only is he trying to get to his axe but he is also moving you away from the entrance of the tent so that you cannot escape! Of course you have no intention of leaving without the ring!

Then an idea springs to mind. The candle has gone out and you are now nearing the bed, above which hangs the only remaining source of light in the tent: the oil lamp. You can see perfectly well in the dark of course…but as far as you know, Scarfells can't! Maybe the warlord's tactic of cutting off your escape route has given you the chance of an unlikely victory!

The lamp is only a few steps away now. If you want to try to destroy it, turn to **226**. If you'd rather prevent the warlord from getting his axe, turn to **260**.

319

The rock plummets to the ground, scoring a direct hit on an unfortunate Scarfell and his steed! Chaos ensues below, but Rical has already peeled off and you follow him behind a nearby ridge to watch.

The Scarfells do not see you and cannot deduce where the rock came from. You notice that they do not even stop to bury their fallen comrade, but continue their journey regardless. You eventually do likewise. Turn to **295**.

320

The rock sails past the Scarfell but he had turned his head away at just that moment and doesn't appear to have seen it. If you want to try again, turn to **199**. If you want to try something else, you could try to grab the Scarfell from the air (turn to **239**).

321

This requires good timing! Roll the die. If you roll a 1, turn to **269**. If you roll a 2 or more, turn to **303**.

322

You fly out of the chasm, dropping your captive near the edge. You may believe his story, but trusting him to help you retrieve a treasure from his own people? That's another matter!

The Scarfell picks himself up from the snowy ground and shakes his fist in anger as you spiral high up into the sky. There is no way he can return to his kinsmen before your mission is complete and you somehow doubt a search party will be sent out for him! Soon he is lost to view beneath you. Turn to **257**.

323

You keep to the wall of the tunnel and try to minimise the noise of your talons on the rocky floor. Spotting firelight up ahead, you advance cautiously towards it and see Rical slumped on the ground, tethered to an iron ring on the wall with thick rope. When you reach your friend, you motion for him to keep quiet, despite his obvious excitement at seeing you. He is still securely tied, but it is short work for you to free him!

Your joy is short lived. When you turn to leave, you see the giant barring the way, a look of fury on his face. He strides towards you and smashes the dispirited Rical to the ground with a swipe of his hand. Unwilling to flee and leave your friend to his fate, you engage the giant in combat, but it is beyond your power to win this particular fight. No Ariax emerges from the cave alive…

324

You don't have to wait long for the right opportunity: a lone Scarfell warrior walks past your hiding place, helmet under his arm, ready to hit the sack. You rush up behind him. Roll the die. If you roll a 4 or less, turn to **241**. If you roll a 5 or more, turn to **286**.

325

Unfortunately things take a nasty turn for the worse. The warlord anticipates your move (either by luck or judgement) and brings his axe up to meet you. The savage weapon slices into your body and you fall to the ground in agony. Mercifully, the Scarfell does not take his time finishing you off…

326

At the end of the tunnel is a cave littered with the skeletons of various unfortunate humanoids. You also discover feathers (not from an Ariax) and the odd rat skittering about. There is nothing else to find here. You now have a choice between going up, out of the ravine? (Turn to **272**) Or further down into it? (Turn to **198**)

327

Unwilling to yield so easily you attack the giant once more, talons slashing and wings beating furiously. But you are no match for him. He flings out another great fist, which you do not see coming in your state of agitation. Your body slams against the mountain rock and the giant deals you a final bone-crunching and fatal blow with his club…

328

Almost afraid to breathe, you run five paces and launch yourself headlong the rest of the way, rolling in the snow behind the shelter of the rock. Just in time! The Moogoll flies overhead, casting a shadow over your position. You can only admire the power and majesty of the thing as it climbs rapidly into the sky, soon lost to view overhead. You stand and brush the snow from your body with relief before resuming your mission. If you have the codeword MOON, turn to **264**. Otherwise, turn to **212**.

329

You creep into the tent. The interior is spacious, lit by dim candlelight which has been left unattended. Crates of dried food lie half open and picked at. Leaning against them are piles of weapons: about a dozen heavy looking two-handed axes and half that number of thick bows. Quivers of arrows are carelessly discarded beside them. To your disappointment, there is no sign of any treasure.

You are just about to leave when a thought occurs to you: you could take some of these weapons and hide them in the mountains. But would this make much indentation on your enemy's strength? If you want to steal the axes, turn to **195**. To take the bows, turn to **275**. Otherwise, there is little else to find in this tent. Will you next head towards the tent with the banner? (Turn to **219**) Or to the other side of the camp? (Turn to **242**). If neither of these appeals to you, you could follow up an earlier idea and start a fire to create a diversion? (Turn to **281**) Or capture a prisoner for interrogation? (Turn to **201**)

330

Your talons rake his flesh and he instinctively draws his hand back. The ring drops to the floor and rolls a little way before settling. Note down the codeword GRUB. You make a move to retrieve it but the warlord catches you off guard as you glance down, rising from his bed and shoving you backwards. Fortunately you are able to recover your balance and now stand facing him. How will you attack? You could:

Pick up the makeshift wooden table next to you and use it as a weapon?	Turn to **214**
Flap your wings frantically and drive him backwards?	Turn to **298**
Or drop to the floor and try to sweep his legs out from under him?	Turn to **341**

331

You attempt to press home your advantage but the warlord kicks out with his legs, hitting you in the midriff. This gives him the chance to get to his feet once more.

If you have the codeword ASH, turn to **232**. If you don't have ASH, but you do have HAFT, turn to **266**. If you have neither of these codewords, turn to **318**.

332

The banner-bearer lowers his standard just in time and you grasp at thin air. "Up!" you gasp to Rical; this is no place to hang around! Note down the codeword SNOW and roll the die. If you roll a 3 or less, turn to **203**. If you roll a 4 or 5, turn to **278**. If you roll a 6, turn to **295**.

333

The wind is stronger up here and you ride the breeze this way and that fruitlessly for about five minutes. Then your keen eyes pick out an unidentified shape far below, half buried by snow. It could be the body of an animal. If you want to investigate, turn to **222**. If you'd rather continue your search for the Scarfells, turn to **256**.

334

The cave goes back a long way and gradually enlarges until you are walking along a tunnel that is three times your height. The smoke collects above you, and you puzzle over what could be creating it. Rounding a corner, you find out. You come face to face with an enormous dragon-like head! Before you can even comprehend what it is, it spurts out a great gout of flame, incinerating you utterly.

335

Fed up with this treacherous man-thing, you decide to show him exactly which species is ruler of the mountains. He seems to forget that you are his only means of escape from the chasm and glares at you with murder in his eyes. Roll the die. If you roll a 1 or 2, turn to **247**. If you get a 3 or more, turn to **218**.

336

"Errr, Xanarel…" says Rical, "I think it's time to go!" As you get to the door you see why: a huge, straggly-haired mountain ogre has appeared on the horizon, dressed in furs and carrying a massive wooden club that looks like a small tree!

You are both airborne long before he can reach you. His howls of rage fade into nothing as you make your way north-west once more. Turn to **209**.

337

You don't wish to alert the entire party, so you drop to the ground with a thud and lie prone, just one leg protruding so that the Scarfell can see. You bank on the fact that he will want to claim you as a prize himself and not involve his fellow Scarfells, but you guess incorrectly: his first reaction is to cry out! You jump up and take off immediately, knowing it would be death to stay. Note down the codeword SNOW (if you haven't already got it).

Ten minutes in hiding pass before you pluck up the courage to try again. To your relief, the same Scarfell is still lagging behind the others. Will you this time fly down, try to grab him and fly him off for interrogation (turn to **239**) or knock him from the yak and drag him behind a rock (turn to **356**)?

338

You glide down the face of the waterfall, which washes into another lake. It is not really deep enough to conceal a body of the size you seek, so you plunge through the curtain of water. There you see, floating face down, the eerily still body of the unfortunate giant!

You run across to the giant's corpse. Both of his hands are submerged and you heave out the nearest one quickly. No ring. You splash round to the other side of the giant, heart pounding, and lift out the second dripping arm.

You stare in disappointment at what you find! The left hand is lacking one finger, crudely hacked off! You let it drop into its watery grave once more and stare upwards in frustration. The Scarfell lied to you! Pausing only to remind yourself never to trust one again, you fly upwards, trailing drips of water below you. Turn to **257**.

339

The guard does not hear you. Inside the tent, you find a spacious interior lit by dim candlelight which has been left unattended. Crates of dried food lie half open and picked at. Leaning against them are piles of weapons: about a dozen heavy looking two-handed axes and half that number of thick bows. Quivers of arrows are carelessly discarded beside them. To your disappointment, there is no sign of any treasure.

You creep about, aware of the Scarfell just a metre away on the other side of the canvas, and are just about to leave when a thought occurs to you: you could take some of these weapons and hide them in the mountains. But would this make much indentation on your enemy's strength? If you want to steal the axes, turn to **195**. To take the bows, turn to **275**. Otherwise, there is little else to find in this tent. Will you next head towards the largest tent? (Turn to **219**) Or to the other side of the camp? (Turn to **242**). If neither of these appeals to you, you could follow up an earlier idea and start a fire to create a diversion? (Turn to **281**) Or capture a prisoner for interrogation? (Turn to **201**)

340

You find a place that is not overlooked and drop quietly to the ground. Then you gingerly lift the edge of the tent and peer under.

The tent is lit by candlelight, though you cannot see the source. But it is not unoccupied; although you can see no-one from your position, you can hear light snores coming from somewhere. There is no sign of the ring as yet, but you decide to investigate further. If you want to creep in, turn to **248**. If you'd rather withdraw and make an incision in the canvas higher up so that you can see in, turn to **311**.

341

The success of this move will depend on your speed, the strength of your blow and a bit of luck! You are only going to get one shot at this! Roll the die. If you roll a 3 or less, turn to **237**. If you roll a 4 or more, turn to **288**.

342

The lamp smashes into pieces and goes out immediately. The Scarfell warlord bellows in rage at you as he is plunged into darkness and you hastily dodge his initial blind attack. If you have the codeword GRUB, turn to **282**. If you do not have this codeword, turn to **299**.

343

"Let's do it!" you cry, and the pair of you fly on in high spirits. About half an hour later, you fly over a familiar sight: it is the Forest of Arcendak, where less than a month ago you both conquered numerous deadly perils on the Fygrinnd. You think of your friend Snyblo, who undertook the test on the same day and has not been heard of since…

Rical points downwards. "Look!" he cries, "There's the Orphus Latix clearing!" You both smile wryly as you remember how easily your task could have been achieved from the air.

Soon Arcendak is lost to view behind you. Further on, something unusual breaks the carpet of clean white snow covering the mountains. A criss-cross of small fissures below you; cracks in the rocky ground that lead like tributaries of a river into a chasm. Steam curls from its depths. If you want to fly down and investigate, turn to **221**. If you want to continue on your way to Musk, turn to **272**.

344

Direct hit! The rock strikes him hard on the back of the head; he loses his balance and falls from his mount onto the snowy ground, unmoving. The yak trundles on, seemingly unaware of what has happened! Keeping your eyes on the rest of the Scarfells continuing on into the distance, you scamper across to your target and drag him out of sight. He is groggy, but not quite unconscious. Turn to **235**.

345

You push up from the rocky bed of the lake but the water makes your take-off sluggish. Roll the die. If you roll a 2 or less, turn to **269**. If you roll a 3 or more, turn to **263**.

346

Ever so slowly and silently, you reach for the rope and grip it in both hands. You lower it over his wrists, but as soon as it touches him he speaks calmly and menacingly. "Ah, so you've come back! But this time I have you!" He tips back his helm, evidently pretending to sleep in order to trap a greedy subordinate, but a look of amazement spreads over his face when he sees you!

"What?" he snarls, the surprise soon turning to anger. *React on instinct*. Will you:

Slash his hand, hoping he will release the ring?	Turn to **330**
Knock the bedside candle over, aiming to start a fire or at least distract his attention?	Turn to **202**
Or attempt to choke him with the rope?	Turn to **359**

347

The chair arcs through the air. The ogre smashes it into pieces with his club as it flies towards him, but you and Rical are already following up. Roll the die. If you roll a 1, 2 or 3, turn to **192**. If you roll a 4 or 5, turn to **227**. If you roll a 6, turn to **294**.

348

"Nightfall? Give me a day at the least!" you cry, unsure of how this bold request will be met. If you have the codeword YAK, turn to **290**. Otherwise, roll the die. If you roll an odd number, turn to **234**. If you roll an even number, turn to **205**.

349

"We'll see!" you declare and pick the man up once more. You fly deeper into the ravine and come to land on a large plateau. A waterfall bursts from the rock nearby, running into a pool that becomes a river very soon afterwards. The river runs off into the distance downhill and round a bend in the cliff. You notice as you near the water, and confirm as you cautiously dip a taloned toe in, that it is warm! How this is possible you do not know, but it explains why it is not frozen!

"That giant's body could've fallen in this river and floated down there," observes your prisoner gruffly, pointing down the slope. You wonder what his motivation is for being seemingly helpful all of a sudden.

Over the edge of the plateau the ravine extends downwards as far as the eye can see. You can therefore see two options. You could follow the river as the Scarfell suggests? (Turn to **296**) Or you could fly deeper into the chasm? (Turn to **252**)

350

The Scarfell camp consists of a ramshackle gathering of about twenty tents, lit by occasional flaming torches thrust into the snowy ground. A few Scarfells wander to and fro on various errands but it looks as though the camp is settling for the night. On the far side you make out a pen for the yaks, currently attended by a couple of guards.

You wonder where you are most likely to find the ring, and narrow down your options. The largest tent flies an icy-blue war banner with gold trim. To investigate this, turn to **219**. You could sneak into the camp and try to eavesdrop in on a conversation or two (turn to **297**). You could quite easily take one of the torches and cause havoc by setting something alight. Maybe this would be a useful distraction? To try this, turn to **281**. Otherwise, you could try to capture a prisoner for interrogation. To follow through on this idea, turn to **316**.

351

Off balance and flustered, he topples backwards and falls to the floor, temporarily vulnerable. If you have the codeword GRUB, turn to **331**. Otherwise, roll the die. If you get a 4 or less, turn to **331**. If the total is 5 or more, turn to **208**.

352

The icy snow chills every feather but you do not feel it. You lie still, not daring to breathe. Roll the die. If you roll an odd number, turn to **229**. If you roll an even number, turn to **274**.

353

The table flies through the air. The warlord looks surprised and parries it with his axe but you are already upon him, slashing ferociously. Blood is drawn, but then your opponent brings his axe up and catches you off guard. The savage weapon slices into your body and you fall to the ground in agony. Mercifully, the Scarfell does not take his time finishing you off…

354

Rical's call brings no response, though for a moment you think that you hear something faint in the depths of the chasm behind you. If you now want to enter the cave, turn to **326**. To ignore the cave and fly deeper down the chasm, turn to **198**. To abandon this whole place and carry on with your journey, turn to **272**.

355

You enter the lake with a small splash. It is not really deep enough to conceal a body of the size you seek, so you plunge through the curtain of water. There you see, floating face down, the eerily still body of the unfortunate giant! Turn to **223**.

356

You land close behind the travelling party and consider the best way to go about this. You could throw a rock at his head and try to knock him out? (Turn to **251**) Or you could run at him and take him by surprise, wrestling him to the ground and muffling his voice with your hand? (Turn to **210**)

357

You hope that the blackness of the night will cover you as you make your move. Roll the die. If you roll a 1 or 2, turn to **258**. If you get a 3 or more, turn to **339**.

358

The warlord stumbles backwards and as his axe remains stuck, he abandons it on the floor. Erase the codeword HAFT. If you have the codeword ASH, turn to **232**. If you do not have this codeword, turn to **318**.

359

You jerk the rope savagely up to his throat and twist his body to get behind him. He splutters for a second, but then grasps the rope calmly with meaty fingers. His strength is immense and he does not react to the pain he surely feels as the rope bites into his jugular!

Slowly, you feel the rope being pulled downwards as he overpowers you and you let go of it to maintain your own balance. You step away and now stand facing him. How will you attack? You could:

Pick up the makeshift wooden table next to you and use it as a weapon?	Turn to **214**
Flap you wings frantically and drive him backwards?	Turn to **298**
Or drop to the floor and try to sweep his legs out from under him?	Turn to **341**

360

Finally, the familiar outline of the Tower of Egratar appears in the distance. As it is the middle of the night there are few Ariax about and you decide to sleep now and explain your extended absence in the morning.

An hour after sunrise, Nimax is irked to find the pair of you relating your tale to an eager group of juvenile Ariax. He strides through them and orders you to follow him to the very same rocky crevasse where you had your initial briefing just yesterday.

Nimax does not believe your story, despite your angry protests considering the dangers you have faced. He scornfully states that, as you did not visit the Horned Mountain, he will recommend further assessment to see if you can be counted fit for the adult ranks of the tribe.

At that point a shadow falls over him. You turn to see the Vzler himself standing over you! "I have had strange news this morning," he says, "and guessed you may be here. Tell me what has befallen you."

You tell your story while the Vzler stands motionless and listens. Nimax stands nearby looking sullen, arms folded. "It is an amazing tale!" proclaims the Vzler as you bring events right up to the present. "Perhaps most surprising to me is Nimax's initial mistake: the Horned Mountain is *east* of here!" he looks sidelong at your mentor with a sardonic smile on his face.

Nimax marches off at this point, face as black as thunder: he deliberately sent you in completely the wrong direction! The Vzler commends you on your success and says that, to him, this kind of achievement marks out a young Ariax for future greatness…

As he takes his leave once more, you follow Rical back into the company of your peers, enjoying the present attention. They are just rewards for your skilful and courageous actions of last night! However, your sense of triumph is not destined to last for long: you are soon to receive fateful news that will change your life forever, as chronicled in book 3 of The Saga of the Ariax:

RAID ON IRO

THE SAGA OF THE ARIAX: 3
RAID ON IRO

Recent events

It is now almost a month since you successfully undertook the coming of age trial known as the Fygrinnd, where you braved the dangers of the Forest of Arcendak to recover a handful of the mysterious herb Orphus Latix. You have since discovered that, thanks to a spell cast on you by a wizard named Vashta who you met along the way, you can speak and understand the languages of other races!

Two days after your recent brush with the Scarfells, your senior master of training, the Vzler, summons you and your friends Rical and Darfak to meet him at the Iriox Ring, an important underground meeting place.

"It is finally time to reveal to you the secret of Orphus Latix," the aged birdman explains. "Orphus Latix is in fact the most powerful plant in the whole of Faltak. If its secret were known outside of our tribe, it would bring the greedy and power hungry from far and wide in search of it. For it is the secret of our longevity, our very survival. He who eats Orphus Latix will be *slow to die...*"

This is astonishing news! The Vzler goes on to explain that the natural lifespan of the Ariax was between fifty and seventy years before the discovery of the powers of Orphus Latix many hundreds of years ago. Now, twice that is commonplace. "The clearing where the Orphus Latix grows is carefully tended as it cannot be made to grow anywhere else. The herb is eaten by every adult Ariax in the Tower of Egratar on the first night of each new year. Tonight, having braved the forest to collect some yourselves, *you* will join us for the very first time!"

Throughout the evening's festivities, all you can think about is the wizard Vashta and his servant Erim. You told no-one, but they took some of the Orphus Latix...

In the morning light, perhaps full of foolish overconfidence, you know what you must do. To keep your tribe's greatest secret, you must fly to a far off city of humans and retrieve that sample of the herb. You must also discover if Vashta has told anyone about it and somehow silence him and his investigations. And *you* must go as you alone can understand and speak the words of men, although you're still not quite sure *how*...

Is that all?

Now turn to **361** to begin...

361

You try to recall all that Vashta and Erim told you. They came from the city of Iro, many miles to the south-east. You remember them recounting a long journey west and then north, 'following the line of the Rune Mountains'. This is good, as it will have taken them a long time to return home, even if they picked up horses when they left Arian. You can fly directly south-east and hopefully catch up with them before or soon after they reach home and have a chance to do anything with the Orphus Latix.

The mountains race by beneath you as the wind sweeps you along. Never have you flown so far from your home! You see a mighty river whose name you do not know churning and gushing its way north through the cracks and crevasses of Arian, but continue south-east, guided by the sun.

You stop only twice to eat and rest on the first day; food is still easy for you to find in the mountains. After spending the night in a cave you resume your journey.

Late on in the second day, you see an incredible sight: the mountains recede and are replaced by rolling brown foothills and then forests of trees you do not recognise. The grasslands become greener and you see strange figures wandering about them, seemingly half-human, half-giant.

You fly for another day, crossing a second mountain range and still pressing on urgently. You discover lowlands on the other side, wooded and populated by strange animals and beasts but no humans as yet.

Finally you spot your first human far below. It is a man dressed in a leather jerkin and tattered trousers, lying alone and seemingly asleep up against a bush in the afternoon sun. He is puny by Scarfell standards but a sword lies beside him so you guess him to be a warrior. Would he be worth questioning about the way to Iro, you wonder?

If you want to wake him, turn to **497**. If you'd like to take his sword first, just in case, turn to **383**. If you decide to fly onwards without talking to the man, turn to **442**.

362

You stand your ground and firmly but politely explain what happened. Other people must have witnessed the event, but no-one comes forth to verify your story. The barrel-maker takes a step forward and eyeballs you, craning his neck to do so. "We don't need ones like you round here," he snarls. "Now pick 'em up!" you feel the eyes of many on the pair of you.

If you decide to concede and help, turn to **464**. To push him away for his impudence, turn to **378**.

363

The man frowns. "Sorry - don't know that name," he says, "Now be off with you!" Note down the codeword ROBE. If you take to the air, in pretence of leaving, turn to **408**. If you stand your ground and protest that this is unjust, turn to **535**.

364

"What?!" splutters Flawn, "This secret will grant great power! Why waste it?!" He narrows his eyes at you as if trying to guess your motives. You decide to change the subject quickly!

If you want to at least pretend to go along with his plan, turn to **499**. To ask him outright to tell you about the secret, turn to **429**. To demand to know where Vashta lives, turn to **520**.

365

You dwarf the little man as you approach him and tap him on the shoulder. He gapes at the sight of you, but regains his cool when he sees your intentions are not malicious.

"No, I don't know this Vashta," he says, peering at you over horn-rimmed spectacles. But before anything further can be said, you both hear a cry. The robed man is being attacked by two hooded robbers! He sprawls on the steps, pathetically stretching a hand out after them as the pair make off down a side street clutching their ill-gotten gains. *React on instinct.* To pursue the robbers, turn to **409**. To turn a blind eye and continue your conversation, turn to **452**.

366

The town square looks much the same as it did earlier. As you stroll through, becoming more and more accustomed to people stepping out of your way in fear (or revulsion), you notice something happening outside the black doorway. An angry dwarf is having a heated argument with a black robed figure whose back is towards you. As you watch, things turn nasty and the pair come to blows, rolling in the dirt and shouting angrily. Erase the codeword SQUARE and replace it with the codeword THORN.

The locals pay no attention to this scuffle. You are just about to leave when you feel a tug on your right wing: it is an ancient old woman with an extremely wrinkled face and but one tooth left in her mouth. "Come away, strange-one!" she cackles. If you want to go with this crone and hear what she has to say, turn to **424**. Otherwise, there are the same four streets leading away as before:

The narrow-looking westerly way?	Turn to **457**
Northwards towards the market?	Turn to **407**
South towards an affluent looking area?	Turn to **393**
Or the widest street, leading roughly east?	Turn to **451**

367

"You broke into Conion the wizard's home in the Disl district of the city. Several city guards observed you entangled in Conion's magic alarm." You appeal that you thought that this was the house of Vashta and mention Finjo, a name which raises eyebrows and draws knowing nods from the panel.

"If you thought that this was your friend's house, why did you not simply ring the bell, which is more customary here in Iro?" asks the noble with the long beard. You choose not to reply.

If you have the codeword KNOCK, turn to **488**. If you do not, but you do have the codeword SWORD, turn to **440**. If you have neither of these codewords, turn to **518**.

368

The study is dominated by a huge desk stuffed full of scrolls and papers. You notice (with amusement) feathers standing in small glass bottles of black ink, used for writing. Shelves crammed with dusty old books and scrolls line the walls and Vashta also appears to have a love of plants, as all sorts grow from various pots and bottles wherever room can be found.

The scrolls that lie open on the table are written in some arcane language that you cannot understand. But a second prominent bundle of papers catches your attention: surely those are Ariax feathers sticking out of the end? You hastily grab the bundle and untie it. The ancient papers are written in a language you can understand and are certainly the ones that led Vashta to Arcendak: you recognise a map of the forest and several references to birdmen. You have no time to read them now though so you roll them up for later.

You are just about to leave the room when you notice in the corner something covered by a thick drape hanging from the ceiling. If you want to pull the drape off and peer underneath, turn to **449**. Otherwise you could try the cellar door (if you haven't already done so) (turn to **462**) or go upstairs (turn to **481**).

369

You grab Sorme firmly by the shoulders and take to the skies. Flight is as normal as walking to you but a completely new experience for your passenger! He whoops loudly in exhilaration, encouraging you to swoop and bank for thrills.

A few miles west takes you into a range of wooded hills, and with your keen eyesight you are first to spot activity below. A band of six or seven warty, green-skinned humanoids are making their way along a stony path towards a cave, stopping only to brawl with each other every so often.

"Are those goblins?" you ask.

Sorme strains his eyes. "Yeah! Put us down over there!" You glide silently down and land undetected behind a wood. "Come on, let's go get 'em!" he smiles, with a wild look of confidence in his eyes. If you decide to help him in his assault on the goblin cave, turn to **513**. If you tell Sorme you'd rather not risk your life on this venture, turn to **470**.

370

Although painful, you reel with the blow and stay on your feet. Finjo is already drawing a dagger from inside his boot, so you ball your fist and punch him in the face. The blow tumbles the thief senseless to the ground; you marvel at his lack of constitution compared to a Scarfell!

You see a man unlocking the front door of the house you so nearly broke in to, and it isn't Vashta. By now, you've seen enough and hurry away. The main road from here twists and turns eastwards. To go this way, turn to **487**. Otherwise, another winding alleyway leads away south-easterly (turn to **393**) or an equally narrow street curves in a north-easterly direction (turn to **407**).

371

The man's face falls. "But it must work!" he cries, and squints into the barrel again. He then begins taking it apart and fiddling with the mechanism inside, holding it very close to his eyes. Realising that he has completely forgotten you, you decide to sidle downstairs and leave him to his work.

From the inventor's house stretch four similar looking streets: north-west (turn to **415**), north-east (turn to **437**), south-west (turn to **554**) and south-east (turn to **493**).

372

You are half starved to keep you subdued and your wings are clipped to prevent flight. An iron ball and chain is affixed to your ankle. You wait and wait for a means of escape, but none presents itself. A few weeks later, your cage is moved onto a cart for transport to another city. Maybe one day you will escape, but by then the secret of Orphus Latix will be known, and expeditions will already have reached the far off Forest of Arcendak. Even if you do free yourself, the resulting shame means that you will be an outcast, and can never return to your tribe.

373

Outside the back door is an alleyway, stinking of filth. At the far end, you see the two thieves scaling a ladder to reach a high window. Perfect! You let out a fearsome screech to curdle the blood and the men turn to see you swooping towards them! You grab the top robber and pull him from the ladder. He drops the bag he was carrying and flails desperately in thin air.

Now what to do? You resolve that you are more likely to get the information you seek from the man who was robbed than from these two, especially when you notice that they are not even fully grown humans!

The second thief has clambered in through the window and disappeared and you let your captive down with an intentional bump at ground level once more. He scarpers as you stoop to pick up the bag he dropped from the rubbish strewn floor. If you have the codeword TALL, turn to **423**. Otherwise, turn to **509**.

374

You hand over the money; after all it has no value to you! The skull-faced man ushers you towards another room which you enter alone. This room is lit only by a very small stub of candle (though you can see in the dark of course), eerily illuminating the figure seated at a small round table. He sits motionless, clad in black robes that cover all but a protruding skeletal jaw. Pungent smelling smoke, which you can see comes from bowls situated around on the floor, encircles the pair of you as you sit down. You also note with interest that there are no other doors in this room.

You wait tentatively for the figure to speak. When he does, he remains unmoving but for the jaw, and the voice is soft and deep. It sounds unrelentingly evil. "You have come from far away...from the north," he intones. There is a pause but you do not react: not that incredible a guess!

"You seek a man who has taken something from you...but not by force," continues the creepy figure. You have that sudden feeling that he is indeed probing your thoughts. Then he speaks a word that makes your blood run cold: "Xanarel!"

Is he really reading your mind? If so, he may uncover what you know about Orphus Latix! If your instincts tell you to flee, turn to **552**. If you want to stay and see what he says next, turn to **410**.

375

The guards allow you to say your goodbyes to Flawn. He embraces you (a custom you find bizarre in your first experience of it) and whispers in you ear to meet him at the Hauter-gate in the eastern wall of Iro at dusk. All is not lost!

As the sun sets, you see a horse and cart appear at the gate, ridden by Flawn and two of his servants. You swoop down from on high where you had been keeping watch and conceal yourself in the cart. Flawn's men throw some grubby old sacking over you and the cart trundles its way back into the city. Turn to **547**.

376

You put your shoulder to the door but even the considerable force of your charge doesn't budge it. In frustration you grasp the handle again and shake it forcefully.

As you rack your brains for another solution, you suddenly feel your arms pinned to your sides! Shining cords of light wrap themselves around your body and wings and you find yourself unable to move! You turn to see Vashta descending the stairs dressed in a long nightshirt, staff held aloft.

"So!" he cries, "I half wondered if one day you would come in search of the…Orphus Latix I think you call it? But forgive me; this is not a secret I wish to lose now, not when I'm so close! Luckily, I prepared for this!" With that, he waves his hands and chants another incantation that makes you lose your senses.

When you awake, you are on a hillside. Why, you can't remember. Still it's a bright sunny morning, the birds are singing and it's time to eat. There is nothing else to trouble you, certainly nothing of your past life, which Vashta has completely wiped from your memory…

377

The main gate towers above you in a wall four or five times your height. There is a steady influx of travellers on the road; some farmers and market traders with carts, others of more dubious intent, but all human.

Two uniformed men stand guard, though they seem to be taking little interest in the comings and goings around them. They wear chainmail and carry spears but their helmets sit on a nearby wall because of the heat. As they see you however, they mutter something to each other and bar your way.

"Now what do *you* want in Iro?" says one man scornfully. "We got rules against things like you!" They chuckle at this apparent joke. What will you reply?

That you seek Vashta the wizard?	Turn to **532**
That you bear important tidings for their ruler?	Turn to **435**
That you have come seeking your fortune?	Turn to **413**
Or if you have the codeword FEATHER, you may wish to tell them of your contact?	Turn to **490**

378

Pandemonium ensues! Several burly marketers throw their weight in to defend their fallen associate and as you fend them off a cry goes up that the city guards are coming! You try to spread your wings but there are just too many people in the way! Note down the codeword MAN.

The brawlers begin to disperse as the guards come through. You hear a voice calling for you to surrender. If you do so, turn to **428**. If you want to try and battle your way out, turn to **542**.

379

"Oh you will, will you?" says the man, clearly suspicious. You lock eyes with him: who holds the power in this conversation? Roll the die. If you roll a 1, 2 or 3, turn to **534**. If you roll a 4 or more, turn to **492**.

380

"Did he now?" says the apothecary, looking down his nose at your answer. "Well, I don't know about that, but there's one thing I do think, knowing old Mr. Vashta like I do, and that's that if you was his servant, you'd more as like be on some severe oath not to tell things like that to folk like me!" He chuckles at his apparent wisdom. "Now can I sell you something, or are you just leaving?"

He doesn't believe your story. You could demand that he gives you Vashta's address? (Turn to **550**) Otherwise, you'll have to leave (turn to **438**).

381

If you have the codeword DUNG, turn to **430**.

A little further down the road you come across a strange sight. A man with tousled hair and a dirty white apron is sat staring sadly at a large heap of horse manure which is piled on the street. It has evidently just spilled from a cart that stands next to it. When he sees you approaching, he stands and speaks to you. "Stranger, I have lost my ring in this here dung-heap!" he says, "And with my back as it is, I can't go digging through it meself! If only you would help me...I can reward you well..."

You look from the man to the dung-heap and back again. A faint look of hope appears in his eyes. If you want to take pity on the man and search for the ring, turn to **479**. If you want to leave him to his own problems and press on, turn to **523**.

382

You open your hand and release the young man. Many pairs of disapproving eyes glare at you from all round and the crowd parts as you walk away. Note down the codeword SQUARE. There are four streets leading away from the town square. Will you:

Take a narrow-looking westerly way?	Turn to **457**
Head north towards what looks like a market?	Turn to **407**
Go south towards an affluent looking area?	Turn to **393**
Or take the widest street, leading roughly east?	Turn to **451**

383

You quickly grab the weapon before nudging the sleeping man with your foot and hovering a short distance away. He is temporarily disorientated and fumbles about for his sword, then sees you with it and scrambles to his feet. You hail him casually, but are not alert enough to the danger: he appeared to be scratching but instead produces a dagger from his clothing and flings it towards you! Roll the die. If you roll a 1 or 2, turn to **482**. If you roll a 3 or more, turn to **555**.

384

You make it clear to the man that you are not interested and he spits on the ground by your feet before melting into the shadows. Note down the codeword STUB.

You continue through this particularly cramped part of town, but the people here seem even more suspicious of you than usual. You realise that you have followed a sort of 'c-shape' loop around and are facing east again. The road continues straight on towards the main town square. To go this way, turn to **487**. Otherwise, roads lead north-easterly where you can see tradesmen's carts (turn to **407**) or south-easterly into a more affluent looking part of the city (turn to **393**).

385

You pick up the crossbow and Mariuk buzzes around you explaining how it works. "This is where you load the bolts," he says, grabbing and waggling a wooden box on the top. "And the mechanism inside automatically loads the next one once you have depressed this trigger."

You study the weapon with interest; you use no missile weapons at all back home. But it is difficult to inspect the weapon properly with its inventor constantly poking and prodding at it. Then: disaster! You had not realised that it was loaded and it goes off in your hand! Roll the die. If you roll a 1, turn to **416**. If you roll a 2 or 3, turn to **521**. If you roll a 4 or more, turn to **544**.

386

You attempt to speak to a group of men in fine attire but they sweep past in a hurry. There is a road that goes north-east from here (turn to **478**) or you could go straight eastwards (turn to **493**) or westwards (turn to **451**).

387

You wake up the next morning feeling gloomy. There's nothing much for it except to wait! Roll the die, adding 3 to the score if you have the codeword ROBE. If you roll a 5 or less, turn to **480**. If you total 6 or more, turn to **524**.

388

At this point Vashta steps forward. "My lords," he starts, bowing low. "If I may say a few words? This fellow, Xanarel, is of an ancient and noble race. We are fortunate indeed to have him in Iro, the first ever of his kind to make contact with us! I am fascinated by his extensive knowledge of the northern kingdoms of Faltak, and his great abilities in herb lore can be of benefit to us as a society if I am just allowed to have him as a guest in my home for a few days. Grant this wish and I guarantee that he will remain in my care and leave as soon as ever his business is completed with me."

Vashta bows low once more and retakes his seat behind you. Quite a lot of exaggeration you think, but you're not complaining! The nobles look impressed by this argument and spend a few moments talking to each other in hushed tones before turning back to you. Turn to **425**.

389

Vashta takes you to his home; a large town-house on the eastern side of Iro. You realise that you had not been more than a few streets away from it during your search! Unlike the rest of the houses on this street, it has three storeys, with each level jutting out over the one below; it looks as though the whole building could topple over at any minute!

Vashta produces a key to get in and leads the way, telling you to mind your head just as you do indeed whack it on the human-sized doorway! Inside you find a modest but well-kept home so Vashta surprises you by dumping his cloak on a chair in the hallway. A servant appears from a side door and you recognise Erim, who proved his courage and bravery battling the hideous toad-creature in the far off Forest of Arcendak!

Erim is astounded but also delighted to see you. He picks up his master's cloak and asks how on Faltak you come to be here. As you explain, Vashta muses, "Ah yes – the book! Come, let me choose you a suitable tome…" You detect a certain note of amusement in his voice at this point.

An hour or so passes and you immerse yourself in the human's strange custom of sitting down to an evening meal. Your host explains to you the purpose of cutlery and plates, and Erim brings three delicious courses before you. "You will wish to stay overnight before setting off on your journey home?" asks Vashta and you thank him humbly, while secretly intending to be far away by sunrise, your mission completed.

The pair of you talk long into the night. You ask Vashta to explain the spell he put on you that enables you to speak and understand other languages and he laughs as he tells you that it was actually a spell he'd never had use of before and he was amazed to find it still working a month later!

You deduce through the evening's conversation that all Vashta's work and experiments are carried out on these premises, but dare not bring up the subject of Orphus Latix for fear of making him suspicious. The thought temporarily crosses your mind to simply torch the whole house and destroy everything in it, but you know the Vzler would disapprove of that!

The servants go home for the night and Erim promises to return early next morning and say a proper goodbye. Vashta offers you a bed upstairs, but you explain that you would prefer to sleep downstairs on a hard surface as you are used to sleeping on rocky cave floors. He finally retires for the night and you wait a good hour or so before beginning your nocturnal search. Out in the hallway you see three main options. You could search Vashta's study on the ground floor (turn to **368**). You could try the door leading to the cellar (turn to **462**). Or you could cautiously ascend the stairs (turn to **481**).

390

The guards are certainly not being very welcoming but they do decide to let you in. You pass under the gate and find yourself walking up a busy main street. Most people look at you with a mixture of shock and disgust on their faces as you walk past; they have never seen the like of you before!

Soon you see the road before you feeding into some sort of gathering place. Turn to **487**.

391

You pick a few more likely characters to question, with no result. Then as you make your way through the crowds a donkey kicks out just in front of you, knocking over a pile of newly constructed barrels. The owner of the animal and the stout barrel-maker had both been facing away from the incident (and each other) when it happened but turn round immediately.

"Hey, watch it ya clumsy oaf!" yells the barrel-maker, and you are shocked to find him talking to you! A few nearby onlookers also look at you disapprovingly! Will you apologise and help pick up his wares? (Turn to **464**) Or will you blame the donkey? (Turn to **362**)

392

"I see!" exclaims the man. "Allow me to introduce myself. My name is Flawn Ghire. I think we share a common purpose! But come, let us not talk here so openly in the street." Note down the codeword BROW.

You let him lead you over to pile of barrels at the edge of the road and sit down. "I know what it is you seek," he continues in hushed tones. "I know that Vashta recently uncovered the secret of the birdmen. I will show you where it is kept if you will help me retrieve it!"

Obviously sharing the Orphus Latix with him is out of the question, but this is still a good lead. If you want to agree to this arrangement immediately, turn to **499**. If you decide to discuss things further and find out exactly what he knows, turn to **429**. If you want to explain that you wish to *destroy* the thing he speaks of, turn to **364**. If you'd rather just demand to know where Vashta lives, turn to **520**.

393

The buildings here are bigger, cleaner and command more space about them than those you have seen so far. Some are clearly not homes as they have open doors and people are coming and going from them freely. Some are adorned with strange symbols and you cannot guess at their meaning. If you have the codeword BOOK, turn to **466**.

The biggest building of all is a mighty sandstone construction with a flight of steps leading up to its entrance. You decide to question one of the men on the steps about Vashta. Will you talk to a little old man with a pile of books in his arms? (Turn to **365**) Or a tall man in plush robes? (Turn to **473**)

394

The man is still cagey in what he says and just tells you a few vague, unimportant things about the wizard. You sense he is holding out for you to spend some more money. If you have more, decide how many coins you wish to give him, cross them off and turn to **522**. If you have no more, or don't want to give him any more, you could demand he tells you what he knows? (Turn to **550**) Or you could just leave (Turn to **438**).

395

Flawn opens his mouth in astonishment and anger at your decision, but you give him a look as if to say 'this could be part of our plan' that silences him. He nods behind Vashta's back and strides out of the building. Erase the codeword WAND and replace it with the codeword STAFF. At that moment a guard appears and tells you to follow him into the Chamber of Iro where you will be judged.

The Chamber of Iro is a huge room dressed with luxurious adornments the like of which you have never seen before. There are plush rugs on the floor and many paintings and tapestries on the walls that depict previous rulers and dignitaries of the city. The crest of Iro, a blue shield criss-crossed in white with a downturned silver gauntlet in its centre hangs proudly on the wall behind a magnificent desk.

You are ushered in your chains to stand in the very centre of the room flanked by two armed guards. Further guards man the doors. Vashta takes a seat behind you with a handful of others who are here to witness today's trials. After a short wait, a door opens at the far end of the room and five noblemen enter, dressed in official red robes. These are the men, known collectively as the Will of Iro, who will decide your fate! If you have the codeword LAW, turn to **447**. If you do not have this codeword, turn to **468**.

396

Your dramatic proclamation creates uproar all around the chamber! The Will of Iro begin debating earnestly at this point and you are taken back to your cell and told that you will be summoned when they have reached a decision.

Roll the die, subtracting 1 from the roll for each one of the codewords HELM, MAN, SPARKS, KNOCK or SWORD that you have. Add 2 to the roll if you have either of the codewords WAND or STAFF. Add 3 to the roll if you have the codeword LAW. If the result is 3 or less, turn to **411**. If you total 4 or 5, turn to **448**. If the score is 6 or more, turn to **530**.

397

You step up to the carving, convinced of its importance. As you investigate, the eyes of the owl appear to glow in the darkness, bathing you in an eerie green light. You step back warily, but the next thing you know you are writhing on the floor in agony, blasted with malicious magical force. You black out and never regain consciousness.

398

"Iro? I'm never going back *there*!" growls the warrior, taking a step towards you. You try to pacify him by pointing out that you didn't suggest he should! He gestures vaguely south and waits in grim silence for you to go, angered by your intrusion. You can see you won't get anything more out of him and take off in that direction, which is where you were headed anyway! Turn to **442**.

399

The time has come to depart the market square. Note down the codeword CIRCLE. The road south leads towards what looks like another busy meeting place. To go this way, turn to **487**. Otherwise you could head generally eastwards (turn to **415**) or south-west, where the streets look narrow and windy (turn to **457**).

400

"It works!" exclaims the man excitedly, throwing his hands in the air in jubilation. He takes the scope from you with reverence and once downstairs places it carefully back on his workbench. You take this opportunity to ask him about Vashta's whereabouts.

"Vashta, eh?" he says to himself. "Big fellow, no teeth?" You confirm that both of these descriptions are false. "Oh, *Vashta* you mean!" he continues. "Yes, I think I know him! Lives…errr…down that way I think!" He points to the south-east but hardly fills you with great confidence.

You thank him and are just about to leave when you feel him pressing a gold coin into your hand 'for your help'. You decide to hold onto it (note it down) as you have seen many of these things changing hands between the humans and they seem to value them.

If you want to follow the inventor's directions, turn to **493**. If you don't trust his memory and would rather go another way, there are roads leading north-west (turn to **415**), north-east (turn to **437**) or south-west (turn to **554**).

401

The apothecary narrows his eyes at you. "So why should I be discussing that person with you then?" he asks suspiciously. Will you claim to be a friend of Vashta? (Turn to **508**) Or demand that the old man answers your question? (Turn to **550**)

402

Note down the codeword SQUARE. There are four streets leading away from the town square. Will you:

    Take a narrow-looking westerly way?   Turn to **457**
    Head north towards what looks like a market?   Turn to **407**
    Go south towards an affluent looking area?   Turn to **393**
    Or take the widest street, leading roughly east?   Turn to **451**

403

At that moment a guard appears and tells you to follow him into the Chamber of Iro where you will be judged.

The Chamber of Iro is a huge room dressed with luxurious adornments the like of which you have never seen before. There are plush rugs on the floor and many paintings and tapestries on the walls that depict previous rulers and dignitaries of the city. The crest of Iro, a blue shield criss-crossed in white with a downturned silver gauntlet in its centre hangs proudly on the wall behind a magnificent desk.

You are ushered in your chains to stand in the very centre of the room flanked by two armed guards. Further guards man the doors. Flawn takes a seat behind you with a handful of others who are here to witness today's trials. After a short wait, a door opens at the far end of the room and five noblemen enter dressed in official red robes. These are the men, known collectively as the Will of Iro, who will decide your fate! If you have the codeword LAW, turn to **447**. If you do not have this codeword, turn to **468**.

404

"You caused a public disturbance when you started a fight with a citizen of Iro," reads the scribe.

You protest that you were provoked and explain the circumstances, to which one of the noblemen retorts, "Of course, we have only *your* word on that. The guard who witnessed it tells a different story!"

If you have the codeword SPARKS, turn to **367**. If you do not, but you have the codeword KNOCK, turn to **488**. If you have neither of these, but you do have the codeword SWORD, turn to **440**. If you have none of these codewords, turn to **518**.

405

There is a sudden shout from behind you. You turn to see Vashta descending the steps dressed in a long nightshirt, staff held aloft. "So!" he begins, "I wondered if that was the reason for…NO!!"

You follow Vashta's gaze to the Jarip, who is hovering upside down near the ceiling clutching a glass bottle of red, swirling liquid, totally absorbed in watching the pretty colours dance around.

"Xanarel!" pants Vashta urgently, with definite terror in his voice, "You shouldn't have let that thing out! You see that bottle it's got? If it breaks, the whole house will be instantly consumed by flames! We've got to get it off him, quickly!"

This could be a trick. You glance at the Orphus Latix, so close but in the other direction. If you stop the Jarip, Vashta will have time to act. He sees your hesitation. "This is no trick! If we survive this, you can *have* the plant! All of it!" he splutters desperately, "I give you my word! But *please* get that bottle!!"

The Jarip looks down at you, grinning manically. You can't tell what it is thinking! Then it lets go of the bottle! *React on instinct*. If you want to catch the bottle, turn to **469**. If you want to go for the Orphus Latix, turn to **496**.

406

You spiral up into the sky just in time and, leaving the unfriendly villagers behind you, speed on towards your destination. Turn to **456**.

407

If you have the codeword BEARD, turn to **421**. If you don't have this codeword, but you have the codeword CIRCLE, turn to **477**. You are in a large, square open area full of people milling about, some with baskets or boxes of produce, others with animals, still more plying their trade as wheelwrights, weavers, carpenters: even a stonemason!

Most of the humans try to keep out of your way and any you attempt to speak to about Vashta shake their heads and hurry on by. Then an unshaven (and unwashed) man in faded black clothing approaches you and says, "I couldn't help but overhearing. I know of the one you seek. Give me gold and I'll tell ya!" If you have some gold coins and want to give him one of them, turn to **483**. If you don't have any or don't want to part with them you can either threaten the man to tell you what he knows? (Turn to **498**) or ignore him and carry on? (Turn to **391**)

408

You fly high up into the afternoon sky, the sheriff left far below you. Then you wheel westwards across the city wall and land on a rocky outcrop overlooking Iro. You rest briefly but decide to return to the city as soon as possible, keeping your eyes open for guard patrols. Airborne once more, you could land in a part of Iro with narrow winding backstreets? (Turn to **457**) Or a more spacious side of town with grand buildings? (Turn to **393**).

409

Note down the codeword BOOK. You sprint down the steps and launch yourself across the street in the direction of the men. As you round the corner, you are just in time to see them shoving their way through the door of a house on the right hand side. In a few strides you are outside the dingy dwelling yourself. *React on instinct*. Will you kick open the door? (Turn to **551**) Or fly to an upstairs window and hope to surprise the men there? (Turn to **537**)

410

"You are destined to witness much death," drawls the voice. "I see sickness on the wind and fire in the sky...bodies tumbling through the air. And there is one close to you who wishes you dead…"

Your mind swims. Roll the die. If you roll a 3 or less, turn to **453**. If you roll a 4 or more, turn to **517**.

411

You have no idea how long you wait. Eventually the same guard returns and leads you back into the chamber. The man on the right of the Will of Iro stands and addresses you.

"The will of Iro is that you be imprisoned for a period of six months and thenceforth banished forever from our city." Your beak drops open in disbelief and anger, and you begin to protest, but three guards take secure hold of you and encumbered by your chains you are in no position to struggle.

You will indeed be set free in half a year, but by then the secret of Orphus Latix will be known and expeditions will already be in the far off Forest of Arcendak. The resulting shame means that you can never return to your tribe: you are destined to be an outcast wandering lands far, far from your home.

412

You very cautiously peer around a few doors to confirm that they are indeed bedrooms, staying away from the one that you can hear Vashta's light breathing coming from. Then it occurs to you that if the Orphus Latix is Vashta's most prized possession, one which he undertook a long and dangerous expedition to recover, could it be possible that he keeps it near to him at all times?

You decide to risk a peek. As you inch the door open a crack, a horrible creaking noise echoes around the silent landing! Vashta stirs immediately and sits up as the moonlight streams in through the window behind him. *React on instinct*. Will you hide? (Turn to **525**) Or try to explain yourself to the wizard? (Turn to **489**)

413

"*Fortune* eh?" scoffs one of the guards. "Wouldn't mind a bit of that neither, eh Rangon?"

"Will folk pay to see such a curiosity?" wonders the other while waving a hand in your direction. They both laugh. Roll the die. If you roll a 5 or less, turn to **519**. If you roll a 6, turn to **390**.

414

"No problem there matey," grins Finjo, cordially. But as you turn to leave, he produces a wooden club from inside his cloak and strikes you hard over the head and shoulders with it. Roll the die. If you roll a 1 or 2, turn to **471**. If you roll a 3 or more, turn to **370**.

415

You follow the road as it continues to snake through the city. If you have the codeword BROW, turn to **458**. Up ahead, you see a man coming towards you with a mass of tangled grey hair pouring from his head and chin, and colourful robes which remind you of Vashta. You decide to ask yet another person for the wizard's whereabouts, but yet another person shakes his head. As he walks away, a tall man with strongly defined features and jet black hair sidles over to you from across the street. "Now why on Faltak are *you* looking for Vashta?" he asks confidently.

"You know him?" you respond.

"Yes, Vashta and I go *way* back. But I ask you again: why are you looking for him?" It is not straightforward to tell from the man's tone whether he regards Vashta as a friend or not. Will you reply:

"He has something I want,"	Turn to **392**
"He's an old friend and I watch to catch up with him,"	Turn to **549**
Or "Never mind why, tell me where he lives!"	Turn to **507**

416

Unfortunately, you had been holding it facing towards you when this happened. The crossbow bolt buries itself in your heart and you slump to the floor in a pool of blood.

417

Wardial himself opens the door and looks immensely pleased to see you. "Come in, come in!" he beams. "If you just go through there, I'll be with you in a moment!"

He points to a nearby door and you step through into a sparsely furnished room – then you are felled from behind by a heavy blow and lose consciousness!

When you awake, you are lying on the floor of a cage lined with straw and fetid animal droppings. Two men are sat talking to each other and drinking from tankards on the far side of the room. You call out to them but they simply laugh at you and one shouts for Wardial to come in.

He does so and you ask what he thinks he is doing. "Well, you see," he explains, "some 'business contacts' of mine are always on the lookout for extraordinary creatures to join their travelling show. And when I saw you, I just knew you'd be perfect for them!"

"You're going to sell me as a caged exhibit for humans to look at for entertainment?" you roar, and demand to be set free. This just draws further cruel laughter from the men on the other side of the bars. Soon they leave the room and you slump dejectedly to the floor of your prison.

Roll the die, adding 1 to the roll for each one of the codewords HELM, MAN, SPARKS, KNOCK or SWORD that you have. If you score a 6 or more, turn to **516**. If the total is 5 or less, turn to **372**.

418

At your reply, the skull-faced man lifts his hands into the air and begins to chant in a hideous guttural growl. Your flesh begins to crawl and you know enough about evil magic to know that you have to get out of there immediately!

You hurry away, recalling the similar actions of the old lady earlier! Once back out in the open air, you shake your head to clear your thoughts, relieved to find that you have not been followed. Will you now go and see the entertainers (if you haven't already done so) (turn to **474**) or leave the town square (turn to **402**).

419

The sneak-thief is good at his profession and soon has the window open without a sound. He pats you on the back and retreats across the street to where Flawn is hidden in the shadows.

You slip into the darkness of a modest but well-kept lounge area. Your keen eyesight scans the room and you pick out the door immediately. It is ajar so you slip into the main hallway. A flight of carpeted steps with a polished handrail leads upwards and a stone passageway leads to what must be the servants' quarters. You see two other doors of interest; an open one that you can see leads to Vashta's study and a second one that you guess leads to a cellar. Will you go upstairs? (Turn to **481**) Try the door to the cellar? (Turn to **462**) Or go into the study? (Turn to **368**)

420

The man in the coach cries out in surprise as you glide in to land beside him. Then he pulls himself together and looks you up and down as you ask your question. He chuckles.

"My dear fellow, this is only a village! Iro is a great city five or six miles yonder!" He points to a road leading south and tells you to follow it if you want to get to Iro.

"Now what manner of beast are you?" he enquires politely. You tell him and in turn ask *his* name. "I am Wardial the merchant," he proclaims proudly, "I am well known about these parts as a wealthy and successful businessman! In fact, I may be in Iro tomorrow – you must come to my house!"

He describes his house to you and tells you it's on the south side of the city. Note down the codeword FEATHER. Not really wanting to waste too much more time here, especially as Wardial seemingly intends to chatter on for a long time, you politely excuse yourself and take off in the direction of Iro once more. Turn to **456**.

421

You are back in the market square *again*! The barrel-maker has finished for the day and sits drinking, but frowns when he sees you.

Suddenly, two men take a firm hold of your arms and you feel a spear point at your back! It is a patrol of the city guard and you did not hear them approach! "You will come with us," states another man, stepping in front of you. When you demand to know why, he simply shakes his head as if unable to believe you would need to ask!

"Struggle and I run you through!" sneers the man with the spear. He digs the spear point painfully into your back as he says this and you decide to go along with them for now.

You are marched through the streets (to the general pleasure of the crowds) until you reach a large sandstone building. You mount a flight of steps leading up to its entrance and are taken to a cell which is locked behind you. Turn to **432**.

422

You drop him in a heap on the ground and decide to lose yourself in the crowd as soon as possible! Will you run east? (Turn to **437**) South-east? (Turn to **478**) Or west? (Turn to **451**)

423

You return to the sandstone building and stride over to where the little old man sits on the steps. He peers at you over horn-rimmed spectacles as you hand him the bag. Inside, he gratefully finds the possessions that had been stolen from him.

"Thank you, stranger!" he exclaims, "Truly one cannot always judge by appearances!" You spend a few moments talking with the old fellow, who introduces himself as Effius Ferrell, a 'nobleman of some standing in Iro' as he himself puts it. He apologises that he does not know Vashta the wizard, but wishes you luck in your search. Note down the codeword LAW.

Eventually Effius bids you farewell and ascends the steps into the building. You look about you and find that this street runs east (turn to **554**) and to the north-west, where it narrows into a densely packed gathering of buildings (turn to **457**). A main street runs due north towards the town square. To go this way, turn to **487**.

424

Away from the crowds, the old woman draws out a necklace full of multi-coloured crystals. She tells you that she is a charmist, and can cast a spell on you that will grant you good fortune for just two gold pieces.

If you have two gold coins and want to give them to her, turn to **467**. If you don't have them, or don't believe her words, you could leave the town square by going:

By the narrow-looking westerly way?	Turn to **457**
Northwards towards the market?	Turn to **407**
South towards an affluent looking area?	Turn to **393**
Or by taking the wide street, leading east?	Turn to **451**

425

"Now before we pass our judgement, *you* have the right to speak feathered one," declares the noble sat in the middle of the five. All eyes are on you as you turn over the possibilities in your head. Will you:

Tell them that you are sure that you can rely on them to be fair in deciding what to do with you?	Turn to **495**
Threaten that if anything happens to you, your tribe will mount an assault on Iro that will leave it devastated (of course, your tribe have no idea where you are, but *they* don't know that!)?	Turn to **396**
Try to persuade them that you do not pose any kind of threat to their city?	Turn to **461**
Or shake your head and defiantly say nothing?	Turn to **553**

426

You take a flying leap and manage to pluck the bottle out of the air as the Jarip howls in disappointment above you. Fortunately the bottle-stopper is in securely, but your momentum carries you painfully into a table and you crash to the floor without the use of your hands to protect you.

Vashta rushes across towards you, but you scramble to your feet and hold the bottle away from him. "Your promise, first…" you say.

With a miserable nod, Vashta slowly walks over to the priceless plant and throws it into a grate. He then touches it with his staff and it ignites, crackling as it burns. There is a solemn silence as the old wizard stands watching the smoke curling up to the ceiling. "That really is all of it," he says sadly, and you know that he speaks the truth.

You suddenly realise that Vashta wasn't joking about the bottle in your hand! You offer it to him and he takes it carefully. "A stupid experiment to make firewater!" he groans. "And as for *you*!" he turns angrily to the Jarip, "You're going back where I found you!"

You decide to make your way out while he is distracted chasing the little creature around the room. Breaking into his cellar and destroying his most valuable work, not to mention stealing his scrolls? It's unlikely that you will be welcomed to stay!

You make your way to the front door and let yourself out. Across the street, Flawn Ghire emerges from the shadows. "Well?" he hisses. You tell him that unfortunately, the secret has been destroyed. Flawn seethes with anger and orders his men to grab you, but you are already spiralling up into the night sky. Turn to **560**.

427

"Me? Well I'm out treasure hunting as usual, always seeking danger and never knowing what tomorrow holds!" he says, relaxing. "Sorme's the name!" You seem to have hit on Sorme's favourite subject (himself) and he begins to tell you tales of glory and riches. You don't like to interrupt by asking where all his wealth *is* exactly, as judging by his clothes he doesn't look particularly rich!

He tells you that he is currently on the trail of a small band of goblins that live in these hills (or more precisely their gold!) and asks if you could help him to locate their cave from the air. He doesn't seem either suspicious of you or interested in why you're here, concerned only with his search. If you want to help him out as he asks, turn to **369**. If you decline and want to be on your way, turn to **442**.

428

You raise your hands skywards and allow the guards to grab you by the arms. "You will come with us," states one man, stepping in front of you. When you demand to know why, he simply shakes his head as if unable to believe you would need to ask!

"Struggle and I run you through!" growls a voice behind you, and he digs his spear point painfully into your back. You decide to go along with them for now.

You are marched through the streets (to the general pleasure of the crowds) until you reach a large sandstone building. You mount a flight of steps leading up to its entrance and are taken to a cell which is locked behind you. Turn to **432**.

429

It soon becomes clear that Flawn Ghire does not know exactly what the secret of the birdmen is and certainly doesn't suspect it to be a *plant*! He needs you to identify it as much as retrieve it! Still, he has information that you need. Will you agree to his deal? (Turn to **499**) Or demand to know where Vashta lives? (Turn to **520**).

430

You are back in the place with the man and his dung-heap. Fortunately it has now been cleared up and there is no sign of him. Then something catches your eye in the distance – surely that's Erim, the servant of Vashta? You barge your way in his direction, but he is walking away from you. Turn to **451**.

431

"Yes…that's just what I'd expect a servant of Mr Vashta's to say, suspicious old gentleman as he is!" says the apothecary. "Very well, here's his Colewort that he wanted." He hands you a bag of dried herbs. "Oh, and he dropped this last time he was in," he adds, and hands you a small silver key on a cord.

You thank the man and leave his shop, unable to ask for directions. You may take the herbs and key with you if you wish (note them down). The cord fits quite snugly round your neck and you conceal the key under your feathers so that it cannot be seen (if you ever have all your possessions taken away from you, no-one will find the key). Note down the codeword PICKLE. From here, three similar looking roads stretch out. You could head west (turn to **554**), north (turn to **381**) or north-west (turn to **478**).

432

You sit on the floor of the cell and look about for a means of escape. The three windowless stone walls and a locked wooden door resist your investigations, and the heavy iron chains on your wrists and ankles will not help! There is only just enough room to lie down and the lack of space bothers you more than the lack of light. The only object in the cell is a bucket; you can guess why this has been provided!

Later on two guards come to the door. One enters and slides a pan of cold food onto the floor. He also takes any gold or herbs you are carrying (cross these off).

"How long are you going to keep me here?" you ask, but the guards do not reply. Not one of the humans you have met here has been surprised that you can speak their language!

You sit picking at the tasteless food, leaving the bits that you cannot identify. Night falls and you grab a few hours of troubled sleep. If you have the codeword WAND, turn to **511**. If you do not have this codeword, turn to **387**.

433

The guards allow you to say farewell to Vashta. He shakes your hand (a custom you remember from your last parting) and you feel a small scroll of paper pressed into your palm. All is not lost!

You fly to a mountainside overlooking Iro and unravel the scroll. Vashta's message reads: "A shame to waste a journey. North gate, sundown. V"

As the sun sets, you see Vashta emerge from the gate on horseback. You swoop down from on high where you had been keeping watch and land beside him. He motions for you to clamber up behind him and pull an old sack over your head, waving away your protestations that you will be seen by reminding you that he is a wizard! You are unsure what magic he conjures, but your journey back into the city is untroubled. Turn to **389**.

434

The window slides open silently and you slip into the darkness of a modest but well kept bedroom, empty of occupants. On the landing you see further doors on either side and at each end is a flight of stairs; one up and one down. If you want to search the upstairs rooms, turn to **412**. To try the stairs leading up, turn to **504**. To go down the stairs at the other end of the landing, turn to **441**.

435

"Oh yeah? And what kind of 'tidings' is that then?" they ask, doubtfully.

"News too important for the likes of you!" you reply, stepping forwards boldly, "Now time is of the essence; let me pass!"

Will the guards fall for your bluff? Roll the die. If you roll a 4 or less, turn to **519**. If you roll a 5 or 6, turn to **390**.

436

Finjo leads you down narrow side-streets until you come upon a bizarre looking house with a crooked tower jutting out from the rooftop. Besides looking out of place with its surroundings, it looks dilapidated; certainly lacking the majesty of the Tower of Egratar back home! Note down the codeword STUB.

"It won't be guarded this time of day," smiles Finjo, "and there's a place you can get in up there!" He points up and you see an open window high up on the south side of the structure. Finjo has no idea of the name of the wizard who lives there, but his intentions are clear: he wants you to burgle the tower! Could this be Vashta's home? If you want to fly up and break into the tower, turn to **533**. If you'd rather tell Finjo you want no part of this, turn to **414**.

437

You reach a bend in the road. Rounding the corner before you trots a horse and rider. The rider is dressed in a fine coat over chainmail armour, wears a silver helm upon his head and carries a long sword at his belt. If you have the codeword SWORD, turn to **527**.

"I am Selgar, chief sheriff of the city of Iro," declares the man with an air of authority. He stops his horse before you. "I have heard news of your activities since arriving in our city. You are to leave immediately and not return!" Note down the codeword SWORD. Will you:

Refuse and protest that this is unjust?	Turn to **535**
Try telling him about Vashta?	Turn to **363**
Or fly away, to return later?	Turn to **408**

438

Note down the codeword PICKLE. You push open the door of the shop and are back out on the street again. From here, three similar looking roads stretch out. You could head west (turn to **554**), north (turn to **381**) or north-west (turn to **478**).

439

"You again?" moans the Jarip. "You'd better be going to let me out this time!"

If you have Vashta's silver key and want to try it in the lock, turn to **512**. If you don't have it, or still don't want to release this creature, you replace the drape (please stop doing this to the poor thing!) and head back out into the hallway. This time will you try the cellar door? (Turn to **462**) or go upstairs? (Turn to **481**).

440

"Selgar, our city's chief sheriff, ordered you to leave Iro yesterday afternoon and not return – is this not so?" asks the scribe. You have to admit that it is, but claim that it was an unjust order.

"That will be for us to decide!" smiles one of the noblemen dryly as the scribe rolls up his scroll once more. Turn to **518**.

441

Downstairs you find yourself in the main hallway. A stone passageway leads to what must be the servant's quarters. You see two other doors of interest; an open one that you can see leads to Vashta's study and a second one that you guess leads to a cellar. Will you try the door to the cellar? (Turn to **462**) Or go into the study? (Turn to **368**)

442

A little later you see below you a collection of maybe fifty huts and other primitive dwellings. You have never seen buildings like this before and many humans walk between them gathering firewood, carrying stores and generally getting on with everyday life. Could this be Iro? You decide to fly down and ask someone if your guess is correct. You observe three possibilities. Would you rather ask:

A farmer tilling a field alone?	Turn to **505**
A rich looking man sitting in a horse-drawn carriage?	Turn to **420**
Or a group of juveniles playing in the dirt?	Turn to **541**

443

"I've lived in Iro all me life!" says the man, dusting off his grubby clothes as you release him. He turns south. "Down there's the town square," he continues, "go through it and you get to the Erro district. Likely you'd find 'igh standing people that way. Otherwise there's a good apothecary by the name of Shem east of Erro – if your friend's really a wizard 'e'd go there I reckon."

You thank the man. He tips his hat before scurrying off. Turn to **391**.

444

"Shame," says Flawn disbelievingly. If you want to make a deal with him and say that you will share the secret if he first tells you where to find Vashta, turn to **379**. If you want to demand he tells you, turn to **520**.

445

You dash through the door and fling yourself to the dusty floor of the back room behind a table laden high with bits of wood. You hold your breath as you hear iron-shod boots thundering past you and out of the back door. When they have gone, Mariuk grabs your arm. "Time for you to go I think!" he puffs, clearly flustered by the presence of the city guards in his home! You oblige! From the inventor's house stretch four similar looking streets: north-west (turn to **415**), north-east (turn to **437**), south-west (turn to **554**) and south-east (turn to **493**).

446

Suddenly, two men take a firm hold of your arms and you feel a spear point at your back! It is a patrol of the city guard and you did not hear them approach! "You will come with us," states another man, stepping in front of you. When you demand to know why, he simply shakes his head as if unable to believe you would need to ask!

"Struggle and I run you through!" sneers the man with the spear. He digs the spear point painfully into your back as he says this and you decide to go along with them for now.

You are marched through the streets (to the general pleasure of the crowds) until you reach a large sandstone building. You mount a flight of steps leading up to its entrance and are taken to a cell which is locked behind you. Turn to **432**.

447

You are shocked to recognise the fourth man who enters! It is none other than Effius Ferrell, the man whose possessions you recovered from the robbery just yesterday! He obviously recognises you too, but says nothing for now. You allow yourself an inward smile; surely he will be able to influence the other men's thinking in your favour! Turn to **468**.

448

You have no idea how long you wait. Eventually, the same guard returns and leads you back into the chamber. The man on the right of the Will of Iro stands and addresses you.

"The will of Iro is that you be released but henceforth banished from our city. The penalty for returning will be death." You sigh with relief, though you know that you will have to return. A guard comes across and sullenly removes your chains. If you have the codeword WAND, turn to **375**. If you have the codeword STAFF, turn to **433**. If you have neither of these codewords, turn to **503**.

449

The drape falls to the floor to reveal a cage the size of your torso. Sitting grumpily inside is a hideous little creature. It resembles a shrunken, bony human, but has a domed head, elongated limbs and bottle-green skin. It leaps nimbly to its feet and grips the bars as it sees you, hopping up and down and staring at you hopefully with deep green eyes. If you have the codeword JARIP, turn to **439**.

"Hurry up! Hurry up!" it squeaks, "Let me out!"

"What are you?" you ask.

"Me? I'm a Jarip!" says the Jarip, "And a wrongfully imprisoned Jarip I might add! Now how are you going to get me out? I'll help you if you help me!"

You pause to consider. "C'mon, c'mon!" wails the Jarip impatiently, "Have you got the key or not?" Note down the codeword JARIP.

If you have Vashta's silver key and want to try it in the lock, turn to **512**. If you don't have it, or don't want to release this creature, you replace the drape (much to the Jarip's disappointment) and head back out into the hallway where you can either try the cellar door (turn to **462**) or go upstairs (turn to **481**).

450

It's no good; she screams! A dozen or so heads turn in your direction. One brave man (a blacksmith) shouts at you to 'leave her alone!' and holds a newly forged sword up towards you, menacingly. Will you slap the weapon away? (Turn to **548**) Or shrug and walk off? (Turn to **399**).

451

You set off down this new street. Suddenly, two men take a firm hold of your arms and you feel a spear point at your back! It is a patrol of the city guard and you did not hear them approach! "You will come with us," states another man, stepping in front of you. When you demand to know why, he simply shakes his head as if unable to believe you would need to ask!

"Struggle and I run you through!" sneers the man with the spear. He digs the spear point painfully into your back as he says this and you decide to go along with them for now.

You are marched through the streets (to the general pleasure of the crowds) until you reach a large sandstone building. You mount a flight of steps leading up to its entrance and are taken to a cell which is locked behind you. Turn to **432**.

452

"Did you see that?" exclaims the man, and hurries over to where the other man has fallen. By their conversation it is clear that they know each other and that you have been forgotten in the drama. Note down the codeword BOOK.

You look about you and find that this street runs east (turn to **554**) and to the north-west, where it narrows into a densely packed gathering of buildings (turn to **457**). A main street runs due north towards the town square. To go this way, turn to **487**.

453

You try to stand up but find that you cannot. The bony jaw appears to be smiling. The dark magic of 'He who knows' will claim another soul…

454

At this point Flawn Ghire steps forward. "Lords of Iro," he starts, bowing low. "May I be allowed to speak? This seemingly bestial creature before you is in fact a learned scholar whom I invited to Iro as my guest! It is my hope that he may broaden my own knowledge which perhaps can then be used to benefit our glorious city! I did not think I did wrong by letting him roam the streets for a time to absorb some of our culture, but if I did then I humbly apologise! I implore you to free him into my custody."

Flawn bows again and retakes his seat behind you. You hope that your expression did not belie the fact that most of this was total rubbish! The nobles spend a few moments talking to each other in hushed tones before turning back to you. Turn to **425**.

455

Suddenly, shining cords of light wrap themselves around your body and wings and you find yourself unable to move! You roll over to see Vashta standing there dressed in a long nightshirt, staff held aloft.

"So!" he cries, "I half wondered if one day you would come in search of the…Orphus Latix I think you call it? But forgive me; this is not a secret I wish to lose now, not when I'm so close! Luckily, I prepared for this!" With that, he waves his hands and chants another incantation that makes you lose your senses.

When you awake, you are on a hillside. Why, you can't remember. Still it's a bright sunny morning, the birds are singing and it's time to eat. There is nothing else to trouble you, certainly nothing of your past life, which Vashta has completely wiped from your memory…

456

It does not take long to reach what, even from a distance you know must be Iro at last. It sits at the end of a mountain range extending from the north and is surrounded by a wall of stone. It is a huge, sprawling mass of buildings – hundreds and hundreds of them. It is an impressive feat of construction, but finding Vashta will be like looking for a feather in a snowdrift!

You circle high above the city, taking in as much as you can before you land. There are several gates allowing passage in and out, the biggest of which is in the west wall where a main road leads off into the distance. There is much human activity below and you see horses and other animals at work too. Some areas of the city are certainly wealthier than others judging by the size and grandness of the buildings. Would Vashta have a big house you wonder?

You decide to rest for the night and start your search in the morning. The only way you will find Vashta is by picking up clues from the humans – you cannot search every building. You sleep on the mountainside wondering just what kind of welcome you will be given…

When you awaken the sun has already climbed half way into the sky: it is mid-morning, a little later than you would like but at least you feel refreshed and ready for anything! How do you plan to enter the city? You observe the humans passing through the city gates, each one stopping to converse with the guards. Perhaps you should seek permission to enter Iro? To try one of the city gates, turn to **377**. If you want to be more understated and land in a back street somewhere near the centre of the city, turn to **526**. To land in the middle of one of the busier areas and really make an entrance, turn to **514**.

457

You are soon walking through a seeming maze of side streets, back streets and alleyways. There are fewer people here but noticeably more filth and rubbish. Rats scamper between drains and even close up you can hardly see through the mud-encrusted windows of some houses! If you have the codeword STUB, turn to **506**.

A disreputable-looking man in a brown cloak and wide brimmed hat is standing on a street corner. He looks you up and down and says, "I'm Finjo.

You *gotta* be the guy Morkos hired for the wizard job!" It is clear that he has mistaken you for someone else, but his mention of the word 'wizard' intrigues you. If you want to tell him that he is mistaken, turn to **491**. If you want to pretend that you're his man (well, bird!), turn to **436**.

458

You recognise this as the place where you met Flawn Ghire, but there is no sign of him now. Do you want to go east? (Turn to **437**) South-east? (Turn to **478**) Or west? (Turn to **451**)

459

"His *servant*, eh?" This takes the old man by surprise, but he looks as if he is just about prepared to accept it. You tell him that Vashta has been very busy recently and hired you to help Erim. You perceive that he knows that name too.

"If you're Vashta's servant then," says the apothecary, looking at you closely, "Where did Vashta go last month? He's been out of the city." Will you reply:

    The mountains of the north?   Turn to **380**

    Or that you can't tell him as it is secret?   Turn to **431**

460

Suddenly the door opens again and there, at last, you see Vashta the wizard! "Well, well, so it's true! I'd heard there was a birdman walking the streets of Iro asking after me!" he beams. Then he notices Flawn Ghire. "Oh. It's you," he says.

You sense the tension between the two men. Vashta ignores Flawn and continues talking to you. "So what brings you here, my fine fellow?"

You explain that, having passed the Fygrinnd, you were given a second task which required you to fly to a human city and bring back a book. In truth, you'd never heard of books before you came to Iro and inwardly congratulate yourself on your quick thinking!

Vashta seems to believe your tale and promises to sort you out with a book later. In return for saving his life in the Forest of Arcendak, he also offers to do what he can here. "No chance of a magical escape though, I'm afraid," he adds. "For one thing, I'd be outlawed in my own city...and also I wasn't allowed to bring my staff inside the building!"

Flawn Ghire, who has stood glowering during all this, gives you a clear "get rid of him!" glare. The two men's dislike for one another is evident, and you're going to have to ask one of them to leave. But will it be Flawn? (Turn to **395**) Or Vashta? (Turn to **494**)

461

The Will of Iro begin debating earnestly at this point, and you are taken back to your cell and told that you will be summoned when they have reached a decision.

Roll the die, subtracting 1 from the roll for each one of the codewords HELM, MAN, SPARKS, KNOCK or SWORD that you have. Add 1 to the roll if you have *none* of the above codewords. Add 2 to the roll if you have either of the codewords WAND or STAFF. Add 3 to the roll if you have the codeword LAW. If the result is 2 or less, turn to **411**. If you total 3 or 4, turn to **448**. If the score is 5 or more, turn to **530**.

462

The cellar door is locked and what's more there's no keyhole! You could try to break it down, though the noise would surely wake Vashta? (Turn to **376**) Otherwise you could go into the study (turn to **368**) or upstairs (turn to **481**)?

463

There is a sickening crunch; the pitchfork has plunged into your back! You fall to the ground in agony. Mercifully the villagers do not take long to finish you off...

464

You are surrounded by strangers you will never see again so you swallow your pride and help out. A few of the bystanders realise what happened and you even hear murmurs of approval! You take the opportunity to enquire after Vashta, but no luck here either. Turn to **399**.

465

You nod and ask him what he knows. This proves to be less than he'd like, but he does offer to show you where Vashta lives if you will help him retrieve the secret.

Obviously sharing the Orphus Latix with him is out of the question but this is still a good lead. If you want to take him up on his suggestion, turn to **499**. If you'd rather just demand to know where Vashta lives, turn to **520**.

466

Neither of the men you saw earlier are still about. You question a man and woman who pass by but, as you have become used to, their answer is negative. As before, this street runs east (turn to **554**), to the north-west, where it narrows into a densely packed gathering of buildings (turn to **457**) and due north towards the town square (turn to **487**).

467

You hand over the money dubiously and the woman cackles with glee. She then closes her eyes and begins to mutter in some strange language while she holds up her necklace and swings it back and forth. You are painfully aware of people staring, and when she has finished you feel no different. You thank her anyway and go on your way.

In actual fact, the old crone was genuine and you now have been enchanted! For the rest of this adventure you may add 1 to every dice roll you are asked to make! Once again there are the same four streets leading away. Your choice is:

The narrow-looking westerly way?	Turn to **457**
Northwards towards the market?	Turn to **407**
South towards an affluent looking area?	Turn to **393**
Or the widest street, leading roughly east?	Turn to **451**

468

One of the noblemen, the one with the long grey beard, nods for proceedings to begin. A young scribe unravels a scroll and clears his throat before reading aloud: "This is Xanarel of Arian. He had not received the appropriate abhuman clearance necessary to enter the city."

"Are there any other charges?" asks another nobleman. The squire turns towards you and consults his scroll again. If you have the codeword HELM, turn to **539**. If you do not, but you do have the codeword MAN, turn to **404**. If you have neither of these, but you do have the codeword SPARKS, turn to **367**. If you have none of the above, but you have the codeword KNOCK, turn to **488**. If you have only the codeword SWORD and not the ones above, turn to **440**. If you have none of these five codewords, turn to **518**.

469

You take a flying leap and manage to pluck the bottle out of the air as the Jarip howls in disappointment above you. Fortunately the bottle-stopper is in securely, but your momentum carries you painfully into a table and you crash to the floor without the use of your hands to protect you.

Vashta rushes across towards you, but you scramble to your feet and hold the bottle away from him. "Your promise, first…" you say.

With a miserable nod, Vashta slowly walks over to the priceless plant and throws it into a grate. He then touches it with his staff and it ignites, crackling as it burns. There is a solemn silence as the old wizard stands watching the smoke curling up to the ceiling. "That really is all of it," he says sadly, and you know that he speaks the truth.

You suddenly realise that Vashta wasn't joking about the bottle in your hand! You offer it to him and he takes it carefully. "A stupid experiment to make firewater!" he groans. "And as for *you*!" he turns angrily to the Jarip, "You're going back where I found you!"

You decide to make your way out while he is distracted chasing the little creature around the room. Breaking into his cellar and destroying his most valuable work, not to mention stealing his scrolls? It's unlikely that you will be welcomed to stay!

You make your way to the front door and let yourself out. You hear a squeal from behind you as the Jarip is caught, but you are already spiralling up into the night sky. Turn to **560**.

470

"Suit yerself!" Sorme cries, "All the more goblins for me!!" And off he runs, waving his sword maniacally above his head and giving a bloodcurdling war cry. You fly up and watch him charging into the goblins who fall back before his ferocity! Shaking your head at the oddity of this human, you turn your attention back to your own quest. Turn to **442**.

471

The blow catches you just right and you crumple to the ground. Finjo thinks nothing of murdering an unconscious birdman right there in the street with his dagger…

472

Incensed by the human's treatment of you, you throw one guard aside as he grabs you by the arm and slash out at a second one to keep him at bay. Having broken their grip, you charge away, narrowly avoiding being impaled by a spear-thrust. Note down the codeword HELM (if you don't already have it). Now will you run south? (Turn to **478**) Or east? (Turn to **381**)

473

You approach the taller of the two men and see him visibly shrink back at the sight of you. But you hold up your hands and try to reassure him that you mean him no harm. Note down the codeword TALL.

"No, I don't know this Vashta," he says, nervously. But before anything further can be said, you both hear a cry. The man with the books is being attacked by two hooded robbers! He lies spread-eagled on the steps, pathetically shaking a bony fist after them as the pair make off down a side street, clutching their ill-gotten gains. *React on instinct*. To pursue the robbers, turn to **409**. To turn a blind eye and continue your conversation, turn to **452**.

474

You see all sorts of unusual behaviour that clearly demonstrates the oddity of humans! One man is showing off his skills at juggling clubs in the air – of what use is that you wonder? Others present themselves as magic users, but most of these are performing simple sleight of hand tricks to get money out of their unsuspecting victims – of which there is a plentiful supply!

Nevertheless, you decide that the magical theme could be a link with Vashta and start mentioning his name to a few of the magicians. Surprisingly, there seems to be no word about him here either, but then you notice a young man in garish robes and a pointy hat almost trembling at the mention of Vashta's name and very quickly beginning to pack up his things as if to leave.

You call out to him but he turns away and continues stuffing things into a battered suitcase. If you want to grab him and find out what is wrong, turn to **546**. If you'd rather leave him be, turn to **510**.

475

You explain to the nobleman that you had come to Iro seeking out the wizard Vashta. "Vashta? And what business have you with *him*?" he enquires.

"You know him then?" you reply excitedly.

The noble continues, "Yes, I know Vashta!" Then he calls a servant over. "Have a scroll bearing my seal delivered to the house of Vashta the wizard," he says, "Have him come here as soon as is possible to meet…an old friend, shall we say?"

You are allowed to wait in the grand entrance hall of the sandstone building (which still no-one has told you the name of!)

Eventually the door opens and there, at long last, you see Vashta the wizard! "Well, well, so it *is* you, Xanarel!" he says. "So what brings you here, my fine fellow?"

You explain that, having passed the Fygrinnd, you were given a second task which required you to travel to a human city and bring back a book. In truth, you'd never heard of books before you came to Iro, but you have had time to concoct this story!

Vashta seems to believe your tale and promises to sort you out with a book later. "But come, let us go to my house!" he exclaims, and leads you to a horse tethered outside. Turn to **389**.

476

Frustrated before even entering the city, you make for the gates anyway. You throw one guard aside as he grabs at you and slash out at the second one to keep him at bay, but seeing more guards tramping down the street towards you, you take to the sky, narrowly avoiding a spear thrown after you. Note down the codeword HELM.

You decide to land discretely in a back street somewhere near the centre of Iro and resolve to keep out of the way of the guards from now on! Turn to **526**.

477

You are in the market place once more. Erase the codeword CIRCLE and replace it with the codeword BEARD. The craftsmen and traders are still at work with their wares and the crowds still flock around them.

You see a young female who you did not notice before. From a hand-barrow, she is displaying a range of robes and cloaks for sale and repair. It's a long shot, but could she know Vashta? You approach her and ask.

As the girl sees you her eyes widen in fear, she takes a step back and her mouth drops open. She appears terrified and could be about to scream! *React on instinct*. Will you back away and leave? (Turn to **399**) Or speak calmly to her and tell her you mean no harm? (Turn to **450**)

478

Up ahead, the street you are walking down is crossed by another. In a niche in this junction nestles a ramshackle little house with cracked windows and soot stained walls. If you have the codeword STOOL, turn to **500**.

The reason that the house catches your attention is that just as you walk by, a puff of black smoke billows from the open front door – could this be evidence of magic, you wonder? If you want to enter the house, turn to **515**. If you want to pass it by, there is a choice of four directions, all pretty similar looking: north-west (turn to **415**), north-east (turn to **437**), south-west (turn to **554**) or south-east (turn to **493**).

479

You plunge your arm into the dung-heap and begin to root around. After about a minute of this disgusting task, you sense something behind you and turn to find the man, along with three of his friends who have joined him, chortling heartily, hands over their mouths to stifle the noise. When they see you looking round, they burst into raucous laughter at their little joke. If you want to grab the trickster and teach him a lesson, turn to **545**. If you'd rather leave him and wash your arm in a nearby animal trough, turn to **523**.

480

A few hours later a guard appears and tells you to follow him into the Chamber of Iro where you will be judged.

The Chamber of Iro is a huge room dressed with luxurious adornments the like of which you have never seen before. There are plush rugs on the floor and many paintings and tapestries on the walls that depict previous rulers and dignitaries of the city. The crest of Iro, a blue shield criss-crossed in white with a downturned silver gauntlet in its centre hangs proudly on the wall behind a magnificent desk.

You are ushered in your chains to stand in the very centre of the room flanked by two armed guards. Further guards man the doors. After a short wait, a door opens at the far end of the room and five noblemen enter dressed in official red robes. These are the men, known collectively as the Will of Iro, who will decide your fate! If you have the codeword LAW, turn to **447**. If you do not have this codeword, turn to **468**.

481

You come to the first floor landing. You see several doors on either side and at each end is a flight of stairs; one up and one down. To search the rooms on this floor (if you haven't already done so), turn to **412**. To try the stairs leading up, turn to **504**. To go down the other set of stairs, turn to **441**.

482

The man's aim is staggering: the dagger pierces your heart. You fall dead onto the grass, so far from your home…

483

You reluctantly press a gold piece into the man's hand (cross this off). He inspects it and pockets it in one swift move. "Thank'ee!" he says, "Now if you want to find your friend Vashta, go that way and keep on going 'till you see a house that obviously belongs to a wizard." You follow where he points (an easterly direction) but when you look back, he has disappeared into the crowd. You wonder exactly how reliable that information was…Turn to **391**.

484

Suddenly, two men take a firm hold of your arms and you feel a spear point at your back! It is a patrol of the city guard and you did not hear them approach! "I'd release 'im if I were you," sneers the man with the spear and you comply. Flawn smoothes down his cloak in an attempt to regain some dignity and strides away. Note down the codeword KNOCK.

"You will come with us," states another man, stepping in front of you. "Struggle and you'll be run through." The spear point digs painfully into your back as he speaks and you decide to go along with them for now.

You are marched through the streets (to the general pleasure of the crowds) until you reach a large sandstone building. You mount a flight of steps leading up to its entrance and are taken to a cell which is locked behind you. Turn to **432**.

485

You feel the apothecary's eyes sizing you up as he muses what to tell you. Roll the die, adding the number of gold coins you just spent to the result. If the total is 4 or less, turn to **394**. If you get a 5 or more, turn to **522**.

486

Something about a building across the street stirs a memory. You stop to think and realise that you are looking at Wardial the merchant's house! If you want to knock at the door, turn to **417**. If you'd rather not, or have done so already, turn to **386**.

487

You find yourself in a huge flagstoned town square and take a moment to look around at the hive of activity about you. If you have the codeword THORN, turn to **446**. If you don't have THORN but you have the codeword SQUARE, turn to **366**.

The humans all seem to be busy. Some are simply crossing the square to get to somewhere else and those who are doing this on a horse and cart or dragging a hand-barrow are causing a general nuisance. Animal droppings litter the ground and you notice pickpockets at work among the wealthier looking citizens. You get a lot of nasty looks from people pushing past and no-one seems to know anything about Vashta.

A group of entertainers has assembled on one side of the square. Then you notice something interesting through a gap in the crowds on the opposite side: a sinister black doorway. Hanging above it is a sign with 'He who knows' painted on it in ornate gold lettering. If you want to find out where this doorway leads, turn to **538**. To go over to the entertainers, turn to **474**. If you doubt either of these will yield a clue you can leave the town square (turn to **402**).

488

"Following a heated exchange, you assaulted an upstanding citizen of Iro named Flawn Ghire and had to be restrained by our guards and brought here. Mr Ghire is of the opinion that his life was in danger!" continues the scribe.

You snort disrespectfully at this last comment and explain that Mr Ghire had been trying to get you to participate in some housebreaking! "That is your word against his!" points out another of the noblemen.

If you have the codeword SWORD, turn to **440**. If you do not have this codeword, turn to **518**.

489

"What on Faltak...?" splutters the old man, his eyes widening as he sees you standing before him in his bedroom. You begin to explain but he cuts you off. "Ah! I know exactly what *you're* doing here!"

Reacting with amazing speed for his age and catching you unawares, he grabs his staff from beside the bed and raises it in the air. You suddenly feel your arms pinned to your sides! Shining cords of light wrap themselves around your body and wings and you find yourself unable to move!

"So!" he cries, "I half wondered if one day you would come in search of the...Orphus Latix I think you call it? But forgive me; this is not a secret I wish to lose now, not when I'm so close! Luckily, I prepared for this!" You try to protest, but he waves his hands and chants another incantation that makes you lose your senses.

When you awake, you are on a hillside. Why, you can't remember. Still it's a bright sunny morning, the birds are singing and it's time to eat. There is nothing else to trouble you, certainly nothing of your past life, which Vashta has completely wiped from your memory…

490

It is clear that one of the men has heard of Wardial and his reputation. He whispers something to his colleague. Roll the die. If you roll a 1, turn to **519**. If you roll a 2 or more, turn to **390**.

491

"Oh, mistaken am I?" sneers the man. "We'll see. How would you like to make yourself a *serious* amount of gold?" Of course the promise of gold doesn't persuade you as the man expects, but you remember he mentioned a wizard and ask him what he's got in mind.

"Oh, no. Details when you're in on the job!" he grins. "Now are you in or out?" If you want to tell him you're in, turn to **436**. If you tell him to count you out, turn to **384**.

492

He tells you that he has decided to trust you. "You'll get to Vashta's house if you keep going in this direction," he says, pointing east. "You can't miss it; it looks as if it's about to fall over; each storey sticking out over the one below!"

You thank him and let him in on the secret he is so desperate to hear. Of course, you tell him a bogus story about a magic necklace that grants extraordinary powers, but this is exactly the kind of thing he wanted to hear so he doesn't challenge you on it. Feeling rather pleased with yourself, you set off alone in the direction he indicated, knowing that if he mounts his own raid on Vashta's house he won't be looking for a plant! Turn to **451**.

493

On a bend of this road you see a busy looking shop with glass windows all along its frontage. A large sign reads 'Shem's Apothecarium' and underneath: 'the finest supplier of herbs and magical ingredients in all of Iro'. If you have the codeword PICKLE, turn to **446**.

You reason that Vashta could well be a customer here and go in to speak to the proprietor. Shem is a plump man with ruddy cheeks and a carefully twirled moustache who is currently in discussion with a very wizard-like client. You look around, staggered at the amount of wild herbs and more outlandish things he has on sale, some of which you recognise and others totally unfamiliar to you! When he has finished, he turns and looks at you warily but without hostility. To gain information, will you:

Ask him directly if Vashta is a customer here?	Turn to **401**
Pretend to be one of Vashta's servants here to collect an order for him?	Turn to **459**
Or if you have some gold coins with you, look around the shop and buy something before bringing the conversation round to Vashta?	Turn to **536**

494

Vashta looks dumbfounded and a little crestfallen at your decision. "Very well," he says and gives you a slightly suspicious look. Has he guessed your intentions?

Flawn smiles as Vashta leaves the room. "You've done the right thing!" he says. Turn to **403**.

495

"Whatever we decide is, by definition, *fair*, birdman!" states the nobleman in the middle, to the agreement of the others. The Will of Iro begin debating earnestly and you are taken back to your cell and told that you will be summoned when they have reached a decision.

Roll the die, subtracting 1 from the roll for each one of the codewords HELM, MAN, SPARKS, KNOCK or SWORD that you have. Add 2 to the roll if you have either of the codewords WAND or STAFF. Add 3 to the roll if you have the codeword LAW. If the result is 1 or less, turn to **411**. If you total 2, 3 or 4, turn to **448**. If the score is 5 or more, turn to **530**.

496

You turn away from the bottle, not fooled by such a simple ruse! But when you hear Vashta's howl of real anguish you know you have made a big mistake. The house and everything in it is instantly destroyed by a massive fireball that the people of Iro discuss for many long years hence. The one consolation is that the secret of Orphus Latix goes with it…

497

You cautiously nudge the sleeping man with your foot and hover a short distance away. He is temporarily disorientated and fumbles about for his sword, then sees you and scrambles to his feet. You hail him casually, but he holds his blade out towards you and growls, "What do you want?" Will you:

  Ask him the way to Iro?   Turn to **398**
  Or ask what he's doing out here on his own?   Turn to **427**

498

You reach out and grab the man by the front of his shirt. Feeling your strength, his eyes widen in fear and a nervous and rather pathetic grin spreads across his face. "I d-don't really know your friend…" he stammers. "But if y-you let me go, I can tell you a bit about Iro that m-might 'elp you!"

You are disgusted by such spineless cowardice, unheard of amongst the Ariax! If you want the man to tell you what he knows, turn to **443**. If you'd rather put him down and get on with things yourself, turn to **391**.

499

"Excellent!" grins Flawn, and holds out his hand to you. You remember Vashta doing the same when last you parted and know to shake his hand in return. Note down the codeword WAND.

"Now I'll meet you back here at sundown," says your co-conspirator. "I have some other business that I must attend to this afternoon. Oh, and keep away from the city guards; 'abhumans' like yourself are not really *welcomed* in Iro."

Flawn Ghire turns and makes his way into a nearby house. You decide not to abandon your search completely and wander the streets of Iro a little more. From here will you go east? (Turn to **437**) South-east? (Turn to **478**) Or west? (Turn to **451**)

500

You peer in at the door but Mariuk is nowhere to be seen. From the inventor's house stretch four similar looking streets: north-west (turn to **415**), north-east (turn to **437**), south-west (turn to **554**) and south-east (turn to **493**).

501

You scramble upstairs and quickly scan the three sparsely furnished rooms you find there but with no result. You can see no trace of the robbers from the windows either; you have lost them. Embarrassed to return to the victim on the steps empty handed, you decide to slip away down a side street to rejoin a main road. Will you head west? (Turn to **457**) Or east? (Turn to **554**)

502

Five minutes pass sat alone until the second door opens again and in walks a man dressed in a long black robe and hood. His face is covered by a mask designed to look like a skull with staring red eyes. He holds out a pale, emaciated hand and in a cracked voice asks for three gold coins.

If you have three gold coins and want to give them to him, turn to **374**. If you don't have this amount, or do not want to pay him, turn to **418**.

503

You fly free, landing on a nearby mountainside to plan your next move. You decide that it would be too dangerous for you to return by day and catch some sleep to prepare yourself for a night time expedition.

Iro looks completely different by night, with its empty moonlit streets. But the very worst examples of mankind roam the streets of Iro at night and you fall foul of a murderous gang, overpowered and slain in an alleyway. You die slumped in the filth of a human city, far from your home...

504

These stairs spiral upwards in a clockwise direction, narrow and difficult for your taloned feet to navigate. At the top is a large room stuffed full of boxes, old rugs and all sorts of other assorted junk. You can see no other doors and little floor space so searching here quietly will not be easy. If you want to try, turn to **531**. If you doubt Vashta would keep the Orphus Latix up here and want to return downstairs, turn to **481**.

505

You attempt as shallow an approach as you can to avoid alarming the farmer. He is a stout fellow however and stands his ground, gripping the shaft of his hoe tightly, ready to defend himself.

When you ask him if this is Iro, he roars with laughter! "*Iro*? Why, this is Athelston, a village! Iro is many, *many* times larger than this! If it's Iro you seek, it's that way, not much more than five miles as the crow flies - oh, er, if y'know what I mean?" He points south, slightly embarrassed by his choice of expression.

You thank the farmer and fly off again heartened by his information. Turn to **456**.

506

You recognise the street corner where earlier you met Finjo. He is nowhere to be seen and the people have as little information on Vashta as before. The main road from here twists and turns eastwards towards the town square. To go this way, turn to **487**. Otherwise, another winding road leads away to the south-east (turn to **393**) or an equally narrow street curves in a north-easterly direction (turn to **407**).

507

The man laughs at your manner. "Come now, I think we may share a common purpose! Allow me to introduce myself. My name is Flawn Ghire. But let us not talk here so openly in the street." Note down the codeword BROW.

You let him to lead you over to pile of barrels at the edge of the road and sit down. "I guess what it is you seek," he continues in hushed tones. "One day I hear that Vashta recently uncovered the far off secret of the birdmen and suddenly *you* appear in Iro!" You try to give nothing away in your expression as Flawn offers to show you where Vashta lives if you tell him what it was that he discovered. Will you:

    Say that you will tell him if he gives
    you the address *first*?   Turn to **379**
    Or use force to get the information from him?   Turn to **520**

508

He frowns, seemingly weighing up whether Vashta would have a friend like you! You take this as a yes, and further your questioning. Roll the die. If you roll a 1 or 2, turn to **543**. If you roll a 3 or more, turn to **522**.

509

You return to the sandstone building and stride over to where the tall man sits on the steps. He nurses his bruised shoulder as you hand him the bag. Inside, he gratefully finds the possessions that had been stolen from him.

"Well...thank you!" he exclaims, "Forgive me that when you ran off I imagined you in league with those rogues, posted here as a distraction!" You spend a few moments talking with the old fellow, who introduces himself as Meekal Mullaw, an 'up and coming noble' in his own words. He apologises that he does not know Vashta the wizard, but wishes you luck in your search. He advises you not to go into the Disl district, as it's full of 'criminal types and ne'er-do-wells!'

Eventually Meekal bids you farewell and ascends the steps into the building. You look about you and find that this street runs east (turn to **554**) and a main street runs due north towards the town square (turn to **487**). The Disl district is to the north-west, a densely packed gathering of buildings. To try this way despite the warning, turn to **457**.

510

You watch the strange man scurry away. As he goes, a gold coin slips from his pocket and rolls towards you. If you choose to pick it up, note it down. Now, will you investigate the black doorway (if you haven't already done so)? (Turn to **538**) Or leave the area? (Turn to **402**)

511

You wake up the next morning feeling gloomy. There's nothing much for it except to wait! Surprisingly this is not too long as, about an hour after you wake, you are taken to (and locked in) a small, well-furnished room and told to sit at a polished wooden table. Minutes later another door opens and Flawn Ghire make an entrance!

"At one point I thought you had reneged on our little agreement!" he says, taking the seat opposite you. "But then this morning one of my servants brought me news that a birdman had been arrested by the city guard. If I help you, I trust you will assist me in return?"

You nod and ask what he can do. He explains that he will be allowed to speak in your defence. Roll the die, adding 3 to the score if you have the codeword ROBE. If you roll a 5 or less, turn to **403**. If you total 6 or more, turn to **460**.

512

The key fits in the lock and opens with a click. "Hee-hee! I'm free!" squeaks the Jarip, a little noisily for your liking. You hurriedly grab his spindly arm with your free hand and ask him to help you find a plant that the wizard stole from you.

"Stealing again? He stole me, you know!" frowns the Jarip, and you let go of his arm as you realise that he is floating in the air beside you. "But he keeps everything like that downstairs." He descends to the carpet and scampers to the door of the cellar, which is locked. The Jarip points, says a word in another language and the door jumps open a crack!

You pull it fully open and follow the Jarip down a flight of stone steps into a huge underground laboratory. Wooden benches punctuate the space and there are bottles, flasks, vials, scientific instruments, books and scrolls scattered *everywhere*: the whole room is very untidy indeed!

The mischievous Jarip begins levitating round the room, immensely enjoying himself by tipping things up, eating herbs left lying around and throwing books. You implore him to stop, but just then he unravels a cloth and out onto the floor tumbles the sample of Orphus Latix that has troubled you for so long! If you have the codeword WAND, turn to **540**. If you do not have his codeword, turn to **405**.

513

"To battle!" cries Sorme in excitement. You are about to suggest a surprise attack but it is too late: Sorme is off, waving his sword maniacally above his head and giving a bloodcurdling war cry. You run after the headstrong human up a hillside to the cave.

The goblins have been alerted by his shouts and charge downhill to meet you with battle cries of their own, brandishing cruel-looking axes and clubs. Sorme meets the first two head on and makes short work of them with his sword. You strike the next goblin down with one blow of your talons. At this, the rest of the band have seen enough and keep running: past you and off down the hill!

You have to grab hold of Sorme's jerkin to stop him pursuing the fleeing creatures! "Okay, okay!" he grumbles, exhilarated by the swift victory. He enters the cave and rummages around the goblins' possessions while you stand guard outside. He returns shortly with a handful of gold coins, of which he counts half out to you. You decline at first, as human money does not interest you, but Sorme asks where you're headed and when you tell him, he advises you they may come in handy. Note down five gold coins if you choose to take them with you. You ask him for directions to Iro and he points due south-east, "Just another five miles or so. But I'd be careful if I were you – they got rules against err…'not-humans'! Better try and stay outta trouble."

You thank him for his generous sharing of the money, smiling inwardly as you can clearly see his pockets bulging with undeclared treasure! Then on with your journey! Turn to **456**.

514

The arrival of an Ariax in their midst certainly causes quite a stir; your landing creates a veritable cloud of dust, straw and dirt! Plump market traders huff and puff out of the way and several nervous souls throw themselves on the ground in fright! Most people regard you with wary interest, but there are audible mutterings of disapproval as well.

Then one brave fishmonger strides forward and yells for you to go back to where you came from and not trouble the people of Iro! He is quite aggressive considering he is a lot shorter than you, his bravery coming from the weight of numbers he (probably correctly) feels are with him on what he says. Much interest surrounds your reaction. Will you simply ignore him and walk away? (Turn to **487**) Or will you shove him over for his nerve? (Turn to **378**)

515

The front door opens into a living room that is also a very cluttered workshop. The little man stood in the centre of the room wears a grubby shirt and trousers with a brown waistcoat and is tinkering with some mechanical apparatus which was the source of the black smoke you saw from outside. You see a second room behind him with a back door that is also open.

You cough to get the attention of the man and he turns and peers at you looking most surprised! "Oh – are you here to collect something?" he says, absent-mindedly. You tell him no and ask after Vashta. He doesn't seem to hear you and introduces himself as Mariuk Semble, master inventor! He apologises for the mess but seems keen to show you one of his latest inventions that 'aren't quite finished yet'. You get the feeling by looking round that most of his stuff would come under this category!

You decide to humour this kindly old fellow, who unlike most of his race doesn't seem bothered by your appearance! Would you like to see a 'far-away scope' that he claims can help you see things that are normally too far away to see? (Turn to **557**) or a 'self-loading crossbow' that he says can fire at a startling rate? (Turn to **385**)

516

Amazingly, just a few hours later, Wardial is back and unlocking your cage! Four city guards accompany him into the room and they seize you roughly and drag you out of the house. "Well, I didn't know you were a wanted criminal!" calls the merchant after you. "Always looking to support the fair upholders of law and order in our city!"

"Oh, and it had nothing to do with the little *reward* on offer, did it?" retorts one of the guards.

You are marched through the streets (to the general pleasure of the crowds) until you reach a large sandstone building. You mount a flight of steps leading up to its entrance and are taken to a cell which is locked behind you. Exchanging one prison for another! Turn to **432**.

517

You try to move your hand and cannot: you realise that the thing before you is trying to take over your mind! It takes great effort but you manage to force yourself upwards with a guttural cry and run out of the building as quickly as you can, slashing out at the skull-faced one as he tries to bar your way.

Outside again in the seemingly dazzling sunlight, you shake your head to clear out the evil that has been inside it. But you are not pursued. Once you have gathered your wits, you could go and see the entertainers (if you haven't already done so) (turn to **474**) or leave the town square (turn to **402**).

518

The scribe turns back towards the table and rolls up his scroll once more. "That is all, my lords," he says. The assembled nobles regard you gravely. If you have the codeword STAFF, turn to **388**. If you have the codeword WAND, turn to **454**. If you have neither of these codewords, turn to **425**.

519

"Nah – you ain't getting in!" snarls the first guard. "On your way!"

If you follow their orders, you could land in a back street somewhere near the centre of Iro (turn to **526**) or land in the middle of one of the busier areas (turn to **514**) Otherwise you could always chose to try and force your way past the guards (turn to **476**).

520

"You *will* tell me what you know!" you snarl, lifting Flawn Ghire off his feet and pulling him close to your sharp beak. Flawn loses his nerve a bit at this and starts yelling for help! You hear the sound of tramping feet approaching in the distance. If you want to flee the scene, turn to **422**. If you want to shake Flawn about a bit first, turn to **484**.

521

The crossbow bolt flies out of the door faster than the eye can see and imbeds itself with a thud in the eaves of a building across the street. Fortunately no-one is hurt but you hear cries of alarm from outside. Then the stern face of a city guard peers in at the doorway and sees you holding the crossbow! *React on instinct.* Will you run into the back room and hide? (Turn to **445**) Or flee out of the open back door? (Turn to **556**)

522

"Yes, Mr Vashta is indeed a customer of mine," admits old Shem. "And he lives not far from my shop! Go right out of here, then take the next right and carry on for a bit until you come to a house where each floor sticks out over the one below. Very distinctive is his home – that's what you get with wizards!"

You thank the apothecary for his help and set off in the direction he showed you. Turn to **451**.

523

The man calls after you but you ignore him. Note down the codeword DUNG. Now, are you heading north-west? (Turn to **437**) east? (Turn to **451**) or south? (Turn to **493**)

524

Surprisingly this is not too long as, about an hour after you wake, you are taken to (and locked in) a small, well-furnished room and told to sit at a polished wooden table. Minutes later another door opens and there, at last, you see Vashta the wizard! "Well, well, so it's true! I'd heard there was a birdman walking the streets of Iro asking after me!" he beams. "So what brings you here, my fine fellow?"

You explain that, having passed the Fygrinnd, you were given a second task which required you to travel to a human city and bring back a book. In truth, you'd never heard of books before you came to Iro, and inwardly congratulate yourself on your quick thinking!

Vashta seems to believe your tale and promises to sort you out with a book later. In return for saving his life in the Forest of Arcendak, he also offers to do what he can here. "No chance of a magical escape though, I'm afraid," he adds. "For one thing, I'd be outlawed in my own city...and also I wasn't allowed to bring my staff inside the building!" Note down the codeword STAFF.

At that moment a guard appears and tells you to follow him into the Chamber of Iro where you will be judged.

The Chamber of Iro is a huge room dressed with luxurious adornments the like of which you have never seen before. There are plush rugs on the floor and many paintings and tapestries on the walls that depict previous rulers and dignitaries of the city. The crest of Iro, a blue shield criss-crossed in white with a downturned silver gauntlet in its centre hangs proudly on the wall behind a magnificent desk.

You are ushered in your chains to stand in the very centre of the room flanked by two armed guards. Further guards man the doors. Vashta takes a seat behind you with a handful of others who are here to witness today's trials. After a short wait, a door opens at the far end of the room and five noblemen enter, dressed in official red robes. These are the men, known collectively as the Will of Iro, who will decide your fate! If you have the codeword LAW, turn to **447**. If you do not have this codeword, turn to **468**.

525

Quick as a flash, you duck back onto the landing and into an adjacent bedroom. Will Vashta think he was dreaming, or will he come looking for you? Roll the die. If you roll a 1, 2 or 3, turn to **455**. If you roll a 4 or more, turn to **559**.

526

You descend into a narrow side street, unoccupied except for a washerwoman gathering clothes from a line. She shrieks and runs inside when you appear from nowhere above her! Behind you is a dead-end, so you decide to head towards the hustle and bustle you see up ahead. Turn to **407**.

527

"You!" barks Selgar the sheriff. "I told you to leave!" Suddenly, two men take a firm hold of your arms and you feel a spear point at your back! It is the city guard! "Now you'll see what happens to those who disobey me! Take him away!" commands the sheriff.

The guard behind you digs his spear point painfully into your back to get you moving and you decide to do as he says for now. You are marched through the streets (to the general pleasure of the crowds) until you reach a large sandstone building. You mount a flight of steps leading up to its entrance and are taken to a cell which is locked behind you. Turn to **432**.

528

Infuriated, you turn to face the guards. One confidently makes a grab for you, but you sidestep and send him tumbling to the floor. You then skilfully hack the head off the second guard's spear as he jabs at you with it! But reinforcements are on their way. You cannot fight them all, and airborne you present an easier target. Note down the codewords DUNG and HELM. Which way will you run? North-west? (Turn to **437**) East? (Turn to **451**) Or south? (Turn to **493**)

529

"Tell me how you know him!" you demand, pulling the man towards you. He glances over your shoulder an instant before you feel a heavy blow to the back of the head which renders you unconscious.

It must have been one of the city guards of Iro who hit you as when you wake up you are slumped on the floor in a prison cell. Turn to **432**.

530

You have no idea how long you wait. Eventually, the same guard returns and leads you back into the chamber. The man on the right of the Will of Iro stands and addresses you.

"The will of Iro is that you be released. You will be free to go if you pledge to adhere to our laws in the future." You thank them and breathe a sigh of relief. A guard comes across and sullenly removes your chains. If you have the codeword WAND, turn to **547**. If you have the codeword STAFF, turn to **389**. If you have neither of these codewords, turn to **475**.

531

You attempt to pick a path through all the clutter, looking desperately for anything that may contain the priceless plant you seek. At one point you knock a golden lamp-stand with you elbow and it wobbles...but remains upright.

On the far side of the attic you see something which intrigues you. It is a wooden carving of an owl trimmed with golden details, which stands almost as tall as you! A space has been cleared before it for some reason (and floor space is at a premium up here!) If you want to examine the owl, turn to **397**. If you want to ignore it and go quietly back down the stairs, turn to **481**.

532

"Never 'eard of him!" declares one guard, pleased with himself. The other looks more dubious, as if he'd rather not meddle with a wizard's business. Note down the codeword ROBE and roll the die. If you roll a 3 or less, turn to **519**. If you roll a 4, 5 or 6, turn to **390**.

533

You soar upwards, hoping not to be seen by anyone in an adjoining street. As quickly as possible, you pull the window outwards and clamber into a circular tower-room with no doors but a trap door in the very centre of the floor.

All around the walls of the room hang many robes and travelling cloaks. As you make for the trap door, their sleeves begin to flap and a heavy red robe floats towards you, animated by themagical power of its wizard owner! It grips you with surprising force and you also feel a cloak wrapping itself around your legs from behind!

It's time to get out! You stagger to the window and just about manage to drag yourself out. Finjo flees at the sight of you hovering high in the sky, disentangling yourself from numerous hostile articles of clothing! Note down the codeword SPARKS.

Unfortunately you have also drawn the attention of several city guards, who shout at you to come down and give yourself up. You have no intention of doing this however and once free fly across the town. Will you land closer to the centre of the city? (Turn to **381**) Or towards the outer wall? (Turn to **493**)

534

"I don't think so!" says Flawn Ghire. "You will betray me!" This taunt causes you to lose your cool a bit!

"You *will* tell me what you know!" you snarl, lifting him off his feet and pulling him close to your sharp beak. Flawn loses his nerve a bit at this and starts yelling for help! You hear the sound of tramping feet approaching in the distance. If you want to flee the scene, turn to **422**. If you want to shake Flawn about a bit first, turn to **484**.

535

"*Unjust*! Who are *you* to decide what is unjust?" barks Selgar. You hear the sounds of running feet behind you and turn to see four armed guards approaching to support their leader. They are almost upon you. Will you fight? (Turn to **472**) Or surrender? (Turn to **428**)

536

You turn towards the nearest display of fresh herbs. Saffron is one gold coin per bundle; Spiderwort is the same price; Speckled Hemlock is two gold coins per sprig. Decide what you will buy, note it down and cross off the money you spend. Now as you pay for your selection will you ask the apothecary about

Vashta? (Turn to **485**) Or will you ask about the herbs you have bought first? (Turn to **558**)

537

With one flap of your powerful wings you are upstairs and in through the window. You quickly scan the three sparsely furnished rooms you find there but with no result. You can see no trace of the robbers from the back windows either; you have lost them. Embarrassed to return to the victim on the steps empty handed, you decide to slip away down a back street. Will you head west? (Turn to **457**) Or east? (Turn to **554**)

538

You make your way straight through the crowds, eyes fixed upon the mysterious black entrance. You walk under the sign and lower your head to pass through the doorway. A long corridor stretches away into the distance, lit by one spluttering candle on the left hand wall. The walls, floor and ceiling all appear to be black. There is silence.

At the end of the corridor, you pull aside a heavy black curtain and enter a small waiting room. A young man and an old lady sit waiting nervously. As it is very dark, and they don't have your Ariax sight, they strain their eyes to make you out. You choose a seat away from them!

The other door in the room opens and a hunched old man staggers in, gibbering unintelligibly to himself. He makes his way out under the curtained entrance. Was he in that state before he went in, you wonder? The old lady looks frightened, and you notice she only has one hand. Suddenly her nerve fails her and she gets up and half runs from the room. The young man follows after her looking concerned, leaving you sitting alone in eerie silence.

If you want to follow the others out of here, you could go and see the entertainers (if you haven't already done so) (turn to **474**) or leave the town square (turn to **402**). If you want to wait and see what happens here first, turn to **502**.

539

"Well for a start, you attacked members of the city guard!" says the scribe. You begin to defend yourself, but it won't get you very far on this point.

If you have the codeword MAN, turn to **404**. If you do not, but you have the codeword SPARKS, turn to **367**. If you have neither of these, but you do have the codeword KNOCK, turn to **488**. If you have the codeword SWORD and none of the above, turn to **440**. If you haven't got any of these codewords, turn to **518**.

540

There is a sudden sound of footsteps behind you. You turn to see Vashta descending the steps dressed in a long nightshirt, staff held aloft. "How did you get out?" he begins, meaning the Jarip, then sees *you* standing there! "So!" he cries, "I half wondered if one day you would come in search of the…Orphus Latix I think you call…NO!!"

You follow Vashta's gaze to the Jarip, who is hovering upside down near the ceiling clutching a glass bottle of red, swirling liquid, totally absorbed in watching the pretty colours dance around.

"Xanarel!" pants Vashta urgently, with definite terror in his voice, "You shouldn't have let that thing out! You see that bottle it's got? If it breaks, the whole house will be instantly consumed by flames! We've got to get it off him, quickly!"

This could be a trick. You glance at the Orphus Latix, so close but in the opposite direction. If you stop the Jarip, Vashta will have time to act. He sees your hesitation. "This is no trick! If we survive this, you can *have* the plant! All of it!" he splutters, desperately, "I give you my word! But *please* get that bottle!!"

The Jarip looks down at you, grinning manically. You can't tell what it is thinking! Then it lets go of the bottle! *React on instinct*. If you want to catch the bottle, turn to **469**. If you want to go for the Orphus Latix, turn to **496**.

541

You swoop down to land near to the group of children. They seem fascinated with rather than scared of you and gather round, jostling you and even pulling at your feathers! You manage to get out of them that you're silly to think this is Iro and that it's 'that way', meaning south.

Out of the corner of your eye you suddenly spot danger: a group of villagers is slowly creeping up behind you with makeshift weapons, obviously seeing you as a threat to their young. At that moment, one throws a pitchfork at you! Roll the die. If you roll a 1 or 2, turn to **463**. If you roll a 3 or more, turn to **406**.

542

Ignoring the voice, you turn and strike out at the nearest guard, knocking aside his spear. Another lunges forwards but you trip him and send him tumbling to the ground. Note down the codeword HELM.

There are too many of them to fight. Seeing an opportunity, you duck another blow and leap sideways into the crowd which parts immediately. Will you run east? (Turn to **415**) Or south? (Turn to **487**)

543

"Sorry – think he came in once, but I don't know him," he says. You cannot be totally sure if he's telling the truth; he moves swiftly on to serve his next customer and you decide there is nothing more to be gained here. Note down the codeword PICKLE.

You push open the door of the shop and are back out on the street again. From here, three similar looking roads stretch out. You could head west (turn to **554**), north (turn to **381**) or north-west (turn to **478**).

544

The crossbow bolt flies with thunderous force into the wooden floorboards between Mariuk's feet and stands quivering there. The inventor looks up at you, and having seen your expression of dismay, roars with laughter! "You see it works then!" he chuckles, undeterred by his close shave. You take this opportunity to ask him about Vashta's whereabouts.

"Vashta, eh?" he says to himself. "Big fellow, no teeth?" You confirm that both of these descriptions are false. "Oh, *Vashta* you mean!" he continues. "Yes, I think I know him! Lives…errr…down that way I think!" he points to the south-east, but he hardly fills you with great confidence.

You thank him and are just about to leave when you feel him pressing a gold coin into your hand, 'for your help'. You decide to hold onto it (note it down) as you have seen many of these things changing hands between the humans earlier on and they seem to value them.

If you want to follow the directions of the inventor, turn to **493**. If you don't trust his memory and would rather go another way, there are roads leading north-west (turn to **415**), north-east (turn to **437**) or south-west (turn to **554**).

545

You grasp the man by the throat, careful to use the arm that *has* been in the dung! He chokes and splutters, the smile gone from his face at once. "'Twas but a joke!" he gurgles.

His friends bravely come to his aid and you are forced to drop the man in order to defend yourself. During the scuffle one of them cries: "The guards!" and a small patrol of chainmail clad, spear-armed guards come rushing down the street. They are almost upon you! Note down the codeword MAN. Will you battle the guards? (Turn to **528**) Or surrender to them? (Turn to **428**)

546

"How do you know Vashta?" you demand of the man, grabbing a handful of his robes. He whimpers at your question but does not reply. Then you hear a gruff voice behind you that warns you to 'let him go'. Will you do so? (Turn to **382**) Or will you ignore it and continue questioning the young man? (Turn to **529**)

547

Flawn Ghire takes you to his home; a large town-house a few streets from where you met. A servant has been watching out for you and opens the door, staring at you in amazement!

An hour or so passes and you immerse yourself in the human's strange custom of sitting down to an evening meal. Your host explains to you the purpose of cutlery and plates, and three delicious courses are brought before you by another servant. Over dinner, Flawn outlines the plans for the night. You offer to do the housebreaking alone (so that you can get the Orphus Latix and make sure Flawn *doesn't*!) and Flawn is quite happy with this arrangement. He doesn't seem keen to 'get his hands dirty'!

The moon is up when Flawn leads you and another man through the deserted streets to Vashta's house at last! Unlike the rest of the houses on this street, it has three storeys, with each level jutting out over the one below; it looks as though the whole building could topple over at any minute! The thought temporarily crosses your mind to simply torch the whole house and destroy everything in it, but you know that Flawn would try to stop you and you are sure the Vzler would disapprove!

From a place of concealment across the street, Flawn Ghire introduces the other man as a 'security expert' who can help you get in. Sneak-thief would be a more honest description, you guess! Flawn points to two possible means of entry but leaves it up to you; an upstairs window that is slightly ajar (turn to

434) or a downstairs window that he claims his 'security expert' could easily access (turn to **419**).

548

You strike with such force that the weapon falls from the blacksmith's hand and clatters to the ground. Almost immediately, two men take a firm hold of your arms and you feel a spear point at your back! It is a patrol of the city guard and you did not hear them approach! "You will come with us," states another man, stepping in front of you.

"Struggle and I run you through!" sneers the man with the spear. He digs the spear point painfully into your back as he says this and you decide to go along with them for now.

You are marched through the streets (to the general pleasure of the crowds) until you reach a large sandstone building. You mount a flight of steps leading up to its entrance and are taken to a cell which is locked behind you. Turn to **432**.

549

"An old friend, eh?" exclaims the man, "That's good – so am I! Allow me to introduce myself. My name is Flawn Ghire. I think I guess why you're here, too! But come, let us not talk here so openly in the street." Note down the codeword BROW.

You let him to lead you over to pile of barrels at the edge of the road and sit down. He continues in hushed tones, "Vashta recently uncovered the secret of the birdmen, didn't he?" He awaits your answer. Will you confirm what he says? (Turn to **465**) Or say that you don't know what he's talking about? (Turn to **444**)

550

"Now I don't much like your tone, stranger!" says the old man in an authoritative voice. "I'm going to have to ask you to leave." You look about at the shocked customers and decide that it would be wise to remain calm; more than one looks like they know magic! Note down the codeword PICKLE.

You push open the door of the shop and are back out on the street again. From here, three similar looking roads stretch out. You could head west (turn to **554**), north (turn to **381**) or north-west (turn to **478**).

551

The feeble door collapses on its hinges at your blow. Inside is a grubby, cobwebbed hallway and living area, but no men. There are stairs leading up and a back door that stands open. *React on instinct*. Will you run up the stairs (turn to **501**) or through the back door (turn to **373**)?

552

"Wait!" commands the unearthly voice. "Do you not wish to hear me speak of your future?" You pause. If this intrigues you, you could retake your seat (turn to **410**). If you choose to leave, you could go and see the entertainers (if you haven't already done so) (turn to **474**) or leave the town square (turn to **402**).

553

The Will of Iro seem surprised by your silence and begin debating earnestly. You are taken back to your cell and told that you will be summoned when they have reached a decision.

Roll the die, subtracting 1 from the roll for each one of the codewords HELM, MAN, SPARKS, KNOCK or SWORD that you have. Add 2 to the roll if you have either of the codewords WAND or STAFF. Add 3 to the roll if you have the codeword LAW. If the result is 1 or 2, turn to **411**. If you total 3, 4 or 5, turn to **448**. If the score is 6 or more, turn to **530**.

554

There are few passers-by down this particular street and those that are there look down on you with contempt and actively avoid you. If you have the codeword FEATHER, turn to **486**. If you do not have this codeword, turn to **386**.

555

You just manage to avoid the dagger and it flies harmlessly past. You manage to keep your composure and ask for directions to Iro in exchange for the man's sword. He points to the south while staring resentfully into your eyes. There's nothing much else to do but drop the blade on the ground and disappear in the direction he indicated. Turn to **442**.

556

You leap over a workbench and sprint outside. A spear flies past your left ear and clatters harmlessly to the street below and you gratefully duck round a corner – straight into another, very surprised guard! You both collapse in a heap and this gives the other guards time to catch up with you!

Two men take a firm hold of your arms and drag you to your feet. "You will come with us," states another man, stepping in front of you.

"Struggle and I run you through!" sneers a guard behind you. He digs his spear point painfully into your back as he says this and you decide to go along with them for now.

You are marched through the streets (to the general pleasure of the crowds) until you reach a large sandstone building. You mount a flight of steps leading up to its entrance and are taken to a cell which is locked behind you. Turn to **432**.

557

You are handed a strange, tubular device made of leather that has a glass lens wedged in at either end. "Come with me!" cries Mariuk, pulling you by the wing to a staircase. Upstairs is a tiny bedroom with a window that looks out over the city.

"Now I've had trouble testing this because of my poor eyesight," explains the little inventor. "And I assume you're not familiar with Iro? Use this and tell me what is mounted on the wall of that big sandstone building yonder!" You look where he is pointing and can clearly see what he means without using the scope: it is a shield adorned with a large silver gauntlet. Even decent human eyesight must be poor in comparison to yours!

You put the far-away scope to your eye and quickly realise that it doesn't work; it's just like looking through a normal pane of glass! Mariuk looks at you expectantly. Will you pretend that his invention works and describe the gauntlet? (Turn to **400**) Or let him down gently as you tell him that his scope doesn't work? (Turn to **371**)

558

The man seems happy to explain. He describes in detail how to properly prepare each purchase for the desired effect while you pretend to be interested. Then you deftly steer the conversation onto the subject of Vashta and his whereabouts. Roll the die, adding the number of gold coins you just spent to the result. If the total is 3 or less, turn to **394**. If you get a 4 or more, turn to **522**.

559

Your luck holds; Vashta does not come into this room. As you hold your breath, you hear him yawn and return to bed. You wait a good ten minutes before you dare to commence your search of the house: that was *too* close! Back out on the landing will you take the stairs leading up? (Turn to **504**) Or the stairs leading down? (Turn to **441**)

560

You put plenty of miles between yourself and Iro before you stop to rest. Choosing a desolate spot in the mountains you sleep, a heavy burden lifted from your shoulders at last!

The return journey is uneventful and this time the only urgency is your desire to be amongst the Ariax once more. What will Rical, Nimax and the Vzler have made of your sudden disappearance?

You break up your trip with periods of intense reading, knowing that you will have less opportunity to do this once you are back home. You discover that the scrolls you took from Vashta's study are the work of an Ariax named Detlaxe. They describe many aspects of his Ariax life which you find familiar and (of course) contain the secret of Orphus Latix that Vashta found so intriguing.

But the rest of Detlaxe's tale astounds you. Hundreds of years ago, in Detlaxe's time, your tribe's Talotrix was named Nevsaron. According to Detlaxe Nevsaron was an inspirational leader, but on top of that he had amazing 'elemental powers': clearly Nevsaron could do *magic*.

You stop reading at this point while your brain digests this information. You were unaware of any Ariax *ever* that could do magic! Detlaxe goes on to say that Nevsaron never revealed where he got his powers from and when he died, his secret went with him. He was buried in an ice tomb high up in a great mountain to the west of your home, which became a sacred place to the Ariax. You wonder why you have not heard any of this before! As you read on, you find the answer.

Then the Scarfells came. They came in huge numbers from the south and chose the very mountain which housed Nevsaron's tomb at its summit for their home as it had a vast natural cave system. Ariax visitors were shocked and appalled to find this intrusion, but were fired on by Scarfell archers if they dared to approach.

This situation created a rift in the Ariax tribe. Some wanted a full scale war; to drive away the Scarfells once and for all! Others said that the outcome would not be worth the cost in Ariax life. They pointed out that the Scarfells didn't know the tomb existed so Nevsaron could rest in peace. The Talotrix,

Hallored, decided to concede the mountain (which of course became known as Musk) to the Scarfells. Detlaxe was firmly in opposition. He tried to stir up a revolt, but could not gain enough support. He became even more angered when it was announced that to prevent future casualties in Nevsaron's name, the story of his life was not to be passed on to future generations.

Detlaxe, disgusted, left the tribe and made his way south, alone. He eventually found himself in a human city called Gangoth, where he came under the tutelage of a wizard named Haraikos Lysk. The scrolls go on to chronicle the next forty years in Lysk's service until the final entry, written in a different hand, which reports that Detlaxe died following a short illness, aged one hundred and eleven.

You can hardly believe what you have read! So many questions swirl around in your brain. Has even Astraphet heard of Nevsaron? What *was* the secret of his magic? Have the Scarfells yet discovered Nevsaron's tomb? And what should you do with this information?

Your heart sings for joy when you finally see the sight of snow-capped mountains on the distant horizon. You soar high up in the sky, knowing that you are less than two days from home! This time cannot pass quickly enough and eventually you see the Tower of Egratar emerging from the morning mists.

Of course it is your friend Rical you seek out first. But as you enter the tunnel that leads to his cave, you immediately sense that something is *very* wrong. Death seems to hang in the air. "What are you doing *here*?" cries the horrified voice of an Ariax gliding in behind you.

The dreadful events that have happened during your absence and the important role you will have in resolving them are detailed in book 4 of The Saga of the Ariax, entitled:

DEATH FROM THE PAST

THE SAGA OF THE ARIAX: 4
DEATH FROM THE PAST

Recent events

You have just returned from a successful mission to the human city of Iro, where you saw to it that a stolen sample of the Ariax's greatest secret, the magic life-prolonging herb Orphus Latix, was destroyed. Whilst there, you stumbled across scrolls containing strange and intriguing legends of the Ariax.

You were away for a week or so. On returning, you go looking for your friend Rical first. But as you enter the tunnel that leads to his cave, you immediately sense that something is *very* wrong. Death seems to hang in the air...

"What are you doing *here*?" cries the horrified voice of an Ariax gliding in behind you. Bewildered, you tell him you've been away and ask him what is going on.

The birdman takes you outside and leads you to a cave full of Ariax in another mountain. The atmosphere is doom laden; you have never known anything like it before. The Vzler (your senior master of training) sees you and comes over to explain what has happened. He sits down wearily.

"I do not know where you have been, young one," he says, "and the time for that tale will come later. But you have returned at a time of great crisis. Two days ago the body of your old friend Snyblo was discovered in the mountains near Arcendak."

Snyblo did not return from your coming of age trial (the Fygrinnd) and had already been presumed dead, but this is still sad news. The Vzler continues, "He died of an ancient and deadly disease, known as Crackbeak, which is very contagious. Unfortunately, before it was identified it had spread like wildfire throughout the tribe."

You shudder when you think that you would certainly have gone to pay your respects to your friend and contracted the disease yourself had you been present.

"The victims of Crackbeak suffer just that; the gradual disintegration of their beak and talons. Death follows within a week. Half of our *entire tribe* already lies dead or dying.... The caves in the other mountain are quarantined with the sick. The one comfort is that neither of the females have yet been affected."

"Rical?" you gasp, dreading the answer. The Vzler nods, sadly.

"He has Crackbeak – but he still lives. Arguttax and his healers are working tirelessly on a cure."

A few hours later, Astraphet assembles a council of every adult Ariax who is still healthy. Before you attend, you stash the scrolls in a safe place where they will not be discovered.

At the assembly you meet up again with your other friend Darfak, but it is a subdued meeting. Arguttax addresses you all. "My friends," he says, "You all know of the desperate situation we find ourselves in. I can at least confirm that there *is* a cure for this disease. Crackbeak has struck our race before, though not in living memory. The cure is a curious mixture of substances and I *could* prepare it...if I had them all."

The Ariax listen in silent anticipation as Arguttax continues. "Most of the herbs required are easily gathered; my apprentices have already scoured Arian and found them. But two ingredients elude us, and now we need your help. One is a rare herb that grows in the frozen icy forests to the far north of here: Elder Mettel is our name for it. The second is the poison from a firebrand snake, and this will be the harder of the two to come by."

Astraphet thanks Arguttax for his team's efforts. "I want every Ariax who is up to this task to prepare themselves to fly out today in search of these things," he says. "You will go in pairs." Astraphet divides the assembly in two, disappointingly separating you from Darfak. The Vzler takes a group to brief about the Elder Mettel; Astraphet himself beckons you and the others who remain (twenty in all) to him.

"You are all aware of the importance of your task," he says gravely, "Time will be of the essence. Arguttax will tell you all we know about your quarry."

"Well, that is not much," confesses Arguttax. "I remember being told that the firebrand snake is so called as it seems attracted by fire. It is a reddish-brown in colour, with distinctive gold blotches down its back. Its habitat is swamps and marshy areas. It is deadly poisonous to Ariax, I'm afraid. Bring back a live reptile if you can and I can milk its venom, or if this is not possible, just collect as much venom as you can."

"How big is this snake?" asks a grizzled veteran behind you.

Arguttax pauses. "That I do not know," he says.

Astraphet thanks him and pairs you up. You are annoyed when your mentor Nimax, who dislikes you and has always been envious of your abilities and successes, is selected to be your partner, but know you must put the success of this mission above such personal differences...

Now turn to **561** to begin...

561

Ten determined pairs of Ariax take to the sky in unison, fanning out and heading swiftly south. To the north lie only mountains. You follow Nimax's lead in silence, covering the miles below at great speed until eventually the other pairs are all out of sight.

For nearly two days you travel, shadowing a similar route to the one you so recently undertook to Iro. Nimax exercises his authority as much as possible during the expedition, deciding when to eat, rest and sleep. You set no watch in the mountains, easily finding inaccessible places in the crags to sleep undisturbed.

There is little conversation between the two of you. The agreed plan seems to be finding a swamp and flying over it with a flaming torch to attract the snake. Nimax tells you not to worry about safely grabbing the poisonous reptile, as he is certain he can do it himself with little difficulty. Despite his position in the tribe, it is clear that he desperately craves the chance to prove himself and is determined to return home the hero!

You sit together eating a mountain yak. "So where exactly did you go last week?" asks Nimax suddenly, chewing on a bone and not looking at you. Because you didn't want to reveal that a sample of Orphus Latix had been lost until you had recovered or destroyed it, you left the tribe without asking permission from Nimax or the Vzler, and without even telling your closest friend Rical where you were going! Will you:

Tell him the truth; that you went to a human city to recover some lost Orphus Latix?	Turn to **607**
Tell him a lie: that the Vzler sent you somewhere on a secret mission?	Turn to **636**
Or tell him that 'it's not important now' and try to avoid the question?	Turn to **700**

562

Your ears strain for the sound. It is coming from the east so gradually you roll over to face that direction. Suddenly, three large wolves with dark green fur burst from the bushes and pounce in your direction, jaws slavering, hungry for your blood! Roll the die. If you roll a 3 or less, turn to **608**. If you roll a 4 or more, turn to **661**.

563

You continue deeper into the wood. The path begins to curve round uphill to the right, but you also notice a set of steps cut into the rock leading downhill and round a bend to the left. If you want to see where the steps lead, turn to **691**. To stay on the main path, turn to **673**.

564

The water has almost magical force behind it, and as you surge upwards, the tentacle whips round you, trying to grasp your leg! Roll the die. If you roll a 3 or less, turn to **716**. If you roll a 4 or more, turn to **610**.

565

You fly deeper into the swamp, landing on a tufty patch of ground for a brief rest. You walk for a bit and come to a collection of what can only be described as nests. Some are on the ground and some are in trees, but there are maybe a dozen of them, made of swamp-weed, reeds and mud. You cannot tell what sleeps within, but you can see a large hairy mound of animal in each one. Note down the codeword TUFT. If you want to investigate the nests more closely, turn to **617**. If you want to creep past and leave them undisturbed, turn to **723**.

566

You quickly decide on the option that will get you out of this stinking swamp-water soonest! Your companion leads you stealthily under the platform, neck deep in sludge, and points out two marsh-goblin guards almost completely submerged, facing the other way.

You creep up behind your one and take him by surprise and the goblin does the same with the other. The battle is short and brutal, but no sooner have you done with one then five more appear as if from nowhere. Surrounded, and fighting in difficult conditions that your opponents are comfortable in, it is only a matter of time before weight of numbers tells and the goblins' spear thrusts begin to count...

567

The power of the creature below you is considerable. It somehow secures a grip with both arms, then you feel the weight of a second beast on you and clutch desperately at a nearby branch as you go down. With a mighty splash, you all plunge into the slimy water. You struggle, but more hairy bodies land on you from the trees. You never resurface.

568

You lie flat and take up a concealed position above the cave. You wait for half an hour but hear nothing but distant underground noises. Then two of the humanoid creatures wander out, morph into wolves and sprint away. If you want to take this chance to creep into the cave, turn to **622**. If you'd rather stay where you are and keep listening, turn to **594**.

569

You briefly introduce yourself and engage the Beotman in his favourite topic. This seems to relax his guard. He invites you into his cave and you sit down on an uneven wooden stool. There are several snakes inside; a large python curled round an outcrop of rock; three or four small green snakes sleeping in a corner; a black one curled up on the table. You assume none of them are poisonous!

"I've seen the firebrand, but never had one here," says your host. "I know that they're scarce, and they like marshy areas. What do you want to know?" You explain why you need to capture one alive as a matter of life and death! "Well, they're about the length of my armspan," he continues and holds out his massive, bear-like arms! "Red-brown colour, with gold patches on its back. As far as I know, the nearest place to find one is in a swamp across the mountains to the east. Follow the mountain river and you'll come to it in a day or two. It's dangerous, but if you're willing to risk it…" Note down the codeword SCALE.

You thank him for his help and, complimenting him on his menagerie of pets, rise to leave. He tells you to wait and roots about in a jumble of bottles at the back of the cave. He produces a vial of browny-yellow liquid which he assures you is an antivenom effective against many types of snake. "I'm not sure if it'll work on a firebrand's bite," he says, "but you never know, it might come in use?" You thank him and decide to take it with you (note down the antivenom).

The Beotman shows you a safe way out of the wood and you are soon back in the skies again, on the next stage of your journey. Turn to **596**.

570

Suddenly you feel a pair of small, sharp fangs nip your forearm! You draw it back instinctively and rub the affected area. The snake that bit you was mildly poisonous, so while your life is not in immediate danger, the bite will leave you feeling a little lethargic for the next few days until the poison works its way out of your system. For the rest of the adventure you must subtract 1 from every die roll you make (unless the text asks whether you have rolled an odd or even number).

Once bitten…you decide to leave the snake pit alone and return to the main path. Turn to **673**.

571

You explain your mission fully to the villagers and this seems to arrest their hostility. A man with a patch over one eye steps forward and speaks. "Forgive our wariness stranger, but we have to guard against those who would trespass in our lands!" You ask why they choose to live here on the edge of a swamp.

Another man replies. "We're farmers really; we cultivate the marshweed and other rare plant life that can only grow in these conditions. Then we sell them on to passing merchants and traders and they sell them on to the wizarding community."

Will you ask directly if they know anything about the firebrand snake? (Turn to **603**) Or will you first make conversation about their lifestyle and business? (Turn to **667**)

572

Your hand-eye co-ordination is spot on; you bring your hand up clutching the snake just behind the head. It snaps viciously at thin air as you wipe some of the mud and slime from its body. You are disappointed to see no splashes of gold anywhere along its back and it really is very brown with little if any red in it at all. You must conclude that this is not the snake you are looking for.

Ruefully you let it go and it slithers away across the mud flats, head held high. Turn to **604**.

573

The mists are especially thick in this part of the swamp, so you take the opportunity to land on a huge log and pick your path carefully on foot. You see a glow up ahead that can only be caused by fire and make your way cautiously towards it.

A small village emerges from the mists! It is built on wooden platforms supported by stilts which keep it above the level of the bog underneath. A ramshackle collection of mud-huts are gathered on top and a number of large flaming torches line the perimeter, presumably to deter the denizens of the swamp.

There does not seem to be anybody about. If your torch has gone out, you can attempt to steal one of the flaming brands (Turn to **663**). If your torch is still alight, will you investigate this strange village more closely? (Turn to **598**) Or will you steer clear of it and go deeper into the swamp? (Turn to **727**)

574

Once more you sweep your torch through the air, close to the ground. Whose plan was this? But then you see a flash of red and gold and a tubular body shoots out of one rock pool and into another. Despite only glimpsing it for a second you recognise your quarry at last: a firebrand snake!

In haste, you drop to the ground and grab at the snake as it surfaces once more. Your torch falls spluttering into the bog. The firebrand begins skating away across the surface of the murky water at great speed and you immediately swoop into the mists in hot pursuit.

Visibility is limited; one moment the firebrand is in sight, the next it vanishes into the haze again. Branches and fronds claw at you as you brush through them. Suddenly there is a loud howling from your right, followed by the sound of several creatures bounding towards you through the trees! If you have the codeword SNAP, turn to **646**. If you do not have this codeword, turn to **659**.

575

On closer inspection you see that the snake was purplish in colour. Nimax is forced to relax the frown he had put on at your failure to react and chooses to say nothing. After ten minutes of combing the area, he finally decides that this is a fruitless job and signals for you to follow him once more. Turn to **614**.

576

One of the greenwolves lands squarely on your back and grabs on to your shoulders, pulling you to the ground. With howls of glee, the others join him. You cannot possibly survive their rending claws and savage bites for long…

577

You wait for a minute or two then hear heavy stomping feet coming in your direction. A Beotman with wild eyes, long straggly hair and a grey snake wrapped around his wrist emerges from the undergrowth. He sees what you have done and looks angry immediately.

"What are you doing, sabotaging my work like this?" he huffs, "Do you think it's easy for someone my size to get up there and set this thing?" You offer to assist him with it and try to explain that you are seeking him out for his help in an important matter, but he interrupts short temperedly.

"Not important to me!" he chuckles. "Not important to me at all! Now begone feathered one, before I call my snakes!"

You try once more to ask for his aid, but this time he glares at you and starts to make a strange hissing sound in the back of his throat. Two or three serpents appear from various parts of the undergrowth, tongues flickering menacingly. It is obvious that you have lost the opportunity to gain knowledge here, so you make your way out of the forest. Turn to **596**.

578

You swoop down to land in an open area in the centre of the village. Your sudden appearance draws suspicious villagers from their homes and you are approached by a group of four men who have grabbed wooden clubs to defend themselves if necessary. They are clearly more used to non-humans than the people of Iro, but still look wary and not particularly friendly.

"What do you want here?" barks the tallest and broadest of the men, standing his ground. Will you:

Tell them that you are going into the swamp but not reveal your mission to them?	Turn to **703**
Tell them the truth about hunting a firebrand snake in the swamp?	Turn to **571**
Or you could take off and head for the swamp without talking to the men?	Turn to **625**

579

You notice that while the creatures approach, they stop short of attacking you. The nearest one paws at the air angrily as if there was an invisible barrier. You suddenly have the idea that maybe it is the bundle of herbs that you hold in your hand, and thrust it towards him. The beast howls in disgust and steps back. The villagers must have discovered that the smell of this herb repels these animals and that's why you saw them tied up and surrounding their valuable crops! Quite clever of them really, you think to yourself!

Using the herb to keep the creatures at bay, you make your way safely through the clearing. Turn to **727**.

580

You spring into action and launch yourself through the air to aid your mentor. But as you reach him he turns and deals with the danger easily, plucking the creature out of the air and holding it at arm's length. He roars with laughter and smirks that he's quite touched by your protectiveness towards him! Feeling foolish, you continue the search.

After ten minutes of combing the area, Nimax finally decides that this is a fruitless job and signals for you to follow him once more. Turn to **614**.

581

The woodland is sparse and airy, and you can see for quite a distance to either side. Before long however the trees become thicker and visibility becomes greatly reduced. It crosses your mind that it would be a good place for an ambush. If you want to press on vigilantly, turn to **654**. To turn back, turn to **630**.

582

You land uncomfortably on the stony ground but at least you avoided the snake which, uninterested in you, makes its way into the undergrowth immediately. You pick yourself up and investigate the pool, but it just seems to be drinking water. As this is a dead end, you decide to rejoin the main path. Turn to **673**.

583

Fire keeps most animals at bay and you are relieved that these seem to be no exception! It is not easy as they are awakening on all sides, but with the aid of your torch you manage to cross the clearing safely and they do not pursue you any further. You hurry on anyway and soon reach another clearing. If you have the codeword TUFT, turn to **727**. If you do not have this codeword, turn to **692**.

584

You fail to spot the snake in time and it sinks its fangs painfully into your calf! You clap your hand to the burning sensation already spreading up your leg and know that you have been bitten by a poisonous one! If you have a vial of antivenom with you, turn to **717**. If not, turn to **657**.

585

You slowly push open the door and peer inside. An intricately constructed wooden throne stands on a raised platform at the far end of the room with long wooden tables stretching out away from it. The discarded food and other rubbish littering the floor is evidence of a recent feast.

You initially think that the room is empty, but then see two of the small creatures skulking in the shadows. They have been scavenging for scraps of food; illegally you guess from their reaction to the door opening! When they see you though, they begin shouting out in gurgling throaty voices. Almost immediately a guard armed with a short spear appears at the door.

Time to leave! You knock the guard to the floor with one blow, but another three crowd the doorway, which is the only exit. A heavy, foul-smelling net is thrown and you become entangled and bundled to the floor.

"Swamp b'longs t'us marsh-goblins!" gurgles a horrible voice behind you. Surrounded by spears, you elect to surrender and are marched out across the platforms to a cell. All your possessions are taken from you and thrown into the swamp, including your torch if you still have it (erase everything you are carrying). Your wrists are uncomfortably bound behind your back. Turn to **682**.

586

During the night, you are shaken awake most unexpectedly! It is the marsh-goblin you helped escape from his kind! You ask him what he wants.

"You fly me t'swamp somewhere?" he gurgles, looking at you hopefully.

Something inside you warms to this repugnant little creature, but you can hardly afford to add time to your journey home. However he may prove useful as a night watchman, and you presume marsh-goblins don't eat snakes... If you want to tell him that you will find him a swamp tomorrow, turn to **653**. If you disappoint him, he trudges off into the distance and you find a new, hidden place to sleep (turn to **706**).

587

You power through the skies and ten minutes later are delighted to see that you guessed correctly: you see the greenwolf pack racing through the grassy plains beneath you. It is clear to you that they do not bear any prisoners: Nimax is either dead or has gone off of his own accord. You think it unlikely that even he would desert you, and have to fear the worst. However, it means you can give up your pursuit of the wolves and get on with the business in hand, alone. Turn to **609**.

588

The trail winds its way up and up into a little clearing that contains a veritable nest of assorted serpents! There must be several hundred snakes of all sizes and colours writhing about in one teeming mass! You catch several glimpses of reddish-brown, but surely there wouldn't be a firebrand *here*, in a forest? If you want to take a closer look, turn to **638**. Otherwise this is a dead end so you will have to retrace your steps and take the other path (turn to **673**).

589

It is slow going through the mist. You land on a tufty patch of earth where you can walk for a bit and come to a collection of what can only be described as nests. Some are on the ground and some are in trees, but there are maybe a dozen of them, made of swamp-weed, reeds and mud. You cannot tell what sleeps within, but you can see a large hairy mound of animal in each one. If you want to investigate the nests more closely, turn to **617**. If you want to creep past and leave them undisturbed, turn to **723**.

590

You slash out with your sharp talons and the creature reels backwards, sinking underneath the water and not resurfacing. Wondering what it was, and how right you were to kill it, you take to the air once more.

You soon come to a thicket of black tanglethorn trees and have the choice of flying to the left of them (turn to **565**) or the right (turn to **573**).

591

You pass a sleepless night, keeping your eyes on both the door of the cell and your fellow prisoner, who dozes slumped in the corner. As the sunlight begins to permeate the writhing mists, you feel yourself being roughly shaken awake.

"Wake up!" gurgles the marsh-goblin. "Guards here soon!" You curse yourself: you had drifted off to sleep after all! Minutes later you hear the sound of the door being unlocked and the pair of you charge at the guard. Roll the die, subtracting 1 from the roll if you have the codeword POINT. If the result is 3 or less, turn to **689**. If it is a 4, turn to **634**. If it is 5 or more, turn to **658**.

592

The momentum of the beasts carries you sideways and as you watch the firebrand disappear into the distance, you find yourself in a desperate battle for your own life! With a mighty splash, you all plunge into the slimy water. You struggle, but more hairy bodies land on you from the trees above and weight of numbers tells. You never resurface.

593

"I've not heard of this snake," confesses the Beotman, to your disappointment. "But years ago I knew a Beotman who dedicated his life to catching and learning about snakes. If anyone would know, it would be he."

As Nimax paces impatiently behind you, seething that he cannot understand a word being said, you ask the Beotman where this snake expert can be found.

"In a cave in a forest somewhere in or around the mountains to the east," is his answer. Note down the codeword FANG.

At this point Nimax rudely interrupts. "Time to go," he says firmly. You bristle, but it is useless to protest so you bid the Beotman farewell. Nimax does not mention your ability, but flies on in sullen silence. Turn to **714**.

594

Your patience finally pays off. Another twenty minutes or so later, two of the green humanoid creatures walk out of the cave and sit down on a rock in the sun. You listen in and they soon start talking about their attack on you earlier. It becomes clear that they only ever saw one birdman (you), which means Nimax had gone before you awoke! Has he deserted you? As you have no idea how to find him, you can only assume that he is continuing the search alone. You resolve to do likewise. Turn to **609**.

595

Your powers of flight enable you to easily outdistance the bear and you have soon left him far behind, both heads roaring furiously in the distance. Turn to **686**.

596

You fly over the mountains, enjoying the familiar panoramic view which reminds you of home. Home…is Rical still alive? The thought spurs you on.

Later you see a youthful river running down from the mountains and decide to follow it. As the sun is setting behind you, you camp for the night first in the relative safety of the mountain heights.

Next morning, you swoop down into the wilderness that lies east of the mountains. You see very little activity below you and just continue following the course of the river as it winds its way here and there through the scrubland.

Early in the afternoon, you finally find what you had been searching for: a huge area of swampland, covered by swirling mists. Then you see a surprising sight: a human village less than a mile from the western edge of the swamp, the first such settlement you have seen all day! Why choose to live in such conditions? Will you enter the village? (Turn to **578**) Or ignore it and head straight for the swamp? (Turn to **625**)

597

Your hand-eye co-ordination is awry and the snake sinks its fangs painfully into your hand! You stuff your hand under your wing to stifle the burning sensation already spreading down your arm and know that the snake was a poisonous one! If you have a vial of antivenom with you, turn to **670**. If not, turn to **657**.

598

You decide to have a closer look at the dwellings on the platform to see what lies within, but will there be any concealed guards? Will you approach by air, which would be faster? (Turn to **652**) Or will you half submerge yourself in the stinking water hoping that this will conceal your approach? (Turn to **693**)

599

You shout out to Nimax that the marsh-goblin is with you, but too late: the creature falls dead to the ground at his feet. Nimax looks down briefly in disgust at the body, then turns his attention to the staked out boot.

He picks it up and peers inside. You expect his congratulations, but instead he steps towards you and thrusts out his sword, which runs straight through your body! You just manage to grunt "Why?" as you fall dying to the grassy floor, but the answer to that you will never know. The last thing you see is Nimax flying off northwards with the precious firebrand snake…

600

You hover out of range and demand answers from the creatures you have pursued so far. But it becomes clear from their reaction to your questions that they only ever saw one birdman (you), which means Nimax had gone before you awoke. Has he deserted you? As you have no idea how to find him, you can only assume that he is continuing the search alone. You resolve to do likewise. Turn to **609**.

601

You conduct your search for about ten minutes, but having checked several snakes of the right colour and found no gold patches on their backs, decide you have pushed your luck far enough here. You leave the snake pit behind you and return to the main path. Turn to **673**.

602

The creature's other hand comes up and you accidentally drop the bundle of herbs, which rain down on the animals below. Almost immediately the hand around your leg releases its grip and you are able to break away. Scattering the remainder of the herbs in your wake, you dive down and grab the firebrand snake which has curled itself around the trunk of a tree. You spiral upwards out of the swamp, elated to have finally captured the key to the survival of a large number of your tribe.

Before long you are many miles nearer the mountains, the firebrand twisting and turning in your hand. You are following the river again with one thought in mind: to get home! The sun has almost set in the distance so you fly down to make camp. You luckily discover a discarded boot nearby that will contain the firebrand, and stake it to the ground securely. Then you settle on the grass (which is far too soft for your liking!) to sleep. You feel reasonably safe; you have seen very little life this side of the mountains.

If you have *both* of the codewords MARSH and REED, turn to **620**. If you have either one but not both of these codewords, turn to **586**. If you do not have either, turn to **706**.

603

The villagers look at one another but shake their heads. They are clearly not experts in swamp reptiles! "If you're really going in there," warns another of the men, "then the only safe path is more or less straight ahead. Somewhere deep within the mists off to the right is a marsh-goblin town - they occasionally mount a raid on us and we have to drive them off. We're not quite as defenceless as we may seem…"

"Oh and don't disturb the Nians!" cuts in the tallest man again. "That's the brutal swamp-monkeys that nest in the trees and on the ground. You don't want to tangle with them: cross one and you have them *all* to deal with!"

You thank the men for their advice. As you take off, the man with the eye patch warns you under no circumstances to take the left hand path as it will lead you into mortal danger…turn to **625**.

604

Further on you fly, ever in search of your elusive quarry. But you see no snakes at all in this part of the swamp. You land again and stand atop an outcrop of spongy earth, surveying the eerie grey scene.

Suddenly you become aware of something approaching you from the right. It is a humanoid head, but warty, brown and ugly, with a pug nose and a mouth of broken jagged teeth. The body is completely submerged in the slimy water and you are not sure, but it sounded like it gurgled at you to 'wait!'

Will you kick water into the face and escape? (Turn to **681**) Order it to come no nearer? (Turn to **697**) Or wait as it requests? (Turn to **651**)

605

You slumber undisturbed in the corner of the cell, but hardly enjoy the best night's sleep of your life! As the sunlight begins to permeate the writhing mists, you feel yourself being roughly shaken awake.

"Wake up!" gurgles the marsh-goblin. "Guards here soon!" Minutes later you hear the sound of the door being unlocked and the pair of you charge at the guard. Roll the die, subtracting 1 from the roll if you have the codeword POINT. If the result is 1 or less, turn to **689**. If it is a 2, turn to **634**. If it is 3 or more, turn to **658**.

606

Just as the firebrand seems within reach, you feel the heavy weight of one of the beasts as it drops down on you from above. With a mighty splash, you both plunge into the slimy water. You struggle, but more hairy bodies land on you from the trees and weight of numbers tells. You never resurface.

607

You tell your story in brief, and as modestly as possible. You can tell that he does not want to believe you, but he is not certain you are lying either. He settles for scoffing at your stupidity to allow the Orphus Latix to be taken and in ever trusting a human in the first place; you never know what they're saying for one thing! Will you enlighten Nimax to the fact that, thanks to Vashta's spell, you *can* actually speak and understand the languages of most creatures, including humans? (Turn to **720**) Or would you rather keep that information to yourself and continue with your mission? (Turn to **647**)

608

You struggle to get airborne and cannot react at a speed to match that of the wolves. The first one is already upon you, savage claws tearing at your flesh. As its companions catch up, you are at least spared a prolonged death…

609

Leaving the wolves far behind, you soar through the sky, refocusing on your mission. In the last few months, you have completed a lifetime's worth of heroic deeds alone, so the disappearance of Nimax does not mean that you abandon all hope for the successful completion of your quest!

The mountains loom closer and closer and you decide to cross them, hoping to find marshier land beyond. If you have the codeword FANG, turn to **643**. If you do not have this codeword, turn to **596**.

610

You manage to break through the wall of sludgy water and gulp in the relatively clear air outside. You hover and watch as the spout splashes back down to the ground in a muddy morass and the tentacle thrashes about for a bit before submerging once more. Unsurprisingly, your torch is drenched and has gone out (note this down).

You decide not to linger for long, and fly onwards. There appears to be two main passages through the vegetation; will you go left, which is the darker route of the two? (Turn to **633**) Or right, which seems to be more overgrown with trees? (Turn to **565**)

611

Somehow you manage to break free and half wade, half drag yourself to freedom. The creature is unwilling or unable to follow you but even so you hurry away from the cave, cursing the mistake which could so easily have cost you your life! Turn to **727**.

612

You stealthily pluck the flaming brand from the wooden hole in which it nestles. You feel lucky not to have been spotted so far, but do you want to push your luck? If you want to investigate the strange village more closely, turn to **598**. To steer well clear of it and go deeper into the swamp, turn to **727**.

613

You swoop safely over the log but have lost a bit of ground on the snake. Then you come to a mass of tangled bushes loaded with large cream-coloured puffballs. The ones that you accidentally disturb with your wing tips burst in clouds of white powder. *React on instinct*. Will you aim to smash a few more of the puffballs as you fly through them and hopefully hinder your pursuers? (Turn to **664**) Or ignore them and concentrate on the chase? (Turn to **642**)

614

The hours pass and morning rolls into afternoon. Then you see a figure wandering the plains far below. It is seemingly half-human, half-giant, and reminds you that you saw some of these at a distance when you were here before. If you have the codeword TONGUE, turn to **660**. If not, will you suggest to Nimax that you fly down and talk to the creature? (Turn to **684**) Or say nothing and continue your journey? (Turn to **714**)

615

Luck is on your side; you instinctively hop backwards and avoid the first falling wolf, which lands awkwardly and howls in pain. This gives you a few seconds head start and you run off as fast as you can down the path! The baying of the other two wolves grows louder and louder as they give chase, and their jaws snap at thin air beneath you as you get airborne just in time! Cursing yourself for losing valuable time in this way, you fly eastwards once more, keen to pick up the trail as soon as possible. Turn to **630**.

616

The wood is airy and clearly well-tended. A variety of birds and land mammals flee before you as you make your way in, following a stony path littered with forest foliage. The path then forks before you. It leads uphill and to the left (turn to **588**) or almost straight on (turn to **673**).

617

You step lightly over to the nearest nest. From here you can see the back of a primate-like head and long-fingered hands. You step back warily, but just then a bat swoops through the clearing and screeches loudly! Note down the codeword SNAP.

The creatures in the nests begin to stir, and the one you had been looking at turns an angry simian face towards you, snarling and revealing sharp teeth. A wave of howls and screeches pours from the trees that surround you, and the nearest of the beasts advances menacingly. If you are carrying a bundle of sweet-smelling herbs, turn to **579**. Otherwise, will you:

Use your talons to keep them at bay?	Turn to **650**
Grab the nearest one and try to throw it into the others?	Turn to **710**
Brandish your torch at them to make them withdraw (if your torch hasn't gone out)	Turn to **583**
Or try to fly away to safety through the mist?	Turn to **674**

618

Luckily you spot the danger and are easily able to avoid the snake. You watch it crawl across the rock and disappear back into the mire.

It is short work to spark your torch back into life (note down that you have relit your torch). You use it to battle against the mists which seem ready to engulf you in this part of the swamp! A few minutes later, you see a cave off to your left. It is half submerged with the filthy swamp water, so that you cannot tell the level of the floor and may have to swim. You could however leave your torch outside, wedged in a cleft in the rock so it would not go out again. If you want to take the trouble to explore this cave, turn to **640**. If you would rather ignore it and continue, turn to **727**.

619

You recognise these creatures as being marsh-goblins, kinsfolk of the one you met earlier on. You continue to creep stealthily around the sides of the buildings. The next hut has no windows, but does have a wooden grille in the door. Peeping through, you see a lone marsh-goblin fast asleep on the floor, his hands also tied behind his back. You guess that this must be the friend the first marsh-goblin spoke of! If you want to try to release him from his prison, turn to **641**. If you want to continue exploring without releasing the goblin, turn to **712**.

620

During the night, you are shaken awake most unexpectedly! It is the two marsh-goblins you helped escape from their kind! You ask them what they want.

"You fly us t'swamp somewhere?" gurgles one, looking at you hopefully.

Something inside you warms to these repugnant little creatures, but you can hardly afford to add time to your journey home. However they may prove useful as night watchmen, and you presume marsh-goblins don't eat snakes... If you want to tell them that you will find them a swamp tomorrow, turn to **677**. If you disappoint them, they trudge off into the distance and you find a new, hidden place to sleep (turn to **706**).

621

"Marshes? Not many in the Beotlands," replies the Beotman, to your disappointment. He describes the one that you and Nimax searched earlier on, but you tell him you've covered that one already.

As Nimax paces impatiently behind you, furious at being unable to understand a word being said, you ask the Beotman in which direction other marshes are most likely to be found.

"Beyond the mountains to the east," is his answer. "There lie perilous lands, many wild woods, swamps and dark caves."

At this point Nimax rudely interrupts. "Time to go," he says firmly. You bristle, but it is useless to protest so you bid the Beotman farewell. Nimax does not mention your ability, but flies on in sullen silence. Turn to **714**.

622

You are once again glad of your ability to see in the dark as you enter the gloomy depths of the cave. A long tunnel slopes down into the heart of the rock, eerily silent at first. Then you hear low, gruff voices but cannot distinguish any words. You edge nearer and peep around the corner to see a large chamber in which is gathered a dozen or so of the greenwolves.

One of them is looking towards the entrance and sees you! With a savage howl, it changes into wolf form and leaps forward, followed by others. You turn and run, but there is not enough room to fly. In a foot race you will be overrun, so you turn to make a brave final stand deep beneath the earth...

623

You wait for a few minutes, but there is no sign of anyone approaching. After ten minutes, you decide to continue deeper into the wood.

The path begins to curve round uphill to the right, but you also notice a set of steps cut into the rock leading downhill and round a bend to the left. If you want to see where the steps lead, turn to **691**. To stay on the main path, turn to **673**.

624

You briefly introduce yourself and the Beotman listens patiently to your tale, his snake winding its way up his arm. When you have finished, he speaks.

"This problem of yours is no affair of mine," he says. "Yet I know of the snake you seek. They're very scarce and they like marshy areas. As far as I know, the nearest place to find one is in a swamp across the mountains to the east. Follow the mountain river and you'll come to it in a day or two. It's dangerous, but if you're willing to risk it... Now you must excuse me, I have things to do." With that, he begins arranging a fire in front of the tree stump.

You thank the Beotman for his help and he wishes you luck in your quest. He points to a safe way out of the wood and you are soon back in the skies again, on the next stage of your journey. Turn to **596**.

625

You soon cover the distance between the village and the swamp. You are going to have to fly low over the stinking morass as the mists make it impossible to see well from above and your best chance of enticing a firebrand is with fire.

With this in mind, you grab a broken branch from the ground and set it alight by striking rocks together. Note down that you are carrying a flaming torch.

Now it is time to enter the swamp. You glide slowly into the mists, sweeping your torch below you and keeping a keen look out. The swamp is teeming with life: insects, snakes and other creatures that you find it harder to identify. You have to keep one eye open for the twisted, blackened swamp-trees that appear without warning from the mists to hinder your progress. That, the pungent smell and the irritating clouds of buzzing insects make this an unpleasant task indeed!

Soon you find yourself having to choose a direction through the almost forest-like vegetation. Will you choose:
    The most well-trodden path, leading to the left? Turn to **680**
    The central way, which looks the most watery? Turn to **668**
    Or the darkest and mistiest pathway to the right? Turn to **589**

626

You lunge forward, but unfortunately in doing so you overbalance and fall into the boggy pool! Although you bring your hand up clutching the snake just behind the head, your torch fell in the water and has gone out if it was still alight (note this down).

The snake snaps viciously at thin air as you wipe the mud and slime from its body. You are disappointed to see no splashes of gold anywhere along its back and it really is very brown, with little if any red in it at all. You are forced to conclude that this is not the snake you are looking for.

Ruefully you let it go and it slithers away across the mud flats, head held high. Turn to **604**.

627

Between your keen eyesight and the goblin's knowledge, you manage to deduce where most of the guards are hidden and plot an escape route through them. Roll the die, subtracting 1 if you have the codeword POINT. If you get a 3 or less, turn to **725**. If you get a 4 or more, turn to **676**.

628

You beat your wings fiercely, hoping gravity help you shake off the foul creature. Roll the die. If you roll a 2 or less, turn to **567**. If you roll a 3 or more, turn to **635**.

629

You scan the surface of the bog as Nimax goes into action with the torch. Suddenly, a purple bat-like creature swoops from a tree behind Nimax, straight towards him! *React on instinct*. Will you attempt to intercept the bat? (Turn to **580**) Or pause and see what happens? (Turn to **678**)

630

You fly hard through the afternoon, overtaking the group that attacked you but immediately observing that they are following the trail of another pack of greenwolves – and this group may have taken Nimax.

You see a mountain range on the horizon with hills that sprawl out before it. Your wings are just beginning to ache with the exertion when you reach a disheartening sight: the tracks terminate at a river which runs through a valley. The wolves are obviously intelligent as they have followed the river for some distance before rejoining the far bank, therefore leaving no tracks. You hope your instincts will be right: will you fly upstream (turn to **701**) or downstream? (Turn to **685**)

631

You stand awaiting a response, but it is not what you expected: out lumbers a huge, two-headed bear! Both heads roar and snarl, and it bounds suddenly towards you with murderous intent! Roll the die. If you roll a 1, turn to **662**. If you roll a 2 or more, turn to **595**.

632

You step as lightly as you can through the clearing, but just then a bat flaps its way through the haze and screeches loudly! Note down the codeword SNAP.

The creatures in the nests quickly begin to stir and the nearest creature turns an angry simian face towards you, snarling and revealing sharp teeth. A wave of howls and screeches pours from the trees that surround you and several more of the beasts advance menacingly. If you are carrying a bundle of sweet-smelling herbs, turn to **579**. Otherwise, will you:

Use your talons to keep them at bay?	Turn to **650**
Grab the nearest one and try to throw it into the others?	Turn to **710**
Brandish your torch at them to make them withdraw (if your torch hasn't gone out)	Turn to **583**
Or try to fly to safety through the mist?	Turn to **674**

633

You glide through the gloom, concerned about relighting your torch as soon as possible. Then you see a large slab of rock protruding from the marsh and land on its slimy pinnacle. Here you can try to reignite the end of your branch.

As you concern yourself with this task, a snake emerges from the swamp and slithers up rock to investigate you. Roll the die. If you roll a 2 or less, turn to **584**. If you get a 3 or more, turn to **618**.

634

You take the guard by surprise and your shoulder charge sends him sprawling to the wooden floor with a gurgling grunt. You hurdle the body and run to the edge of the platform, the footsteps of your fellow inmate scampering behind you. Then you hear the splatter of swamp-muck all around as the guards in the mire below surface to investigate the commotion!

You cannot leave the goblin here to die, and turn to grab him and take him with you. As you do this however, he is struck in the back by a spear thrown from below - he loses his balance and topples head first into the swamp!

Stifling a cry you leap upwards, narrowly avoiding a similar fate as spears fly through the thick air. Then you are gone, grabbing one of the flaming torches from its niche as you pass. Note down that you have a lit torch once more, and turn to **727**.

635

To your relief, the hand around your leg releases its grip and you are able to break away. You circle the tree, spot the firebrand once more and bravely dive down, finally grabbing the snake which has curled itself around the trunk.

You spiral upwards out of the swamp, elated to have at long last captured the key to the survival of a large number of your tribe. The shrieks and screeches from below you gradually fade away.

Before long you are many miles nearer the mountains, the firebrand twisting and turning in your hand. You are following the river again with one thought in mind: to get home! The sun has almost set in the distance so you fly down to make camp. You luckily discover a discarded boot nearby that will contain the firebrand and stake it to the ground securely. Then you settle on the grass (which is far too soft for your liking!) to sleep. You feel reasonably safe; you have seen very little life this side of the mountains.

If you have *both* of the codewords MARSH and REED, turn to **620**. If you have either one but not both of these codewords, turn to **586**. If you do not have either, turn to **706**.

636

Nimax listens to your story with seeming indifference. "Hmmph!" he snorts. "That'd be just like that old fool to choose someone so young and unsuitable for such a task! Someone prone to fabricating tall tales…" as he passes this last comment he turns and meets your gaze; he did not believe your account of your mountain adventure last month and it is clear that he suspects you of lying this time too. He is in two minds though because of his evident contempt of the Vzler, a birdman you had believed to be universally respected up until now.

Your dislike for Nimax only grows following this exchange. Turn to **647**.

637

You get to your feet and scan the plains for the cause of the sound. It is coming from the east and in horror you see three large wolves with dark green fur burst from the bushes in front of you and pounce in your direction, jaws slavering, hungry for your blood! Roll the die. If you roll a 1, turn to **608**. If you roll a 2 or more, turn to **661**.

638

Cautiously you reach in and lift a few of the snakes to better see beneath. Roll the die. If you roll a 2 or less, turn to **570**. If you roll a 3, turn to **666**. If you roll a 4 or more, turn to **601**.

639

You fly to the right spot and slowly descend into the water, waist deep before you gratefully feel solid rock beneath your feet. You reach out and pick up one of the eggs, which you immediately discern to be empty. Turning it over in your hands, you see that you are only holding a fragment of the entire shell.

But you have been observed. Something throws a barbed hunting spear at your back! Although the throw is wayward, the weapon slices your wing, hampering your movement. For the rest of this adventure, you must subtract 1 from any die rolls you make (unless the text asks whether you have rolled an odd or even number).

You turn to deal with the creature, but are only in time to see a gloomy figure submerging. You continue on our way. Turn to **573**.

640

The water may smell as bad as anything you have ever smelt in your life, but at least it is not too deep. You have to bow your head to enter the cave mouth, submerged to just below your waist. You are just deciding that there seems no end to the tunnel, when you feel rather than see under the water a heavy, hairy body squeeze past you and wrap a powerful limb around your waist! *React on instinct*. Will you try to muscle your way free (turn to **675**) or strike at it with your talons? (Turn to **704**)

641

The door is only locked by a crude bolt on the outside, so you are easily able to open it. The prisoner within wakes up at the noise and stares in wide-eyed fear at the sight of you! You stride across the cell and sever his bonds with one slash of your talons, a deed which confuses him even more!

You quickly explain about the other marsh-goblin you met and he looks overjoyed. "Got get away!" he croaks in a whisper. "Or I dead tomorrow!" Note down the codeword REED.

Fortunately, none of the guards have been alerted. You grab the goblin by the shoulders and he gives a gurgling cry as you take to the sky and put some space between you and the goblin town.

A safe distance away, you set the trembling creature down on a patch of dry ground, but he immediately slips into the slimy marsh which is more to his liking! You ask him if he knows anything about snakes, but he shakes his head.

You decide you have wasted enough time with these creatures and wish him luck as he swims off. He is heading out of the swamp to freedom, but unfortunately you know that your path lies deeper *into* it! Turn to **727**.

642

Just ahead, the firebrand slithers with amazing speed up into the jagged branches of a large, leafless tree. You know you must get at it somehow, but are mindful of the bloodthirsty hollering that if anything is gaining on you! *React on instinct*. Will you leap into the branches of the tree (turn to **728**) or swoop to the far side of it and try to intercept the snake there? (Turn to **713**)

643

You remember the advice given to you by the Beotman; the snake expert's cave must be close by. You decide to slow your flight and scan the rolling hills and valleys that pass beneath you, and soon you see a cave cut into the side of a hill. A rocky path winds up to it from a little wooded dell. If you want to swoop down and investigate the cave, turn to **715**. If you want to land outside and announce your presence by calling out, turn to **631**. If you don't think that this is the right cave and want to continue searching elsewhere, turn to **686**. If you'd rather not waste time searching for this character and want to cross the mountains now, turn to **596**.

644

A short, fat, reddish-brown snake flashes across the soggy ground before you, and for a second your heart leaps – but then you remember that the firebrand is as long as a Beotman's armspan, and this one is nowhere near that! Ruefully, you watch it plunge into a pool to the left of the pathway. Turn to **604**.

645

The floor is quite solid but is only wood lashed together with reeds, twined together for strength. You are able to get your talons in between the cracks and sever enough of these fastenings to loosen a couple of floorboards and pull them up, all quietly enough to avoid detection.

Your goblin companion is full of excitement at the prospect of escaping his imprisonment and leads the way, slipping into the murky depths just a few feet below. You are far less enamoured with the prospect but force yourself into the muck and floating debris alongside him.

"Which way?" you whisper.

"Guards everywhere," replies the goblin, "hidden in water!" When you look closely, you can just see the top of a slimy head glistening in the available light, or the distinct gleam of a metal spear. How will you suggest making your escape?

Trying to sneak past the guards?	Turn to **627**
Fighting your way out?	Turn to **566**
Or waiting until the nearest guards leave?	Turn to **705**

646

You glance to the side and see the same snarling, gnashing primates that you saw in the nests earlier on! They have picked up your scent and now look to kill you and feast on your flesh! Roll the die. If you roll a 4 or less, turn to **592**. If you roll a 5 or more, turn to **699**.

647

As evening draws in, the mountains recede and are replaced by rolling brown foothills and then forests of unfamiliar trees. You can tell from Nimax's obvious interest that he has never seen anything like this before, but he does not speak of it.

Eventually, Nimax spirals down to ground level to find somewhere to sleep for the night. He orders a watch to be held now that you are out of the mountains taking the first duty himself and waking you up for yours halfway through the night. After an uneventful time spent lost in your thoughts, you set off once more across the grasslands.

In the late morning, Nimax is first to spot a stream flowing down from the hills and follows it to a marsh small enough that, even standing at the edge, you can see to the far bank. Nimax lights a tree branch by striking two flints together and directs you to watch carefully, ready to grab the firebrand snake should it appear, while he flies low over the surface.

You look about for the best vantage point. Will you station yourself on the side overgrown with vegetation? (Turn to **671**) Or the bare banks of the opposite side? (Turn to **629**)

648

You slowly drift backwards...exactly as the creature wanted! Three of the greenwolves are waiting for you in the leafy branches of a tree! Roll the die. If you roll a 3 or less, turn to **576**. If you roll a 4 or more, turn to **665**.

649

The Beotman is a little disappointed, but you explain your reason for urgency

"I've seen the firebrand, but never had one here," he tells you. "They're scarce and they like marshy areas. Red-brown in colour, with gold patches on its back. They're about the length of my armspan," he continues and holds out his massive, bear-like arms! "As far as I know, the nearest place to find one is in a swamp across the mountains to the east. Follow the mountain river and you'll come to it in a day or two. It's dangerous, but if you're willing to risk it..." Note down the codeword SCALE.

You thank the Beotman for his help and he wishes you luck in your quest. He shows you a safe way out of the wood and you are soon back in the skies again, on the next stage of your journey. Turn to **596**.

650

You step forwards and slash at the nearest creature, which howls even louder and draws back in pain. You hope that this will warn the rest of them off, but it seems to have the opposite effect! More and more appear from all around you, and as if on a signal, they suddenly attack as one and you are swamped with long armed, hairy bodies, biting and tearing at your flesh. You go down fighting...

651

Intrigued but on guard, you stand your ground. The creature in the mire clambers with difficulty onto the rock on which you stand. It is a short, squat humanoid, and you see its trouble: its hands are tied behind its back!

"What are you?" you ask, sensing no immediate danger. But the creature ignores your question and implores you in a gurgling, throaty voice to break his bonds. First you want to know why he is tied up!

"Huh!" he snorts, causing a clod of goo to run from his nostrils. "Prisoned by king back *there*," he indicates behind him with a nod of the head.

If you want to free the strange creature, turn to **688**. If you'd prefer not to get involved, you can head off either generally to the left (turn to **565**) or to the right, the direction the thing indicated he had escaped from? (Turn to **573**)

652

You fly as quietly as possible over the wooden slats and peer in at a long, low hole in the wall of one of the largest huts. Sleeping inside, snoring disgustingly are thirty or forty warty, brown, pug-nosed humanoids! Though clearly physically weaker than you, in numbers they could be dangerous.

If you have the codeword MARSH, turn to **619**. If you do not have this codeword, turn to **712**.

653

A wide smile of yellowed, broken teeth spreads across his face at your promise. But first you need to sleep!

Later that night you are woken by the sound of battle! You scramble to your feet to witness your marsh-goblin companion defending himself with a branch. You are shocked when you see that his opponent is none other than...Nimax! Nimax bears a long steel sword which he uses to cut the goblin's weapon down to size. If you are wearing a golden snake charm, turn to **694**. If you do not have this object, turn to **599**.

654

A dozen steps further down the path is all it takes for your fears to be confirmed: you feel a droplet of what turns out to be saliva drip on you from above! You look up into the rabid eyes of three of the greenwolves! Roll the die. If you roll a 3 or less, turn to **576**. If you roll a 4 or 5, turn to **708**. If you roll a 6, turn to **615**.

655

The snake drops to the ground in two parts; your blow has severed it completely! You examine the pool more closely; it seems to be just drinking water. This is a dead end, so you turn to return to the main path. Roll the die. If you roll an odd number, turn to **679**. If you roll an even number, turn to **673**.

656

You fly onwards, but there is no sign of any snakes in this part of the swamp either. Then the path you are following becomes totally submerged and you fly over a large area of bog that looks suspiciously like quicksand.

Suddenly there is an explosive surge of water below you and you are engulfed and driven upwards in a column of filthy water! An enormous tentacle lashes back and forth within, slapping you hard across the back. *React on instinct*. Will you try to fly forwards through the wall of water? (Turn to **687**) Or upwards and out of the spout that way? (Turn to **564**)

657

The poison is fast acting. You stagger on, but within minutes consciousness has left you and you fall forwards into the swamp, dead.

658

You take the guard by surprise and your shoulder charge sends him sprawling to the wooden floor with a gurgling grunt. You hurdle the body and run to the edge of the platform, the plodding footsteps of your fellow inmate behind you. Then you hear the splatter of swamp-muck all around as the guards in the mire below surface to investigate the commotion.

You cannot leave the goblin here to die, so grab him roughly by the shoulders to take him with you. He wails as you soar up into the mists and you hear the whoosh of spears flying through the thick air. But you are gone, even having the presence of mind to grab one of the flaming torches from its niche as you pass! Note down that you have a lit torch once more.

A safe distance away, you set the trembling creature down on a patch of dry ground, but he immediately slips into the slimy marsh which is more to his liking! You ask him if he knows anything about snakes, but he shakes his head.

You decide you have wasted enough time with these creatures and wish him luck as he swims off. He is heading out of the swamp to freedom, but unfortunately you know that your path lies deeper *into* it! Note down the codeword REED and turn to **727**.

659

You glance to the side and see angry primate-like animals leaping through the trees towards you, snarling and baring their sharp teeth. A wave of howls and screeches pours from the trees all around you; these creatures have picked up your scent and now look to kill you and feast on your flesh!

Horrified at this twist of fate at the critical moment, you fly with all your speed: you mustn't lose the firebrand! The trees thin, but your pursuers seem able to move almost as fast as you can fly! Suddenly a huge log looms up out of the mist, right in your way. *React on instinct.* Will you fly over the log (turn to **613**) or under it? (Turn to **719**)

660

Nimax slows down to fly beside you, points downwards and calls across sarcastically, "Well, there's a native! Why don't you ask him the way?" He laughs at his little joke. He evidently didn't believe what you said about Vashta's spell!

Although you have never before spoken with this kind of creature, you are confident that you will be able to and bank away, swooping down to land before the figure. You only wish you could see Nimax's face as he follows you, landing a good distance further back.

You hold up your hands to indicate that you come in peace, but the huge man-like being does not look like the sort to easily scare. He is a head taller than you, dressed in patchwork leather clothing, with stumps of blunt teeth lining a lower jaw that juts out. He brushes the long, straggly black hair from his eyes with a meaty hand, but does not speak.

You greet him politely and introduce yourself. "Ariax, eh?" he says, thoughtfully.

You confirm this and ask what manner of being you are addressing. He smiles. "I am one of the Beotmen!" he declares. Seeing your unfamiliarity he adds, "An ancient and noble race, one of the oldest in all of Faltak. We are a solitary lot, but roam here and there, at one with the nature of the Beotlands, where you now stand."

You sense Nimax's irritation at your progress and decide to ask a question to advance your quest. Will you ask:
    Whether there is any marshland nearby?   Turn to **621**
    Or about the firebrand snake?   Turn to **593**

661

You manage to overcome your shock and scramble airborne as the wolves reach the spot where you had been sleeping. They paw angrily at the dirt. But where is Nimax, who was on watch?

You gaze down at the strange green wolves and look about for any sign of Nimax. You see none. Then you notice below you that something extraordinary is happening: two of the greenwolves at first appear to be rearing up on their hind legs, but a few seconds later they have in fact morphed into two-legged, green-skinned, wolf-faced humanoids! In their new voices they mock you and call for you to come down.

Your mind races. Could Nimax be their prisoner? Eventually you decide that even though he is not your favourite Ariax, he is one of your kind and you are going to at least try to discover his fate by pursuing the greenwolves, who have given up on you and raced off.

They have a head start, but you can fly like the wind when needs must. You saw a group of them fleeing to the east, and set off in hot pursuit in this direction, heart racing in your chest. You soon pick up their trail, their paw prints showing up clearly in the sponginess of the plains. Then they must have split up; you see one set of tracks has peeled off from the main group and headed north into a small wood. The majority of the pack continued east. If you wish to pursue the smaller group, turn to **581**. To ignore them and continue following the others, turn to **721**.

662

You take to the air, but feel yourself being pulled back by the left leg! You look down and see one of the bear's heads has its jaws clamped around your calf while the other still snarls ferociously! You kick out and strike with your talons, but it is in vain. The bear rears up on its hind legs and uses its sharp claws to drag you down into the dirt. From there, you have no chance of survival.

663

You glide almost silently across to the nearest torch and attempt to take it from its housing, temporarily illuminated. Roll the die. If you roll an odd number, turn to **698**. If you roll an even number, turn to **612**.

664

It takes little effort to slash out at the puffballs as you pass, and clouds of white dust explode in the air. From the screeching and chattering noises behind you, the chasing pack are clearly not enjoying it!

Just ahead, the firebrand slithers with amazing speed up into the jagged branches of a large, leafless tree. You know you must get at it somehow, but are mindful of the bloodthirsty hollering that continues and, if anything, is gaining on you from behind! *React on instinct*. Will you leap into the branches of the tree (turn to **606**) or swoop to the far side of it and try to intercept the snake there? (Turn to **713**)

665

Just in time you sense the danger and avoid the leaping form of one of the wolves. It howls as it falls to the ground, rolling in a heap between two of its fellows. You hover out of range and demand answers from the rest of the pack. But it becomes clear from their reaction to your questions that they only ever saw one birdman (you), which means Nimax had gone before you awoke. Has he deserted you? As you have no idea how to find him, you can only assume that he is continuing the search alone. You resolve to do likewise. Turn to **609**.

666

You conduct your search for about five minutes, checking several snakes of the right colour but finding no gold patches on their backs. Then you hear heavy feet stomping in your direction. A Beotman with wild eyes, long straggly hair and a grey snake wrapped around his wrist emerges from the undergrowth. He sees what you are doing and immediately looks angry.

"What are you doing, interfering with my snakes like this?" he huffs, and pulls you roughly away by the shoulder. You try to explain that you are seeking him out for his help in an important matter, but he interrupts short temperedly.

"Not important to me!" he chuckles. "Not important to me at all! Now begone feathered one, before I call my snakes!"

You try once more to ask for his aid, but this time he glares at you and starts to make a strange hissing sound in the back of his throat. Two or three serpents rise from the nest, tongues flickering menacingly. It is obvious that you have lost the opportunity to gain knowledge here, so you make your way out of the forest. Turn to **596**.

667

Unfortunately, the suspicious villagers regard this innocent line of conversation as intrusive and begin to suspect that you are a saboteur! Of course you could hardly be less interested in their crops, but your protests only serve to confirm their suspicions!

You persevere with your questioning, but the men are having none of it, and you concede that you'll get nothing more from them. As you take off, the man with the eye patch shouts at you to under no circumstances take the left hand path as it will lead you into mortal danger…turn to **625**.

668

This route is indeed sodden; in fact it is just a mass of pools and bogs connected by streams of grey-brown mud. If you have the codeword SCALE, turn to **644**. If you do not have this codeword, turn to **711**.

669

The cell door is opened and you are shoved roughly inside. Your arrival awakens a lone marsh-goblin who had been slumped asleep, his hands also tied behind his back. You realise that this must be the friend the first marsh-goblin spoke of! This one stares in wide-eyed fear at the sight of you!

When he realises that not only do you mean him no harm but you may be able to help him escape, he croaks in a whisper, "Got get away! I dead tomorrow!"

You cannot reach whatever it is binding your wrists, but you *can* reach the goblin's bonds. You cut through them with one swipe of your beak. Then he returns the favour for you, using his teeth to bite through your restraints. You turn your attention to escape.

The prison cell has no windows, but does have a wooden grille in the door. Although when you peep through you see no guard immediately outside, they surely cannot be far away. After a hasty discussion, you think of three possible ways to escape. Do you want to:

Try to break down the door?	Turn to **718**
Rip up some floorboards and escape via the swamp below?	Turn to **645**
Or surprise the guards when they open the door and overpower them?	Turn to **726**

670

You hurriedly unstopper the vial and gulp down the bitter tasting fluid within. Almost immediately your head seems to explode with a blinding pain and you black out.

You have no idea how long you are unconscious, but are mightily relieved that when you do awake, the pain has all but gone from your head, arm and hand. The bad news is that your torch has rolled into a pool and gone out (note down that your torch is out). Still, you're alive! You pick yourself up and get on with your mission. Turn to **604**.

671

You prowl around the boundary of the mire, eyes peeled for activity. A minute or so later, you see out of the corner of your eye something large and snake-like sliding through the reeds and into the bog! *React on instinct.* Will you reach out and grab it (turn to **707**) or wait to see if you can make it out more clearly first (turn to **575**)?

672

Once airborne, you soon spot what disturbed your sleep: a pack of large wolves with dark green fur! The wolves reach the spot where you had been sleeping and paw angrily at the dirt. But where is Nimax, who was on watch?

You gaze down at the strange green wolves and look about for any signs of a struggle. You see none; and no blood either. Then you notice below you that something extraordinary is happening: two of the greenwolves at first appear to be rearing up on their hind legs, but a few seconds later they have in fact morphed into two-legged, green skinned humanoids! In their new voices they mock you and call for you to come down.

Your mind races. Could Nimax be their prisoner? Eventually you decide that even though he is not your favourite Ariax, he is one of your kind and you are going to at least try to discover his fate by pursuing the greenwolves, who have given up on you and raced off.

They have a head start, but you can fly like the wind when needs must. You saw a group of them fleeing to the east, and set off in hot pursuit in this direction, heart racing in your chest. You soon pick up their trail, their paw prints showing up clearly in the sponginess of the plains. Then they must have split up; you see one small set of tracks has peeled off from the main group and headed north into a small wood. The majority of the pack continued east. If you wish to pursue the smaller group, turn to **581**. To ignore this trail and continue east, turn to **721**.

673

The path twists and turns as it ascends deeper into the wood, eventually arriving at the mouth of a cave. Sitting on a tree stump outside is a Beotman with wild eyes, long straggly hair and a grey snake wrapped around his wrist. He looks up as you hail him politely, nodding in acknowledgement but saying nothing. What would be the best way to engage this fellow in conversation?

Tell him about the outbreak of Crackbeak which ravages your tribe?	Turn to **624**
Ask him directly about the firebrand snake?	Turn to **569**
Or tell him about the Beotman you met yesterday who directed you here?	Turn to **702**

674

You decide there is no sense giving your life battling these vicious creatures, and break through the ever present layer of mist into the sky above. The air tastes sweet and fragrant compared to the foulness below, but you know that you cannot loiter for long.

You fly deeper into the swamp before descending into an empty clearing. If you have the codeword TUFT, turn to **727**. If you do not have this codeword, turn to **692**.

675

You desperately try to get a handhold on the rocky ceiling of the cave to help you break the terrible grip of the thing that is surfacing below you! Roll the die. If you roll a 2 or less, turn to **724**. If you roll a 3 or more, turn to **611**.

676

Somehow your luck holds and you reach the outskirts of the marsh-goblin town undetected. There you grab one of the flaming torches stuck into the wooden platform (note down that you have a lit torch once more) and pull yourself gratefully out of the swamp onto a rock.

Your fellow escapee seems more than happy to stay in the mire! You ask him if he knows anything about snakes, but he shakes his head. You decide you have wasted enough time with these creatures and wish him luck as he swims off. He is heading out of the swamp to freedom, but unfortunately you know that your path lies deeper *into* it! Note down the codeword REED and turn to **727**.

677

Wide smiles of yellowed, broken teeth spread across their faces at your promise. But first, you need to sleep!

Later that night you are woken by the sound of battle! You scramble to your feet to witness your marsh-goblin companions locked in combat with an intruder in the camp! You are shocked when you see that this intruder is none other than...Nimax! Nimax is wielding a long steel sword, and as you watch, he uses it to cut down his first opponent!

The other goblin is just behind him. He runs bravely at Nimax unarmed and throws himself onto his back. You shout out that the little creature is with you, but too late: he shrugs the marsh-goblin from his back and hacks him down with another savage blow.

Nimax looks down briefly in disgust at the bodies, then assumes a battle-ready stance, sword tip pointed out towards you!

You can hardly believe what is happening: you are next! Are you destined to meet your end here in the wilds, at the hands of a treacherous enemy whose crime will never be discovered?

Not today! As Nimax advances on you, you see the mortally wounded marsh-goblin at his feet stretch out a feeble hand and grasp the battered old boot! With his last ounce of strength, he drags out the irritable, hissing firebrand and tosses it weakly towards your former mentor. Nimax winces in pain as the reddish-brown serpent clamps its fangs down on his calf, then he stumbles sideways, clutching at his leg. You remember Arguttax's words about the firebrand: 'It is deadly poisonous to Ariax, I'm afraid.'

You are shaken to your senses by the sight of the firebrand shimmying away across the grass and leap after it at once. This time it is a far easier task to catch the wriggling thing and within a few minutes it is safely back within your grasp once more. You return to the scene of carnage that was your camp.

The two marsh-goblins lie dead where they fell, but of Nimax there is no sign. You circle the area from the skies, expecting to find him dying somewhere not far away, but you see not a trace; it is as if he has completely vanished.

You shudder. If it hadn't have been for your goblin companions, Nimax may well have murdered you in your sleep. For that reason, you take the bodies to the nearest river and lower them carefully in, hoping it will return them to their swampy homeland. Turn to **730**.

678

Nimax turns his head just in time and deals with the danger, plucking the creature out of the air and holding it at arm's length. He glares at you as if to enquire why you weren't covering his back, but you ignore him.

After ten minutes of combing the area, Nimax finally decides that this is a fruitless job and signals for you to follow him once more. Turn to **614**.

679

As you turn, you see a Beotman with wild eyes, long straggly hair and a grey snake wrapped around his wrist stood watching you, looking angry.

"We have a snake killer!" he says. He grabs you by the shoulder and pulls you roughly away from the pool. You try to explain that you are seeking him out for his help in an important matter, but he interrupts short temperedly.

"Not important to me!" he chuckles. "Not important to me at all! Now begone feathered one, you are testing my non-violent nature!"

You have no desire to come to blows with a Beotman! It is obvious that you have lost the opportunity to gain knowledge here, so you make your way out of the forest as respectfully as you can. Turn to **596**.

680

You fly over a pathway of flattened mud and trampled reeds. Here and there, a large stone has been rolled deliberately in place to enable passage across a pool. You soon come to a vast spread of wetland which stretches off to your left as far as the eye can see (which isn't that far in these mists). Various crops are being grown here, almost certainly by the humans in the village as there are human tools stuck into the earth awaiting their owner's return.

Your torch attracts no snakes of any kind. As you make your way across the fields, you see that tall wooden poles have been positioned around the perimeter of the clearing, from the top of which hang bundles of herbs. They have a potent smell, and you wonder for what reason they have been put here. If you want to take one of the bundles down, turn to **696**. If you decide to leave them alone, turn to **656**.

681

The face disappears underwater as you spatter it with wet mud, and you take to the air once more. You soon come to a thicket of black tanglethorn trees and have the choice of flying to the left of them (turn to **565**) or the right of them (turn to **573**).

682

The cell door is opened and you are shoved roughly inside. Your arrival awakens a lone marsh-goblin who had been slumped asleep, his hands also tied behind his back. He stares in wide-eyed fear at the sight of you!

You cannot reach whatever it is binding your wrists; but you *can* reach the goblin's bonds. "If I free you, will you do the same for me?" you ask, taking a risk. He nods, still dumbstruck at your appearance, let alone comprehending the fact that you may be able to help him get out of here!

You cut through the ropes easily with one swipe of your beak and turn so that he can do the same for you. Fortunately, he does return the favour, using his teeth to bite through your restraints. You turn your attention to escape. "Got get away!" he croaks in a whisper, "Or I dead tomorrow!"

The prison cell has no windows, but does have a wooden grille in the door. Although when you peep through you see no guard immediately outside, they surely cannot be far away. After a hasty discussion, you think of three possible ways to escape. Do you want to:

Try to break down the door?	Turn to **718**
Rip up some floorboards and escape via the swamp below?	Turn to **645**
Or surprise the guards when they open the door and overpower them?	Turn to **726**

683

You decide that before you go any further you need to sort out the fire situation but there is no dry wood or anything like rock to strike a spark on here. You fly up through the mist, intending to find what you need in the lands surrounding the swamp. From above you see several reddish glows through the fog which look suspiciously like fire and decide to investigate.

A small village emerges from the mists! It is built on wooden platforms supported by stilts which keep it above the level of the bog underneath. A ramshackle collection of mud-huts are gathered on top and the glow you saw was a number of large flaming torches that line the perimeter, presumably to deter the denizens of the swamp.

You glide almost silently across to the nearest torch and attempt to pluck it from its housing, temporarily illuminated. Roll the die. If you roll an odd number, turn to **698**. If you roll an even number, turn to **612**.

684

Nimax looks across at you. "Good idea!" he smirks, sarcastically, "Be my guest!" He has no knowledge of your ability to speak and understand the languages of other races and fully expects you to make a fool of yourself!

So it comes as a bit of a surprise to him when this is not what happens! Although you have never before spoken with this kind of creature, you are confident that you will be able to and bank away, swooping down to land before him, Nimax landing a good distance behind you.

You hold up your hands to indicate that you come in peace, but the huge man-like being does not look like the sort to easily scare. He is a head taller than you, dressed in patchwork leather clothing, with stumps of blunt teeth lining a lower jaw that juts out. He brushes the long, straggly black hair from his eyes with a meaty hand, but does not speak.

You greet him politely and introduce yourself. "Ariax, eh?" he says, thoughtfully.

You confirm this and ask what manner of being you are addressing. He smiles. "I am one of the Beotmen!" he declares proudly. Seeing your unfamiliarity he adds, "An ancient and noble race, one of the oldest in all of Faltak. We are a solitary lot, but roam here and there, at one with the nature and animals of the Beotlands, where you now stand."

You sense Nimax behind you fuming that he cannot understand what is being said and decide to ask a question to advance your quest. Will you ask:
    Whether there is any marshland nearby?   Turn to **621**
    Or about the firebrand snake?   Turn to **593**

685

After twenty minutes the river runs underground. There are no signs of any tracks leading away: you chose the wrong direction! You return upstream as fast as you can, hoping that your mistake will not be too costly!

Eventually you find what you had been searching for: you pick up the trail again, higher up in the hills. You follow it to the greenwolves' camp: a cave in the hillside. Outside is a clearing surrounded by a ring of trees; one of the wolves is standing there in humanoid form. He does not see you, and as you watch he changes once more and races away down the hillside. Is Nimax in the cave, or has he been taken somewhere else? Will you:
    Creep into the cave to see what you can find?   Turn to **622**
    Hide and see if you can overhear
    the greenwolves talking?   Turn to **568**
    Or screech to get their attention and try to
    bargain with them for Nimax's life?   Turn to **729**

686

You divert your course northwards further up into the mountains, and remember that you are looking for a cave in a forest of some sort.

There is little woodland to be seen here, but finally you do find a small wood nestled in a natural hollow between crags, grassy and verdant. Is this the one? As you descend, you see two paths leading through the wood, one from each direction. Do you want to enter the wood from the more mountainous east side (turn to **709**) or from the west? (Turn to **616**)

687

You manage to break through, but the effort of fighting the flow causes you to stumble and fall face first onto the marshy ground. You pick yourself up and watch as the spout splashes back down to the ground in an deluge of mud and the tentacles thrash about for a bit before submerging once more. Unsurprisingly, your torch is drenched and has gone out (note this down).

You decide not to linger for long and fly onwards. There appear to be two main passages through the vegetation; will you go left, which appears the darker route of the two? (Turn to **633**) Or right, which seems to have the most trees? (Turn to **565**)

688

You receive no thanks for freeing him; the creature just stands there flexing his joints. You decide to hover out of his reach and repeat your previous question. "Marsh-goblin," he glugs, and tells you that he escaped from the marsh-goblin town but his friend is still back there, a prisoner!

Marsh-goblins evidently do not share the same code of honour as you: he seems resigned to his friend's fate and is not planning a 'death or glory' rescue attempt! In fact, he half believes that *you* have come to rescue his friend, and starts burbling away about guards hidden in the water!

You ask him if he knows anything about snakes, but he shrugs unintelligently. In fact, now that you have served his purpose, he makes off in the direction you have come from. Note down the codeword MARSH. From here, you can head generally to the left (turn to **565**) or to the right, the direction the goblin indicated his town was in? (Turn to **573**)

689

Your charge knocks the guard from his feet but as he stumbles you become entangled in his legs and also fall to your knees. This gives the other guards who had been following up the chance to strike at your unprotected back with their barbed spears. Your body is unceremoniously kicked into the swamp.

690

You kick out frantically; this mission is too important to be ended now that you are so close! Roll the die. If you roll a 1, turn to **567**. If you roll a 2 or more, turn to **635**.

691

The steps meander round the corner, widening as they go. At the bottom is a large flat slab of rock, surrounded by thick trees. The rock contains what looks like a natural pool of still water. As you stand before it, a blue snake suddenly breaks the surface and flies towards you at chest level! *React on instinct.* If you want to slash out at the snake, turn to **655**. If you want to try and dodge aside, turn to **582**.

692

The next clearing is surrounded by waterways and is criss-crossed by the streams that feed and link them. You find no snake activity at all, but then you do see in the distance a cluster of large eggs, apparently floating in the water. If you want to try and recover some of the eggs, turn to **639**. If you choose to ignore them and carry on deeper into the swamp, turn to **573**.

693

You attempt to breathe as little as possible as you make your way slowly through the thick mud. You are approaching the wooden platform when you suddenly realise with a shock that you are being watched by several warty, brown, pug-nosed faces! A heavy, foul-smelling net is thrown and entangles you, then you feel several slimy bodies throwing themselves on top of you, trying to push you under!

You have greater physical strength than these creatures, but caught in the net, with weight of numbers against you and being in their natural environment, you are losing the battle. Fortunately, they do not attempt to drown you, but drag you roughly onto their platform.

"Swamp b'longs t'us marsh-goblins!" gurgles a horrible voice behind you. Surrounded by spears, you elect to surrender and are marched out across the platforms to a cell. All your possessions are taken from you and thrown into the swamp, including your torch if you still have it (erase everything you are carrying). Your wrists are uncomfortably bound behind your back. If you have the codeword MARSH, turn to **669**. If you do not have this codeword, turn to **682**.

694

You shout out to Nimax that the marsh-goblin is with you, but too late: he slays the unarmed creature in cold blood! Nimax looks down briefly in disgust at the body, then turns his attention to the staked out boot. He picks it up and has a quick look inside, but instead of congratulating you, he tosses the boot aside and assumes a battle-ready stance, sword tip pointed out towards you!

You can hardly believe what is happening: you are next! Are you destined to meet your end here in the wilds, at the hands of a treacherous enemy whose crime will never be discovered?

Not today! As Nimax advances on you, the firebrand pops out of the boot! Nimax winces in pain as the reddish-brown serpent clamps its fangs down on his calf, then stumbles sideways, clutching at his leg. You remember Arguttax's words about the firebrand: 'It is deadly poisonous to Ariax, I'm afraid.'

You are shaken to your senses by the sight of the firebrand shimmying away across the grass and pursue it at once. This time it is a far easier task to catch the wriggling thing and within a few minutes it is safely back within your grasp once more. You return to the scene of carnage that was your camp.

The marsh-goblin lies dead where he fell, but of Nimax there is no sign. You circle the area from the skies, expecting to find him dying somewhere not far away, but you find no trace of him: it is as if he has completely vanished.

You shudder. If it hadn't been for your goblin companion, Nimax may well have murdered you in your sleep. For that reason, you take the body to the nearest river and lower it carefully in, hoping it will return him to his swampy homeland. Turn to **730**.

695

You pick up a branch and hurl it upwards. The bag and the bells are easily dislodged from their position in the trees and tumble clattering and clanging to the ground. Roll the die. If you roll an odd number, turn to **623**. If you roll an even number, turn to **577**.

696

You easily unattach the herbs and hold them in your free hand by the knotted rope with which they were fixed to the pole. Nothing happens. If you decide to take them with you, note down that you are carrying a bundle of sweet smelling herbs. Turn to **656**.

697

You issue your command, but the thing in the water pays no heed and continues to approach. Will you strike it with your claws? (Turn to **590**) Or wait to see what it does next? (Turn to **651**)

698

You grab the torch and are just banking up into the sky once more when a heavy, foul-smelling net is thrown over you and you are dragged, struggling, into the swamp below!

Three or four squat, humanoid creatures rise from the murky mire and begin pulling you in. You glimpse warty, brown, pug-nosed faces through the netting.

You have greater physical strength than these creatures, but tangled in the net, with weight of numbers against you and in their natural environment, you are losing the battle. Fortunately, they do not attempt to drown you, but drag you roughly onto their platform.

"Swamp b'longs t'us marsh-goblins!" gurgles a horrible voice behind you. Surrounded by spears, you elect to surrender and are marched out across the platforms to a cell. All your possessions are taken from you and thrown into the swamp, including your torch if you still have it (erase everything you are carrying). Your wrists are uncomfortably bound behind your back. If you have the codeword MARSH, turn to **669**. If you do not have this codeword, turn to **682**.

699

Luckily you have a small head start, but horrified at this twist of fate at the critical moment, you fly with all your speed: you mustn't lose sight of the firebrand!

The trees thin, but your pursuers seem able to move almost as fast as you can fly! Suddenly a huge log looms up out of the mist, right in your way. *React on instinct.* Will you fly over the log (turn to **613**) or under it? (Turn to **719**)

700

"*I'll* decide whether it is important right now," snaps Nimax angrily, turning his gaze upon you. "*You* are answerable to *me*!" You had better think quickly! Will you tell him the truth (turn to **607**) or lie? (Turn to **636**)

701

Eventually you pick up the trail again, heading higher into the hills. You follow it to the greenwolves' camp: a cave in the hillside. Outside is a clearing surrounded by a ring of trees; one of the wolves is standing there in humanoid form. He does not see you, and as you watch he changes once more and races away down the hillside. Is Nimax in the cave, or has he been taken somewhere else you wonder? Will you:

Creep into the cave to see what you can find?	Turn to **622**
Hide and see if you can overhear the greenwolves talking?	Turn to **568**
Or screech to get their attention and try to bargain with them for Nimax's life?	Turn to **729**

702

You recount your tale and the Beotman seems interested. He asks you to describe the other Beotman carefully. Evidently Beotmen are quite content with their own company but do occasionally form friendships with others of their race.

"You have spoken with Gurther!" he exclaims. "He and I are old friends, though we have not seen one another for forty seasons! Actually, I was thinking of Gurther just last week! I could use his advice in a little matter concerning herbs. Always had a great knowledge of herbs did Gurther."

You politely introduce the subject of your task. "Snakes, is it?" he replies. "Well...I'm sure I can help you there...and if you'll find Gurther and ask him something for me, I've got something I can give you that may be very useful."

You mull it over. It would take an extra day to complete this task – can you spare this precious time? If you want to accept the Beotman's offer, turn to **722**. If you tell him that unfortunately every hour could be crucial to your quest, then ask him more about the firebrand, turn to **649**.

703

"Going into the swamp, eh? And I bet we can guess *why*!" snarls the tall man in reply, turning to the other men. They nod grimly.

It is as if they have some secret hidden in the swamp that they suspect you of coming to steal! It surely cannot be a *snake* you reason, but when you protest that you don't know what they are talking about the men look even more hostile! You persevere with your questioning, but the men are not interested in helping you and you concede that you'll get no more information from them.

As you take off, the man with the eye patch shouts at you to under no circumstances take the left hand path as it will lead you into mortal danger...turn to **625**.

704

You blindly lash out, hoping to break the terrible grip of the thing that is surfacing below you! But in the thick, slimy water, your blows have less speed and ferocity than usual. Roll the die. If you roll a 4 or less, turn to **724**. If you roll a 5 or more, turn to **611**.

705

You wait patiently in the shadows, the cold marsh water feeling icily revolting in your feathers. After nearly an hour of miserably watching the guards (who seem happy to stay there forever) they do finally begin to move! Soon the way is clear for you to follow the goblin out from under the town and away, hidden by the mists! You even have the presence of mind to grab one of the flaming torches from its niche as you pass! Note down that you have a lit torch once more.

At a safe distance, you pull yourself gratefully out of the swamp onto a rock. Your fellow escapee seems more than happy to stay in the mire! You ask him if he knows anything about snakes, but he shakes his head.

You decide you have wasted enough time with these creatures and wish him luck as he swims off. He is heading out of the swamp to freedom, but unfortunately you know that your path lies deeper *into* it! Note down the codeword REED and turn to **727**.

706

You drift off to sleep, unaware that you are destined never to see another dawn. Later on in the night you are treacherously murdered as you lie defenceless by none other than your missing mentor Nimax! It is scant consolation to you that the firebrand *will* make its way safely back to your tribe and Rical will live…

707

You stumble forwards, entering the revolting morass with a large splosh. Without stopping, you hurl yourself forwards and clutch at the snake but you are too slow; it has eluded you. Nimax laughs unkindly at the sight of your wings and lower body dripping with all manner of filth as you drag yourself out again. After ten minutes of combing the area, he finally decides that this is a fruitless job and signals for you to follow him once more. Turn to **614**.

708

The first lands on your shoulders and its claws rend your flesh, but you manage to hurl it off. The second leaps too far and slashes your back without getting a grip on you. You run for your life, the baying of the other two wolves growing louder and louder as they give chase, their jaws snapping at thin air beneath you as you get airborne just in time!

But you have been wounded and are bleeding heavily from several different places. You land and tend to your injuries the best you can, but for the rest of the adventure you must subtract 1 from every die roll you make (unless the text asks whether you have rolled an odd or even number). Cursing yourself for losing valuable time in this way, you fly eastwards once more, keen to pick up the trail as soon as possible. Turn to **630**.

709

The wood is verdant and pleasant; it is also clearly well-tended. A variety of birds and land mammals flee before you as you make your way in, following a stony path littered with forest foliage. You notice a bag made of thick rope netting hanging high up in a tree. Four rusty bells dangle beneath it.

Then you have an idea: you're not sure of its purpose, but if this was set up by the Beotman you seek you might be able to summon him by knocking the bag down from the trees and jangling the bells! If you want to try and do this, turn to **695**. If you want to leave it and continue into the forest, turn to **563**.

710

You react faster than the recently awoken creatures, grabbing the nearest one by the forearm and hurling it upside down into another two. This only serves to increase the volume of the screeching! While they are temporarily distracted, you race through their midst and cross the clearing safely. Although they do not seem to want to pursue you any further, you hurry on anyway and soon reach another clearing. But this has come with a cost: you dropped your torch in the struggle and it is not safe to retrieve it, even assuming it is still alight! Note down that your torch has gone out. If you have the codeword TUFT, turn to **727**. If you do not have this codeword, turn to **692**.

711

Suddenly you see a flash of reddish-brown and a short, fat snake whizzes across the ground just before you! You instinctively make a grab for it! Roll the die. If you roll a 2 or less, turn to **597**. If you roll a 3 or 4, turn to **626**. If you roll a 5 or 6, turn to **572**.

712

You pass a prison cell containing another of the sleeping creatures, then come to the largest hut of all – and this one has no 'window' openings at all. You can just hear a quiet scrabbling noise from within. If you want to open the door slightly and peer in, turn to **585**. If you decide that you have had enough of creeping round here and want to fly away again, turn to **727**.

713

You swoop round the tree and pull up sharply as you sight the snake – but then you feel a clawed hand stretching up to grab your leg from below! You glance down into the snarling face of the primate. If you are carrying a bundle of sweet smelling herbs, turn to **602**. Otherwise *react on instinct*. Will you try to break the grip by flying upwards (turn to **628**) or by kicking out at the beast (turn to **690**)?

714

The evening draws in. Nimax stops for a brief rest and announces that he has decided to go east. "If we keep going in one direction," he says, "then sooner or later we are bound to find a river or something. I expect that we will discover vast areas of swampland eventually." You suspect that he is trying to keep his own spirits up more than worry about you!

When night falls, Nimax insists on taking first watch again. You are tired so that's fine by you!

Hours later, your eyes flick open. What is that sound? It is like a low growling some way off. Will you lie still where you are and listen? (Turn to **562**) Stand up and look about? (Turn to **637**) Or take to the air immediately, where you will see better but can also be seen? (Turn to **672**)

715

You enter the cave, which is bare except for straw and various animal bones strewn across the floor. A second cave adjoins the first; when you peer in you see a huge, two-headed bear! Hearing you, both heads turn and roar savagely, and it bounds suddenly in your direction with murderous intent! Roll the die. If you roll a 3 or less, turn to **662**. If you roll a 4 or more, turn to **595**.

716

Smack! You feel the tentacle wrap around you at least twice. There is a momentary pause; then you are dragged straight down and below the surface with staggering force. You cannot match the power of the unseen beast below; only your bones resurface, a few days later…

717

You hurriedly unstopper the vial and gulp down the bitter tasting fluid within. Almost immediately your head seems to explode with a blinding pain and you collapse and black out.

You have no idea how long you are unconscious, but are mightily relieved that when you do awake, the pain has all but gone. You try to shake the dizziness from your head and refocus on the task ahead.

It is short work to spark your torch back into life (note down that you have relit your torch). You use it to battle against the mists which seem ready to engulf you in this part of the swamp! A few minutes later, you see a cave off to your left. It is half submerged with the filthy swamp water, so that you cannot tell the level of the floor and may have to swim. You could however leave your torch outside, wedged in a cleft in the rock so it would not go out again. If you want to take the trouble to explore this cave, turn to **640**. If you would rather ignore it and continue, turn to **727**.

718

You take a short run up and put your shoulder to the door. It shudders and some of the wood cracks, but it does not break. You try again and the cracks widen. Suddenly an angry looking marsh-goblin face appears at the grille. He holds up his spear and growls, "Do again and get m'spear, see?" Note down the codeword POINT.

The guard moves away but won't have gone far. You will need to try another plan. Will you rip up some floorboards and escape via the swamp below? (Turn to **645**) Or surprise the guards when they open the door and overpower them? (Turn to **726**)

719

You dive under the log - into brambles and thorns that you did not see! They rip at your flesh but you ignore the pain and soon emerge on the other side. You curse that you have lost some ground on the snake. Then you come to another mass of tangled bushes, these ones loaded with large cream-coloured puffballs. The ones that you accidentally disturb with your wing tips burst in clouds of white powder. *React on instinct*. Will you aim to smash a few more of the puffballs as you fly through them and hopefully hinder your pursuers? (Turn to **664**) Or ignore them and concentrate on the chase? (Turn to **606**)

720

Nimax doesn't attempt to disguise his scorn "Of course you can!" he laughs sarcastically. There is no way to prove this to him just now and nothing to be gained by getting angry, so you simply shrug and repeat that it is true. This latest episode does little for your relationship with your travelling companion! Note down the codeword TONGUE and turn to **647**.

721

You fly hard through the afternoon, overtaking the group that attacked you but observing that they are following the trail of another pack of greenwolves – and this group may have taken Nimax.

You see a mountain range on the horizon with hills that sprawl out before it. Your wings are just beginning to ache with the exertion when you reach a disheartening sight: the tracks terminate at a river which runs through a valley. The wolves are obviously intelligent as they have followed the river for some distance before rejoining the far bank, therefore leaving no tracks. You hope your instincts will be right: will you fly upstream (turn to **587**) or downstream? (Turn to **685**)

722

You agree and the Beotman looks pleased. He hands you three plants and asks you to ask Gurther about their properties. "Tell him it's for Burunduss," he adds, giving his own name for the first time.

You nod and immediately take to the air, speeding westwards to where you last saw Gurther. After a tiring search, you finally find him sitting beneath a tree, in the process of lighting a fire. You ask about the plants and he is able to tell you what Burunduss wants to know with little difficulty.

You arrive back at the home of Burunduss the following morning and share your news. "Excellent!" he exclaims, "You are a true friend of the Beotmen. Now for my part of the bargain. Tell me exactly what you seek." You explain that you need to capture a firebrand snake as a matter of life and death!

"I've seen the firebrand, but never had one here," says your host. "I know that they're scarce, and they like marshy areas. Red-brown in colour, with gold patches on its back. They're about the length of my arm," he continues and holds out a massive, bear-like arm. "As far as I know, the nearest place to find one is in a swamp across the mountains to the east. Follow the mountain river and you'll come to it in a day or two. It's populated by savage packs of swamp primates called Nians; avoid them at all costs! Note down the codeword SCALE.

You thank him for his help. He tells you to wait and roots about in a jumble of bottles at the back of the cave. He produces a vial of browny-yellow liquid which he tells you is an antivenom, effective against many types of snake. You thank him again and decide to take it with you (note down the antivenom).

"But wait a while longer!" he adds. He rummages about for a second time and shows you what looks like a golden chain. He puts it over your neck and it sits comfortably around your shoulders. Up close you see that it is actually a very thin golden snake swallowing its own tail!

"This is an ancient snake charm," explains Burunduss. "I was given it by my grandfather many years ago. I cannot really explain its powers; it does not necessarily deter snakes from biting you if they feel threatened. But when I am wearing it, snakes sometimes react very strangely, as if charmed somehow. I need it no longer." Note down that you are wearing a golden snake charm.

You thank Burunduss yet again for his help and he wishes you luck in your quest. He shows you a safe way out of the wood and you are soon back in the skies again, on the next stage of your journey. Turn to **596**.

723

You decide that it would be wise not to disturb these creatures, whatever they are! Roll the die. If you roll a 3 or less, turn to **632**. If you roll a 4 or more, and have the codeword TUFT, turn to **727**. If you roll a 4 or more and do not have the codeword TUFT, turn to **692**.

724

It is no good; the thing in the water gets a good grip and has the strength of ten Ariax! You thrash wildly, trying desperately to break free, but you are dragged slowly and surely underwater, where you soon feel the power of the thing's mighty jaws…

725

You almost make it. The mists swirl around you and dry land is in sight when a barbed spear is hurled with deadly accuracy into your back by a hidden assailant. You stumble forwards and fall face down into the mud, and the guards see to it that neither of you make it one step further…

726

You explain your plan to the goblin and he nods, bowing to your greater strength and intellect. The pair of you settle down to wait, as he tells you the guards will not return until well after daybreak. If you want to try to get some sleep, turn to **605**. If you think it would be too dangerous and want to try and stay awake, turn to **591**.

727

You reach a point in the swamp where the brown muck all around you bubbles and pops with continual squelches and glugs. If your torch is alight, turn to **574**. If your torch has gone out and not been relit, turn to **683**.

728

You clutch the trunk of the tree, spot the firebrand once more and climb almost frantically towards it, finally grabbing the snake which has curled itself around a branch.

You spiral upwards out of the swamp, elated to have at long last captured the key to the survival of a large number of your tribe. The shrieks and screeches from below gradually fade away.

Before long you are many miles nearer the mountains, the firebrand twisting and turning in your hand but unable to strike. You are following the river again with one thought in mind: to get home! The sun has almost set in the distance so you fly down to make camp. You luckily discover a discarded boot nearby that will contain the firebrand, and stake it to the ground securely. Then you settle on the grass (which is far too soft for your liking!) to sleep. You feel reasonably safe; you have seen very little life this side of the mountains.

If you have *both* of the codewords MARSH and REED, turn to **620**. If you have either one but not both of these codewords, turn to **586**. If you do not have either, turn to **706**.

729

You give out your loudest call. Moments later, three of the greenwolves bound out and revert to humanoid form. They look at you with their cruel yellow eyes and have the look of the wolf about them even on two legs.

"Come down!" snarls one of them in mock friendliness as you hover out of range. You demand to know what they have done with Nimax.

One of the creatures advances towards you, denying having ever seen a being like you before. You get the impression from his long winded answer that he is trying to distract you from something. Will you back off but remain at the same height (turn to **648**) or hover higher in the air? (Turn to **600**)

The return journey passes without incident. As before, the Tower of Egratar is the first sign of home that you see and your spirits are lifted at the sight of it. But will you be in time?

You glide in to land at the entrance to the cave where your quest began over a week ago. All heads turn towards you and when you produce the firebrand from the boot there are cheers and shouts the like of which have not been heard in Arian for many a long year!

The Vzler, Arguttax and Astraphet himself hear the commotion and come to the cave to investigate. "Is this the one?" Astraphet asks Arguttax.

"I think so!" replies Arguttax as you gladly hand the hissing reptile over!

Everyone wants to praise and congratulate you at once! But you have other thoughts and you are secretly grateful when the Vzler takes your arm and leads you through the throng to his own private chambers, deep within another mountain.

Away from the noise, the Vzler bids you to sit down and rest. His usual serious expression relaxes into a broad smile that you have not seen before! "I am reminded of my prediction following your encounter with the Scarfells," he says, "I think 'future greatness' were my words? But even I could never have imagined…"

Despite your achievements, it is still amazing to hear the Vzler speak of you like this. You thank him respectfully, but are desperate to hear news of Rical.

"Rical is very ill," says the Vzler gravely. "But thanks to you he may yet recover! Two teams returned from the north with the Elder Mettel three days ago. Most of those who were sent searching for the firebrand have already returned, empty handed. Two, like you, returned alone…"

You hang your head in reverence for the dead. "And…Nimax?" prompts the Vzler.

"He was…bitten by the firebrand," you say, looking at the floor. There is a silence. You cannot bring yourself to tell him the whole truth. Nimax is certainly dead by now and the news of his treachery can do no good. In these times of trouble, no more bad news is needed.

Over the next few days, Arguttax works tirelessly to prepare the cure for Crackbeak and finally announces that he has succeeded! The remaining search parties return – and you were the only one who brought back a firebrand snake! You spend much of your time with Darfak, who was one of those who unsuccessfully sought the Elder Mettel.

Finally you are able to visit Rical for the first time since before your trip to Iro. He is very weak, and his beak and talons horribly scarred, but you are assured they will heal in time. The tales of your adventures keep him (and others) going for long periods of their recovery, though the visit to Iro and the truth about Nimax you keep only for Rical.

A great feast is thrown in honour of all those who recently risked their lives for the survival of the tribe. Later that night, you pay the Vzler another visit. You have decided to discuss with him the scrolls that you recovered from Vashta's study…

The fateful consequences of this conversation and the latest dangerous adventure which results is chronicled in book 5 of The Saga of the Ariax, entitled:

ICE IN THE TOMBS

THE SAGA OF THE ARIAX: 5
ICE IN THE TOMBS

Recent events

A great feast is thrown in honour of all those who recently risked their lives searching for the cure for Crackbeak. Later that afternoon, you pay a visit to the Vzler. You tell him you have something important and secret to show him and he takes you to his private chambers, caves situated deep in one of the mountains. There he hears your astonishing story. You tell him how you met Vashta the wizard in the Forest of Arcendak and about the spell he cast on you. You tell him how Vashta took some of the Orphus Latix (which you didn't realise at the time was a priceless Ariax secret!) You tell him how you flew alone to the city of Iro and saw to it that the plant was destroyed and the secret retaken!

"I do not doubt your word, Xanarel," says the Vzler, marvelling at your story. "You are truly an exceptional young Ariax! This explains your... *disappearance*!" You had gone to Iro in secret and were away for a week! Then you produce the scrolls that you found in Vashta's house.

The Vzler pores over them. They are written in the language of men, so he cannot understand a word. As you begin reading them to him, he listens without interruption. The scrolls are the work of an Ariax named Detlaxe. They describe many aspects of his Ariax life which you find familiar, and (of course) contain the secret of Orphus Latix that Vashta found so intriguing.

But the rest of Detlaxe's tale is the bit you have been eager to share. Hundreds of years ago, in Detlaxe's time, your tribe's Talotrix was named Nevsaron. According to Detlaxe Nevsaron was an inspirational leader, but on top of that he had amazing 'elemental powers': clearly Nevsaron could do *magic*.

"I had thought that no Ariax was ever able to do magic!" you say.

"That is what I too believed," replies the Vzler, clearly intrigued. "Read on!"

Nevsaron never revealed where he got his powers from and when he died, his secret went with him. He was buried in an ice tomb high up in a great mountain to the west of your home, which became a sacred place to the Ariax.

Then the Scarfells came. They came in huge numbers from the south and chose the very mountain which housed Nevsaron's tomb at its summit for their home as it had a vast natural cave system. Ariax visitors were shocked and appalled to find this intrusion, but were fired on by Scarfell archers if they dared to approach.

This situation created a rift in the Ariax tribe. Some wanted a full scale war; to drive away the Scarfells once and for all! Others said that the outcome would not be worth the cost in Ariax life. They pointed out that the Scarfells didn't know the tomb existed so Nevsaron could rest in peace. The Talotrix, Hallored, decided to concede the mountain (which of course became known as Musk) to the Scarfells. Detlaxe was firmly in opposition. He tried to stir up a revolt, but could not gain enough support. He became even more angered when it was announced that to prevent future casualties in Nevsaron's name, the story of his life was not to be passed on to future generations.

Detlaxe, disgusted, left the tribe and made his way south, alone. He eventually found himself in a human city called Gangoth, where he came under the tutelage of a wizard named Haraikos Lysk. The scrolls go on to chronicle the next forty years in Lysk's service until the final entry, written in a different hand, which reports that Detlaxe died following a short illness, aged one hundred and eleven.

Finally you finish reading. The Vzler says nothing; this is all as new to him, one of the oldest and most senior birdmen, as it is to you! He wanders across the cavern and stands deep in thought for several minutes. You again wonder about the origin of the ugly scar across his back. Eventually he turns to face you again, and you detect a wild glint in his eye.

"Tonight," he says, slowly and deliberately, "I am going to Musk. I am going to find Nevsaron's tomb! Coming?"

Now turn to **1** to begin…

1

Even after all you've been through in the last few months, you feel a new thrill of excitement. Searching for a long lost Ariax secret under the very noses of your greatest enemies? You instantly agree to the Vzler's plan!

"We will tell no-one, not even Astraphet," says the Vzler. "He will counsel me not to go, especially now during our time of vulnerability. But I am confident that we will return safely before sunrise. The Scarfells have no reason to mount much of a watch at night."

Going undercover of darkness makes sense. Last time you tangled with the Scarfells, the fact that you could see in the dark and they couldn't was vital in your escape.

You fly for an hour and a half or so due west, over mountains painted in vibrant evening hues. The Forest of Arcendak passes underneath you.

Eventually the Vzler glides down to land on a mountain peak. He indicates Musk on the horizon, and in the fading light you gaze upon the dreaded mountain home of your enemies for the first time.

Suddenly there is a thud and a wooden spear embeds itself in the rock just to your left! You both look up. "Scarfells!" snarls the Vzler, and you see that he is right: two of them, mounted on giant eagles and armed with more spears, swooping overhead.

To your surprise the Vzler then yells: "Run - now!" and turns and scrambles away on foot down the slopes behind you! You had always imagined the Vzler to be bold and fearless in the face of danger! What if the Scarfells return home and alert the whole of Musk to your presence? If you trust the Vzler's judgement and follow him, turn to **126**. If your instincts tell you otherwise you could attack the Scarfells, hoping that the Vzler will back you up (turn to **75**).

2

You manage to squeeze yourself into a cleft in the rock, covered in shadow. The Scarfells conduct a brief search of the cave but do not see you. Then you feel that growing surge of energy from deep inside you again; your new powers are searching for a physical outlet. Will you try to resist and force them away again? (Turn to **185**) Or will you release them and attempt to use them on your enemies? (Turn to **135**)

3

You continue along the winding tunnel, which eventually feeds into a set of roughly cut stone steps leading upwards. As you ascend, you detect smoke in your nostrils. The steps lead into a deserted cavern with a very high roof. Another set of steps leads up and out on the far side. The blackened remains of three Scarfell bodies lie smouldering atop a decorated stone plinth in the centre of the chamber indicating that the Scarfells cremate their dead.

Looking up, you see the stars twinkling in the night sky. A natural hole in the roof of the cave is why it has been chosen for its purpose. You fly up, but you are too big to squeeze through. You catch a tantalising breath of clean air amid the smoke: will you ever get to stretch your wings outside again? You must force such gloomy thoughts from your mind! You have been in tighter spots than this…haven't you?

You find yourself intrigued by the curling smoke and have a strange desire to hover in it and feel its power. But you hear what sounds like a cough from the tunnel ahead of you. You freeze, hearing nothing else. Did you imagine it? If you want to give in to your yearning and fly into the smoke, turn to **143**. If you'd rather cautiously approach the steps, turn to **97**. To go back the way you came, turn to **54** if you have the codeword YELL or **6** if you do not have this codeword.

4

The sleepers remain undisturbed and you reach the tunnel safely. Unfortunately it only leads to another similar bedchamber, with no exits! You silently curse your bad luck; you must turn back and pass through the cave again! Roll the die. If you roll a 3 or more you are safe again (turn to **19**). If you roll a 1 or 2 however, turn to **179**.

5

You come to a wooden door on the left hand side of the passage. A metal grille and heavy lock suggest that this is a prison cell. The key is in the lock.

You peer in. Slumped on the floor, cold and mournful looking, is a Scarfell prisoner. His eyes flick open and he sees you just before you duck out of sight. "Wait!" he calls in a rasping whisper.

You freeze, but he calls out to you again, louder this time. To prevent him alerting anyone, you return to view. Is the enemy of my enemy my friend, you wonder? He looks amazed to see you, and brushes his untidy shock of brown hair from his eyes. "You can understand me?" he asks, pulling himself to his feet, and you nod. "Unlock this door!" he says. "I know a secret way outta Musk!"

You consider. You've no idea what his punishment is due to be; he may be that desperate that he'd help you. But can you trust a Scarfell? If you want to take a chance and release him from captivity, turn to **165**. If you'd sooner try to make it on your own, turn to **79**.

6

The steps wind round as they descend, but are always wide enough for your taloned feet. Far off in the distance, you fancy that you hear the clanging of a bell being struck. It is not a comforting sound and reminds you that you are surrounded on all sides by hated foes! Note down the codeword OX. At the bottom of the steps is a tunnel that runs off into the gloom in two directions. Both look pretty similar to you. To go left, turn to **41**. To go right, turn to **72**.

7

Nothing happens; you have failed to channel your powers at this most critical of times. If you have the codeword ARMS, turn to **167**. If you do not have this codeword, will you:

Try to flee the room?	Turn to **208**
Attack Gargrimm, who stands nearest to you?	Turn to **139**
Or grab his axe and try to magically fracture it?	Turn to **217**

8

You step back quickly. The huge man flails at thin air, loses his balance and topples to the floor, where he lies crumpled in a heap! You automatically assume a battle ready stance, but there is no need – he is asleep, snoring softly! Thankful that your race does not need to drink intoxicating liquid to enjoy themselves, you head for the opening on the other side of the tavern. Turn to **125**.

9

You enter the chamber. The chill winds of Arian have not been able to permeate this deep and a thick layer of cobwebs and centuries of dust covers everything. The smell of decay hangs in the air. But it is the great rocky plinth in the centre of the cavern that immediately draws your attention. Despite the covering of grime, it is clearly an Ariax skeleton, and there is only one possibility: it is Nevsaron himself! Your mind reels in awe as you remember first reading about this legendary birdman, and now here you are in his presence. You stand respectfully in silence, the faint sound of the wind outside the only disturbance.

If you want to take a closer look at the body, turn to **83**. If you want to search around the rest of the chamber first, turn to **67**.

10

You turn immediately to leave but three burly Scarfells appear at the entrance to the cave. Their axes are drawn and they grin menacingly in anticipation of the bloodshed. You battle bravely to the end, but fall, deep within the inner sanctum of your foes.

11

You come to a dirty-looking kitchen. Massive spits stand over empty fire-pits, clearly indicating the Scarfell's staple diet! You notice meat-cleavers and cooking knives left lying amid general food waste on the wooden tabletops and great chunks of meat hanging from the ceiling on hooks.

A sudden movement draws your attention to a nearby wooden table and you see a pair of inquisitive eyes peer nervously over the tabletop. It is a small boy clutching a stolen chicken-leg! His eyes widen in fear: clearly he has never seen an Ariax before! *React on instinct.* Will you grab him? (Turn to **219**) Or run? (Turn to **137**)

12

Your blow catches the torturer across the chest but as he staggers back he flails out an arm and knocks you off balance against the wall. You stare up at the icicle laden ceiling and in a split second feel your powers at work once more. The icicles pour down like molten lava, forming frozen solid bars across the tunnel and cutting you off from your enemy! Breathing heavily, and not quite sure how you did it, you stumble away from the scene as the torturer hurls insults and threats at you from behind the barrier. Turn to **207**.

13

The furs are heavy with the familiar scent of wolf and bear. You have just seconds to conceal yourself! Roll the die. If you roll a 1 or 2, turn to **174**. If you roll a 3 or more the Scarfells pass; turn to **131**.

14

The guards are bewildered by the darkness and you screech loudly for effect as you attempt to writhe free! Roll the die. If you roll a 1 or 2, turn to **109**. If you roll a 3 or more, turn to **202**.

15

You stand up resolutely to the King's furious probing, maintaining eye contact and saying nothing. But you can find no way to free yourself from your manacles. No power is forthcoming and bound in this way it will be impossible to escape. Soon the King will tire of you and then only death awaits…

16

The spear cracks in half as it smashes into a boulder. As you rise to your feet, you see the Vzler locked in combat with the second Scarfell. Again the man is no match for the bird and you marvel at the Vzler's strength and prowess.

The eagles are put to flight and you stand amidst the bodies of your fallen enemies. Turn to **196**.

17

You feel the power of the rock building to a painful crescendo inside you. Just for a moment, you can indescribably *understand* the very nature of the rock beneath your feet and command it to do your bidding. You grimace; your mind feels like it is being stretched to bursting point. Suddenly there is a terrific rumbling noise and the whole chamber begins to tremble. "Xanarel!" cries the Vzler anxiously, but you are already trying to stop it before it gets out of control!

Blocks of stone and ice begin showering from the roof of the tunnel. You close your eyes and try to focus your mind. With a mighty effort you manage to regain control as one final burst of energy leaves you, sending chunks of rock flying violently down the tunnel and out of the cave. You slump to the ground.

"Well…" begins the Vzler, but he cannot find the words. You look up into his concerned face and reassure him that whatever just happened inside you has passed.

"Time to go I think," says your mentor, pulling you to your feet. "If there *are* any night guards, that would certainly have alerted them." You pick your way carefully down the tunnel once more, but as you reach the entrance, a huge dark shape passes across the sky in a rush of wind. You step back, dismayed, as you see a mighty creature curl round in the air. It is shaped like a huge scaly snake, light blue-green in colour, with the head of a dragon and large, bat-like wings. Smoke curls from its nostrils and you tremble: you have seen one of these beasts once before in the mountains of Arian and barely escaped with your life: it is the most feared creature from Ariax legend, the Moogoll!

"Get back!" you cry, "Moogoll!" The Vzler shudders. A roar from outside tells you that you were seen. But what will you do? If you want to suggest retreating into the tomb, turn to **142**. If you want to try and speed past the Moogoll to freedom, turn to **53**. If you want to try and summon your powers and use them against it, turn to **119**.

18

You first strike out at the axe to knock it from his grasp before driving your fist into his face. But this Scarfell is made of tougher stuff than you imagined. Not only does he retain his grip on the axe, but your punch does not stop him from slashing out as you push past. The axe cuts deep into your side and you fall to your knees, unable to defend yourself from the man's ferocious follow up…

19

The tunnel winds its way uphill for quite a while before terminating at an open door. You peer round it into a room shrouded in darkness. No torches are lit here, but of course *you* can still see.

This chamber appears to be a meeting room of some kind. A massive stone table stands in the middle of the room surrounded by oak chairs. Furs and drapes adorn the walls, a contrast to the bare rock you have become accustomed to so far. Empty goblets and flagons are scattered across the tabletop. There are two other tunnels leading away from the meeting room, but you stiffen as you hear voices from…somewhere. You cannot ascertain their direction. If you want to concentrate and listen, turn to **144**. If you'd sooner get out of here, you could take the larger tunnel (turn to **199**) or the smaller tunnel? (Turn to **78**)

20

You rush to the doors and press your palms up against them, closing your eyes and trying to draw power from the wood. Nothing happens; you can feel none of the force that you have experienced before. Then you hear voices somewhere behind you. Glancing back, you see nothing. If you want to persevere with the doors, turn to **86**. If you'd rather leave this exposed position for the wider tunnel to the left, turn to **59**. To head for the tunnel to your right, turn to **74**.

21

You step up to the gates and flatten your palms against them, running your hands over the metal surface which begins to warm to the touch as you concentrate your energy upon it. You feel the power flowing down your arms and suddenly, with a terrible creaking, cracking noise, the entire gate breaks in two and falls to the ground with a resounding clang! Note down the codeword FRACTURE.

Behind the gates is a small cell area which you guess is for holding prisoners (or animals) prior to a battle being fought here. It is a dead end, anyway. If you have the codeword AXE, turn to **57**. If you do not have this codeword you elect to hurry on before the noise brings enemies to you (turn to **93**).

22

You launch yourself straight at the burly figure of the King, fancying your chances with the advantage of sight. Your talons scrape his face and he bellows in pain, sweeping his arms out in your general direction. But this exchange has given Gargrimm time to get to the window and throw back the shutters. The first rays of the morning sun give just enough light to see by and you suddenly find yourself fighting a one-on-one battle with the most powerful Scarfell of them all! As reinforcements appear on the steps behind you, you realise that this is a battle you cannot win…

23

The nearest Scarfell has time to hurl another spear in your direction as you close in. You bank to avoid it at the last second. Roll the die. If you roll a 3 or less, turn to **181**. If you roll a 4 or more, turn to **88**.

24

The anger and sorrow you feel at this time seems almost to be fuelling you; as you close your eyes you feel indeterminate powers rising from the pit of your stomach. You back away down the tunnel, unsure of what to do. If you want to unleash your powers immediately, turn to **135**. If you want to try and gain a little mastery over them first, turn to **162**.

25

You freeze out of sight, senses straining for the first signs of movement coming your way. Roll the die. If you roll a 1 or 2, turn to **178**. If you roll a 3 or more, turn to **105**.

26

You soon come upon a short set of steps cut out of the rock, snaking their way upwards. Around the next bend you reach a point where a side tunnel splits off to the right from the one you are in. Eerily, there is no sound from either direction. If you want to continue along the main passage, turn to **157**. If you'd like to follow this new branch, turn to **69**.

27

You hurry off down the tunnel. The Scarfell does indeed begin clamouring for the guards (shouting 'filthy bird-scum' at the top of his voice) but there is no immediate response. Turn to **207**.

28

Note down the codeword AXE. Your speed allows you to cross the chasm much more quickly than the Scarfells and you plunge into the tunnel on the far side. If you have the codeword OX, turn to **107**. If you do not have this codeword, turn to **72**.

29

Now you must get free from these guards! Will you try to slip out of their grasp? (Turn to **14**) Or will you attempt to take them by surprise and slam their heads together, hoping to break loose that way? (Turn to **50**)

30

There is a barely audible clink as you liberate the keys from their home (note down that you have them). You immediately turn your attention to escape, but as you round the corner out of sight, you hear another set of footsteps approaching from in front of you! *React on instinct*. Will you hide in the shadows (turn to **140**) or try to take out the newcomer as soon as he comes into view? (Turn to **188**).

31

It is not easy to clamber down the shaft, but you are intrigued. At one point your foot slips when a clod of loose rock comes away with it and you fall painfully down into a rocky tunnel which stretches out in front of and behind you. Turn to **91**.

32

You are able to glide across the cavern, gaining a head start on your pursuer. If you have the codeword YELL, turn to **54**. If you do not have this codeword, you rush out and decide to take the steps you saw earlier (turn to **6**).

33

You screw up your eyes and throw back your head as the exhilarating power flows through your arms. When you look, you see that you have frozen the liquid in mid-air, creating a solid, unmoving wave of ice! Then as soon as it came upon you, the power ebbs away again. Note down the codeword ICE. You glance about, but can see or hear nothing; a false alarm? Turn to **121**.

34

You notice the temperature dropping steadily as you continue down this tunnel. Soon you come to another set of steps, these very much steeper and more roughly cut than the last.

Another dark tunnel leads away at the bottom of the steps. You notice that this tunnel is less frequently lit than the others. Ice glistens along the walls, stalactites hang from the roof and your breath begins to puff out in clouds. Nevertheless you decide to press on in case the boy behind you raises the alarm. Maybe there is a grate or something down here that you can escape through? The tunnel suddenly forks. You can hear the occasional sound of clanking metal down the right hand branch; nothing at all from the left. Will you go right (turn to **158**) or left? (Turn to **5**)

35

Nothing happens and you silently curse your ill fortune at this crucial time. The feelings you had for earth and flames have ebbed away and the Scarfells grab their weapons. If you have the codeword ARMS, turn to **167**. If you do not have this codeword, will you:

Try to flee the room?	Turn to **208**
Attempt to refocus your powers on extinguishing the torches?	Turn to **117**
Attack Gargrimm, who stands nearest to you?	Turn to **139**
Or grab his axe and try to fracture it as you did with your bonds?	Turn to **217**

36

You close in and manage to strike a telling blow: the Scarfell topples from his mount and plunges to his death on the rocky mountainside far below. Glancing across, you see that the Vzler has dealt with his opponent in a similar fashion and you glide down to meet him.

"A little more trust in me would be appreciated, Xanarel…" he chides, but he is not angry. He explains his actions: the Vzler had been far from fleeing; he was trying to draw the Scarfells into a channel where they could be ambushed! You apologise, but the Vzler merely chuckles to himself. He is certainly cool under pressure – you were both nearly killed! Turn to **196**.

37

The flames incinerate everything in their path. You are burned to a crisp.

38

The Scarfell is a wily opponent and anticipates your move moments before you strike. He dodges aside and delivers a crippling blow with his axe. Mercifully, his follow up finishes you off…

39

These stairs take you into a rubble-strewn rocky tunnel. Perhaps it's the strange odour of decay and perhaps it's the ominous looking bones scattered about, but you sense danger up ahead. If you want to go back down the stairs and continue down the main tunnel, turn to **19**. If you want to press on and investigate, turn to **91**.

40

Unfortunately, while you are examining your find a Scarfell enters the cavern. He stealthily creeps up behind you and buries his axe in your defenceless back. You never know what hit you.

41

The temperature is definitely rising sharply as you progress in this direction. Then you come to a surprising sight. The passage opens up into a vast open space; a chasm torn right out of the heart of the mountain. The bottom of the pit is out of sight far below in the gloom, but this is certainly where the heat is coming from. You are unsure what could be causing it: some kind of furnace?

Through the heat haze you can make out a natural rocky bridge spanning the crevasse wide enough for two to walk abreast. There is an indentation running down the middle where years of heavy Scarfell footfalls have worn it away.

If you want to fly down and investigate the source of the heat, turn to **64**. To fly across the chasm to the tunnel on the other side, turn to **146**. To cross using the bridge, turn to **201**.

42

You stare at the flame and allow your mind to focus. You become almost transfixed by the dancing orange light and before you know it, the candle flame is streaming upwards, reaching almost to the ceiling! How did you do that? You imagine the flame reducing to normal and it obeys your mental command. You experiment further, snuffing out the flame and attempting to relight it with your magic. But nothing happens; it seems you can control fire, but not create it.

Buoyed by your findings, you decide to hurry back into the main tunnel before you are discovered. Turn to **115**.

43

Your blow catches the guard right and he crumples to the floor, unconscious. You are already fleeing the scene, vaulting over the unfortunate man before his absence is noticed. Turn to **168**.

44

This cave is far deeper than it first looked. You pick your way through the stalagmites that grow up from the floor and come to a dark tunnel. The eerie silence is punctuated by the occasional howl of wind from outside and the odd droplet of water which shakes itself free from the stalactites above you.

Up ahead you see a natural low archway of rock that you have to duck your head under to pass through, but before you do, something in the arch catches your attention. It is a stone tablet that has been fitted into a niche cut out of the rock. On it is carved ancient symbols and emblems, and although you cannot understand their precise meaning, they are clearly Ariax in design. This must be it: Nevsaron's tomb! If you want to call the Vzler, turn to **184**. If you want to have a look round by yourself first, turn to **9**.

45

You feel the power of fire building to a painful crescendo inside you. Just for a moment it seems you can *understand* the very nature of fire, a source of which is somewhere nearby. You grimace; your mind feels like it is being stretched to bursting point. Suddenly there is a terrific sensation of heat running down your arms and a fireball bursts from your left hand! It billows up to the ceiling and disappears! "Xanarel!" cries the Vzler anxiously, but you are already trying to stop it before it happens again!

You close your eyes and try to focus your mind, but can already feel more power building up within you. As a second, much bigger burst of flame leaves you, surging violently down the tunnel and out of the cave, you manage to regain control. You slump to the ground.

"Well..." begins the Vzler, but he cannot find the words. You look up into his concerned face and reassure him that whatever just happened inside you has passed.

"Time to go I think," says your mentor, pulling you to your feet. "If there *are* any night guards, that would certainly have alerted them." You pick your way carefully down the tunnel once more, but as you reach the entrance, a huge dark shape passes across the sky in a rush of wind. You step back, dismayed, as you see a mighty creature curl round in the air. It is shaped like a huge scaly snake, light blue-green in colour, with the head of a dragon and large, bat-like wings. Smoke curls from its nostrils and you tremble: you have seen one of these beasts once before in the mountains of Arian and barely escaped with your life: it is the most feared creature from Ariax legend, the Moogoll!

"Get back!" you cry, "Moogoll!" The Vzler shudders. A roar from outside tells you that you were seen. But what will you do? If you want to suggest retreating into the tomb, turn to **142**. If you want to try and speed past the Moogoll to freedom, turn to **53**. If you want to try and summon your new powers and use them against it, turn to **119**.

46

You make your way cautiously down the dark tunnel which is gradually bending round to the left. It appears to be naturally formed and you recall from Detlaxe's scrolls that the mountain's many cave systems was one of the main reasons for the Scarfells settling there in the first place. Every so often a torch has been set in a sconce on the wall, the flames casting ghostly shadows all about.

Your heart is beating fast. The Vzler is dead and you are alone in the heart of the domain of your mortal enemies. If you are discovered, you can expect no mercy.

You have no further sensations of the powers of the elemental crystal. You are sure that swallowing it has granted you magical powers like Nevsaron, but you will need to learn how to control and direct them.

You pass large darkened rooms on both sides of the passage. Inside you can hear the sounds of Scarfells breathing heavily in sleep, with the occasional snore or grunt. You pass by stealthily, keeping to the shadows where possible and always alert for sounds of activity ahead. The fact that it is night and most of the Scarfells are asleep is your main hope for escape!

In the next cave is a Scarfell who is wide awake, sitting with his back to you. You had assumed the room to contain more sleepers and duck back instinctively. You peer round the corner and see that the man is sat at a desk, writing on a large scroll by the light of a candle; he must be a scribe.

Just at that moment a side door in the cave opens. Another Scarfell strides in and starts angrily berating the scribe. You duck back again and the shouting suddenly stops. Did the man see you? If you want to freeze and prepare yourself to ambush anyone who comes out of the cave, turn to **25**. If you want to run on down the passage, as quietly as you can, turn to **156**.

47

Fixing the boy with your fiercest stare, you make it clear to him that Ariax *are* the cold blooded killers he was taught they were! Roll the die. If you roll a 1 or 2, turn to **212**. If you roll a 3 or more, turn to **98**.

48

The torturer is a formidable opponent and a malicious grin spreads across his face as he recognises that you are going to do battle. Roll the die. If you roll a 1, 2 or 3, turn to **145**. If you roll a 4 or more, turn to **12**.

49

You swoop back up to the bridge. The Scarfells have gone so you make your way to the tunnel on the far side, hoping that they have presumed you dead. If you have the codeword OX, turn to **107**. If you do not have this codeword, turn to **72**.

50

Both men are as tall as you and broader still, but you take a deep breath and make a mighty effort to haul them together. Roll the die. If you roll a 1, 2 or 3, turn to **109**. If you roll a 4 or more, turn to **202**.

51

Frustrated that your powers seem to have deserted you in the face of impending death, you unleash a defiant outburst from the ceiling. The men below are taken aback! "You speak in the tongue of the Scarfells?" cries Gargrimm. "Impossible!"

You laugh down at him and leave him to puzzle over this mystery. He calls up to you again, "Such a curiosity must be brought before the King! He will want to see you before you die! Surrender to me!" As he speaks, three more Scarfells enter the cave, carrying the same kind of hunting spears that you have seen before. Caught between a rock and a hard place! If you surrender to Gargrimm, turn to **203**. If you stay where you are and try to play for time, turn to **133**.

52

You hurl yourself to the rock, intending to roll straight back onto your feet if you can. The Scarfell lets another spear fly. Roll the die. If you roll a 1, turn to **181**. If you roll a 2, turn to **169**. If you roll a 3 or more, turn to **16**.

53

The situation is desperate and you have to act swiftly. You run three steps to the entrance and launch yourself into the night sky. But the Moogoll moves with unbelievable speed and agility. It twists in the air, surges towards you and clamps its great jaws around you with deadly accuracy. You snap like a twig between razor sharp teeth. Death is instantaneous.

54

You make your way quickly down the tunnel. You round the next bend…and come face to face with three fully armed Scarfells! You lash out instinctively at the nearest one who falls back, blood streaming from a wound to his neck. But the second flings his hunting axe at your retreating form and it bites deep into your back. You tumble to the rocky floor, easy prey for your bloodthirsty foes…

55

You are on the move quickly, prepared to practise your magic at a later, safer opportunity! You hurry down the tunnel and come to a flight of stairs that lead up on the left hand side. If you want to go upstairs, turn to **39**. To carry on down the tunnel, turn to **19**.

56

You keep your eyes fixed on the torturer as you edge across to the other side of the chamber. Suddenly he turns round and you freeze, hoping that the shadows will hide you. You sigh with relief when the burly man appears to be walking past you, but then he darts sideways and grabs you with vice like hands!

"Now what have we got 'ere then?" growls the torturer. You struggle, but his strength is immense! He violently thrusts you sideways and plunges your head in a trough of ice-cold, filthy water. He is going to try and drown you in his ducking pool!

You must fight! You must escape before water fills your lungs and you drown! You must…but then you stop. Your lungs feel funny, like they are already filled with water! But you are still alive: you can feel the torturer's stubby fingers around your neck and the chill of the water in your feathers!

It must be your elemental powers! Not only are you safe from the effects of fire, but you can breathe underwater too! If you want to go limp and play dead, turn to **130**. If you want to slash out at the torturer's legs with your talons, turn to **213**. Or if you have the codeword ICE, you may choose to use your powers as you did before (turn to **92**).

57

The time you have spent dallying in the arena has given the Scarfells from the bridge time to catch up with you. As you hear them enter and turn to do battle, one of them hurls his throwing axe into your arm. You strive to defend yourself from the battle-hardened warriors, but wounded and outnumbered you stand little chance…

58

The weapon just misses you and clatters into the wall. As soon as you get to the exit, you know that there is no way out here; there are guards lurking not far down the passage, evidently not permitted into the King's chamber, but waiting there for Gargrimm's return. You must think fast! Will you:

Attempt to refocus your powers on extinguishing the torches?	Turn to **117**
Attack Gargrimm, who is now closest to you?	Turn to **139**
Or grab his axe and try to fracture it as you did with your bonds?	Turn to **217**

59

As you make your way down this tunnel, the unmistakeable sound of baying dogs assails your ears, along with an accompanying smell! The floor here is strewn with straw and excrement! You come to a large cavern on the right that stretches you cannot tell how far into the distance. There are indeed a multitude of dogs (and wolves) housed within. Two Scarfells stand talking at this end of the cavern.

You can just about make out snippets of their conversation and allow yourself a small smile: one of the men is telling the other that he's heard a birdman is loose in Musk! It becomes less pleasant to listen to them discussing with relish the prospect of your death, so you decide to sneak past the opening while they are distracted. The noise recedes as you proceed deeper into the mountain. Turn to **125**.

60

You surge upwards to the attack, surprising the Scarfell with your boldness. But he skilfully yanks on the reins and his mount rears back in the air, shaking you off. This gives him the few seconds he needs to line up his next attack, and as you battle to fend off the eagle's rending talons, you fail to see the spear-strike coming that ultimately kills you...

61

You concentrate your mind and stretch out your talons and wings as you hover in the smoke. You are not quite sure how, but as you urge it on, you can feel the amount of smoke increasing accordingly! You wonder if you can thin it out and will it to happen. Within a minute, the smoke has all but gone! You clench your fist and try to force the smoke to billow out once more. It does! Note down the codeword SMOKE.

With a jolt, you suddenly notice that you are not alone! A Scarfell has entered the chamber, armed with a deadly looking war-axe, looking perplexed at what he sees. Before he can cry out, you direct the smoke directly towards him in as much density as you can. The man chokes as he is enveloped in the black cloud and you allow yourself a smile as you swoop safely past him and up the steps on the far side of the cavern. Once in the tunnel you attempt to create more smoke from thin air as an experiment but nothing happens; you must need some to be naturally present in the first place. Turn to **19**.

62

You go as slowly as you dare, senses straining for the first sounds of trouble. Roll the die. If you roll a 1 or 2, turn to **179**. If you roll a 3 or more, turn to **4**.

63

You hasten down yet another tunnel. Rounding a bend, you come across a wooden doorway which is ajar. You can see instantly that this is a weapons storeroom. If you want to look inside and maybe take a weapon, turn to **173**. If you want to hurry onwards, turn to **115**.

64

You swoop almost vertically into the gloom. After your initial dive the heat becomes sweltering, but having survived the fires of the Moogoll, this holds no fear for you!

Eventually you come to a number of vents cut out of the rock. The heat coming from these is intense. You fly closer and ascertain that they release heat from a huge underground forge. You could squeeze through one of the vents into the furnace if you wish. To do this, turn to **159**. Otherwise you can fly back up to the tunnel on the other side of the chasm (turn to **146**).

65

The situation still looks grave and you don't see how you can escape this one without using your magic again. Under such pressure as this, you concentrate and attempt to summon more of the energy that has been so useful so far.

This time you feel something almost immediately! Mightily relieved, but aware of the presence of your enemies so close by, you close your eyes to focus your mind. For the first time since you ate that fateful crystal, options seem to present themselves. You feel the rock beneath your feet tingling; the slight breeze from the cracks in the shutters is heightened against your beak; the fiery torches on the walls blaze brightly in your mind's eye. How will you choose to direct your powers? Will you:

Try to enhance the breeze, extinguish the torches and plunge the room into darkness?	Turn to **117**
Try to make the flames rise into torrents of fire towards your enemies?	Turn to **194**
Or channel the power down your legs and rupture the floor on which the Scarfells stand?	Turn to **160**

66

With a mighty crash, the table overturns and tumbles into the path of the dogs. But this does little to deter them. The first leaps over it, saliva streaming from its vicious jaws. *React on instinct*. Will you fly up to the roof of the cave (turn to **176**) or run for the exit (turn to **82**)?

67

You wonder if any of Nevsaron's possessions or treasures were entombed with him. But you find nothing; the chamber is empty except for the body itself. You investigate a cleft in the rock right at the back of the cave and to your surprise find that it goes back much farther than you would think. In fact, it appears to be the entrance to some kind of tunnel! You squeeze in and explore. The tunnel leads steeply downwards and soon comes to a set of steps that have been deliberately cut into the rock: a back entrance into Musk perhaps? Note down the codeword STONE.

Very nice, but not the reason you're here! You decide to return to the mouth of the cave and call the Vzler. He eagerly swoops over to join you, sensing the excitement in your cry! You lead him to where Nevsaron lies and he shakes his head in wonder. "So it is true...and this discovery is all down to you, Xanarel!" he says, quietly. Turn to **211**.

68

You attempt to wedge yourself in behind an outcrop of rock, but it is not quite big enough to conceal your wings as well. The Scarfells see you and ready themselves for battle. Burning anger wells up inside you for the loss of the Vzler and you let this fuel you as you make your last stand, cornered in Nevsaron's tomb.

69

A little further onwards, you detect the unexpected smell of herbs on your nostrils. An unlit and uninhabited cave opens up on your right and you see that you were correct; bundles of herbs and mountain plants of all sorts hang from hooks around the walls. You also see a wooden door on the far side of the cave. If you want to try the door, turn to **90**. If you want to stop to investigate the herbs, turn to **216**. If you want to ignore the cave and carry on down the passage, turn to **120**.

70

As you deliver your threat, you fix the boy with an evil stare, but he has grown up knowing cruel treatment as the norm! Will he crack? Roll the die. If you roll a 4 or less, turn to **212**. If you roll a 5 or more, turn to **98**.

71

You make your way round another wide bend. You could easily bump into someone here, so you proceed with caution. The tunnel ends in a small room lit (and heated) by a single brown candle stood on a table. All around the room are the trappings of a pest-controller: numerous traps, baits and sticks which proudly display the corpses of mice and rats.

This is a dead end. You are about to leave, but the candle draws your attention, almost hypnotically. Something inside you wants you to stay and stare into it. If you give in to this urge, turn to **42**. If you ignore it and return to the main passageway, turn to **115**.

72

This passageway looks well used; there are more torches burning here and it is wider and altogether more airy. You arrive in a roughly circular cavern, again deserted, whose floor is covered in sawdust and dried blood. One other exit is situated on the far side from where you stand. All around the floor area is a high wall made of huge stone blocks, and above and beyond this are semi-circular rows of wooden benches. You deduce that this must be a fighting arena. To your right, set into the wall below the seats, is a pair of iron gates.

Will you fly up and investigate the seating area? (Turn to **108**) Try the gates? (Turn to **123**) Or escape the unpleasant feeling of this place and go down the tunnel? (Turn to **93**)

73

There is enough smoke for you to work your magic and you find it easier than before to mentally command it to swell and increase. You continue to will more and more smoke until the angry shouts of the Scarfells are replaced by choking and coughing. They are in no condition to fight now and you take your chance to run in the general direction of the window. Fortune is on your side, and when your talons feel the wooden shutters, you rip them away just as the men realise what is happening.

But it is too late. You launch yourself into the early morning air, overjoyed at the sight of the sun rising over the horizon in the direction of home. The space, the cool air, the sight of snow: all are wondrous! You are free! Turn to **220**.

74

The tunnel narrows until you have difficulty squeezing your wings through. It then rises and widens, zig-zagging its way onwards. You hear voices up ahead and proceed with extreme caution, passing through a recess into a cave shaped roughly like a cross which seems to be a guard post. The group of Scarfells you heard are standing in the opposite spoke of the cross to you, closeted around a table. The other exit is in the branch of the cross between you and them, so it should be straightforward enough to sneak past.

As you begin to do so, you notice a bunch of keys hanging from a spike hammered into the wall. The guards are not looking; would it be worth the risk to take a few steps towards them and steal the keys? If you want to try this, turn to **110**. If you decide it would be an unnecessary risk, turn to **218**.

75

Confused by his apparent cowardice, you yell to the Vzler to join you in battle. As you fly straight for the nearest eagle, the Scarfell rider flings his spear. Roll the die. If you roll a 1 or 2, turn to **181**. If you roll a 3, turn to **210**. If you roll a 4, 5 or 6, turn to **118**.

76

"Are you sure?" asks the Vzler. You cannot quite tell if he is pleased or disappointed by your decision. He takes a deep breath, pauses and pops the crystal into his mouth, swallowing hard. At first nothing happens. Then he staggers back against the rocky wall, eyes screwed up in pain. You go to help him but he waves you away. It is fortunate that he did! He suddenly flings out his arms and screeches incredibly loudly. There is a terrific rumbling noise and the whole chamber begins to tremble! Note down the codeword SHAKE.

Blocks of stone and ice begin showering from the roof of the tunnel. You press yourself up against the wall, unsure what to do. It is clear that the Vzler is struggling to control some sort of huge energy building up inside him. With a mighty effort he manages to regain control as one final burst of energy leaves him, sending chunks of rock flying violently down the tunnel and out of the cave. He slumps to the ground.

"Time to go I think," you say, as you help him to his feet. "If there *are* any night guards, that would certainly have alerted them!" He nods, a dazed expression on his face. You pick your way carefully down the tunnel once more and as you reach the entrance, a huge dark shape passes across the sky in a rush of wind. You step back, dismayed, as you see a mighty creature curl round in the air. It is shaped like a huge scaly snake, light blue-green in colour, with the head of a dragon and large, bat-like wings. Smoke curls from its nostrils and you tremble: you have seen one of these beasts once before in the mountains of Arian and barely escaped with your life: it is the most feared creature from Ariax legend, the Moogoll!

"Get back!" you cry, "Moogoll!" The Vzler shudders. A roar from outside tells you that you were seen. But what will you do? If you want to suggest retreating into the tomb, turn to **142**. If you want to try and speed past the Moogoll to freedom, turn to **53**.

77

You have confidence in your ferocity: you have always been a deadly fighter! Roll the die. If you roll a 1 or 2, turn to **38**. If you roll a 3 or more, turn to **136**.

78

You make your way down a long, straight tunnel with a sharp bend at the end. As you near this, you are excited to feel a breeze that can only be coming from outside, but you can also hear two or three Scarfells talking not far around the bend. Could this be one of the lookout posts, manned even at night? You can think of no other logical alternative. Will you:

Rush around the corner, to burst through the guards to freedom?	Turn to **106**
Poke your head round the corner for a second to spy out the land?	Turn to **171**
Or stay put and listen to the conversation before making a decision?	Turn to **182**

79

You begin to head off down the tunnel. "Stop!" cries the prisoner, then a threatening tone comes into his voice. "If ya *don't* lemme out, I'll shout this place down! You'll be caught for sure!" If you want to relent and unlock the door, turn to **165**. If you ignore him, turn to **27**.

80

Trying to keep your cool under pressure, you concentrate on channelling the energy down through your legs. The Scarfells get halfway towards you before there is an almighty sound like a giant's hammer splintering rock. Black cracks rapidly snake out across the bridge from your feet, widening and intertwining as they go. The Scarfells are startled but see the danger; they turn tail and run back the way they came.

They almost make it. You jump in the air as with a resounding din, the entire bridge comes apart and huge blocks of masonry plunge into the chasm. The Scarfells cry out in anguish as they fall to their doom in a cloud of dust and rock. Note down the codeword RUBBLE.

That was exhilarating! But was it also foolish? It certainly created a terrific commotion! You fly across the rift to the tunnel on the other side, enjoying the momentary freedom of flight. If you have the codeword OX, turn to **107**. If you do not have this codeword, turn to **72**.

81

The wily veteran nimbly deflects your strike. This gives the King time to act and he charges into you with full force. You are thrown, winded, against the rocky chamber wall. You drag yourself to your feet, but fighting alone against the most powerful Scarfell of them all is beyond even you. As reinforcements appear on the steps behind you, you realise that this is a battle you cannot win…

82

You make it to the opening, but then another Scarfell appears before you! He is unarmed and taken by surprise: he had only come looking for his helmet, left here yesterday! "Stop him!" bellows the dog-handler from somewhere behind you. *React on instinct*. Will you try to barge your way past the man? (Turn to **195**) Or propel yourself up to the roof of the cavern? (Turn to **176**).

83

Nevsaron lies serenely, empty eye sockets staring up into nothingness. You sense the power of this great birdman and feel an unexplainable affinity with him; a sense of destiny even. It is a sombre moment.

You decide to return to the mouth of the cave and call the Vzler. He eagerly swoops over to join you, hearing the excitement in your cry! You lead him to Nevsaron's body and he shakes his head in wonder. "So it is true…and this discovery is all down to you, Xanarel!" he says, quietly. Turn to **211**.

84

You focus your mind and stretch out your talons and wings to urge on the smoke. Roll the die. If you roll a 4 or less, turn to **198**. If you roll a 5 or more, turn to **113**.

85

You continue along this passage as it zigzags its way steadily through the mountain. Then it feeds into a large cave which is clearly used as a kitchen. Work has finished for the night however and there is no-one about. You notice many unfamiliar cooking implements on the wall hanging beside meat-cleavers and carving knives. Drapes half cover store room entrances and you catch the faint odour of pickled food.

Lying unattended on a table is a joint of meat which you tuck into ravenously. You will need to be at full strength if you are going to escape! Large cauldrons of water are suspended over fire pits ready for tomorrow's meals and for some reason you feel yourself attracted to them. As you approach, you feel a strange sensation in the pit of your stomach. It isn't hunger; it is as if some strange power is drawing you in. If you want to try and rouse your magic and see what happens, turn to **206**. If you think it could be dangerous and want to leave the kitchen through the other exit, turn to **121**.

86

You ignore the sounds and try again, willing the timbers to crack underneath your palms. But the door is thicker than you know and again you experience failure. Unfortunately as you are lost in concentration, two Scarfells approach quietly from behind. They have no idea what you are doing (and don't care either). The only thing they have on their minds is your death, a task they all too easily accomplish…

87

You use the experience you gained on the bridge to try to summon the same type of power again and after a few seconds you manage it! The floor begins to tremble and shake, then cracks begin flowing out from your feet, speeding in the direction of your bewildered foes who hastily leap aside to avoid the crevasses. "What witchcraft is this?" roars the King. Note down the codeword POWER and erase the codeword ARMS (if you have it).

You cannot keep this up indefinitely; you can already feel the drain on your energy. It is time to press home your advantage. Will you:

Try to flee the room?	Turn to **208**
Tell the King that if he doesn't let you go free you will destroy the entire mountain?	Turn to **153**
Attempt to refocus your powers on extinguishing the torches?	Turn to **117**
Attack Gargrimm, who stands nearest to you?	Turn to **139**
Or grab for his axe and try to fracture it as you did with your bonds?	Turn to **217**

88

The spear whistles past, brushing your wing as it goes but not causing any damage. You grapple with the Scarfell and he is suddenly forced to cling on to his mount! You strike a telling blow and he topples from the saddle, falling to his doom on the mountainside far below. Glancing across, you see that the Vzler has returned and dealt with his opponent in a similar fashion. You glide down to meet him.

"A little more trust in me would be appreciated, Xanarel…" he chides, but he is not angry. He explains his actions, and you realise that the Vzler had been far from fleeing; he was trying to draw the Scarfells into a channel where they could be ambushed! You apologise, but the Vzler merely chuckles to himself. He is certainly cool under pressure – you were both nearly killed! Turn to **196**.

89

You manage to squeeze yourself into a niche of rock right at the back of the cave and to your surprise find that it goes back much farther than you would think. In fact, it appears to be the entrance to some kind of tunnel! There's nothing else for it: you squeeze in and explore. The tunnel leads steeply downwards and soon come to a set of steps that have been deliberately cut into the rock: a back entrance into Musk perhaps?

The Scarfells behind you will find the remains of Nevsaron and the Vzler but have no knowledge of your presence. But as you crouch in the shadows to wait for the sound of the Scarfells to go, you fall through a concealed hole in the ground, landing with a bump in a passageway below!

Annoyingly, there is no way back up again. There is not enough room to spread your wings and it is too high up to jump. The walls are climbable, but not near enough to the hole to be able to access it. In fact, unless you knew the hole was there, you don't think you would even be able to see it! You reason that this is how Nevsaron has remained undisturbed all these years.

Then it dawns on you. You are trapped inside Musk and need to find another way out! You have been in some tight spots in the recent months...but nothing to compare with *this*!

From the outside you remember seeing lookout posts dotted around the mountain. Of course there's also the front door! But both are sure to be guarded and you have no clue as to their direction! Best foot forward Xanarel, you think to yourself. The passageway stretches out in two directions and both look similarly uninviting! Will you take the way you happen to be currently facing (turn to **46**) or will you turn round and go the other way? (Turn to **150**)

90

You get to the door easily enough, but groan when you open it: it is merely a store cupboard. You scan it quickly but there is nothing of interest, just the ordinary tools of the herbalist's trade. A distant noise alerts you to the presence of Scarfells. If you have the codeword YELL, turn to **10**. Otherwise, you hurry down the main passage (turn to **120**).

91

Suddenly you freeze – is that voices you can hear? If it is they are talking quietly as if they do not wish to be overheard. Then they stop. You think they came from behind you, but cannot be totally sure in these echoey subterranean passageways. But you *are* sure that you do not wish to meet the owners of the voices. If you want to go on in the direction you are facing, turn to **129**. If you want to turn back, turn to **54**.

92

Keeping your head underwater, you try to relax and focus your powers as you did in the kitchen upstairs. Nothing happens at first, but then you are delighted to feel an energy building up inside you and feeding into your submerged head! The water all around you begins to bubble gently, then two spouts of water rise slowly upwards and form into hands. The torturer releases you and backs away in confusion and fear. You stand and turn about, dramatically gesturing towards the Scarfell and commanding the hands. This is enough for him! He runs from the chamber, back down the tunnel the way you came in. Chuckling to yourself and again marvelling at the awesome abilities you now possess, you let the hands disperse in a mini torrent which splashes down all around you. You take the other way out of the torture chamber, shaking water droplets from your feathers. Turn to **207**.

93

The tunnel leads to a crossroads. Note down the codeword ROCK. If you want to take the left hand branch, turn to **152**. To try the right hand branch, turn to **78**. To continue straight on, turn to **74**.

94

You must act fast; the Scarfells are enraged and fearlessly search for you in the dark. Will you:
        Attack the King as he blunders towards you?   Turn to **22**
        Try to avoid them both and get to the window?   Turn to **175**
        Or if you have the codeword SMOKE, you
        could try to use your powers as you did before?   Turn to **73**

95

You make your daring bid for freedom as suddenly as possible, trying to take the Scarfell by surprise. You screech loudly as you swoop towards the startled man blocking the way, but he is a battle-hardened veteran and not one to shirk a challenge! He brings his arms up to defend himself and stands firm in the face of your attack. Although you manage to force your way past, you trip and bash your knee. The delay is enough for the slavering hounds to be upon you, where they are able to do what they do best with fallen prey…

96

It is hard going, and after only a few steps upwards your foot slips again when a clod of loose rock comes away with it and you fall. You knock your head on one wall and your leg painfully on the opposite one before landing on the floor of a rocky tunnel which stretches out in front and behind you. Turn to **91**.

97

It is fortunate that you were cautious! You are half way up the steps when a fully armed Scarfell warrior appears at the top! A look of amazement passes over his features, soon replaced by one of fury! *React on instinct*. Will you:

    Use your beak and talons to attack?   Turn to **77**
    Meet him as he comes down the steps
    and hurl him from them?   Turn to **163**
    Or flee, back out the way you came in?   Turn to **32**

98

Fear spreads across the young boy's face and he stammers his reply: "T-that way leads to ice-dungeons...don't go there!"

You ask him for the quickest way out. "D-down that way," he gibbers, pointing to the way you came in. You consider that he may then go and alert someone, but draw the line at murdering a child, even a Scarfell! So you warn him never to speak of this encounter or you will come back for him, then let him go. But which way now? If you want to go in the direction that the boy indicated, turn to **107**. If you want to carry on the way you were going, which he said led to 'ice dungeons', turn to **34**.

99

As the torturer turns away, his guard is dropped and you take this opportunity to strike! Roll the die. If you roll a 1 or 2, turn to **145**. If you roll a 3 or more, turn to **12**.

100

You meet the Scarfells in the middle of the bridge where they can only attack one at a time. The first swings his axe; you nimbly avoid it, overbalance him and send him plummeting to his doom down the chasm! The second decides to leap onto you and bring you back down to earth. In the struggle, you both tumble off the bridge and into the darkness. It is only a matter of time before your panic stricken opponent loses his grip and follows his comrade into the depths.

You catch your breath, fly back up to the bridge and take the other exit from the cavern. If you have the codeword OX, turn to **107**. If you do not have this codeword, turn to **72**.

101

You gain the opening and bound down the steps. Unfortunately, you almost bump into the two Scarfell guards who were waiting in the passage below! You lash out, but one of them drives you up against the rocky wall and gets you by the arm. The other is quick to help and you soon find yourself pinned in their vice like grip. They march you back into the presence of the King. Note down the codeword ARMS and turn to **65**.

102

Your blow knocks the guard from his feet and he staggers back against the rocky wall. But he retains his composure, and as you attempt to flee the scene he sticks out a leg and catches you by your ankle. You only stumble for a second, but this gives the man time to launch himself towards you and call for support. As you both tumble to the floor, you can already hear the sound of tramping feet behind you; feet that bring with them only death…

103

You manage to cling on and haul the surprised Scarfell from his mount. He falls senseless to the rock below.

The eagles are put to flight and you stand amidst the bodies of your fallen foes. The Vzler mops his brow as he receives your adulation for his quick thinking, but you too are congratulated for your part in the battle. Turn to **196**.

104

You nervously pop the crystal into your mouth and try hard to swallow it. It takes a moment to go down, feeling like an uncomfortably large morsel of food.

Nothing happens immediately. Then all of a sudden you feel an intense burning sensation in the pit of your stomach, which changes bizarrely to a feeling of coolness then rapidly becomes an immense and unpleasant churning. You stagger back against the wall of the cave, eyes screwed up in pain.

Something is going on in your mind too; a bizarre tapestry of thoughts and images flashes through your consciousness. In a moment you feel the freedom of the ocean depths; the power and age of the mountain rock; the rage of a roaring inferno; the vitality of a youthful forest. It is an intense experience. Then it as if two of these elements (fire and rock) are almost competing for your attention; as if their individual forces are seeking for a release. If you want to try to focus on the fire, turn to **45**. If you want to focus on rock instead, turn to **17**. If you want to attempt to hold back both elemental powers, turn to **190**.

105

No-one emerges from the cave; you remain undetected. But you have already decided not to linger *anywhere* in Musk for long! A little further on, the tunnel splits into two identical looking branches. Will you take the left hand branch (turn to **69**) or the right (turn to **191**)?

106

You mentally prepare yourself for action and take a deep breath. But no sooner have you rounded the corner then you notice a big problem: a heavy iron portcullis spans the tunnel, cutting you off from what is indeed a look-out post! You see three astonished Scarfell guards framed clearly in the night sky. One grabs a bow and begins to notch an arrow; another heaves a huge double-handed axe from against the wall and the third makes for a lever which must control the mechanism.

You skid to a halt and make an immediate decision: to flee! Fortunately the portcullis is heavy and rises slowly, giving you time to escape. As you make your way back down the tunnel, you notice a smaller side tunnel that you hadn't seen before. *React on instinct*. If you want to duck down this way, turn to **54**. If you want to continue back the way you came, turn to **114**.

107

You notice that the passageways on this level are wider and less well kept. You frequently have to pick a path through piles of rubbish. You can hear nothing at all as you creep quietly along.

The tunnel leads into a huge chamber which dwarfs any you have discovered so far. Twelve mighty tables of oak line the room, served by long, low wooden benches. Scraps of discarded food cover much of the tabletops along with mugs of unfinished drink. There are rats here too, making sure nothing goes to waste. Two other tunnels lead out of this dining hall and from one of them you feel warmth. As you ponder the options, you feel your new powers drawing you to the nearest table. Is this a safe place to experiment though? If you want to go over to the table, turn to **151**. If not will you opt for the warm tunnel (turn to **41**) or the regular one (turn to **63**)?

108

There is nothing extraordinary to be found here, though the rubbish and spilt flagons of drink on the floor suggest that the fighting is a social occasion. You return to the arena floor. If you have the codeword AXE, turn to **57**. If you do not have this codeword, will you investigate the gates? (Turn to **123**) Or leave through the tunnel on the far side? (Turn to **93**)

109

Despite your greatest efforts, the Scarfells manage to hold firm. You continue to struggle, but then feel the fearsome force of the King's axe. Mercifully, he grants you a quick death...

110

You never know when keys will come in handy! You focus on the thievery in hand. Roll the die, subtracting one from the roll if you have the codeword FETCH. If the total is 3 or less, turn to **148**. If it is 4 or more, turn to **30**.

111

You brush away the thick-stranded curtain and make your way into the cave. Many more webs impede your progress and you wonder that you see nothing of any spiders at all. You also find nothing to indicate that this is a tomb. You are about to leave when you nearly fall into a hole in the floor! It too is covered in layers of webbing and seems to lead into some sort of naturally occurring shaft. If you want to pull away the web and enter the shaft, turn to **161**. If you want to leave well alone and try the other cave, turn to **44**.

112

You secrete yourself just outside the remains of Nevsaron's tomb, determined to avenge the Vzler's death. But there are more Scarfells than you anticipated. You strike down the first to pass and grapple valiantly with the next, but as reinforcements join the fray, there can only be one outcome to this battle...

113

You are not quite sure how, but as you concentrate, you can feel the amount of smoke increasing! You clench your fist and will it to billow out in the direction of your enemy. It does! Note down the codeword SMOKE.

The Scarfell chokes as he is enveloped in the black cloud and you allow yourself a smile as you drift safely past him and up the steps on the far side of the cavern. Once in the tunnel you attempt to create more smoke as an experiment, but nothing happens. You must need some to be present in the first place. Turn to **19**.

114

Note down the codeword FETCH. If you have the codeword ROCK, turn to **192**. If you do not have this codeword, turn to **199**.

115

The tunnel twists through the mountain, rejoins another and begins to slope steeply, winding round to the left before levelling out again. Eventually you come to a T-junction. On the wall in front of you is a pair of colossal double-doors made of oak and studded with iron bolts. They must be fully three times your height and as wide as they are high! Your first thoughts are that this is the main entrance to Musk, but you cannot be halfway down the mountain yet and they are by no means *that* big!

If you want to try and open the doors, you could inspect what looks like a mechanical winding mechanism to the left of the doors, turn to **193**. To see if you can summon your powers to help you, turn to **20**. If you'd rather go for one of the passages instead, will you go down the wider tunnel, to the left? (Turn to **59**) Or the narrower tunnel, to the right? (Turn to **74**)

116

You swoop to the attack! Roll the die. If you roll a 1 or 2, turn to **166**. If you roll a 3 or more, turn to **100**.

117

With just seconds to act, you will the breeze to whip up and plunge the chamber into darkness. If you want to direct the power through your arms and hands, turn to **214**. If you want to close your eyes and direct the power through your head, turn to **187**. (If you have the codeword ARMS, you *must* choose the second option.)

118

The spear flies harmlessly past you. If you want to grapple with the nearest eagle-rider, turn to **23**. If you want to take cover in case more spears are thrown, turn to **141**.

119

You stand near the entrance to the cave and see the Moogoll turn in the air and swing round towards you again. Resolutely you stand your ground and will the elemental crystal to work its magic once more. But nothing happens; you feel no power this time. You turn to run, but it is too late: the entire cave suddenly becomes a raging inferno as the Moogoll's fiery breath engulfs everything within! If you have the codeword SHAKE, turn to **37**. If you do not have this codeword, turn to **215**.

120

The passage begins to slope gently downwards. A side tunnel opens up on the right which leads to a set of stairs down. If you want to take this new branch and head for the stairs, turn to **6**. To continue in the direction you are going, turn to **3**.

121

You leave the kitchen and follow a short passageway. You soon come to a flight of stairs that lead up on the left hand side. If you want to go upstairs, turn to **39**. To carry on down the tunnel, turn to **19**.

122

You suddenly hear a yell of surprise and turn to see an axe wielding Scarfell warrior has just entered the room. You have no time to feel fortunate that he alerted you to his presence: you decide to flee while he is still a distance away! Note down the codeword YAP and *react on instinct*. Will you run for the warmer tunnel (turn to **41**) or the other (turn to **63**)?

123

The gates are, as you expected, locked. But as you stand before them you feel a strange sensation and an urge to *connect* with the iron somehow. If you want to press your hands up against the gates, turn to **21**. If you want to suppress this urge, and hurry out of the arena by the other exit, turn to **93**.

124

In desperation, you launch yourself bravely at the burly figure of the King. But this man became leader of a tribe of ruthless and deadly warriors with good reason; this is the meanest, most powerful Scarfell of them all! He shrugs off your initial attack, and as reinforcements appear on the steps behind you, you realise that this is a situation you are not going to get out of alive...

125

You emerge from the gloom into a large, well-lit cavern served by this entrance and a similar one on the far side of it. It appears to be a communal living area for a large number of Scarfells: tables and benches are positioned randomly around the room, dotted between with log-circle seating areas. Plates, tankards and food waste lie scattered about, along with the odd broken weapon or discarded piece of armour. But there is no-one here at this time of night (or morning; you really have lost track of time in this accursed city).

Suddenly you hear the sound of barking dogs coming from the entrance behind you and about half a dozen blood-crazed hounds bound into the room! The noise increases when they pick up your scent! A running Scarfell soon follows them in, urging on his dogs and commanding them to rip you apart! *React on instinct*. Will you run for the other exit (you should have just enough head start to make it)? (Turn to **82**) Pause to kick one of the tables over into the path of the dogs? (Turn to **66**) Or fly up to the roof of the cavern, out of reach? (Turn to **176**)

126

Something tells you that the Vzler is no coward. You spin round and follow him as he runs down the mountainside, darting sideways into a narrow channel. There he stops and pulls you roughly behind him, edging back to the point where he disappeared from the Scarfells' view.

As the first Scarfell banks his steed eagerly around the corner, he does not expect the Vzler to be standing right there! The experienced birdman strikes suddenly and with devastating accuracy, smashing the surprised man from his mount and rendering him unconscious on the rocky ground below! "Choose your ground to fight on!" pants the Vzler. Your instincts were right!

The second eagle-rider joins the fray and descends from behind. Will you:
    Try to grapple with him like the Vzler did?   Turn to **189**
    Grab a nearby branch to use as a weapon?   Turn to **154**
    Or dive to the side to avoid the attack?   Turn to **52**

127

You feel the spear brush the edge of your wing as it flies past and breaks against the rocky wall behind you! But it has given you the seconds you needed to focus your energies. The cavern begins to tremble once more; large rocks detach themselves from the roof and fall among the Scarfells. As they retreat, you attempt to reign in the power, but by the time you have, an immovable barrier blocks your escape route!

You slump down, physically and mentally drained by your experiences. There seems like no way out. Your only hope is to use your powers to blast your way through before the oxygen runs out! You sit down to rest at the back of the cave. To your surprise you find that it goes back much farther than you would think. In fact, it appears to be the entrance to some kind of tunnel! You are delighted with your good fortune and decide to squeeze in and explore. The tunnel leads steeply downwards and you soon come to a set of steps that have been deliberately cut into the rock: a back entrance into Musk perhaps?

This tunnel leads to a dead end, but as you investigate you fall through a concealed hole in the ground, landing with a bump in a passageway below!

Annoyingly, there is no way back up again. There is not enough room to spread your wings, and it is too high up to jump. The walls are climbable, but not near enough to the hole to be able to access it. In fact, unless you knew the hole was there, you don't think you would even be able to see it! You reason that this is how Nevsaron has remained undisturbed all these years.

Then it dawns on you. You are trapped inside Musk and need to find another way out! You have been in some tight spots in the recent months...but nothing to compare with *this*!

From the outside you remember seeing lookout posts dotted around the mountain. Of course there's also the front door! But both are sure to be guarded and you have no clue as to their direction! Best foot forward Xanarel, you think to yourself. The passageway stretches out in two directions and both look similarly uninviting! Will you take the way you happen to be currently facing (turn to **46**) or will you turn round and go the other way? (Turn to **150**)

128

You cough as you emerge from the smoke into the comparatively clean air of the rest of the cave. As you glance across to the steps you intend to take, a fully armed Scarfell warrior appears at the top! A look of amazement passes over his features, soon replaced by one of fury! *React on instinct*. Will you:

    Use your beak and talons to attack?   Turn to **77**
    Meet him as he comes down the steps
    and hurl him from them?   Turn to **163**
    Or flee out of the cave the way you came in?   Turn to **32**

129

You soon enter a large circular cavern lit by ten flaming torches. There are four wooden doors on the far wall from where you stand. Seeing some sort of runic writing carved into each one, you cross the chamber to read them. A mistake. Above the entrance you came in through is an outcrop of rock formed like a natural balcony leading to another tunnel. Standing atop it is a Scarfell woman armed with a bow and arrows, taking a short cut to join a sentry post. Female Scarfells are just as ruthless as the males and have equally deadly aims with their bows; from this range one arrow is all she needs to end your life.

130

You struggle for a while, then allow your muscles to relax and your whole body goes limp. After a minute or so the torturer hauls your body back up again and dumps it on the floor of the cave, chuckling evilly to himself. Will you take the chance to attack while his back is turned? (Turn to **99**) Or remain still until he leaves the cave? (Turn to **200**)

131

You hurry onwards down the next tunnel, wondering if you will *ever* find a way to escape from this labyrinth! You pass more sleeping quarters undetected and come to a point where a second tunnel crosses the one you are in. You could carry on straight ahead (turn to **125**), turn sharp left (turn to **59**) or take the right-hand way (turn to **168**)?

132

You grit your teeth in silent delight as the wind suddenly whips up around the room and the torches simultaneously splutter and die, leaving curling wisps of grey smoke in their wake. If you have the codeword ARMS, turn to **29**. If you do not have this codeword, turn to **94**.

133

One last chance! As you attempt to stall your enemies with more talk, you recall every past sensation in a desperate attempt to muster *something*. But just as you think you can feel a glimmer of power, the Scarfells below throw their spears. Two hit home and you plummet downwards, the humiliating jeers of your foes the last sounds that you hear…

134

There are some rough-and-ready hand-and-footholds to cling to as you attempt your ascent. Roll the die. If you roll a 2 or less, turn to **96**. If you roll a 3 or more, turn to **149**.

135

You fling your arms out towards your foes and urge your powers on. The cavern begins to tremble once more; large rocks detach themselves from the roof and fall among the Scarfells. As they retreat, you attempt to reign in the power, but by the time you have, an immovable barrier blocks your escape route!

You slump down, physically and mentally drained by your experiences. There seems like no way out. Your only hope is to use your powers to blast your way through before the oxygen runs out! You sit down to rest at the back of the cave and to your surprise find that it goes back much farther than you would think. In fact, it appears to be the entrance to some kind of tunnel! You are delighted with your good fortune and decide to squeeze in and explore. The tunnel leads steeply downwards and you soon come to a set of steps that have been deliberately cut into the rock: a back entrance into Musk perhaps?

This leads to a dead end, but as you investigate, you fall through a concealed hole in the ground, landing with a bump in a passageway below!

Annoyingly, there is no way back up again. There is not enough room to spread your wings, and it is too high up to jump. The walls are climbable, but not near enough to the hole to be able to access it. In fact, unless you knew the hole was there, you don't think you would even be able to see it! You reason that this is how Nevsaron has remained undisturbed all these years.

Then it dawns on you. You are trapped inside Musk and need to find another way out! You have been in some tight spots in the recent months…but nothing to compare with *this*!

From the outside you remember seeing lookout posts dotted around the mountain. Of course there's also the front door! But both are sure to be guarded and you have no clue as to their direction! Best foot forward Xanarel, you think to yourself. The passageway stretches out in two directions and both look similarly uninviting! Will you take the way you happen to be currently facing (turn to **46**) or will you turn round and go the other way? (Turn to **150**)

136

The Scarfell tumbles out of your way and you are able to leap over him as he falls down the steps. You don't look back as you speed onwards! Turn to **19**.

137

Not waiting for him to scream or yell out, you give him a menacing stare and sweep past. You hope that he'll sneak back to bed and keep his mouth *shut*! Turn to **34**.

138

You raise your arms in surrender, banking on the torturer's natural desire to prolong your life for his sadistic pleasure to give you an opportunity to maybe use your powers and escape.

"Now what 'ave we 'ere then?" says the torturer. He grabs you and firmly twists your arm behind your back, then frogmarches you to his torture chamber which is down the other branch of the tunnel that you saw. You do not have time to take in all the various cruel-looking torture equipment as the torturer violently thrusts you sideways and plunges your head in a trough of ice-cold, filthy water. He is going to try and drown you in his ducking pool!

You must fight! You must escape before water fills your lungs and you drown! You must...but then you stop. Your lungs feel funny, like they are already filled with water! But you are still alive: you can feel the torturer's stubby fingers on your feathered neck and the chill of the water on your face!

It must be your elemental powers! Not only are you safe from the effects of fire, but you can breathe underwater too! If you want to pretend to drown, turn to **130**. If you want to slash out at the torturer's legs with your talons, turn to **213**. If you have the codeword ICE, you may choose to use your powers as you did before (turn to **92**).

139

You turn your full ferocity on Gargrimm who brings his axe up smartly to defend himself. Roll the die, adding one to the roll if you have the codeword POWER. If you roll a 3 or less, turn to **81**. If you roll a 4 or more, turn to **183**.

140

You press yourself flat and keep as still as possible; surely you will be seen? But no: a guard strides past you into the chamber without even glancing aside! Relieved at your little bit of good fortune, you hurry on. Turn to **168**.

141

You dive behind a nearby outcrop of rock and out of the corner of your eye see the Vzler returning to help you. A second spear is thrown, this time in his direction. He shows surprising agility for his age as he avoids it and has the presence of mind to quickly retrieve the weapon and send it speeding back at the Scarfell who is spurring him war-eagle right at him! The spear misses but forces the man to abort his attack and bank sharply away.

The Vzler has momentarily gained the upper hand for the pair of you but the other Scarfell is already swooping down at him. If you want to press home the advantage by attacking this Scarfell, turn to **177**. If you want to take one each and head off the first one, turn to **204**.

142

You hurry out of sight of the creature and see that the Vzler is noticeably shaken too. There is a roaring sound, and the entire cave suddenly becomes a raging inferno as the Moogoll's fiery breath engulfs everything within! If you have the codeword SHAKE, turn to **37**. If you do not have this codeword, turn to **215**.

143

You drift into the smoke, which appears to twist and wrap itself around you as you enter. You feel a similar strange churning feeling in your chest and stomach as before and warmth begins to radiate through your body. The smoke is beginning to thicken and increase even though there is no fire below! It is an unusual sensation; powerful and slightly dangerous... If you want to break out of the smoky cloud, turn to **128**. If you want to try and urge your powers on again, turn to **61**. To simply float and see what happens, turn to **170**.

144

You close your eyes and concentrate. Snippets of clear conversation reach your ears: it is three Scarfells who seem to be grumbling about the guard duty they are undertaking at night. But these men are not within your normal earshot. As the voices fade you realise that they were being magically brought to you from outside and you are somehow aware that it came from the smaller tunnel leading from this chamber!

You regain your senses fully. Will you take the smaller tunnel and investigate the guard post? (Turn to **78**) Or the larger tunnel and avoid the men? (Turn to **199**)

145

You draw first blood; your talons raking across the torturer's exposed flesh. But he barely seems to register the pain and you see his lip curl into a cruel sneer. You attempt to dodge his fist at the last second as it is propelled towards your face, but it catches you a glancing blow that knocks you off balance into a brazier of hot coals behind you. The heat does you no damage but the torturer takes the chance to pick up a deadly looking two-headed halberd from its place on the wall. You are cornered. You fight valiantly, but the torturer handles the weapon expertly and uses it to spill your innards onto the torture chamber floor…

146

After so long walking through dark, rocky tunnels it is nice to be able to stretch your wings and glide through the (albeit stuffy) air. As you near the other side of the chasm you hear a cry and glance over your shoulder to see two Scarfells emerging from the tunnel entrance behind you. If you want to turn and do battle with the men as they run onto the bridge towards you, turn to **116**. If you want to fly away from them and escape, turn to **28**.

147

You do your utmost to ignore the King's furious rant and gaze resolutely forwards, gripping the manacles behind your back as best you can. You mentally call forth the powers you felt earlier when you broke the iron gates.

Suddenly you are struck with terrific force about the head! The King is enraged by your insolence and has lashed out! You tumble to the rocky floor of the cave: he has the strength of a frost bear!

But perhaps this is the catalyst you needed: you feel your powers rising! Your hands are getting warmer and so are the manacles you hold! As you stagger to your feet, you speculatively urge on similar magic to the bonds around your ankles and to your indescribable joy, feel it happening! It rapidly builds and builds until with a dramatic cracking sound, the metal warps and breaks! You throw out your arms and screech as both sets of manacles are flung across the room! The Scarfells look aghast, yet still they block your way to the window, and freedom. Will you:

Attack the King, who stands nearest you?	Turn to **124**
Try to summon more of your powers?	Turn to **65**
Or run for the archway behind you and attempt to get out that way instead?	Turn to **101**

148

You stretch to get the keys but alas! You accidentally dislodge the bunch and they fall tinkling to the ground! You immediately turn to run but a guard appears behind you with a hunting horn. A sharp blast follows, and as you pass a side tunnel a Scarfell rushes out and you collide with each other. The chasing guards find the pair of you sprawled on the floor, and ensure that only one of you gets up…

149

It is not easy, but you manage to make the climb successfully. You decide that this is certainly not what you were looking for and head for the other cave. Turn to **44**.

150

You make your way warily down the dark tunnel. It appears to be naturally formed and you recall from Detlaxe's scrolls that the mountain's many cave systems was one of the main reasons for the Scarfells settling there in the first place. Every so often a torch has been set in a sconce on the wall, the flames casting ghostly shadows all about.

Your heart is beating fast. The Vzler is dead and you are alone in the heart of the domain of your mortal enemies. If you are discovered, you can expect no mercy.

You have no further sensations of the powers of the elemental crystal. You are sure that swallowing it has granted you magical powers like Nevsaron, but you will need to learn how to control and direct them.

You pass large darkened rooms on both sides of the passage. Inside you can hear the sounds of Scarfells breathing heavily in sleep, with the occasional snore or grunt. You pass by stealthily, keeping to the shadows where possible and always alert for sounds of activity ahead. The fact that it is night and most of the Scarfells are asleep is your main hope for escape!

Soon you reach a fork in the passage. The main tunnel curves round to the right (turn to **26**) or a smaller tunnel branches off to the left (turn to **85**).

151

As you press your palms flat onto the surface of the table you can feel the age of the piece. Some sort of energy begins to course through your fingers and the oak begins to emit a straining, creaking sound. Roll the die. If you roll an odd number, turn to **40**. If you roll an even number, turn to **122**.

152

You pass three short side-tunnels which you can see lead to sleeping quarters for many Scarfells. Then you come to an animal-skin drape hung across the main passage. Hearing nothing, you cautiously peep around it and see a high-ceilinged cave full of furs, pelts and more dried animal-skins. They are piled up in heaps in no apparent order.

You cross the cave but suddenly freeze: you can hear loud voices coming up the passage behind you! *React on instinct*. Will you:

    Dive into the furs and hide?   Turn to **13**
    Run for the exit ahead of you?   Turn to **131**
    Or fly up and hide in the shadows of the ceiling? Turn to **186**

153

Despite the recent demonstration of your abilities, the King roars with laughter. "No-one has *ever* infiltrated Musk and lived to tell the tale, bird-scum!" he snarls. "And I can guarantee that you are not about to become the first!" He hefts his gigantic axe up into a battle stance as he speaks and fixes you with a malevolent, determined stare. You must subtract 1 from the next die roll you make in this adventure. Will you:

    Try to flee the room?   Turn to **208**
    Attempt to refocus your powers
    on extinguishing the torches?   Turn to **117**
    Attack Gargrimm, who
    approaches to your right?   Turn to **139**
    Or grab for the King's axe and try to
    fracture it as you did with your bonds?   Turn to **217**

154

Making the most of natural resources: the Vzler would certainly approve! Just in time you lift the heavy branch and heft it in the direction of the swooping Scarfell. The eagle grasps it in its claws and wrenches it from your hands, but it has deflected the attack. As he circles round for another sweep, you see the Vzler pull the wooden spear from the rock and hurl it into the Scarfell's side with deadly accuracy. He topples from his steed with a cry of agony.

The two riderless eagles are soon lost to view in the distance. Turn to **196**.

155

You have only seconds to find a suitable place to hide: you scan the cave desperately. Roll the die. If you roll a 2 or less, turn to **68**. If you roll a 3 or 4, turn to **2**. If you roll a 5 or 6, turn to **89**.

156

Will the Scarfell's ears pick up the faint clatter of your talons on the rock? Roll the die. If you roll a 4 or less, turn to **205**. If you roll a 5 or more, turn to **105**.

157

The tunnel continues to twist its way through the mountain and eventually you come to a large natural opening on your left. Inside you see about a dozen Scarfells sleeping on mattresses stuffed with straw and covered in animal-skin blankets. Snores and grunts punctuate the silence.

You are about to pass by without hesitation when you notice another tunnel opening on the far side of the room. Is this worth investigating, or is the risk of crossing the room too great? If you want to sneak through the sleepers, turn to **62**. To continue along the main tunnel, turn to **19**.

158

You go carefully, extra wary of trouble in this inhospitable half-light. Shortly you come to a low ceilinged cave and observe the source of the clanking that you heard: a torture chamber! All sorts of cruel looking torture equipment is evident: whips; cages; a rack; a brazier of hot coals with more than one branding iron and several sets of metal pincers and bladed implements whose function you can only shudder to imagine!

The torturer stands with his back to you fiddling with some sort of apparatus, but he is so bulky you cannot see past him! Despite the temperature he is bare-chested and he wears a black hood that exposes only his eyes and mouth. Across to your right is another exit to the torture chamber. If you want to sneak across to it while the torturer's back is turned, turn to **56**. If you'd rather go back to the fork and try the left hand branch, turn to **5**.

159

You manage to force your way through the opening into a white hot raging inferno. The light is blinding, but the heat does not even singe your feathers! As you make your way across the burning coals, you spot a couple of iron grates which must be where the Scarfell blacksmiths insert the metal they wish to heat for shaping.

Then one of the grates opens and a long steel rod is thrust in, narrowly missing you! A mischievous idea forms immediately in your mind and you grab the rod and yank it hard towards you! The Scarfell at the other end gives a cry of shock and lets go, and a moment later two nervous faces peer in at the opening. You choose this moment to screech dramatically and clamber out of the flames through the grate. The two Scarfells flee in panic, believing you to be some sort of demon!

You emerge into a now deserted forge. You decide not to dwell here long, as surely the men will return soon with their disbelieving comrades! You jog up a set of steps to the only exit and after a short way come to a T-junction from where you can go left (turn to **74**) or right (turn to **115**).

160

A good idea if you can manage it! If you have the codeword RUBBLE, turn to **87**. If you do not have this codeword, turn to **35**.

161

You carefully lower yourself into the gloom and find a ledge there to support you. But before you can look around the ledge cracks under your weight and you fall down a sort of vertical zig-zag in the rock! You suffer many bumps and bruises in stopping your descent. Looking up you can see only blackness. You have two choices: do you want to try to climb up (turn to **134**) or down (turn to **31**)?

162

You are determined to control your power: you would rather avoid a repeat of your last experience! But as you concentrate, the first Scarfell sees you and lets fly his hunting spear in his eagerness for blood! Roll the die. If you roll a 2 or less, turn to **181**. If you roll a 3 or more, turn to **127**.

163

You attempt to use your adversary's weight against him and sweep him off balance. Roll the die. If you roll a 1, turn to **38**. If you roll a 2 or more, turn to **136**.

164

As you abandon your trial the fist splashes back down to earth, ordinary water once more. You dive for cover behind a bench and lie prone. But after a minute or so you realise that it was a false alarm; you are still alone.

You pick yourself up and return to the cauldron, but try as you might you cannot repeat the build up of power you experienced just moments ago.

Disappointed by the situation, you decide the time has come to exit the kitchen. Turn to **121**.

165

You apprehensively turn the key in the lock and open the door. The man claps you on the shoulder in thanks. "Good work!" he grins, displaying a selection of cracked, brown teeth. "This way!"

You follow him down the passageway and he chooses a left hand fork at the next junction. "I'm not goin' that way," explains the Scarfell. "Oh no. I gotta find Dugroth – he's the only one what can clear me name! But for you – up there's a nice way out. Best of luck!" and he is gone, scampering light-footedly down the other tunnel.

You consider your options. You have no idea what leads in either direction and the Scarfell could well be lying. But you have to check out what he says anyway and hope for the best.

You creep down the gloomy passage. You go carefully, extra wary of trouble in this inhospitable half-light. Shortly you come to a low ceilinged cave which is clearly a torture chamber! All sorts of cruel looking torture equipment is evident: whips; cages; a rack; a brazier of hot coals with more than one branding iron and several sets of metal pincers and bladed implements whose function you can only shudder to imagine! So this is where the unfortunate you freed would have ended up!

Suddenly a bulky torturer appears out of the darkness and bars your exit! Despite the temperature he is bare-chested, and wears a black hood that exposes only his eyes and mouth. He is so wide that it is impossible to run past him from where you stand! *React on instinct.* Will you fight your way past him? (Turn to **48**) Or surrender and hope a way of escape will present itself? (Turn to **138**)

166

One of the Scarfells reads your dive perfectly and swings out his axe. The blow catches you in the side, and the pain causes you to lose control and plummet almost vertically into the gloom. You clutch your injured side (trailing crimson blood) and just manage to regain control before you hit anything. You hover in the air, looking up at the shadowy outline of the bridge high above. The wound is not deep and you manage to staunch the flow of blood, but you cannot properly treat it now. For the rest of the adventure you must subtract 1 from every die roll you make (unless the text asks whether you have rolled an odd or even number).

As you take stock of your surroundings, you notice that the heat is sweltering. Having survived the fires of the Moogoll, this holds no fear for you!

A number of vents are cut out of the rock. The heat coming from these is intense, but you fly closer and ascertain that they serve a huge underground furnace. You could squeeze through one of the vents into it if you wish. To do this, turn to **159**. Otherwise you can fly back up to the tunnel on the other side of the chasm (turn to **49**).

167

The King has noticed that you are up to something and deduced that you have magic powers. He decides to take no chances. "Bring him forth!" he orders and you are powerless as you are dragged towards him and executed…

168

You are descending down a sloping tunnel. You pass under a crude wooden sign which mysteriously bears the symbols of a tankard, a yak and a wheel into a huge cavern. Large numbers of barrels are located at the rear; many benches and small tables are scattered haphazardly around and about. The whole place is a mess, with spilt drink and mounds of rubbish everywhere. A few sleeping Scarfells lie draped over some of the benches, lolling about as if dead. Some still have tankards clutched in their hands. They have presumably been drinking large quantities of ale, the smell of which lingers in the air.

You assess that you can cross without danger, none of these men being in a fit state to even notice you! But then you hear something, and turn to see a semi-conscious Scarfell with half open eyes staggering towards you, muttering something in a slurred voice. *React on instinct*. Will you step back to avoid him? (Turn to **8**) Or slash out at him as he gets nearer? (Turn to **209**)

169

The spear punctures your right wing and you screech in pain. As you rise to your feet and withdraw the offending weapon, you see the Vzler locked in combat with the second Scarfell. Again the man is no match for the bird and you marvel at the Vzler's strength and prowess.

The eagles are put to flight and you stand amidst the bodies of your fallen foes. The Vzler is keen to assess your injury. It is not severe, but you must subtract 1 from the next two die rolls you make in this adventure. Turn to **196**.

170

You drift calmly for another minute or so before suddenly noticing with a jolt that you are not alone! An axe wielding Scarfell has entered the chamber, looking perplexed at what he sees. *React on instinct*. To flee the cavern as quickly as possible, turn to **32**. To try and use your powers to direct the cloud of smoke towards him, turn to **84**. Or you could swoop forward and either attack with your talons and beak (turn to **77**) or try to throw him from the steps (turn to **163**).

171

This turns out to be a good idea! With a quick glance, you see that a heavy iron portcullis bars the way to the outside world. Three Scarfell guards are on the other side of it. If you had run around the corner you would have been seen; instead your presence remains unknown to them. But there is no way through here so you turn back. If you have the codeword ROCK, turn to **192**. If you do not have this codeword, turn to **199**.

172

The susceptible young boy stares into your eyes with a look of terror as his worst nightmares unfold before him! Roll the die. If you roll a 1, turn to **212**. If you roll a 2 or more, turn to **98**.

173

The small cave is well stocked with death-dealing equipment! You decide not to take too long here (Ariax rarely use weapons at all) but may choose a shield and a small hand-axe to arm yourself with (note these items down if you want to take either or both of them). If you have the codeword YAP or FETCH, turn to **40**. If you have neither of these codewords, turn to **115**.

174

The Scarfells enter the cave and begin to cross it. You just allow yourself to think that you are going to remain undetected, when one gives a shout! Unluckily, one of the others is an archer who is carrying a loaded crossbow. He plumps for some target practise and is unerringly accurate with his shot. You are killed instantly.

175

The King's rage is intense: even Gargrimm retreats to avoid being struck by his mighty axe! You manage to make it to the window, but it takes two attempts to pull back the wooden shutters. Gargrimm anticipates your move and flings himself at your legs, hauling you roughly to the ground. The King sees you illuminated in the early morning light, strides towards you and delivers his axe. You are cut almost in two...

176

You are relieved to be momentarily safe from the animals, but how are you going to escape? Both exits to the cave have Scarfells in them: an unarmed man to your right and two new arrivals in the tunnel entrance you came through. The man in the centre of the cavern (addressed as 'Gargrimm' by one of the newcomers) is surrounded by his salivating animals. This is indeed a sticky spot to find yourself!

Your magic seems to be your best (maybe only) hope so you close your eyes and try to call forth something of the feelings of power you have experienced before. But there is nothing. Fear begins to creep into your mind: is this your last stand?

Will you be bold and swoop for the exit barred by only one man? (Turn to **95**) Or shout down at the Scarfells, stalling them until you can summon your powers? (Turn to **51**)

177

The Vzler steps deftly away to avoid the charge, and the pair of you take the eagle-rider down in a pincer attack. Without pause for a rest, you follow the Vzler as he carries the fight to the remaining Scarfell in the air. The man throws his last spear waywardly and finds himself facing two determined Ariax in an aerial duel! He swings his axe at you and misses, giving the Vzler the opening to dismount him and send him plunging to the mountainside below.

The two of you glide down to land together, exhilarated with your quick victory. "A little more trust in me would be appreciated, Xanarel..." chides your mentor, but he is not angry. He explains that, far from fleeing, he was trying to draw the Scarfells into a channel where they could be ambushed! You apologise, but the Vzler merely chuckles to himself. He is certainly cool under pressure – you were both nearly killed! Turn to **196**.

178

The shouter's head pokes inquisitively out into the tunnel! You react first and your fist connects solidly with his puzzled face, sending him toppling backwards to the floor. The cry of the scribe echoes round the enclosed space as you flee the scene. Note down the codeword YELL. A little further on, the tunnel splits in two. *React on instinct.* Will you take the left hand branch (turn to **69**) or the right (turn to **191**)?

179

One of the men was lying awake the whole time. Your talons make only the faintest clattering sound on the bare rock, but he sits up and allows his eyes to adjust to the darkness of the cave. He picks out your movement and gives a shout which rouses several other sleepers. You make an instant decision to flee, but one of the waking Scarfells intercepts you and brings you crashing to the ground. Even dazed as they are by sleep, you cannot hope to battle through odds like this...

180

The Scarfells exclaim in unison and back away from the flames as they dramatically rear up and lick the ceiling. You cannot keep this up indefinitely; you can already feel the drain on your energy. It is time to press home the advantage. Note down the codeword POWER and erase the codeword ARMS (if you have it). Will you:

Try to flee the room?	Turn to **208**
Tell the King that if he doesn't let you go free you will destroy the entire mountain?	Turn to **153**
Attempt to refocus your powers on extinguishing the torches?	Turn to **117**
Attack Gargrimm, who stands nearest to you?	Turn to **139**
Or grab for his axe and try to fracture it as you did with your bonds?	Turn to **217**

181

The spear sinks into your body with a sickening squelch, piercing your heart. It is the last sensation you ever feel...

182

The guards are discussing their night-time vigil and the fact that whereas normally they have nothing to report, tonight they saw the Moogoll. You grimly recall your own terrible encounter with the beast. Then one of them says something about 'the portcullis' and this alerts you.

This eavesdropping does at least confirm that your guess was correct and it is a possible escape route. If you want to rush around the corner and burst through the guards to freedom, turn to **106**. To poke your head round the corner for a second to spy out the lie of the land first, turn to **171**.

183

You swipe his resistance aside in your fury and his axe drops to the floor with a clang of metal on rock. You now have space to act. Will you turn your attentions to the King? (Turn to **124**) Or will you attempt to call on your powers to extinguish the torches? (Turn to **117**)

184

You step back outside into the open air and call as loudly as you dare into the night sky. The Vzler eagerly swoops over to join you, sensing the excitement in your cry!

Together, you enter the chamber. The chill winds of Arian have not been able to permeate this deep and a thick layer of cobwebs and centuries of dust covers everything. The smell of decay hangs in the air. But it is the great rocky plinth in the centre of the cavern that immediately draws your attention. Despite the covering of grime, it is clearly an Ariax skeleton, and there is only one possibility: it is Nevsaron himself! Your mind reels in awe as you remember first reading about this legendary birdman, and now here you are in his presence. You stand respectfully in silence, the faint sound of the wind outside the only disturbance.

The Vzler shakes his head in wonder. "So it is true…and this discovery is all down to you, Xanarel!" he says, quietly. Turn to **211**.

185

You manage to overcome the urge to unleash your powers, remembering the devastation they caused last time. But the Scarfell scouts stand between you and escape. Burning anger wells up inside you for the loss of the Vzler and you let this fuel you as you make your bid for freedom. It is a brave attempt, but there are more Scarfells than you realised, and as you try to surge through them you are hauled to the icy floor of the cave. Axes fly and your life is ended here in Nevsaron's tomb…

186

You are relieved that the height of the cave gives you a chance of concealment. Roll the die. If you roll a 4 or more the Scarfells pass (turn to **131**). If you roll a 1, 2 or 3 however, you are spotted (turn to **174**).

187

You focus as well as you can in the circumstances. Roll the die, adding 2 to the roll if you have the codeword POWER, but subtracting 2 from the roll if you have the codeword ARMS. If the total is 4 or less, turn to **7**. If the total is 5 or more, turn to **132**.

188

It is another guard (as you guessed) who strides into the chamber. You smash your fist into his face in an attempt to take him out as quickly and quietly as possible. Roll the die. If you roll a 4 or less, turn to **102**. If you roll a 5 or more, turn to **43**.

189

Eager to prove that you are capable of pulling your weight in this battle, you bravely take the fight to the enemy. Roll the die. If you roll a 1 or 2, turn to **60**. If you roll a 3 or more, turn to **103**.

190

You grimace; your mind feels like it is being stretched to bursting point. Suddenly there is a terrific rumbling noise and the whole chamber begins to tremble. "Xanarel!" cries the Vzler anxiously, but you are already trying desperately to stop it before it gets out of control!

Blocks of stone and ice begin showering from the roof of the tunnel. You close your eyes and try to focus your mind. With a mighty effort you manage to regain control as one final burst of elemental energy leaves you, sending chunks of rock flying violently down the tunnel and out of the cave. You slump to the ground.

"Well..." begins the Vzler, but he cannot find the words. You look up into his concerned face and reassure him that whatever just happened inside you has passed.

"Time to go I think," says your mentor, pulling you to your feet. "If there *are* any night guards, that would certainly have alerted them." You pick your way carefully down the tunnel once more, but as you reach the entrance, a huge dark shape passes across the sky in a rush of wind. You step back, dismayed, as you see a mighty creature curl round in the air. It is shaped like a huge scaly snake, light blue-green in colour, with the head of a dragon and large, bat-like wings. Smoke curls from its nostrils and you tremble: you have seen one of these beasts once before in the mountains of Arian and barely escaped with your life: it is the most feared creature from Ariax legend, the Moogoll!

"Get back!" you cry, "Moogoll!" The Vzler shudders. A roar from outside tells you that you were seen. But what will you do? If you want to suggest retreating into the tomb, turn to **142**. If you want to try and speed past the Moogoll to freedom, turn to **53**. If you want to try and summon your powers and use them against it, turn to **119**.

191

You find that this tunnel becomes gradually narrower and narrower until it ends abruptly at a blank rock-face. It is a dead end. You will have to retrace your steps to the last junction and go left. If you have the codeword YELL, turn to **54**. If you do not have this codeword, turn to **69**.

192

You soon find yourself back at the crossroads. The left hand branch (as it is now) leads back to the arena. If you want to go straight across, turn to **152**. To make a right hand turn, turn to **74**.

193

You wrap both hands around the metal handle mounted on the wall and lean in to it with your entire weight. But it budges only marginally and emits a loud grating noise as it does. It must take several Scarfells working together to open these doors!

You can move it no further. If you now want to try using your powers on the door, turn to **20**. If you worry that the Scarfells may investigate the noise you can exit through the wider tunnel (turn to **59**) or the narrower one (turn to **74**)?

194

An ambitious plan, but one that will certainly pay dividends if you can pull it off! Roll the die, adding 2 to the roll if you have the codeword POWER, but subtracting 2 from the roll if you have the codeword ARMS. If the total is 4 or less, turn to **35**. If the total is 5 or more, turn to **180**.

195

You put everything into a shoulder charge and collide with great momentum into the Scarfell. But you lose your footing as you do this and crumple into a heap on top of him. The delay is enough for the slavering hounds to be upon you and they are able to do what they do best with fallen prey…

196

After a brief rest, the Vzler leads you back on your way. He insists that the brush with the Scarfells is put firmly out of mind, and turning back is not even mentioned. The sun has all but gone by the time you glide down to a rocky hollow on a mountainside overlooking Musk.

Now much closer, Musk is an ominous sight. It stands alone surrounded by icy plains, as if even the other mountains shun its presence. Your keen eyesight picks out a few Scarfells tending to yaks kept in pens around the mountain's base. They are preparing for nightfall. The main entrance faces you directly: a pair of colossal oaken doors. They stand ajar at the present, the only visible way in at ground level, but you have no intention of going in! You also see a number of lookout posts dotted about the mountain face; natural caves manned by Scarfell guards. They cannot see you in the darkness, and you are thankful.

"Detlaxe indicated that Nevsaron's tomb was 'high up' in the mountain," recalls the Vzler. "That is good. Come: now is the moment. Follow me."

You take a wide, sweeping arc through the sky, descending steeply to the snowy peak of Musk undetected. As you land, you see numerous caves. The Vzler suggests splitting up to cover double the ground and wishes you good luck before making his way carefully along a mountain path.

You turn your attention to your own search. You decide to ignore the smaller caves and look for one that befits such a dignitary as Nevsaron. Ten minutes later and you have found two possibilities: a cave whose entrance is covered with cobwebs (turn to **111**) or one supporting an impressive array of stalactites and stalagmites? (Turn to **44**)

197

You remember the secret passage you discovered earlier and know that you have no choice. You squeeze into it again and jog down the tunnel to the steps. This time you take them.

The Scarfells behind you will find the remains of Nevsaron and the Vzler but have no knowledge of your presence. But as you crouch in the shadows to wait for the sound of the Scarfells to go, you fall through a concealed hole in the ground, landing with a bump in a passageway below!

Annoyingly, there is no way back up again. There is not enough room to spread your wings and it is too high up to jump. The walls are climbable, but not near enough to the hole to be able to access it. In fact, unless you knew the hole was there, you don't think you would even be able to see it! You reason that this is how Nevsaron has remained undisturbed all these years.

Then it dawns on you. You are trapped inside Musk and need to find another way out! You have been in some tight spots in the recent months…but nothing to compare with *this*!

From the outside you remember seeing lookout posts dotted around the mountain. Of course there's also the front door! But both are sure to be guarded and you have no clue as to their direction! Best foot forward Xanarel, you think to yourself. The passageway stretches out in two directions and both look similarly uninviting! Will you take the way you happen to be currently facing (turn to **46**) or will you turn round and go the other way? (Turn to **150**)

198

Aggravatingly, nothing happens. The Scarfell runs towards you, axe raised. *React on instinct*. If you want to tackle him head on, turn to **18**. To flee back the way you came before he reaches you, turn to **32**.

199

The tunnel leads to a set of steps leading down. You are just debating whether to turn back or take them when far off in the distance you fancy that you hear the clanging of a bell being struck. This helps you to make up your mind!

The steps wind round as they descend, but are always wide enough for your taloned feet. At the bottom is a Y-shaped tunnel that runs off into the gloom in two directions. Both look equally unwelcoming. To go left, turn to **11**. To go right, turn to **107**.

200

You open your eyes just a fraction when you hear the torturer's footsteps recede into the distance. He is gone. Cautiously you get to your feet again and shake yourself to dry your feathers a bit. Then you make your way through the torture chamber and out of the other side. Turn to **207**.

201

As you walk across the rocky bridge, you feel a peculiar sensation in your feet. By now you know that this sort of thing is your newfound magic powers seeking an outlet! Then you hear a cry and glance over your shoulder to see two Scarfells emerging from the tunnel entrance behind you! But that feeling in your feet is spreading up your legs… If you want to attempt to unleash your powers and break the bridge, turn to **80**. If you don't trust your ability to control your powers just yet, you could either fly away down the other tunnel (turn to **28**) or turn and do battle with them as they run onto the bridge towards you? (Turn to **116**).

202

The two men cry out as you get free, but you have just seconds to act; the Scarfells are enraged and fearlessly search for you in the dark. Will you:

    Attack the King as he blunders towards you?   Turn to **22**
    Try to avoid them and head for the window?   Turn to **175**
    Or if you have the codeword SMOKE, you could
    try to use your powers as you did before?   Turn to **73**

203

Although this is the last thing you would ever normally think of doing, it is better than hanging around up here to be used as target practice for the spearmen!

You glide downwards and are immediately set upon by the Scarfells, who roughly take hold of you and pin you to the ground. They take anything you were carrying and toss it away. "Manacles!" cries Gargrimm, who appears to have authority over the others.

Your arms are twisted behind your back and a pair of iron cuffs clipped round them. Your feet are similarly bound. All the while, the Scarfells jeer and shout all manner of abuse at you, revelling in the fact that you can understand. You blank them out, determined to deny them the pleasure of a reaction. You are only relieved that they do not mention the Vzler. Clearly the news of his death has not reached these particular Scarfells, yet.

You are set on your feet and led away by Gargrimm. Two guards follow behind you, prodding you painfully in the back with their spears when you lag behind (and occasionally when you don't). You are taken via a series of labyrinthine tunnels further up and up through Musk until you reach a flight of steps. The guards seem reluctant to continue.

"Up there!" orders Gargrimm, with a hint of sadistic pleasure in his voice. He puts a hand on your shoulder and shoves you forwards. You mount the steps and pass under a stone arch into a large room, luxuriously decorated (for Musk). Furs hang from the walls in between torches and a variety of broken weapons and other war trophies which attest to many triumphs in battle.

On a raised platform of rock on the far side of the room is a magnificent throne of oak and stone. Sitting upon it, dressed in a studded leather tunic, heavy hobnailed boots and a wolf-pelt cloak is a giant of a man, with gold rings on every finger and a necklace of animal teeth. His huge black beard is flecked with white, as is his hair and eyebrows. As he rises and descends the steps towards you, you look upon his cruel face and feel that this man could tear down walls of rock with his bare hands if he so wished. This is the King of the Scarfells.

"What is the meaning of this?" he bellows at Gargrimm, who clearly fears his master but tries not to show it.

"Your majesty! I have captured this intruder in the animal quarters. I…"

But the King interrupts, angrily. "Why wasn't it killed immediately? You'll suffer for this indiscretion!"

Gargrimm takes a step back and attempts to placate the tyrant by explaining about your ability to understand and talk their language. But your attention has been taken by a pair of heavy wooden shutters, barred from the inside, which you can tell from the faint breeze leads to the open air!

Have the Scarfells led you to your best chance of escape? Just the small matter of two sets of manacles and two of the most powerful Scarfells barring your way! The King takes a step in your direction and begins to bark questions at you about your ability, why you are here and how you got in. If you have the codeword FRACTURE, turn to **147**. If you do not have this codeword, turn to **15**.

204

You propel yourself into the air to intercept your opponent. Roll the die. If you roll a 3 or less, turn to **60**. If you roll a 4 or more, turn to **36**.

205

Your heart leaps into your mouth as you hear a voice behind you calling out in alarm. But you have already gone. Note down the codeword YELL. A little further on, the tunnel splits in two. *React on instinct*. Will you take the left hand branch (turn to **69**) or the right (turn to **191**)?

206

Although still wary about the power running through you, you hold your hands out above the surface of the water and feel the magical energy flow into them. To your amazement, the surface of the water slowly begins to churn; then a watery fist begins to rise upwards as you will it!

You are concentrating hard – but then you hear a noise from somewhere behind you. *React on instinct*. If you want to ignore the sound and stay in the moment, turn to **33**. To hide, turn to **164**. To flee the kitchen through the other exit to the one you came in through, turn to **55**.

207

The tunnel merges with another that leads back into the icy depths behind you, but you are more interested by a set of steps ahead of you that lead up to a warmer part of Musk. You follow the new tunnel undisturbed and it begins to swing round to the right. Soon after this, at a point where a side passage leads off to the left, you make a strange discovery: a sharpened wooden stick protrudes from a cleft in the floor to about waist height and impaled atop the stick is a dead rat. This gruesome marker seems to belong to the side passage. If you wish to investigate this way, turn to **71**. To ignore it and follow the main route, turn to **115**.

208

You are on the right side of the room to escape this way. But the King anticipates your move and flings a spear from the wall towards you. Roll the die, adding 1 to the roll if you have the codeword POWER. If you roll a 2 or less, turn to **181**. If you roll a 3 or more, turn to **58**.

209

The Scarfell makes no attempt to defend himself and your blow fells him easily. He lies still and your first thought is that he is unconscious. But you notice with surprise that he is still muttering under his breath and is merely dazed. Then he begins snoring softly!! Thankful that your race does not need intoxicating liquid to enjoy themselves, you head for the opening on the other side of the tavern. Turn to **125**.

210

The spear punctures your left wing and you screech in pain. It is not life threatening, but is certainly debilitating. You must subtract 1 from the next two die rolls you make in this adventure. You struggle to ignore the pain: the danger is not over yet! If you want to grapple with the nearest eagle-rider, turn to **23**. If you want to take cover in case more spears are thrown, turn to **141**.

211

The Vzler approaches the corpse and begins to examine it. "Yes…a mighty Ariax indeed!" he observes. "And undefiled. It is certain that the Scarfells have not been here – in fact *no-one* has been here for centuries, I would say…but what is this?"

The Vzler leans over the corpse, then suddenly and unexpectedly stretches out an arm and reaches right into the midriff of the skeleton! When he withdraws his hand, you notice that he is holding a flawless crystal about the size of an eyeball.

You both marvel at the wondrous artefact. As you gaze into it, you can see colour, ever changing. At first it appears a deep blue-green, but that then becomes a vibrant orangey-red. Then it changes to deep hues of brown and green before being replaced by a lighter blue-white. The colours swirl and merge into each other seamlessly. Even to an Ariax, it is obvious that this crystal is magic.

"Xanarel," says the Vzler, breaking the silence. "I believe that this is what gave Nevsaron his 'elemental powers'! I think he discovered this crystal – though I've no idea from *where* – and he must have *swallowed* it!"

The Vzler's idea is logical. No-one could ever guess Nevsaron's secret. And there this precious crystal has lain, unblemished for centuries, as the flesh decomposed around it!

"I think," states your mentor, solemnly, "that it should be *you*, Xanarel; you who discovered this lost secret, you who are the future of our beleaguered tribe (for I am its past), *you* who should inherit Nevsaron's legacy."

"You mean for me to swallow this crystal?" you repeat, awestruck and a little apprehensive.

The Vzler nods. "If you so wish." He smiles encouragingly.

You take a deep breath. If you want to swallow the crystal, turn to **104**. If you decline and offer it to the Vzler instead, turn to **76**.

212

The boy suddenly begins wailing loudly and bursts into tears! Cursing inwardly, you drop him to the floor and turn tail, running hard out of the kitchen before you are discovered. Turn to **34**.

213

Determined to show this Scarfell exactly what Ariax are made of, you lash out twice, drawing blood with each swipe. The torturer cries out gruffly in pain but pulls you out of the water and flings you against the wall as if you were light as a feather. Your head hits a spur of rock and, head swimming, you look up to see the torturer bearing down on you with a massive two-handed axe. Unusually for a torturer, your death is made swift...

214

You focus as well as you can in the circumstances. Roll the die, adding 2 to the roll if you have the codeword POWER. If the total is 2 or less, turn to **7**. If the total is 3 or more, turn to **132**.

215

The force of the blast knocks you from your feet and you feel the flames washing over you. In the few stunned seconds that follow you realise that you are not dead; In fact, you're pretty sure that you aren't even hurt! Was it an illusion?

You turn to the Vzler, but the sight that greets your eyes sickens you to the core. Next to you lies a charred skeleton, the odd blackened feather still smoking. The Vzler is dead.

The power of the elemental crystal has made you impervious to fire. But there is no relief; only grief and anger that it should be you who is spared and not that of your mentor...your *friend*: the Vzler.

The terrifying roar of the Moogoll outside stirs you back into action. You also hear the screech of more than one eagle, and even more surprising, Scarfell voices shouting to each other! A group of eagle-riders is coming in to land at the cave mouth, somehow untroubled by the Moogoll!

There is no time to figure out this new puzzle: you need to act quickly! The Scarfells must have come to investigate what the great serpent had seen! If you have the codeword STONE, turn to **197**. If you do not have this codeword, will you hide from (turn to **155**) or ambush (turn to **112**) the incoming Scarfells?

216

You are no herb expert, yet as soon as you handle each bundle you intuitively know its exact properties: your magic at work again! As you sift through the collection you come to realise that the best of these are remedies for minor ailments; many more are totally useless.

If you have the codeword YELL, turn to **10**. Otherwise roll the die: if you roll a 1 note down the codeword YELL. You can now try the door (turn to **90**) or continue down the main passage (turn to **120**).

217

You can still feel the residual power in your arms and it is becoming increasingly easy to summon your powers every time you use them. The metal axe-head breaks apart in your grasp, but for a second your defences are down. Gargrimm delivers a punch to your ribs which winds you and as you stagger sideways gasping for breath, the King grabs a hunting spear from the wall. He drives it two-handed into your midriff with a sickening crunch. You cry out in agony and fall mortally wounded to the floor. Luckily he does not take long to finish you off…

218

You cross the open area in the middle of the cave, but hear the sound of footsteps approaching from in front of you as you near the other exit! *React on instinct*. Will you hide in the shadows? (Turn to **140**) Or prepare to ambush the newcomer as soon as he comes into view? (Turn to **188**)

219

Quick as a flash, you dart towards the boy and take hold of the collar of his tunic as he tries to scamper away. You decide to try to get directions out of him as well as 'persuade' him not to alert his far more dangerous relatives! What do you feel would be the most effective angle to take? Will you:

Play on your appearance and
claim to be a monster? Turn to **172**
Threaten him with death if he will not help you? Turn to **47**
Or say that you will tell on him for
stealing if he doesn't help? Turn to **70**

220

You find amazing speed in your wings: is it your imagination after so long underground, or your elemental powers at work again? Either way, the snow whips by beneath you at a startling rate. It is within the hour that the welcome sight of the Tower of Egratar appears before you once more. Home at last.

But this is not a joyous homecoming. How are you going to explain your latest disappearance and the death of the Vzler? And what about your magic powers? You decide that you must talk to the Talotrix, Astraphet.

Seeing the expression on your face, Astraphet grants you a personal audience. You have never spoken one-to-one with your leader before and you find yourself scrutinised by his wise and powerful eyes. Astraphet has a great burden on his shoulders following the recent events, and you are about to increase it!

"I bring tidings of woe," you begin, respectfully. "The Vzler is dead."

Astraphet does not react at first. He takes a deep breath and closes his eyes. Finally he speaks. "Tell me all," he says.

You briefly recount your trip to Iro a few weeks ago and the reason for it. If Astraphet is surprised by this news he hides it well. You tell him of the scrolls you found and of your decision to share its revelations with the Vzler. You explain how the Vzler determined that the pair of you would set out in secret to find Nevsaron's tomb. At this Astraphet nods. Then he frowns. "So the Scarfells killed him?"

"No…it was…a Moogoll." You lower your voice. The creature is known and feared throughout Arian.

"A Moogoll…" murmurs the Talotrix to himself. "I do not doubt that you speak the truth. You Xanarel have again faced deadly peril and come through it, where this time even the Vzler did not. I read in your face that you feel his loss almost as I, his friend of many years. Now more than ever we need young Ariax like you who can help steer the future of our decimated race. And I am beginning to feel as the Vzler did, that you may yet have a *significant* future ahead of you, young Xanarel…"

You allow yourself a humble smile. You are relieved that you did not have to disclose your newfound magic powers; you will work on them over the coming months in secret and reveal them when the time is right. Now, you feel only waves of exhaustion washing over you; sleep is your foremost desire.

But your tribe is soon to face a threat that will eclipse even the recent terrible events, chronicled in book 6 of The Saga of the Ariax:

EGRATAR FALLS

THE SAGA OF THE ARIAX: 6
EGRATAR FALLS

New rules for book 6 and 7

Following your discovery of some ancient Ariax scrolls, you and the Vzler journeyed to the Scarfell city of Musk in search of the forgotten tomb of a former Talotrix called Nevsaron. You found it, and gained mysterious magic powers when you ate an elemental crystal. Tragically the Vzler was then killed during your escape.

A month has passed since your return from Musk. During this time you have spent many hours alone in the mountains, experimenting with your magic, without telling even your closest friend Rical what you were doing. You have learnt much, but know that you still have more to discover. On first swallowing the crystal, you could barely control the energy coursing through you. It seemed to come and go at random. You eventually established that the magic was being drawn from the natural elements (such as fire or wood) that you were in physical contact with or near to, and you could then manipulate these elements, though not create them from nothing. After much dedicated practise, you are now able to summon or contain your power at will, given time to concentrate.

There is an amazing amount you can now do. You can run and fly much faster than before. Even a blazing inferno cannot harm you and you can breathe underwater as easily as in the air. You can crack or crumble stone, rock, wood and metal, channelling the power through your hands or feet. You can mentally command fire, smoke, water and the wind as you wish (on a moderate scale) and have just begun experimenting on plant life as well. You can identify the properties of herbs and plants just by touching them. Once or twice you have been able to hear the voices of people out of normal earshot, brought to you on a magical airstream. You have found this difficult to practise and it is one of your more wayward abilities.

When you wish to use your magic during the adventure, you will usually be told you need to roll the die to see whether you can summon the required power in time. The text will indicate what you need to roll to succeed, as from experience you will have a rough idea of the difficulty level. Use this information to judge whether it is wise to attempt to use a given power in the circumstances. Failure could leave you exposed in a potentially dangerous situation! Also be wary: you have found that overuse of your magic can leave you feeling drained and weak! Note that you *can* use a feat to pass a magic roll.

Magic points

To aid you with your magic, you start book 6 with 6 magic points. Whenever you have to make a magic roll, you may first choose to expend 1 or more magic points: each magic point adds one to the die roll you are about to make. You must decide how many points to spend *before* you make the roll, and you lose the magic points whether or not they affect the outcome of the roll. Magic points unused at the end of book 6 cannot be carried over to book 7, though you start that adventure afresh with 6 magic points.

Recent events

The sun floods Arian with its dawn rays. As usual, you were up before daybreak, taking the opportunity to grab a few peaceful hours alone in the mountains to work on your magic before your many tasks of the day begin.

You are still a distance away from your home when you first realise that something is wrong. You listen carefully and unbelievably you hear the battle-screeches of dozens of Ariax…and the familiar harsh cries of Scarfells!

You fly with all speed, bewildered by the almost implausible news your ears bring to you. You land and look up the hundred metres or so from where you stand to the top of the Tower of Egratar. There you can see giant eagles, tamed steeds of the Scarfells, wheeling and circling in the bright sunlight! You have seen the Scarfells riding these huge birds before, but never have they dared to attack your home!

Then you see why they dare. Drifting menacingly out of the glare, you see a vision of nightmares: a massive serpent-like creature, with the head of a dragon and large, bat-like wings. It is a Moogoll! You have seen a beast like this twice before (if not the same one), the last time near Musk. Somehow the Scarfells have found a way to control this terrifying monster!

Claws clatter on rock high above you as the Ariax muster for battle. Many birdmen are already airborne, launching themselves from their caves and bravely battling the Scarfells in the sky to defend their home.

As you look on, you see a *second* Moogoll wrapping itself around the Tower of Egratar, constricting and breaking it apart! Massive blocks of stone tumble through the air as the entire top half of the tower is toppled before your very eyes! Then the other Moogoll begins to bathe the mountainside with its flaming breath! It is a scene of utter chaos. This is a carefully planned and devastating attack, designed to obliterate your entire race!

Is this the end of the Ariax?

Now turn to **221** to begin…

221

Your heart is pounding furiously in your chest. Dozens of Scarfells armed with hunting spears sweep through the scattered birdmen, controlling their eagle steeds with considerable skill. As the Moogolls pour their deadly fire into cave mouths, the Scarfells follow up, landing at the cave entrances and charging in to finish off the survivors on foot. The sky is littered with chunks of rock and the falling bodies of both Ariax and Scarfell; no quarter is being asked or given!

Never before has a situation felt so desperate or so hopeless. But with your magic, surely there is something you can do? You think quickly. If he still lives, Astraphet is most likely to be found in the remains of the Tower of Egratar, where the fighting seems fiercest. Should you try to rally round your leader? On the other hand, if you join the aerial battle, you could better assess the overall situation and perhaps help to tip the balance. Maybe this would be more useful? Of course your instincts tell you to seek out your great friend Rical (still on the long road to recovery from Crackbeak) in the caves of healing and stand side by side with him once more. Not an easy decision! Will you:

Fly to the Tower of Egratar?	Turn to **251**
Try to find Rical?	Turn to **271**
Or join the dogfight in the skies around Arian?	Turn to **347**

222

A first chance to put all those long hours of practice into action – and you fail to summon your powers just when you need them! You are frowning in frustration and only just avoid an eagle swooping in behind you! Its claws slash your back, drawing blood, and you tumble to the floor. Adrenalin will keep you going, but the pain will hinder your actions. For the rest of this adventure, you must subtract 1 from any die rolls you make (unless they relate to the actions of a *group* of Ariax and not you individually: to indicate this the word group will appear in the same sentence as 'roll the die' or you will be asked to roll the die more than once).

As you pick yourself up from the rubble-strewn floor, you hear a horrific screech from behind you. Turning, you see the flailing form of Astraphet falling forwards with an axe buried in his back; a cowardly blow struck from behind! Note down the codeword TOR.

A wave of despair passes over the open beaked witnesses. One plucky youth recovers quickly and deals a savage blow to the murderer. This shakes you into action, and you instinctively find yourself impelled to take the lead. *React on instinct*. Will you cry for the remaining Ariax to:

Follow you and flee down the stairs?	Turn to **333**
Fly away from the scene?	Turn to **407**
Or stand and fight, defending Astraphet's body?	Turn to **375**

223

The power begins to build in your legs, coursing downwards into the rock below but it is happening too slowly: unless you act, you will be struck down! Instinctively you try to topple the Scarfells from the ledge, avoiding their murderous axes as you do. Roll the die. If you roll a 3 or less, turn to **266**. If you roll a 4 or more, turn to **309**.

224

You manage to put the peril of your situation temporarily to the back of your mind and concentrate on Rical's voice. At first, nothing. Then you pick up your friend's familiar tones, talking to his companions and unaware you are listening. In the moments that you dare remain motionless, you learn that the Ariax are barricaded in, but a party of Scarfells is between you and them bearing flaming torches to light their way in the darkness.

Your followers are impatient and there is no time to explain. Will you rush to find your friend (turn to **427**) or go cautiously (turn to **259**)?

225

You do not find the Scarfells you were searching for: they find you! You are spotted by an archer in a concealed position on the mountain below and the first you know of him is when an arrow embeds itself deep into your back! The pain causes you to black out, and amazingly a second arrow finds its mark before your body hits the ground...

226

You glide in and snatch the bundle from the horror-struck Scarfell. As you climb into the sky, the sackcloth falls away and a high-pitched squeal emanates from below you! You are amazed to find that you are holding a steel cage containing a hideous little creature! It resembles a shrunken, bony human, but has a domed head, elongated limbs and bottle-green skin. It leaps deftly to its feet (despite being in transit) and stares up at you hopefully with deep green eyes. It is a Jarip!

You encountered one of these mischievous, magical creatures once before in the wizard Vashta's house in Iro. But can this thing really be controlling the giant Moogolls? If you have the codeword GROUP, turn to **298**. If you do not have this codeword, turn to **363**.

227

You stretch open your mind and attempt to soak up the searing Moogoll fire washing over you. The feeling is exhilarating; never before have you experienced so much power at once! As the flames die out, you have a second to glimpse the astounded faces of your enemies and the bewilderment of your followers before you pour out the fire, channelling it through your arms with an explosion of power directly towards a cluster of Scarfells swooping in from your right. They are utterly incinerated in mid-air to the cheers of the Ariax who witness the display. If you have the codeword OPEN, turn to **290**. If you do not have this codeword, turn to **356**.

228

The Jarip squeals once more and wriggles like anything as you catch hold of his spindly arm. He settles down once he realises that he cannot escape your grip. "We're going in!" you cry.

You part the smoke with your magic, remembering from your previous visit that the Orphus Latix grows in a clearing near the centre of the forest. You deviously plot to find a similar looking plant somewhere else and fool the Jarip into taking it. You doubt that he will be able to distinguish the truth as he can only have a rough description from Vashta's memory to go by. A cunning ruse!

"Somewhere about here, I think," you say with authority, and glide down into the chaos that is the Forest of Arcendak. Visibility is incredibly limited, and you haven't the strength to keep clearing the smoke for long. Panicked forest animals are fleeing for their lives about your feet, and although it cannot harm you, the roaring sound of the fire is deafening. Every so often a flaming branch breaks off and comes crashing down nearby. Then, as you stumble uphill into a clearing, a different roaring sound is heard, and you turn in surprise to witness a fully grown frost bear, coat aflame, pounding straight towards you! *React on instinct*. Will you scramble quickly into the air (turn to **355**)? Or will you use your magic to drive a cloud of smoke in front of the animal to ward it off (needing to roll a 2 or more to succeed) or a curtain of flame for a similar effect (needing to roll a 3 or more)?

If you successfully divert the smoke, turn to **419**. If you redirect the fire, turn to **291**. If you fail either magic roll, turn to **373**.

229

You feel a sudden brutal impact from behind and are smashed to the ground, temporarily winded! At that moment a wooden spear flies over your head and breaks in two on the rock above you!

You glance up and see a wounded but still armed Scarfell clambering down the mountainside. Gravelax (for it was he who knocked you out of the path of the spear) picks himself up, runs forwards and pulls the man from the cliff, plenty of strength still remaining. The Scarfell is hurled past you, bouncing off the mountainside like a rag doll.

"Sorry," says Gravelax, as the rest of your gathering follows him up onto the summit. But there is no need to apologise; it is plain that the veteran Ariax has just saved your life! Gravelax receives the congratulations of Rical and the others, while you take a moment to recover your composure. But there is no time for rest!

You survey the scene. Most of the Scarfells that still can are now fleeing into the distance and the Moogolls have gone altogether. Here and there, small bands of Ariax are finishing off the dismounted Scarfells who are still lurking about dangerously.

You glide round the mountain to the side facing the remains of the tower. There you come across a group of three birdmen. "It's Scancaro!" calls one of your followers.

The birdman hailed as Scancaro is glad to see you. He is the only one of the three who is not critically wounded. His injured comrades clearly cannot be moved and he asks for help to defend them until the final Scarfell has gone.

If you want to leave some of your birdmen with Scancaro, decide how many (though you decide to keep Gravelax and Rical with you at least) and turn to **263**. If you want to reassure him that the Scarfells are on the run and leave with your group intact, turn to **313**.

230

Your throw is deadly; you are amazed by the added range and accuracy your powers give you. The Scarfell target is skewered and thrown from his steed, which banks away sharply.

The two Ariax are a few years older than you but recognise you and look up to you as some sort of leader. The nearest one hands you one of the other spears (which you can note down if you wish to take) while the other asks what to do next. Keep a careful track of the number of Ariax followers you have, starting with these two. Will you lead them:

To the summit of the Tower of Egratar in search of Astraphet?	Turn to **341**
To the cave of your friend Rical?	Turn to **389**
Into the aerial battle still raging above you?	Turn to **286**
Or towards a scorched and blackened cave entrance close by to look for survivors?	Turn to **349**

231

You hastily split your force to do the best you can. As you reach the brink, you see more Scarfell eagle-riders are indeed swooping in. Will you throw a spear at them (if you have one)? (Turn to **257**) Call for the Ariax to fall back and regroup? (Turn to **285**) Or you could try to crumble the roof and block the Scarfell's entrance using your magic (needing a 3 or more to succeed). If you manage this, turn to **425**. If you try but fail the roll, turn to **359**.

232

You hurry along but the feeling of invasion and defilement lingers all around. You pass through an undamaged cave which leads out into a tunnel sloping upwards to the left (turn to **302**) or downwards to the right (turn to **402**)?

233

You instruct the others to hold this position as you brave the aerial dangers and fly up to the smoking ruin which once dominated the skyline. At the summit, you overlook a scene of devastation. The bodies of at least twenty Ariax warriors are strewn amidst the rubble along with a similar number of Scarfells: the defenders did not give their lives cheaply.

Although there is no longer any fighting in this position, it is still not a safe place to linger. You stumble through the wreckage and sadly discover what you had feared: the unmistakable form of Astraphet lying face down with a Scarfell axe still lodged deep in his back. Your leader is dead, struck down by a cowardly blow from behind.

You slash out at a Scarfell survivor who attempts to ambush you, killing him instantly in your fury. With a heavy heart you return to your growing warband and break the bad news. There is open dismay at first, but you rally them with a rousing promise of victory and revenge. Turn to **247**.

234

Your chosen few are given their task and land a tantalising distance from the enemy. But instead of charging forwards as you hoped, the archers below hurriedly prepare their bows for firing. Can the Ariax judge the range of the weapons? Roll the die and compare the result to the number of Ariax in the group you sent out. If you roll equal to or under the number of Ariax, turn to **281**. If the number you roll is higher than the number of birdmen by 1 or 2, turn to **344**. If the number you roll is higher than the number of birdmen by 3 or more, turn to **418**.

235

Your efforts come to nothing, leaving you looking rather indecisive to the onlookers. However it does serve as the distraction needed to tip the balance in favour of the Ariax; they leap the barricade in a bold counter attack and after a brief scuffle the Scarfells are defeated and slain.

Rical is out of breath and clearly not fit to fight, but nevertheless he stumbles across to thank you for your help. Sadly two of the other Ariax were killed in the melee. You tell Rical to seek refuge in the caves deeper in the mountain, and that you intend to turn the tide of this battle...somehow! The other surviving Ariax elects to come with you; despite being older than you are, your reputation goes before you. Keep a careful track of the number of Ariax followers you have, starting with this one. You promise Rical you will see him later and head back into the fray. Turn to **386**.

236

From somewhere deep inside you call forth hidden energies and even you are surprised by the degree of your success! Many of the fires suddenly billow back into life in dramatic fashion and you are actually able to command some of them to surge towards the Scarfells, who fall back in fear. Some quick-witted Ariax deduce what you have done, incredible as it seems, and press home the attack.

You have granted the defenders new heart and gained them the momentary advantage. Note down the codeword BURN and turn to **415**.

237

You lead your force directly into a group of Scarfells to the left hand side of the room, scattering them in several directions. Three Scarfells have been killed but sadly so too have two birdmen (deduct them from your number of followers). You look around at the impact you have made. Turn to **415**.

238

You soon find yourself in a large cavern, deep inside the mountain. By the huge variety of herbs, potions and other medical paraphernalia it is clear that this is one of Arguttax's chambers. Work lies abandoned as Arguttax's team must have rushed out to fight. This is no time to go ransacking the workshop of a senior birdman but you see a freshly prepared poultice of healing herbs so if you have suffered an injury (which causes you to have to subtract 1 from die rolls) you may use the poultice and no longer suffer that penalty.

Another exit offers a short cut out into the open air once more. Turn to **421**.

239

You swoop into the valley and it doesn't take long to affirm that there is no suspicious activity here. But every second you waste will cost further Ariax lives. Will you continue your search alone (turn to **393**) or return to the rendezvous point as arranged and see if anyone else has had any success (turn to **351**)?

240

You land on a section of rock far above your target, close your eyes and will the familiar energy of your magic through your feet with as much power as you can muster. Roll the die. If the total is 1 (or less), turn to **352**. If you get a 2, 3 or 4, turn to **262**. If your score is 5 or 6, turn to **311**.

241

The Jarip whines in frustration at your decision, then slumps down grumpily in his cage. "Call off the Moogolls!" you bark, and although you can see no particular movement from your captive, the giant dragon-snakes do slowly begin to twist away from the mountains. Note down the codeword RAZE and turn to **269**.

242

Once again your magic saves your life. You burrow your talons into the ground and feel the energy flowing through your hands and feet. Suddenly there is a burst of power surging through the soil, and earth, roots and stones shower upwards. The little creatures shriek and howl as they are thrown into the air and the remainder of the following pack divert their course away from you. Soon they are gone, leaving you to pick up your dirty and battered body from the mud. Amusingly, you have created an Ariax shape depression in the earth where you lay!

You continue to battle through the flame heading in the direction of the centre of the forest but you are unable to tell whether this is the same part of Arcendak that you visited before. You come across a mighty rock face with a lip at the top. The path you are on continues with the cliff to its right. This place seems strangely familiar; your head is swimming and you cannot be certain but you feel sure you are near the Orphus Latix glade. You struggle to remember which way it is. If you want to fly up to the top of the cliff, turn to **256**. If you want to stay on the path, turn to **299**.

243

Somehow the man manages to turn his head out of the way and you deal him only a glancing blow. He hangs on grimly and carries you down the cliff with him locked in a death embrace. Your head strikes a rocky outcrop on the way down, and you know no more.

244

You swoop down to land at the summit, where you overlook a scene of devastation. The bodies of at least twenty Ariax warriors are strewn amidst the rubble, along with a similar number of Scarfells: the defenders did not give their lives away cheaply.

There is no longer any fighting in this position, but it is still not a safe place to linger. You stumble through the wreckage, and sadly discover what you had feared: the unmistakable form of Astraphet lying face down with a Scarfell axe still lodged deep in his back. Your leader is dead, struck down by a cowardly blow from behind. Note down the codeword TOR.

If you want to check for survivors, turn to **396**. To descend the steps to the lower level (they are just about passable), turn to **314**. To leave this carnage behind you and take to the skies once more, turn to **421**.

245

Looking around, the battle of Egratar has swung in your favour and your efforts have played no small part in tipping the balance! You watch two weary but still very determined Ariax finish off the final Scarfell. A temporary calm fills the room, but the noise of combat from outside serves as a reminder of your peril.

You are reunited with any Ariax you brought with you and your ranks are swelled with four new additions, all keen to follow you in the fight (note down that these four Ariax are with you). One tall, burly old birdman (who reminds you a little of the Vzler in stature) introduces himself as Gravelax, a veteran warrior who tells you he has admired your recent daring and courage. Note down the codeword GRAVELAX.

The roof in here is unstable and could collapse so you decide to get outside as quickly as possible. If you have both the codewords TIME and TOR, turn to **247**. If you have the codeword TIME but not the codeword TOR, turn to **360**. If you have neither codeword, will you lead your group:

To the cave of your friend Rical?	Turn to **389**
Into the aerial battle still raging outside?	Turn to **286**
Or towards a scorched and blackened cave entrance below to look for survivors?	Turn to **349**

246

You fail in your attempt; the torches flicker but do not go out. The Scarfells decide on your group as the more immediate threat and turn towards you with axes raised. One of your followers is killed as battle is joined (subtract one from your number).

You kick out at a charging opponent and knock the wind out of him. This gives you the seconds needed to act and you redouble your efforts with the fire; it would give you a much needed advantage! Roll the die again. If you roll a 3 or more this time, turn to **350**. If you fail for a second time, one more birdman is slain, but at last you manage it (turn to **350**).

247

"We have to find out how the Scarfells are controlling these accursed Moogolls," you say, to common agreement. "They must have some sort of magic at work, hidden nearby."

"Then let's find it and destroy it!" cries a young birdman impetuously, but he is right.

You lead your followers to a safe place removed from the battle. "I hate to deplete our forces further," you say, "but apart from a full scale retreat, which could turn into a massacre, this is our only hope! Split up and search the surrounding region. *Be careful!* Report back here before long."

Eagerly you set off alone, newly focused and determined. The others peel away and glide low across the mountain faces. You dive more or less straight ahead at first, keeping near to the ground, out of sight of the eagle-riders who are not far off. You are following a low valley, whose untouched snowy beauty betrays no invader. You notice a channel off to the left, cutting between two very close outcrops of rock. To investigate this way, turn to **317**. To continue across the valley and in to the next, turn to **288**.

248

Despite the danger of this enterprise, the Ariax with you are quickly becoming battle-hardened and nod at your plan. They pair up swiftly and take to the skies, taking the long route round so as to come at the enemy without being seen. Then the crash-dive begins! Roll the die separately for each *pair* of Ariax you have in your group (including yourself in a pair). Every 2 or more you roll is one Scarfell plucked from the ground. If there are an odd number of you, roll once more for the spare birdman, needing a 4 or more this time.

If your Ariax succeed in grabbing 3 or more Scarfells, turn to **345**. If they get 2, turn to **414**. If they only grab 1, or none at all, turn to **297**.

249

The Scarfells wheel their steeds round to face you as you lead the charge! Roll the die. If you roll a 2 or less, turn to **320**. If you roll a 3 or more, turn to **380**.

250

The spear sinks into your body with a sickening squelch, piercing your heart. It is the last sensation you ever feel...

251

As you near the tower, you see that only the bottom two floors remain. It is hard to comprehend that this glorious and ancient structure is now in ruins! Hand-to-hand fighting is being fought fiercely on both levels. Will you join the fray on the exposed top level (turn to **348**) or surge in through the broken walls of the lower level (turn to **314**)?

252

You react immediately, hoping to take the burly Scarfells by surprise. Roll the die, adding 2 to the roll if you are carrying a Scarfell spear. If the total is 4 or less, turn to **315**. If you get a 5 or more, turn to **376**.

253

Your scout is soon a diminishing speck in the distance, swooping up to the once proud Tower of Egratar. In horror, you suddenly notice one of the serpentine Moogolls twisting round the mountainside below him and spewing forth its burning flame! The unfortunate birdman is roasted in mid-air as you watch helplessly! Deduct one Ariax from your group.

There is a sombre silence. But there is no time for mourning now. Will you attempt the mission yourself? (Turn to **233**) Or all go together? (Turn to **360**)

254

You lead the raiding party to a high cleft in the mountain, out of sight of the target below. Note down the codeword GROUP.

Unfortunately, there is no obvious answer to the question of *how* these men are controlling the Moogolls, but by now you are sure that they are. You had secretly hoped to see a Scarfell with some sort of magic staff or jewel brandished in the serpents' direction which you could swoop down and snatch!

"What's the plan?" whispers someone behind you. After a hasty discussion you have narrowed down the options, but the choice it seems is yours. You could plan a direct attack (turn to **304**), or try to split the Scarfells by sending some of your force to distract them (turn to **338**)? Alternatively you could use your magic, either to land before them and crack the ice on which they stand or land above them and splinter the mountain face, raining devastation from the sky. Both would require your full power and the effect would be difficult to predict. If you want to try to crack the ice, turn to **331**. To fracture the mountainside, turn to **240**.

255

You nearly succeed. But one of the archers has recovered amazingly quickly, notched an arrow and fired as you are distracted by your task. You are struck from very close range and killed instantly.

256

You swoop upwards, recalling the memories of last time when you had Vashta and Erim for company. You land on the cliff top and find yourself in another dark, tunnel-like path leading away. You blunder exhaustedly along in the gloom hoping for some good fortune. Then at last you come to a clearing you well remember. On the summit of a small flattened mountain you find the glade where Orphus Latix grows!

The crop is burning! In alarm you drop to your knees, desperately trying to salvage as much as you can. Already at least two thirds of the plants have been destroyed! Frustration and despair begins to creep in as you remember the Vzler telling you at the Fygrinnd that the life-prolonging plant will *only* grow in the Forest of Arcendak!

You collect as much Orphus Latix as you can, but there is nothing you can do to prevent the flames claiming the rest. The only consolation is that at least you now know that once and for all the secret is safe from Vashta's hands…Turn to **430**.

257

Your throw is as accurate as before and the Scarfell falls backwards over the precipice. But this is one enemy out of dozens, and you have lost your spear. You may not use it again if you see the option (unless you had two of course!)

If you have the codeword TIME, turn to **327**. If you do not have this codeword, turn to **358**.

258

Unbeknown to you, up ahead lies a Scarfell ambush! But one of the Scarfells proves too eager for blood and gives away their position a fraction early. His axe strike whistles across your face, mere inches from your beak! You retaliate immediately, lashing out and sending him reeling back in pain. A second opponent emerges from the shadows and battle is joined. The skirmish is short and decisive; both men are quickly dispatched.

After a brief rest to catch your breath, you continue down the tunnel. It leads to living quarters for some of the apprentice craftsbirds. But there is no-one about and on finding a short cut back outside, you elect to go and see how the battle is going. Turn to **421**.

259

You strain your ears for any sign of your friend as you creep forwards. Roll the die, subtracting 2 if you have the codeword CRY. If you roll a 1 (or less), turn to **336**. If you roll a 2, turn to **303**. If you roll a 3 or more, turn to **403**.

260

You let savage fury fuel your assault as you lash out at your foes. How will your arrival affect the situation?

Roll the die once separately for each Ariax with you (if you have any). Do not add the numbers together. If you roll any 6s, turn to **328**. If the highest number you roll is a 5, turn to **295**. If you do not roll anything higher than 4, or are alone, turn to **237**.

261

You shake your head in frustration as any sign of your foes continues to elude you. If you give it up and hope someone else has had more luck, turn to **398**. To continue your search, roll the die again. If you roll a 2 or less, turn to **225**. If you roll a 3 or more, turn to **383**.

262

There is a dull rumbling sound which builds into a roar as your magic splits the mountain rock apart! Gravity does the rest and blocks of stone begin to rain down among the Scarfells. One looks up and spots you standing amid the avalanche, a sight which confuses him greatly!

If you have the codeword GROUP, turn to **390**. If you do not have this codeword, will you focus your concentration on what you are doing? (Turn to **368**) Or take the opportunity to summon your followers? (Turn to **394**)

263

Scancaro is grateful for your aid (deduct the number you chose from your number of Ariax). He has done the best he can at patching the wounds of the fallen Ariax and offers the rest of you a sip from a healing draught he has with him (being a trainee of Arguttax). The brown liquid burns your throat as it goes down but revives you somewhat: you may add 1 to the die next time you are asked to roll it. Unfortunately, a quick glance at Rical confirms he thinks as you do that neither of Scancaro's friends will make it...Turn to **313**.

264

Unfortunately the Scarfell sees you as you retreat and quick as a flash hurls his spear in your direction. Roll the die. If you roll a 1 (or less), turn to **250**. If you roll a 2 or 3, turn to **332**. If you roll a 4 or more, turn to **300**.

265

You fling yourself to the ground, landing with a painful bump on the wreckage of the tower. The eagle screeches as it sweeps overhead but luckily its rider has no remaining spears to throw.

You rise shakily to your feet and assist your new comrade to do the same. Do you want to follow the stairs down to the level below? (Turn to **314**) Or take to the skies once more? (Turn to **421**)

266

You gain a grip and heave backwards but the second Scarfell sees his opportunity! As his comrade tumbles helplessly over you with a cry of anguish, the other binds his arms around your left wing and arm. Unable to fly, you frantically thrash about but only succeed in taking you both over the edge! The doomed Scarfell is determined to take you with him! You cannot free yourself from his death embrace and the pair of you plummet to the unforgiving rocks below…

267

You hurry with all speed, hoping that even with your delay your followers have not given up and returned to the main battle. But alas: this is what has happened! Roll the die and subtract the number you roll from the number of birdmen in your group (note down your deduction). If you rolled equal to or more than the number of birdmen you had, and are therefore now alone, you return to the Scarfells (turn to **289**). If you still have followers you hurriedly explain what you have seen before flying into action (turn to **254**).

268

There is a dull rumbling sound which builds into a roar as your magic ruptures the ice, snaking black crevasses racing away from your feet. The two attackers are thrown to the ground and the others begin to look worriedly about them and shout indistinguishable things to each other.

If you have the codeword GROUP, turn to **390**. If you do not have this codeword, will you focus your concentration on what you are doing? (Turn to **368**) Or take the opportunity to rejoin your followers? (Turn to **394**)

269

It is important to somehow try and organise the defence of Arian. As you reassess what has happened since your departure, you can see both sides have suffered heavy casualties. Is there anything further you can do?

Just then, you feel a sensation that you have not felt since you wandered the dark halls of the Scarfell city of Musk. There, as your new magic first began to reveal itself, you had urges and sensations of power when you were in the vicinity of certain elements. These sometimes led to the discovery of new abilities (but at times left you in positions of danger too). Now you feel drawn somehow to the increasingly undirected bursts of flaming breath from the Moogolls: indisputably an intense source of elemental energy! If you were to fly into it and harness this power (as fire cannot hurt you), could you use it as a weapon? If you want to try this, turn to **400**. If you decide it is too risky and want to suppress the urge, turn to **319**.

270

You are too slow: the massive bulk of the animal charges you down and you are crushed under its great weight. You fall, one more casualty in the death of the Forest of Arcendak...

271

You safely skirt the war in the air and swoop into the cave where Rical is recuperating, fortunately untouched thus far by Moogoll fire. But not far down the tunnel you stop, hearing raised Scarfell voices! Are you too late?

You creep into the main entrance cave of this system. There is a dim light so the advantage of seeing in the dark is of no benefit here. You make out the familiar figure of Rical with three other Ariax defending some sort of hastily erected barricade from two Scarfells wielding their customary war-axes. Although they have numbers, the Ariax defenders are not experienced warriors as you now are!

You have a second to act before being detected. The direct approach would be to either attack the nearest Scarfell from behind (turn to **374**) or charge into both at once and knock them over (turn to **340**). If you'd rather use magic, you could try to shake the rocky floor of the cave under the Scarfell's feet (needing to roll a 3 or more to succeed) or send energy coursing through the stone walls and shower your foes with rocks from above (needing to roll a 4 or more to be successful).

If you successfully shake the floor, turn to **420**. If you bring the roof down on their heads, turn to **401**. If you fail either magic roll, turn to **235**.

272

This is the most intense carnage you have ever witnessed! You have to be constantly alert for fresh attackers coming at you from all angles whilst also looking out for stricken comrades and opportunities to repel new invaders!

As you battle your way across the dust and rubble-strewn floor, you hear a horrific screech from the left. Turning, you see the flailing form of Astraphet falling forwards with an axe buried in his back; a cowardly blow struck from behind! Note down the codeword TOR.

A wave of despair passes over the open beaked witnesses. One plucky youth recovers quickly and deals a savage blow to the murderer. This shakes you into action, and you instinctively find yourself impelled to take the lead. *React on instinct*. Will you cry for the remaining Ariax to follow you and either flee down the stairs (turn to **333**) or fly away from the scene (turn to **407**)? Or will you tell them to stand and fight and defend Astraphet's body? (Turn to **375**)

273

You punch the air with momentary delight as one huge stone slab drops heavily onto both of the Scarfells, crumpling them senseless to the floor! But there is no time to celebrate now! If you have the codeword BURN, turn to

245. If you do not have this codeword, but do have the codeword SCORCH, turn to **397**. If you have neither of these codewords, roll the die. If you roll a 4 or less, turn to **323**. If you roll a 5 or more, turn to **397**.

274

You hurry with all speed, hoping that your followers have not delayed in their return. Roll the die once separately for each birdman in your group. Every 1 you roll represents that birdman not being present when you arrive (note down these deductions from your group). If you rolled a 1 for *every* birdmen you had and are therefore now alone, turn to **289**. If you still have followers you hurriedly explain what you have seen (turn to **254**).

275

You are quietly impressed by the steely determination your race shows in the face of adversity. Despite their losses, they battle on and even seem to be gaining the upper hand! You then notice some unusual activity at the rear of the struggle. One Scarfell seems intent on moving a large object covered in brown sackcloth away from the fight. A second who is not involved in combat is distracted by his concern for stashing away some hand-sized item which you cannot see. You decide to take a chance that one of these things is what you are looking for. Will you try to grab the sackcloth-covered object (turn to **226**) or the smaller, hidden item (turn to **318**)?

276

You stretch open your mind and attempt to soak up the searing Moogoll fire washing over you. Unfortunately, the exhilarating sensation takes your eye off the great serpent at just the wrong moment: its jaws clamp round you with a sickening crunch and your body is snapped in two…

277

Your talons stretch out as you desperately attempt to break the Scarfell's grip. Roll the die. If you roll a 2 or less, turn to **243**. If you roll a 3 or more, turn to **411**.

278

It is impossible to be aware of danger from every direction; you have been targeted by a swooping eagle rider who aims his spear at you. Roll the die. If you roll a 1, turn to **250**. If you roll a 2, turn to **365**. If you roll a 3 or more, turn to **426**.

279

As you ponder which way to go, a young birdman behind you tells you that these caves are where Arguttax works. "Down that way and right at the next junction," he informs you, pointing to the right hand tunnel. If you wish to follow his directions, turn to **238**. If you'd rather explore the other tunnel instead, turn to **232**.

280

The size of your force is enough to brush aside the resistance and you sweep through them, flying right to the summit, where you overlook a scene of devastation. The bodies of at least twenty Ariax warriors are strewn amidst the rubble, along with a similar number of Scarfells: the defenders did not give their lives away cheaply.

There is no longer any fighting in this position, but it is still not a safe place to linger. You stumble through the wreckage and sadly discover what you had feared: the unmistakable form of Astraphet lying face down with a Scarfell axe still lodged deep in his back. Your leader is dead, struck down by a cowardly blow from behind.

There is open dismay among your group at first, but you rally them with a rousing promise of victory and revenge. Turn to **247**.

281

A few arrows go close but there are no casualties. You notice that the disturbance has provoked some unusual activity at the rear of the group of Scarfells. One man seems intent on moving a large object covered in brown sackcloth away from the perceived danger. Is this what you're looking for? As the Scarfell's attention is distracted, you work your way behind him and when you spot a chance to move, you decide to take it. Turn to **226**.

282

You hover in the air, strangely calm and confident in the face of the enemy. Roll the die. If you roll a 1 (or less), turn to **366** (unless you have the codeword RAZE, in which case turn to **305** instead). If you roll a 2, turn to **305**. If you roll a 3 or more, turn to **379**.

283

You make your move and disappear into the inferno, leaving the surprised Jarip hovering in the air behind you. You use your magic to part the smoke, remembering that the Orphus Latix grows in a clearing near the centre of the forest. Visibility is incredibly limited and you will not be able to sustain your smoke clearing magic for ever. Panicked forest animals are fleeing for their lives about your feet and although it cannot harm you, the roaring sound of the fire is deafening. Every so often a flaming branch breaks off and comes crashing down nearby.

Then, as you stumble through a channel of rock into another clearing, you find yourself suddenly covered by a horde of humanoid creatures! They are only waist height to you, with brown-skinned bodies covered in hair or fur and small wooden spears in their hands. They are fleeing the inferno and in their hurry topple over a ridge right on top of you! *React on instinct.* You could beat your wings and lash out to try and fight them off (turn to **405**). You could lie still and play dead, hoping they continue on their way (turn to **346**). Or you could use your magic to create an explosion of earth all around you to fling the little creatures away (needing to roll a 4 or more to succeed). If you successfully cause the earth to erupt, turn to **242**. If you fail this magic roll, turn to **306**.

284

You wish this other group good fortune and hear them swoop up into the sky behind you. You decide to take the rest up the nearest mountainside. Turn to **339**.

285

The Ariax react to your command and are soon gathered in a much more cohesive unit. The flow of Scarfells assaulting the gap in the walls is lessening. You step backwards and assess the other, smaller breaches. Turn to **415**.

286

The skies are thick with aerial duelling; everywhere you look birdmen and eagle-riders swoop past each other, exchanging deadly blows. But the ever present threat of the Moogolls overshadows all as they continue to snake their way around the mountain bringing death and destruction wherever they go. You have nothing to fear from their fiery breath, but you still don't fancy getting too close to those jaws!

Just then, one of the terrible creatures glides round the corner directly towards you! Will you lead your following into cover (turn to **417**) or yell "Scatter!" (turn to **329**)?

287

You close your eyes and send forth a magical wind. There comes an answering cry of confusion which you recognise as a Scarfell voice. This is the signal for your attack and, fighting blind, they stand little chance against the dark-sighted Ariax.

The skirmish is short. When it is over, you are reunited with Rical, who had been defending a makeshift barricade with two others. Sadly, a third Ariax lies unmoving on the rocky floor. Rical is out of breath and clearly not fit to fight, but nevertheless he stumbles across to thank you for your timely assistance. You tell him to seek refuge in the caves deeper in the mountain, and that you intend to turn the tide of this battle…somehow! The other two Ariax elect to come with you; despite being older than you are, your reputation goes before you (add them to your number of followers). You tell Rical you will see him later, and head back into the fray. Turn to **421**.

288

Over another ridge, through another channel, across another of Arian's beautiful vistas: still no result. You are confident your keen eyesight would pick out the enemy if this was the right area. But every second you waste will cost further Ariax lives. Will you continue your search alone (turn to **393**) or return to the rendezvous point as arranged and see if anyone else has had any luck (turn to **351**)?

289

You survey the scene. With the odds stacked against you, you decide you will need to use your magic. You could land before them and crack the ice on which they stand or land above them and splinter the mountain face, raining devastation from the sky. Both would require your full power and the effect would be difficult to predict. If you want to try to crack the ice, turn to **331**. To fracture the mountainside, turn to **240**.

290

Then tragedy strikes. Even as the last of the flame disappears into the morning sky, one of the Moogolls twists round behind you, controlled by a hidden enemy. Its jaws clamp round your body with a sudden sickening crunch and you are snapped clean in two…

291

Despite your fatigue, you manage to create a curtain of fire which surges dramatically up from the ground. The bear roars angrily but diverts its charge in a new direction. Turn to **391**.

292

You swoop down quickly, picking up two unbroken spears from the snow-covered rock. Before you have time to talk to the birdmen however, you hear the screech of an eagle and see two Scarfells hurtling towards the three of you, spears poised to be thrown! *React on instinct*. Will you stand firm and throw a spear first, aided by your magic? (Turn to **326**) Or shout: "Take cover in the rocks!" (Turn to **364**)?

293

With an almighty sound like rolling thunder, deep cracks surge from around your feet, and you direct them to break off a large hunk of masonry that your enemies stand on. With a horrified cry, the Scarfells lose their balance, and although one manages to save himself by leaping forwards, the other three are cast backwards to their doom down the cliff face! When it came to it, your magic didn't let you down! You may add 1 to the die on your next two magic rolls.

Suddenly you hear a horrific screech from behind you. Turning, you see the flailing form of Astraphet falling forwards with an axe buried in his back; a cowardly blow struck from behind! Note down the codeword TOR.

A wave of despair passes over the open beaked witnesses. One plucky youth recovers quickly and deals a savage blow to the murderer. This shakes you into action, and you instinctively find yourself impelled to take the lead. *React on instinct*. Will you cry for the remaining Ariax to follow you and either flee down the stairs (turn to **333**) or fly away from the scene (turn to **407**)? Or will you tell them to stand and fight, and defend Astraphet's body? (Turn to **387**)

294

Even you are surprised at the speed in which your magic works this time. Just as the Scarfells swing their axes, you jump backwards into mid-air and the crumbly ledge on which you stood breaks off and plummets down the sheer drop below it. Your two foes follow it down.

If you have the codeword BURN, turn to **245**. If you do not have this codeword, but do have the codeword SCORCH, turn to **397**. If you have neither of these codewords, roll the die. If you roll a 4 or less, turn to **323**. If you roll a 5 or more, turn to **397**.

295

Your force crashes into a scattered group of Scarfells to the left hand side of the room. The fighting is swift and bloody; three Scarfells are killed but sadly so too is one birdman (deduct him from your number of followers). You look around at the impact you have made. Note down the codeword SCORCH and turn to **415**.

296

Your shout is met with a distant response; certainly an Ariax voice, but you cannot tell if it was Rical or not. Note down the codeword CRY. You could try to summon the magic which allows you to hear far off voices (needing a 4 or more to succeed). If you manage this, turn to **224**. If you decide not to, or fail the roll (you may only try once), will you advance as quietly as possible (turn to **259**) or rush forwards to find your friend (turn to **427**)?

297

Your attack has only briefly disrupted the Scarfells and you have lost the element of surprise! You notice a couple of archers struggling to untangle their bows from their baggage and make the instant decision to launch a hit and run attack.

To see who gets the best of this skirmish, you will need to roll the die twice separately; first for the Scarfells and then for the Ariax. Add 5 to the Scarfell roll. Add the number of Ariax in your group (including you) to the Ariax roll, and a bonus 1 if you managed to carry one of the Scarfells away a moment ago. Add another 1 if you are armed with a spear and want to use it (but you lose the spear if you do). Also add 1 to the Ariax roll if you have the codeword BATTLE.

If the Scarfell total is higher than the Ariax total, turn to **429**. If the scores are level or the Ariax win by 1 or 2, turn to **353**. If the Ariax roll is higher by 3 or more, turn to **409**.

298

You hold up your trophy and signal for the others to follow you. The angry curses of the Scarfells quickly fade away and you come to rest in a secluded part of the mountain.

"What in Arian is it?" wonders the nearest birdman. You offer a brief explanation before questioning the captive creature.

"Are you controlling those things, Jarip?" you ask. The Jarip nods.

"Yes, yes, now let me out I'm freezing!" he squeaks. "I'll send them away, I will!"

"Can we trust this thing?" asks the same Ariax as before; a question you had just been asking yourself. When you released the one you met before it *did* keep its word and help you break into Vashta's cellar, though its subsequent mischief also almost caused the whole of Vashta's house to go up in flames!

You could quite easily free the Jarip by fracturing the metal bars with your magic. If you want to do this, turn to **325**. If you'd rather force him to get rid of the Moogolls first, turn to **241**.

299

You stumble round the crag, feeling your way with an outstretched arm. The noise of the fire is growing in intensity. Perhaps this is the reason why you fail to hear a pack of crazed wolves racing along the path in your direction! The first animal springs at you, its momentum knocking you to the floor. You are then set upon by the rest and torn to pieces in a frenzied flurry of claws and fangs…

300

The spear whistles past harmlessly and splinters on the wall next to you. As you instinctively duck back, an Ariax behind you rushes forward and kicks out at the thrower, sending him hurtling to his doom down the cliff face! There is now a chance to escape. Will you head:

To the summit of the Tower of Egratar in search of Astraphet?	Turn to **341**
Into the aerial battle raging above you?	Turn to **286**
Or towards a scorched and blackened cave entrance close by to look for survivors?	Turn to **349**

301

This takes precise timing, and you nearly make it. You launch yourself up into the air and succeed in pulling the shocked Scarfell onto the debris below. He fights back with fists like balls of iron, but unfortunately his plight has been spotted by a second warrior swooping in behind him. This man slashes out with his axe as he passes, almost severing your right wing! The pain is intense and gives your foe beneath you ample opportunity to turn the tables on you. As the second Scarfell banks round again, you realise that you are destined to be just one more casualty of this horrific assault…

302

You hurry up the tunnel and come to a small cave where the body of a single Ariax lies slumped over a rock. He has suffered minor burns but is only unconscious. You manage to bring him round and he explains that he and two companions took refuge here from the Moogoll fire. You help him to his feet but he immediately rushes up a set of steps on the other side of the cave. The charred remains he finds there fill him with despair: his friends are dead.

His is one of many tales of grief that will be told today. But for now, he agrees to join your faction in their joint effort against the enemy (note him down). He shows you a way outside. Turn to **421**.

303

Unfortunately the Scarfells had posted a rearguard, leaving one of their number hidden in a niche to ambush such a support party as yours. He leaps out as you pass, cutting down one of your followers with his axe! You react first, striking down the enemy before he has a chance to swing again, but the birdman is dead (subtract one from your group).

Is death lurking around every corner? You try to regulate your breathing, and in the lull feel your elemental powers at work: instinctively you sense that there is a source of fire not much further up this tunnel, though it is out of sight at the moment. You could use your magic to extinguish it if you wanted as surely it is more Scarfells lighting their way in the dark? If you want to extinguish the flame, turn to **287**. If you'd rather make sure it is not of Ariax origin first, turn to **367**.

304

Hurriedly, you discuss battle strategy. The two best suggestions are to mount a hit and run divebomb attack (turn to **324**) or to swoop down and try to grab individual Scarfells and take them away (turn to **248**)?

305

Despite your self-belief, nothing happens! You now find yourself horribly exposed and only just avoid a chunk of rock which an enterprising Scarfell flings at you! Then a second, similar projectile is thrown from behind, striking you painfully in the leg! Though a nasty gash, the wound is not life-threatening. Next time you are asked to roll the die, subtract 1 from the result.

As you glide to a less exposed position, you once more feel a surge of intrigue towards the Moogoll fire. If you want to give in this time and attempt to harness its power, turn to **400**. To resist the urge a second time and try to create a magical gale to blow the Moogolls off course instead, turn to **366**.

306

As you struggle within the stampede of the little creatures, a volley of spears is thrown at you from close range. You crumple dead onto the floor of the Forest of Arcendak.

307

You are alone again; it seems you are destined to survive while others around you fall. But as you dwell on these grim thoughts for just the merest of seconds, a Scarfell spearman picks you as his target from a blind spot behind you. The spear pierces your body and you see it emerge from your abdomen. You fall to the ground, gurgling blood…

308

The numbers against you don't look good so you turn to leave. But you have been targeted by a swooping eagle rider who aims his spear at you. Roll the die. If you roll a 1 or 2, turn to **365**. If you roll a 3 or more, turn to **426**.

309

Using all your experience, you time the move to perfection and send the first Scarfell hurtling over your back and down the sheer drop behind. You immediately grapple with the second and manage to drag him close enough to the edge to send him following after.

If you have the codeword BURN, turn to **245**. If you do not have this codeword, but do have the codeword SCORCH, turn to **397**. If you have neither of these codewords, roll the die. If you roll a 4 or less, turn to **323**. If you roll a 5 or more, turn to **397**.

310

You fly as high as you dare, ever watchful eyes urgently scanning the panorama below. Roll the die. If you roll a 3 or less, turn to **225**. If you roll a 4, turn to **261**. If you roll a 5 or more, turn to **383**.

311

There is an awesome cracking sound as the full force of your power surges through you. Huge boulders and rocks launch into the air, arcing downwards and smashing into the Scarfell group. Two are killed instantly, but you notice that despite this, one man seems most protective of a large object covered in brown sackcloth, moving it away from the danger zone. Is this what you're looking for? As the Scarfell's attention is distracted, you work your way down towards them and when you spot a chance to move, you decide to take it. Turn to **226**.

312

At the last moment you remember to toss the caged Jarip to a surprised Ariax nearby, who catches it…just! Then you stretch open your mind and attempt to soak up the searing Moogoll fire washing over you. The feeling is exhilarating; never before have you experienced so much power at once! As the flames die out, you have a second to glimpse the astounded faces of your enemies and the bewilderment of your followers before you pour out the fire, channelling it through your arms with an explosion of power directly towards a cluster of Scarfells swooping in from your right. They are utterly incinerated in mid-air to the cheers of the Ariax who witness the display.

You feel you really should release your prisoner now, as he *is* directing the enormous serpents away from your home. You take the cage in both hands, and impress the watching crowd for a second time as they see the metal bars fragment in your bare hands. Squeezing out, the little creature hovers in the air beside you for a moment, grinning. "You're making quite a habit of freeing me, aren't you?" he winks, and as he flies off you realise that this is the very same Jarip you met in Iro! Turn to **356**.

313

You leave Scancaro behind and land amidst the smoking ruins of Egratar. You have repelled the enemy, but at what cost? In the sober silence that follows, you try to take in everything that has happened. To think that a tiny Jarip could enable the Scarfells to do all this! And what a coincidence that it was the very one that Vashta held captive, so far away!

A coincidence? What if Vashta sent the Jarip north to collect a second sample of the life-prolonging herb Orphus Latix, the secret of which you have risked your life to protect? Although you destroyed his maps and scrolls, the wily wizard could conceivably have drawn the plant from memory! And didn't the Jarip complain about the cold? Arian can't be its natural habitat!

"Arcendak…" you manage to blurt out, and to the astonishment of the gathered Ariax, you run to the edge of the outcrop of rock and swoop into the air, headed westwards. You hear Rical calling for you to wait, but no Ariax can match your magically enhanced air-speed!

Your heart pounds in your chest at the thought of a renewed threat to your tribe's greatest secret. Now more than ever you will need the magic plant's power! But even before the forest first appears on the horizon you can see that something is terribly wrong. Dense black smoke is coming from your destination: the Forest of Arcendak is burning! The Moogolls have struck one final blow for the Scarfells, this time unintentionally!

You may not have much time; you must brave the inferno and gather whatever remains of the crop; you could not hope to use your magic to melt enough ice to extinguish the blaze!

Then you spot the Jarip below you! It is heading straight for the flames, as untroubled as you are by the heat and smoke. You notice that the Jarip does not seem to breathe anyway; it has no nostrils! "So, Vashta *did* send you!" you yell, raising your voice to compete with the noise of the blaze.

The Jarip looks round and squeaks in surprise, but you can tell your guess is correct. If you want to grab the creature and keep it where you can see it, turn to **228**. If you'd rather swoop past it and get to the Orphus Latix first, turn to **283**.

314

You arrive in what was once the grand entrance chamber on the lowest level of the Tower of Egratar. The ceiling is more or less intact (though raining dust from many cracks) but large holes have been blown out of the walls and small fires burn unchecked all around.

Amidst this destruction, it is talon versus axe. A dozen or so Ariax are battling at least as many Scarfells and the fallen from either side lie amongst the wreckage. What will you do to influence the conflict? Will you charge in and add your numbers to the Ariax defenders? (Turn to **260**) Try to cover some of the breaches in the wall and prevent further Scarfell reinforcements arriving? (Turn to **358**) Or use your magic to whip up the fire, using it as a weapon? If you choose to try this, roll the die. If you roll a 2 or less, turn to **369**. If you roll a 3 or 4, turn to **424**. If you roll a 5 or 6, turn to **236**.

315

You make solid contact with the first man's legs, but it is as if they are made of rock! He stumbles and falls on top of you, constricting your movement and leaving you open to attack from the other Scarfell. They are in no mood for anything other than a swift kill…

316

In a situation like this, you need to rally round your leader: Astraphet the Talotrix. No-one recalls seeing him but the logical place he would be is defending the Tower of Egratar. Will you:

Send a scout to seek Astraphet? Turn to **408**
Keep the group together and all go? Turn to **360**
Or go alone, risking only yourself? Turn to **233**

317

You bank and swoop skilfully through the gap, emerging into another wide valley. On the far side of this is one of the largest mountains you know of in the area, where of late you have often sought refuge to practise your magic. There are more deep valleys to search on either side of it. Will you fly to the left (turn to **239**) or the right (turn to **428**)?

318

You creep into position, swoop in and seize the item from the man, who cries out in surprise and nearly falls over! As you climb out of range of the archers you see that you are carrying a small hatchet, quite ordinary in appearance. Surely this can't be what you have been looking for?

You look towards the Moogolls. They continue to circle the mountainside breathing death and destruction upon the Ariax. You note that the Scarfells remain untroubled by the beasts; there is nothing magical about the axe you hold.

In frustration, you splinter the weapon in your bare hands using your magic and the pieces are carried away by the wind. If you want to immediately make an attempt to grab the sackcloth-covered bundle, turn to **362**. If you want to use a gust of magic wind to blow it free from the Scarfell's grasp, you will need to roll a 4 or more on the die. If you try and succeed, turn to **399**. If you try and fail, turn to **255**. The other option is to break off the attack and take stock of the situation (turn to **422).**

319

Deliberately tangling head on with a Moogoll? Surely the situation isn't that desperate? You find yourself instead flying to the smoking remnants of the Tower of Egratar, where a significant number of Ariax are making a stand. They are outnumbered by the Scarfells who have encircled them and are closing in. A ring of fire dances around the perimeter of the ruins and you wonder if you could channel all your energy into whipping these flames up into a blaze to use against the Scarfells?

Landing nearby, you focus your mind and feel the flames. A gathering of maybe ten more eagle-riders are gliding in. Will you unleash your power now, targeting the Scarfells fighting the Ariax? (Turn to **282**) Or will you wait for the reinforcements to get up close before discharging your energy? (Turn to **410**)

320

You cut through the eagle riders – but fly straight into a trap! Four of their comrades are hidden in the surrounding rocks armed with reclaimed spears. As you swoop past, they leap out and simultaneously deliver their weapons. You are one of the targets and their aim is true. You crash onto the rock, dead.

321

You see the man's eyes widen as he realises what you are doing and there is a resounding clang as you crash into his armour. He stumbles backwards, but grabs onto you and attempts to take you with him! *React on instinct*. Will you strike him with your talons? (Turn to **277**) Or flap your wings to try and shake him off? (Turn to **357**)

322

You quickly bring your spear into the ready position and hurl it at the eagle. But the huge bird is amazingly agile and banks left to avoid it; the spear sails harmlessly off into the distance (you may not use it again). Fortunately this attack has diverted the great bird in a different direction towards a new target.

There is nothing else to be done here. Will you run downstairs (turn to **314**) or return to the skies (turn to **421**)?

323

Looking around, the battle of Egratar is being won but at great cost. A temporary calm fills the room, but the noise of combat from outside serves as a reminder of your peril.

You are reunited with any Ariax you brought with you, and your ranks are swelled with two new additions, exhausted but keen to follow you in the fight (note down that these two Ariax are with you).

The roof in here is unstable and could collapse so you decide to get outside as quickly as possible. If you have both the codewords TIME and TOR, turn to **247**. If you have the codeword TIME but not the codeword TOR, turn to **360**. If you have neither codeword, will you lead your group:

To the cave of your friend Rical?	Turn to **389**
Into the aerial battle still raging outside?	Turn to **286**
Or towards a scorched and blackened cave entrance below to look for survivors?	Turn to **349**

324

Your suggestion gets a positive reaction from the others; they obviously favour the direct approach for dealing with the enemy! You lead the Ariax in formation high up behind the Scarfells to approach unseen. Then you give the order and begin plunging down through the air towards your target.

To see who gets the best of this skirmish, you will need to roll the die twice separately; first for the Scarfells and then for the Ariax. Add 5 to the Scarfell roll. Add the number of Ariax in your group (including you) to the Ariax roll, and a bonus 1 if you managed to carry one of the Scarfells away a moment ago. Add another 1 if you are armed with a spear and want to use it (but you lose the spear if you do). Also add 1 to the Ariax roll if you have the codeword BATTLE.

If the Scarfell total is higher than the Ariax total, turn to **429**. If the scores are level, or the Ariax win by 1 or 2, turn to **353**. If the Ariax roll is higher by 3 or more, turn to **409**.

325

You feel confident that the Jarip will hold no loyalty to the Scarfells once released and take the cage in both hands. As the metal bars fragment in your bare hands, beaks drop open in amazement all around. Squeezing out, the little creature hovers in the air beside you for a moment, grinning. It frowns upwards at the Moogolls and to your relief they immediately begin to twist away from the mountains of your home.

"You're making quite a habit of freeing me, aren't you?" he winks, and as he flies off you realise that this was the very same Jarip you met in Iro! Turn to **269**.

326

Once again you show nerves of steel in a moment of critical danger! Roll the die. If you roll a 1 or 2, turn to **381**. If you roll a 3 or more, turn to **230**.

327

Your defence of the breach has diverted three incoming eagle riders who bank away and seek fresh targets. You turn your attention to the interior of the tower. Turn to **415**.

328

Your force smashes easily through the ranks of the Scarfells on the left hand side of the room. Four barbarian invaders are toppled from the heights and the balance begins tipping in favour of the defenders. Note down the codeword BURN and turn to **415**.

329

Your followers react quickly and dart in all directions in a flurry of feathers! You on the other hand fly directly in line with the creature, hoping to draw its flame in your direction. Roll the die; if you roll higher than the number of Ariax in your group (not including you) you all avoid the fire and regroup nearby (turn to **421**). If you roll equal to or less than the number of birdmen, one is tragically caught in the flame and roasted (deduct him from your tally). Roll the die again as before (with the new number of Ariax) and lose a second birdman if you are unlucky again. If all of your followers are killed, turn to **307**. If not, do not roll a third time, but turn to **421**.

330

Your experiences have sharpened your reflexes and you easily avoid the spear, which clatters into the rock beside you without breaking. You pick it up and send it back to its owner, who is struck square in the chest. He tumbles backwards out of his saddle and falls down the mountainside.

The wounded Ariax acknowledges that you have saved his life and in return he pledges you his 'loyal service'! Keep a careful track of the number of Ariax followers you have, starting with this one. Will you now head:

To the summit of the Tower of Egratar in search of Astraphet?	Turn to **341**
To the cave of your friend Rical?	Turn to **389**
Back into the aerial battle still raging above you?	Turn to **286**
Or towards a scorched and blackened cave entrance close by to look for survivors?	Turn to **349**

331

You wait until you feel the power beginning to build in your legs before gliding down as close to the enemy as you dare and unleashing the destructive force into the ice. The Scarfells are at first amazed by the boldness of a single birdman appearing from nowhere to face them, but soon pull themselves together. Two grab their axes and begin to charge towards you, bellowing battle cries. Roll the die. If you roll a 3 or less, turn to **404**. If you roll a 4 or 5, turn to **268**. If you roll a 6, turn to **378**.

332

The spear whistles past you. You hold your nerve, stride forwards and shove the thrower to his doom down the cliff face. But the Scarfell has claimed his kill: the spear stands lodged in the body of an Ariax behind you (lose one follower already!) If you have no more Ariax with you, turn to **307**. If you had more than one birdman with you, you have to move on! Will you head:

To the summit of the Tower of Egratar in search of Astraphet?	Turn to **341**
Into the aerial battle still raging above you?	Turn to **286**
Or towards a scorched and blackened cave entrance close by to look for survivors?	Turn to **349**

333

As your talons clatter down the cracked stone steps to the lower level, you find that three Ariax warriors have followed you. Your reputation goes before you and they see you as a leader, even though older than you. Keep a careful track of the number of Ariax followers you have, starting with these three. Turn to **314**.

334

You try to topple the Scarfells from the ledge, avoiding their murderous axes as you do. Roll the die. If you roll a 2 or less, turn to **266**. If you roll a 3 or more, turn to **309**.

335

You follow the passage deeper into the mountain until you reach a point where it feeds into a larger tunnel running across it. From here you can go left (turn to **370**) or right (turn to **238**)?

336

Fate seems to favour the Scarfells today. You lead the way around a blind corner – straight into an ambush! You do not see the Scarfell who claims your life, but at least his strength is such that your death is swift…

337

There is nothing to report from the other Ariax scouts; your enemy continues to elude you. Maybe it was a wild goose chase anyway and the secret behind the Moogoll-control was never to be found out here? You decide to return to the fighting and see what else can be done. Note down the codeword OPEN and turn to **269**.

338

Even though it is a role fraught with danger, you are not short of volunteers to brave the Scarfell's anger…and arrows! Choose how many birdmen you will send out on this mission and note it down. You must send at least one and cannot go yourself. Will you direct your distracters to:

Occupy the archers' attention from the sky?	Turn to **384**
Or land and draw some of the Scarfells out into battle, splitting their force in two?	Turn to **234**

339

At the summit you turn to await the arrival of the others. Then disaster strikes. A wounded but still armed Scarfell picks you as his target from a blind spot above you. His spear sinks into your back with a sickening squelch: it is a mortal wound. You breathe your last in the arms of your despairing friend Rical…

340

One of the men senses something at the last minute and turns round but it is too late. You smash into the pair, knocking one from his feet and sending the other reeling backwards! The defenders need no further encouragement; they scramble over their emplacement and finish the job! But it has come at a cost. The Scarfell who reacted has opened a nasty looking wound in your side and you are forced to sit down and see to it. Your head swims momentarily but it will heal given time. Even so, for the rest of this adventure, you must subtract 1 from any die rolls you make (unless they relate to the actions of a *group* of Ariax and not you individually: to indicate this the word group will appear in the same sentence as 'roll the die' or you will be asked to roll the die more than once).

Rical is out of breath and clearly not fit to fight, but nevertheless he stumbles across to thank you for your intervention: there were no Ariax casualties in this skirmish. You tell Rical to seek refuge in the caves deeper in the mountain, and that you intend to turn the tide of this battle…somehow! The three other Ariax elect to come with you; despite being older than you are, your reputation goes before you. Keep a careful track of the number of Ariax followers you have, starting with these three. You tell Rical you will see him later and head back into the fray. Turn to **386**.

341

Note down the codeword TIME. As you near the tower, still finding it hard to comprehend that this glorious and ancient structure no longer exists, you see that only the bottom two levels remain. Hand-to-hand fighting is being fought fiercely on both. Will you join the melee on the exposed top level (turn to **244**) or swoop in through the broken walls of the lower level (turn to **314**)?

342

You are not going to be beaten now, not when yet again your tribe is depending on you! With a surge of energy, you manage to break through the pack of half-sized creatures and up into the trees. Your battered body aches and you have suffered several minor wounds, but you force yourself to go on.

You battle through the flame, heading in the direction you estimate the centre of the forest to be. You come to the bottom of a mighty rock face with a lip at the top. The path you are on continues with the cliff to its right. This place seems strangely familiar; your head is swimming and you cannot be certain but you feel sure you are near the Orphus Latix glade. You struggle to remember which way it is. If you want to fly up to the top of the cliff, turn to **256**. If you want to stay on the path, turn to **299**.

343

These men are trained warriors and this assault has been planned for months. They stand firm in their position, even when some of their number are slain. One Scarfell hurls his axe at you as you hover out of reach and roars in satisfaction at the sight of your mortally wounded body plummeting towards the ground with the weapon still embedded in your throat…

344

You are quietly impressed by the steely determination your race shows, willingly putting their own lives at risk for the greater good of the tribe. Your

Ariax frustrate the Scarfells, who begin to ration their arrows. The birdmen close in!

You then notice some unusual activity at the rear of the group. One man seems intent on moving a large object covered in brown sackcloth away from the approaching Ariax. A second is distracted by his concern for stashing away a hand-sized item which you cannot see. You decide to take a chance that one of these things is what you are looking for. Will you try to grab the sackcloth-covered object (turn to **226**) or the smaller, hidden item (turn to **318**)?

345

There is consternation as half of the entire group of Scarfells is suddenly plucked from the ground and taken away! You notice that despite this, one Scarfell seems most protective of a large object covered in brown sackcloth, moving it away from the danger area. Is this what you're looking for? As the man's attention is distracted, you work your way down towards them and when you spot a chance to move, you decide to take it. Turn to **226**.

346

Every nerve in your body is jangling as the creatures trample over you. But your luck holds: they hurry onwards, paying no heed to what is (in their eyes) just another casualty of the fire. Although filthy, battered and bruised, you are still alive!

You pick yourself up from your prone position and continue to battle through the flame, heading in the direction you estimate the centre of the forest to be but unable to tell whether this is the same part of Arcendak that you visited before. You come to the bottom of a mighty rock face with a lip at the top. The path you are on continues with the cliff to its right. This place seems strangely familiar; your head is swimming and you cannot be certain but you feel sure you are near the Orphus Latix glade. You struggle to remember which way it is. If you want to fly up to the top of the cliff, turn to **256**. If you want to stay on the path, turn to **299**.

347

You thread your way between the deadly aerial duels helping where you can, your speed and agility in the air matchless. You help a young Ariax to dismount a Scarfell, only for the birdman to be skewered by a new enemy surging in from behind. The fighting is swift and bloody.

You look around and see two Ariax far below who have landed and are collecting spears that have thankfully missed their targets. This seems like a good idea! But then you also notice a lone warrior not far away struggling with a spear through his wing. Will you go to his aid? (Turn to **416**) Or will you join the scavengers gathering weapons below you? (Turn to **292**)

348

You swoop down to land at the summit, where you overlook a scene of utter chaos. Maybe twenty combatants remain alive on each side of the skirmish, and in the centre of it all you see your leader Astraphet. You glide in to join the fray, but more Scarfells are also on their way! Will you attempt to fight your way through to Astraphet? (Turn to **272**) Or try to use your magic to break a chunk of the tower's edge away, sending the Scarfells tumbling to their doom (needing a 3 or more to succeed)? If you try this and are successful, turn to **293**. If you fail this roll, turn to **222**.

349

You lead the way to the cave, and quickly assemble in its rocky sanctuary. There is a horrible burnt smell about the place and ashy deposits coat the floor. Finding no survivors, you follow the tunnel down to a T-junction. Roll the die; if you roll less than or equal to the number of Ariax in your group (not including you), turn to **279**. If you roll higher than the size of your group, you have the choice of going left (turn to **232**) or right (turn to **335**)?

350

With a dramatic gust, the torches simultaneously splutter and die, plunging your enemies into darkness. Fighting blind, the Scarfells stand little chance against the dark-sighted Ariax.

The skirmish is short. When it is over, you are reunited with Rical, who had been defending a makeshift barricade with three others. Sadly, one of the Ariax lies unmoving on the rocky floor. Rical is out of breath and clearly not fit to fight, but nevertheless he stumbles across to thank you for your intervention. You tell him to seek refuge in the caves deeper in the mountain and that you intend to turn the tide of this battle…somehow! The other two Ariax elect to come with you; despite being older than you are, your reputation is spreading (add them to your number of followers). You tell Rical you will see him later and head back into the fray. Turn to **421**.

351

You soon arrive at the appointed place; but do any of your comrades have news? Roll the die separately for each birdman in your group. Every 1 that you roll is a birdman who does not return, either taking overlong, returned to the main battle…or worse. Make the necessary deductions. If none of your followers came back, turn to **307**.

Now roll the die once more and add the number of Ariax who have returned to your group. If your total is 5 or less, turn to **337**. If it comes to 6 or more, turn to **413**.

352

Nothing happens at first. You redouble your efforts and finally feel the familiar power building up inside you. But the delay proves costly. A Scarfell far below has pointed you out as a target for the archers. Three well aimed arrows whistle upwards and two find their mark. You tumble down the mountainside and your body lands crumpled in the midst of your enemies.

353

Both sides suffer losses in the encounter: two Ariax have been killed (deduct these from your number). If this wipes out your entire group, turn to **307**. Otherwise you have a snap decision to make – fight or flee? *React on instinct.* If you give the order to withdraw, turn to **371**. If you want to press on with the attack, turn to **275**.

354

This is going to be tricky; there's still no knowing exactly which way the great serpent will turn! Roll the die. If you roll a 1 (or less!), turn to **276**. If you roll a 2 or more, turn to **227**.

355

You desperately try to drag your fatigued body skywards, out of the reach of the deadly teeth and claws of the frost-bear. Roll the die. If you roll a 2 or less, turn to **270**. If you roll a 3 or more, turn to **391**.

356

"Xanarel!" comes the cry of a familiar voice behind you. You turn and greet your great friend Rical, who swoops across and lands at your side. With the Moogolls disappearing in the distance, it is a joyous reunion!

"Incredible: there's no knowing what you're going to do next!" Rical laughs, patting your shoulder. The secret of your magic powers is well and truly out now!

But the day is not yet won. Many Scarfells have sensed that the game is up and have taken to their steeds, heading westwards back to Musk. They have not achieved total annihilation of the Ariax, but certainly came close! Groups of them continue to fight on, some because they have lost their mounts; others as they are in a battle-frenzy and fighting to the death!

There is still work to be done to cleanse your home. Will you:

Attack a nearby group of Scarfell eagle-riders who show no sign of retreating?	Turn to **249**
Begin searching caves for stranded enemies?	Turn to **395**
Or round up as many Ariax as possible before taking further action?	Turn to **423**

357

The Scarfell's feet leave the ground and you are suddenly jolted downwards with his weight. The strength in your wings is immense however; the man's grip weakens and you are able to disentangle him. He drops like a stone down the mountainside. There is now a chance to escape. Will you head:

To the summit of the Tower of Egratar in search of Astraphet?	Turn to **341**
Into the aerial battle still raging above you?	Turn to **286**
Or towards a scorched and blackened cave entrance close by to look for survivors?	Turn to **349**

358

One particular Scarfell hovering not far away picks you out as the target for his final spear. You just sense something at the last moment and attempt to dive aside to avoid it. Roll the die. If you roll a 2 or less, turn to **250**. If you roll a 3 or more the spear flies harmlessly past (turn to **327**).

359

Small cracks open up in the roof and spread outwards in all directions but too slowly: by the time the first chunks fall, the lead Scarfell has already flung his axe at you. At this close proximity there isn't the time or room to avoid it. The impact knocks you off your feet and you fall backwards onto the rubble, dead.

360

You decide to look for Astraphet in the upper reaches of the tower. But as you swoop in you see it is occupied by a small Scarfell force. You elect to drive through them and clear them out! Roll the die, adding the number of Ariax in your group to the roll (including yourself). If the total is 6 or less, turn to **343**. If it is 7 or more, turn to **280**.

361

You stay well below the line of white mountains which loom imposingly on either side of you. Roll the die. If you roll a 1, turn to **225**. If you roll a 2, 3 or 4, turn to **261**. If you roll a 5 or more, turn to **383**.

362

Luckily the archers had not anticipated that you would return immediately! Roll the die. If you roll a 4 or less, turn to **255**. If you roll a 5 or more, turn to **226**.

363

The angry curses of the Scarfells are quickly lost behind you, and you come to rest in a secluded part of the mountain.

"Are you controlling those things, Jarip?" you ask. The Jarip nods.

"Yes, yes, now let me out I'm freezing!" he squeaks. "I'll send them away, I will!"

You return homewards, wondering exactly what to do with it. On the way, you are spotted by your fellow searchers and reunited with your group. They stare at the Jarip with fascination! "What in Arian is it?" wonders the nearest birdman. You offer a brief explanation before questioning the captive creature further.

"Can we trust this thing?" asks the same Ariax as before; a question you had just been asking yourself. When you released the one you met before it *did* keep its word and help you break into Vashta's study, though its subsequent mischief also almost caused the whole of Vashta's house to go up in flames!

You could quite easily free the Jarip by fracturing the metal bars with your magic. If you want to do this, turn to **325**. If you'd rather make him get rid of the Moogolls first, turn to **241**.

364

The two other Ariax react quickly and there is a handy gap in the rocks which turns out to be a shallow cave. The spears thud down into the ground behind you, but you are unhurt. The Scarfells are forced to pull their steeds up sharply and wheel away in another direction, giving you time to catch your breath.

The two Ariax are a few years older than you, but recognise you and look up to you as some sort of leader. The nearest one asks what to do next. Keep a careful track of the number of Ariax followers you have, starting with these two. Will you lead them:

To the summit of the Tower of Egratar in search of Astraphet?	Turn to **341**
To the cave of your friend Rical?	Turn to **389**
Into the aerial battle still raging above you?	Turn to **286**
Or towards a scorched and blackened cave entrance close by to look for survivors?	Turn to **349**

365

There is a sharp cry of pain from behind; one of the Ariax has been killed by a well-aimed spear thrown from below! (Reduce your number of followers by one already!) Will you lead the survivors:

To the cave of your friend Rical?	Turn to **389**
Into the aerial battle which still rages outside?	Turn to **286**
Or towards a scorched and blackened cave entrance close by to look for survivors?	Turn to **349**

366

Your focus is fully on the nearest Moogoll as you unleash the force of your magic. Unfortunately, this means that you have taken your eye off the other one, which rises up beneath you. A warning shout comes too late: the huge jaws clamp round you with a sickening crunch and your body is snapped in two…

367

You curse your foolishness when you discover that your initial guess was correct: of course it's the Scarfells! Under pressure, how quickly can you extinguish the flames? Roll the die. If you roll a 2 or less, turn to **246**. If you roll a 3 or more, turn to **350**.

368

You focus on your magic like never before and finally start to see results. You notice unusual activity at the rear of the Scarfell group as they hurry to reorganise themselves. One seems intent on moving a large object covered in brown sackcloth away from the area. A second Scarfell is distracted by his concern for stashing away a hand-sized item which you cannot see. You decide to take a chance that one of these things is what you are looking for. Will you try to grab the sackcloth-covered object (turn to **226**) or the smaller, hidden item (turn to **318**)?

369

You call forth hidden energies and many of the fires suddenly billow into life. You struggle to command them but the nearest Scarfells fall back in fear. Some quick-witted Ariax deduce what you are doing, incredible as it seems, and press home the attack. You have granted the defenders the momentary advantage. Turn to **415**.

370

The passage twists its way downwards into the depths of the mountain. It is pitch black down here, but of course you can all see as clearly as if it was day. You then feel your elemental powers stirring once more: instinctively you know that there is a source of fire not much further up this tunnel, though out of sight at the moment. Surely it is more Scarfells lighting their way in the dark? If you want to extinguish the flame, turn to **392**. If you'd rather investigate cautiously in case it is of Ariax origin, turn to **412**.

371

You lead the survivors away to regroup. A fateful decision. As you climb into the sky, a volley of arrows is fired from below. Your body is pierced in vital places by not one but *two* of the deadly shafts and you are dead by the time you hit the ground…

372

You decide that this is not the time to divide your forces, but to gather together to rid your home of the enemy. A few of the birdmen nod respectfully at your decision and you lead them up the nearest mountainside to a different vantage point. If you have the codeword GRAVELAX, turn to **229**. If you do not have this codeword, turn to **339**.

373

Nothing is happening and you are forced to forget that plan and throw yourself aside to save your life! Roll the die. If you roll a 4 or less, turn to **270**. If you roll a 5 or more, turn to **391**.

374

The man senses something at the last minute and turns round but it is too late. You slash out at him and he staggers back against the rocky wall. The defenders need no further encouragement; they scramble over their emplacement and finish the job. But it has come at a cost; one of the Ariax lies grievously wounded at the hands of the other Scarfell.

Rical is out of breath and clearly not fit to fight, but nevertheless he stumbles across to thank you for your help. You tell Rical to take the fallen birdman to the refuge of the caves deeper in the mountain and that you intend to turn the tide of this battle…somehow! The two other Ariax elect to come with you; despite being older than you are, your reputation is spreading. Keep a careful track of the number of Ariax followers you have, starting with these two. You tell Rical you will see him later and head back into the fray. Turn to **386**.

375

Your rallying call has the desired effect and the defenders channel their despair and anger into the fight. The body count begins to rise rapidly but although you are personally getting the best of it, it becomes clear as more Scarfell reinforcements arrive that this is a losing battle. You find yourself back to back with one other birdman and decide to get out while you both still live. He meets your gaze, and despite being older than you are, clearly recognises you and looks up to you as a leader. Keep a careful track of the number of Ariax you have with you, starting with this one.

Will you head down the stairs? (Turn to **314**) Or out into the open air? (Turn to **278**)

376

You accomplish your plan in some style, using the momentum of the first Scarfell against him and sending him into the abyss behind you. The second man receives a blow to the ribs which winds him and he is soon sent following headlong after his comrade!

If you have the codeword BURN, turn to **245**. If you do not have this codeword, but do have the codeword SCORCH, turn to **397**. If you have neither of these codewords, roll the die. If you roll a 4 or less, turn to **323**. If you roll a 5 or more, turn to **397**.

377

The brave scout takes to the sky and you stand sentry like watching him get smaller and smaller in the distance. He is back safely in a matter of minutes, but his expression is grave. You listen in silence as he recounts his tragic news: Astraphet's body is among the dead at the top of the tower, though judging by the number of enemies surrounding him, he did not give his life cheaply. There is open dismay among your group at first, but you rally them with a rousing promise of victory and revenge. Turn to **247**.

378

You feel an intense surge of magical energy; black cracks begins to appear in the ice around your feet and snake with surprising speed towards the amazed and horrified Scarfells, widening as they reach them. The two who were charging at you are forced to throw themselves to the side with cries of alarm as the ground crumbles beneath them!

You then notice some unusual activity at the rear of the group. One Scarfell seems intent on moving a large object covered in brown sackcloth away from the danger. A second is distracted by his concern for stashing away a hand-sized item which you cannot see. You decide to take a chance that one of these things is what you are looking for. Will you try to grab the sackcloth-covered object (turn to **226**) or the smaller, hidden item (turn to **318**)?

379

Your timing is impeccable: the flames rise upwards and you have a second to glimpse the astounded faces of your enemies and the bewilderment of your followers before you direct them towards a cluster of Scarfells swooping in from your right. They are roasted in mid-air to the cheers of the Ariax who witness the display.

If you have the codeword RAZE, turn to **385**. If you do not have this codeword, but have the codeword OPEN, turn to **290**. If you have neither of these codewords, turn to **356**.

380

Morale is as high as it has been all day among the Ariax; you sweep through the enemy, cutting them down without suffering a single loss! Without pause for respite, you lead your victorious band up the nearest mountainside to a different vantage point. If you have the codeword GRAVELAX, turn to **229**. If you do not have this codeword, turn to **339**.

381

At the last moment, the eagle manages to bank left and avoid the deadly projectile. You hastily prepare your second spear, but too late: the eagle grasps it in its talons and tries to yank it from your hand! As you struggle, you fail to see the rider swing his axe. It slices your neck open and the crisp white mountain snow is stained red with the blood of your fallen body...

382

You lead the way around a blind corner – straight into an ambush! The birdman at your side is unlucky enough to be on the wrong side of the tunnel and is cut down by a vicious axe strike. Reduce the number of Ariax in your group by one. If he was your only follower, turn to **307**.

There are quite a few of them it seems and you instinctively flee down a side tunnel. There is no sound of pursuit; only when you stop do you realise that you are bleeding from a wound in your side. For the rest of this adventure, you must subtract 1 from any die rolls you make (unless they relate to the actions of a *group* of Ariax and not you individually: to indicate this the word group will appear in the same sentence as 'roll the die' or you will be asked to roll the die more than once).

The attack and sudden loss of life has clearly shaken the others. You decide to seek the freedom of the open air once more to raise their spirits and find the way out easily enough. Turn to **421**.

383

Just as you are beginning to give up hope, you find exactly what you have been searching for! You dive down onto a rocky ledge from where you can survey the activity without being seen yourself.

You are high up on one side of a concealed valley. A group of six Scarfells stand or sit about in a dell on the other side. Your pinpoint eyesight observes a selection of baggage but no eagle mounts. It is a cunningly chosen little nook: the men are hard to spot from a distance, but are in fact not far (as the Ariax flies) from the Tower of Egratar and command a view of the aerial battle. Surely there can be no other reason for their presence here except that they are controlling the Moogolls, but how? You can see no obvious answer and infuriatingly your magic power to carry their voices to you reveal only snatches of conversation and nothing of any use.

If you want to go back and try to pick up the rest of your group, hoping they have waited for you, turn to **267**. If you want to attempt to stop them alone, turn to **289**.

384

You are almost bemused by the sight of these birdmen, who have had little experience of warfare before today, banking and wheeling fearlessly through the air in front of the archers! Roll the die once separately for each Ariax you sent; each 1 you roll represents an unfortunate who is struck down by the deadly Scarfell arrows (deduct him from your number). If all of your followers are killed and you are left alone, turn to **307**.

The Scarfells are enraged and draw their weapons. There appears to be a dispute however, as some want to charge at the flying birdmen while others try in vain to keep the group together. You take the opportunity to order the attack and plunge down through the air towards your target.

To see who gets the best of this skirmish, you will need to roll the die twice separately; first for the Scarfells and then for the Ariax. Add 5 to the Scarfell roll. Add the number of surviving Ariax in your group (including you) to the Ariax roll. Add another 1 if you are armed with a spear and want to use it (but you lose the spear if you do). Also add 1 to the Ariax roll if you have the codeword BATTLE.

If the Scarfell total is higher than the Ariax total, turn to **429**. If the scores are equal, or the Ariax win by 1 or 2, turn to **353**. If the Ariax roll is higher by 3 or more, turn to **409**.

385

You feel you really should release your prisoner now, as he *is* directing the enormous serpents away from your home. You take the cage in both hands, and impress the watching crowd again as they see the metal bars fragment in your bare hands. Squeezing out, the little creature hovers in the air beside you for a moment, grinning. "You're making quite a habit of freeing me, aren't you?" he winks, and as he flies off you realise that this was the very same Jarip you met in Iro!

If you have the codeword OPEN, turn to **290**. If you do not have this codeword, turn to **356**.

386

As you reach the cave mouth you see another Scarfell dismounting from his steed up ahead. He has not seen you yet and you have the chance to act first. Will you charge at him to try to knock him over the cliff? (Turn to **321**) Or duck back and ambush him as he blunders up the tunnel? (Turn to **264**)

387

Your rallying call has the desired effect and the defenders channel their despair and anger into the fight. The body count begins to rise rapidly but although you are personally getting the best of it, it becomes clear as more Scarfell reinforcements arrive that this is a losing battle. You cut a path through to the three other surviving birdmen and decide to get out while you still live. One meets your gaze, and despite being older than you are, clearly recognises you and looks up to you as a leader. You wave your arm in the direction of escape and the others nod immediately. You are in command! Keep a careful track of the number of Ariax you have with you, starting with these three.

Will you lead them down the stairs? (Turn to **314**) Or out into the open air? (Turn to **308**)?

388

An incomplete wall section nearby provides you with some kind of cover but you realise that the men are still going to reach you more or less together. You must change strategy quickly! *React on instinct.* To try and knock the men over the edge, turn to **334**. To use your magic to break off the ledge on which you will soon all stand, you need to roll a 3 or more. If you succeed, turn to **294**. If you try and fail this roll, turn to **223**.

389

You safely skirt the war in the air and swoop into the cave where Rical is recuperating, fortunately untouched thus far by Moogoll fire. You are met by silence. Will you call out Rical's name? (Turn to **296**) Signal for quiet and lead the way? (Turn to **259**) Or rush to discover his fate? (Turn to **427**)

390

There is a sudden screeching sound behind you: here comes the cavalry! Your Ariax have decided now is the moment to strike and dive to the attack while the Scarfells are in disarray! You give an answering battle-cry and swoop down through the air towards your target.

To see who gets the best of this skirmish, you will need to roll the die twice separately; first for the Scarfells and then for the Ariax. Add 3 to the Scarfell roll. Add the number of surviving Ariax in your group (including you) to the Ariax roll. Add another 1 if you are armed with a spear and want to use it (but you lose the spear if you do). Also add 1 to the Ariax roll if you have the codeword BATTLE.

If the Scarfell total is higher than the Ariax total, turn to **429**. If the scores are equal, or the Ariax win by 1 or 2, turn to **353**. If the Ariax roll is higher by 3 or more, turn to **409**.

391

The bear thunders past, lost in the smoke. You take a deep breath but cannot afford to rest here!

In the next clearing you spy a bush with leaves which vaguely resemble those of the Orphus Latix. As you feign delight at your find, you also loosen your grip slightly so that the Jarip can wriggle free. It takes the bait, grabbing a handful of the plant and speeding off into the smoke. Your cries for him to come back go unanswered...exactly as hoped!

You continue to battle through the flame, heading in the direction you estimate the centre of the forest to be. You come to the bottom of a mighty rock face with a lip at the top. The path you are on continues with the cliff to its right. This place seems strangely familiar; your head is swimming and you cannot be certain but you feel sure you are near the Orphus Latix glade. You struggle to remember which way it is. If you want to fly up to the top of the cliff, turn to **256**. If you want to stay on the path, turn to **299**.

392

You close your eyes and calmly generate a magical breeze to whip down the passage and snuff out the fire. This provokes a clamour of Scarfell voices and you know that your guess was correct! You lead the charge and discover three intruders. Fighting blind they are easily dispatched by your force.

Immediately you press on even deeper into the mountain. Then you feel a breeze coming from up ahead and find yourself at another cave mouth leading out into the open air. Time to get airborne again! Turn to **421**.

393

You attempt to put the time delay out of your head and concentrate on the task in hand. Will you keep low, where you have more chance of seeing the enemy before they see you? (Turn to **361**) Or fly high, where this risk is greater but you can search a wider area? (Turn to **310**)

394

You peel off, hoping that your followers will have been looking for you and the sound of your magic will have attracted their attention. Roll the die; if you roll a

1, two of the Ariax in your group do not rejoin you; if you roll a 2, one does not show up. If you roll a 3 or more, all your birdmen return. Make any deductions necessary. If this roll has taken away *all* of your followers, turn to **307**. Otherwise, note down the codewords BATTLE and GROUP and decide how you are going to press home the advantage. Will you plan a direct attack? (Turn to **304**) Or try to split the Scarfells by sending some of your force to distract them? (Turn to **338**)

395

Urging your birdmen to be careful, you manage to root out two Scarfells who were lurking in a burnt out cave and put to flight three eagles which were circling aimlessly around the mountain peaks. Sure that the immediate area is clear, you lead the weary Ariax up the nearest mountainside to a different vantage point. If you have the codeword GRAVELAX, turn to **229**. If you do not have this codeword, turn to **339**.

396

You pick your way respectfully through the carnage, expecting the worst. But you see a faint stirring, and crouch at the side of a wounded Ariax who is only just regaining consciousness. With help, you lift him to his feet and drag him under cover of the biggest remaining fragment of wall. He gathers his wits amazingly quickly and is keen to join your growing band of birdmen (add him to the number of followers you currently have).

Suddenly a cry from behind alerts you to the imminent arrival of an eagle-rider. *React on instinct*. Will you:

Throw a spear at it (if you have one)?	Turn to **322**
Attempt to pull the man from his mount with a well-timed strike?	Turn to **301**
Or dive prone on the ground?	Turn to **265**

397

Looking around, the battle of Egratar has swung in your favour and your efforts have played no small part in tipping the balance. You watch two weary but still very determined Ariax finish off the final Scarfell. A temporary calm fills the room, but the noise of combat from outside serves as a reminder of your peril.

You are reunited with any Ariax you brought with you and your ranks are swelled with two new additions, both keen to follow you in the fight (note down that these two Ariax are with you). One tall, burly old birdman (who reminds you a little of the Vzler in stature) introduces himself as Gravelax, a veteran warrior who tells you he has admired your recent daring and courage. Note down the codeword GRAVELAX.

The roof in here is unstable and could collapse so you decide to get outside as quickly as possible. If you have both the codewords TIME and TOR, turn to **247**. If you have the codeword TIME but not the codeword TOR, turn to **360**. Otherwise, will you lead your group:

To the cave of your friend Rical?	Turn to **389**
Into the aerial battle still raging outside?	Turn to **286**
Or towards a scorched and blackened cave entrance below to look for survivors?	Turn to **349**

398

You are soon at the appointed place; but do any of your comrades have news? Roll the die; this is the number of birdmen in your group who do not return, either taking overlong, rejoined the main battle...or worse. Make the necessary deductions. If none of your followers come back, turn to **307**.

Now roll the die once more and add the number of Ariax who have returned to your group. If your total is 5 or less, turn to **337**. If it comes to 6 or more, turn to **413**.

399

Perhaps it is frustration which fuels your effort? The wind surges from your talons and whips off the sackcloth, sending it dancing away into the distance. You are amazed at what you see underneath: a steel cage containing a hideous little creature! It resembles a shrunken, bony human, but has a domed head, elongated limbs and bottle-green skin. It leaps deftly to its feet and stares at you hopefully with deep green eyes. It is a Jarip!

You encountered one of these mischievous, magical creatures once before, in the wizard Vashta's house in Iro. Without hesitation you dive through the air, grab the metal cage and pull up sharply. The sluggish Scarfell guard yells and curses but you are far out of range before he can prepare his bow for firing. You look down at the strange little creature. Can this thing really be controlling the giant Moogolls? If you have the codeword GROUP, turn to **298**. If you do not have this codeword, turn to **363**.

400

The temptation is too strong; you swoop directly towards the nearest Moogoll, ignoring the cries of horror from the Ariax behind you. If you have the codeword RAZE, turn to **312**. If you do not have this codeword, turn to **354**.

401

You feel the adrenalin pumping through your body as you throw your hands dramatically to the ceiling and watch as it cracks and crumbles exactly as you will it. The Scarfells look up open-mouthed but react too slowly: a huge rock detaches itself and crushes both men! When it came to it, your magic didn't let you down! You may add 1 to the die on your next two magic rolls.

Rical is out of breath and clearly not fit to fight, but nevertheless he stumbles across the barricade to congratulate you. "You can explain how you did *that* later!" he chuckles. Due to your intervention there were no Ariax casualties in this skirmish.

You tell Rical to seek refuge in the caves deeper in the mountain and that you intend to turn the tide of this battle…somehow! The other three Ariax elect to come with you; despite being older than you are, your reputation goes before you. Keep a careful track of the number of Ariax followers you have, starting with these three. You tell Rical you will see him later and head back into the fray. Turn to **386**.

402

You hurry down the passageway, ears straining for signs of danger. You come to a cave in which two Ariax and one Scarfell lie dead on the ground. Any survivors have long gone. You notice the Scarfell's spear lying next to his body and may choose to take this with you if you wish (note it down if you do).

You press on even deeper into the mountain. Eventually you feel a breeze coming from up ahead and find yourself at another cave mouth leading out into the open air. Time to get airborne again! Turn to **421**.

403

Suddenly you hear something: only the faint scrape of a boot on rock but enough to alert you to the presence of an ambush up ahead! Pre-warned, it is easy to deal with. You whisper your knowledge to the others and stealthily creep to the blind corner around which your enemy hides. Then on the signal, you turn the tables completely and surprise *them*! The fighting is swift and bloody, but results in nothing but minor injuries to any Ariax.

Is death destined to lurk around every corner? You regulate your breathing again, and in the lull feel your elemental powers at work once more: instinctively you know that there is a source of fire not much further up this tunnel, though it is out of sight at the moment. Surely it is more Scarfells lighting their way in the dark? If you want to extinguish the flame, turn to **287**. If you'd rather make sure it is not of Ariax origin first, turn to **367**.

404

The ice beneath your feet does indeed begin to buckle and crack, but not nearly as dramatically as you had hoped. The two charging Scarfells are still a way off so you determine to give it a few more seconds. But you had not counted on the fact that the archers in the main group of Scarfells would fire on you even though their comrades are in the way! An arrow suddenly flies between them and thuds directly into your chest, killing you instantly.

405

There is a frantic flurry of feathers amidst the little brown bodies shoving and striking! Roll the die. If you roll a 4 or less, turn to **306**. If you roll a 5 or more, turn to **342**.

406

You howl in pain as the spear strikes you in the left thigh. You glide to the ground in agony, but thankfully the eagle wheels away and flies off in search of a fresh target.

You look down to the bloody wound in your leg: it is painful but not life threatening and you patch it up quickly as best you can. For the rest of this adventure, you must subtract 1 from any die rolls you make (unless they relate to the actions of a *group* of Ariax and not you individually: to indicate this the word group will appear in the same sentence as 'roll the die' or you will be asked to roll the die more than once).

The wounded Ariax hurries across to where you sit. He acknowledges that you have saved his life and in return pledges you his 'loyal service'! Keep a careful track of the number of Ariax followers you have, starting with this one. Will you now head:

To the summit of the Tower of Egratar in search of Astraphet?	Turn to **341**
To the cave of your friend Rical?	Turn to **389**
Back into the aerial battle still raging above you?	Turn to **286**
Or towards a scorched and blackened cave entrance close by to look for survivors?	Turn to **349**

407

As you scramble airborne, you find that three Ariax warriors have followed you. Your reputation has spread and they see you as a leader, even though they are older than you. Keep a careful track of the number of Ariax followers you have, starting with these three. Now roll the die. If you roll a 2 or less, turn to **365**. If you roll a 3 or more, turn to **426**.

408

One brave soul immediately volunteers for the task. You urge him to be careful and to report back as soon as possible. Roll the die. If you roll a 2 or less, turn to **253**. If you roll a 3 or more, turn to **377**.

409

The Ariax strike with deadly force and all pull up safely; it is a resounding victory! Three Scarfells lie dead but despite this, one survivor seems more concerned with a large object covered in brown sackcloth, moving it away from the danger area. Is this what you're looking for? As the man's attention is distracted, you work your way down towards him and when you spot a chance to move, you decide to take it. Turn to **226**.

410

You wait a few more spine tingling moments and feel strangely calm and confident as you begin to release your power. Roll the die. If you roll a 2 or less, turn to **366** (unless you have the codeword RAZE, in which case turn to **305** instead). If you roll a 3 or 4, turn to **305**. If you roll a 5 or more, turn to **379**.

411

You manage to grab hold of a lump of rock protruding from the wall and use the leverage to kick out against the hapless man. He loses his hold on you and falls down the cliff face. You have thoughts only for returning immediately to the fray! Will you head:

To the summit of the Tower of Egratar in search of Astraphet?	Turn to **341**
Into the aerial battle still raging above you?	Turn to **286**
Or towards a scorched and blackened cave entrance close by to look for survivors?	Turn to **349**

412

You signal for quiet and proceed further down the tunnel. Roll the die. If you roll a 2 or less, turn to **336**. If you roll a 3, turn to **382**. If you roll a 4 or more, turn to **258**.

413

One of the Ariax has the news you have been hoping for! He tells you that he found a group of six Scarfells in a little dell not far from the Tower of Egratar. Apparently it commands a view of the aerial battle. This must be it: why else would they set up an observation point like this and not get stuck into the fighting? There's only one thing for it: off you go immediately! Turn to **254**.

414

Two men are plucked from the ground and carried away in the air, limbs flailing. You cannot help but chuckle to yourself at the sight, but then notice some unusual activity within the remaining Scarfells. One seems intent on moving a large object covered in brown sackcloth away from the scene. A second is distracted by his concern for stashing away a hand-sized item which you cannot see. You decide to take a chance that one of these things is what you are looking for. Will you try to grab the sackcloth-covered object (turn to **226**) or the smaller, hidden item (turn to **318**)?

415

You spot an opportunity to give a precariously positioned Scarfell a shove over the precipice, but when you turn back you see that you have attracted the attention of two more battle-crazed Scarfells who run over the debris towards you with murderous intent. You have seconds to act. Will you drop to the floor and try to knock the onrushing men off balance? (Turn to **252**) Back away towards the edge and draw them in one at a time? (Turn to **388**) Or attempt to use your magic to dislodge some loose blocks of masonry from the ceiling onto their heads (needing to roll a 3 or more to be successful)? If you try this and succeed, turn to **273**; if you fail, turn to **359**.

416

You call out to your wounded comrade, who turns towards you with a look of concern upon his face. You carefully withdraw the spear and inspect the wound, which is not too bad. He is still able to fly but the incident has shaken him up. Just then, another eagle-rider closes in and throws his spear. Roll the die. If you roll a 1, turn to **250**. If you roll a 2, turn to **406**. If you roll a 3, 4, 5 or 6, turn to **330**.

417

Spotting a decent looking overhang of rock, you frantically direct the retreat as the hideous Moogoll closes in. Then you feel the deadly flame gushing towards you. Roll the die; if you roll equal to or more than the number of Ariax currently in your group (not including you) they all make it to safety. If you roll less than the number of Ariax, then the number you rolled is the number of Ariax that *survive* (adjust your numbers accordingly).

The creature passes, arching back up in search of new targets, and you lead the shaken survivors in the other direction. Turn to **421**.

418

The Scarfell arrows all fall wide of the mark. The archers become enraged and turn to their axes. But clearly some of the Scarfells want to charge at the birdmen while others are trying in vain to keep the group together. You take the opportunity to order the attack, and plunge down through the air to support your warriors on the ground.

To see who gets the best of this skirmish, you will need to roll the die twice separately; first for the Scarfells and then for the Ariax. Add 5 to the Scarfell roll. Add the number of surviving Ariax in your group (including you) to the Ariax roll. Add another 1 if you are armed with a spear and want to use it (but you lose the spear if you do). Also add 1 to the Ariax roll if you have the codeword BATTLE.

If the Scarfell total is higher than the Ariax total, turn to **429**. If the scores are equal, or the Ariax win by 1 or 2, turn to **353**. If the Ariax roll is higher by 3 or more, turn to **409**.

419

You manage to achieve your aim but will it deter the onrushing frost-bear? Roll the die. If you roll a 2 or less, turn to **270**. If you roll a 3 or more, turn to **391**.

420

You feel the adrenalin pumping through your body as you channel the energy through your legs and cause the very floor to rumble and judder. The effect for all but you is terrifying as there is no explanation for the sudden tremor! The Scarfells sprawl on the ground, off balance and bewildered, and you call forth the defenders, who were not at the epicentre of the quake. The battle is soon won. When it came to it, your magic didn't let you down! You may add 1 to the die on your next two magic rolls.

Rical is out of breath and clearly not fit to fight, but nevertheless he stumbles across the barricade to congratulate you. "You can explain how you did *that* later!" he chuckles. Sadly one of the defenders lies grievously wounded at the hands of the Scarfells: one must have got a lucky strike in. You tell Rical to take him to the refuge of the caves deeper in the mountain and that you intend to turn the tide of this battle…somehow! The two other Ariax elect to come with you; despite being older than you are, your reputation goes before you. Keep a careful track of the number of Ariax followers you have, starting with these two. You tell Rical you will see him later and head back into the fray. Turn to **386**.

421

The fighting must have been raging for half an hour by now and the mountains are dotted with black scorch-marks. Still the defenders fight on and still the Scarfells assail them. If you have the codeword TOR, turn to **247**. If you do not have this codeword, turn to **316**.

422

This indecisive action meets almost immediately with disaster. Your hesitation has given one of the archers a chance to pick you out as a target and his aim is true. You fall face down to the ground in a cloud of powdery snow…

423

You hurry round the mountainside and collect two younger Ariax who had been isolated and are more than happy to swell your ranks. Then one of the older birdmen suggests splitting the group in two and offers to lead the smaller of them himself. You could cover a wider area in the same time and they could rejoin you later with any new recruits. If you agree to this suggestion, turn to **284**. If you say that you'd rather keep together in numbers, turn to **372**.

424

From somewhere deep inside you call forth hidden energies and are delighted by the degree of your success! Many of the fires suddenly billow into life and you are actually able to command them to surge towards the Scarfells, who fall back in fear. Some quick-witted Ariax deduce what you have done, incredible as it seems, and press home the attack.

You have granted the defenders new heart and gained them the momentary advantage. Note down the codeword SCORCH and turn to **415**.

425

You reel backwards as the power courses through your outstretched arms. Three loose blocks of stone break free from their positions and drop to the ground, spreading dangerous looking cracks across the remaining wall in every direction. The fact that you are responsible for this event seems to have gone almost unnoticed amid the commotion in the tower but the eagle riders *do* notice and pull their steeds away from the danger! Turn to **415**.

426

You make it out into the open air unscathed. Your followers look to you for direction and you must decide quickly where you can be of most use. Will you lead them:

To the cave of your friend Rical?	Turn to **389**
Into the aerial battle which still rages outside?	Turn to **286**
Or towards a scorched and blackened cave entrance close by to look for survivors?	Turn to **349**

427

With the chaos and carnage you have witnessed outside, desire to see Rical and fight side by side with him wins over cautiousness. Roll the die, subtracting 2 from the roll if you have the codeword CRY. If you roll a 1 or less, turn to **336**. If you roll a 2, 3 or 4, turn to **303**. If you roll a 5 or more, turn to **403**.

428

You glide effortlessly on the breeze. As soon as you top the ridge, you see that you have made a wise (or fortunate) choice: there is Scarfell activity below! You dive down onto a rocky ledge from where you can observe what is happening without being seen yourself.

You are high up on one side of a concealed valley. A group of six Scarfells stand or sit about in a dell on the other side. Your pinpoint eyesight observes a selection of baggage but no eagle mounts. It is a cunningly chosen little nook: the men are hard to spot from a distance, but are in fact not far (as the Ariax flies) from the Tower of Egratar and command a view of the aerial battle. Surely there can be no other reason for their presence here except that they are controlling the Moogolls, but how? You can see no obvious answer and infuriatingly your magic powers to carry their voices to you reveal only snatches of conversation and nothing of any use.

If you want to go back and pick up the rest of your group, turn to **274**. If you want to attempt to stop them alone, turn to **289**.

429

The combat is brief and ugly: within seconds you can see that, despite the speed and ferocity of the Ariax, the battle-axes and brute strength of the Scarfells have given them the best of it. You furiously battle on, slashing out at one man and kicking the axe from the hand of a second.

But the momentum has swung against you. As the survivors rally for a second push, the archers have readied their weapons and unleash a deadly volley of arrows into your midst. Distracted by an opponent, you cannot avoid the one that kills you …

430

You escape the forest through the gap in the trees. But exhaustion sets in; your wings feel heavy and every muscle cries out for a rest. Your magic is all but spent and even the heat and the smoke begin to affect you. You somehow struggle out of the inferno but as soon as you feel the crisp mountain snow underfoot and the chill Arian breeze on your face, you can do nothing more than collapse unconscious to the ground, the precious plant clutched to your chest.

The Scarfells have been defeated. But you do not yet realise the full cost of victory and you are soon to find that even more trials lie ahead. There is much work still to be done in book 7 of The Saga of the Ariax, entitled:

SURVIVAL OF THE ARIAX

THE SAGA OF THE ARIAX: 7
Survival of the Ariax

New rules for book 6 and 7

If you have not read book 6 of the Saga of the Ariax: 'Egratar Falls', refer to the new rules at the beginning of that book before reading book 7.

Recent events

You open your eyes and look around. You are lying in an unfamiliar cave with a dozen or so Ariax sitting around resting and conversing quietly. As you slowly come to your senses, the memories of the horrific Scarfell attack come flooding back to you. With the help of two giant, fire-breathing serpents called Moogolls, they destroyed the Tower of Egratar and slaughtered the Ariax in droves! Only the use of your magic prevented your tribe from being wiped out!

A nearby birdman notices that you are awake and summons two visitors. You smile; your old friend Rical and the veteran warrior Gravelax, who saved your life during the battle, are at your side once more.

Rical recounts how he and Gravelax found you lying unconscious, face down in the snow just outside the Forest of Arcendak. You recovered an armful of the Orphus Latix from the forest, which had been set alight by the fiery breath of the Moogolls. It is now the following morning.

Just twenty-four survivors are with you in this shallow cave system many miles north of your former home. It has already been named 'New Arian'. When you ask if that is all that remains of your once three-hundred strong tribe, Gravelax nods sadly.

"Astraphet and Arguttax were both killed in the fighting," says Rical. "Darfak too…" he adds, hanging his head as he relays the sad news about your friend.

You struggle to absorb the enormity of the tragedy. Things have never looked blacker for the Ariax: leaderless and all but annihilated. Is this the end…or a new beginning?

Now turn to **431** begin…

431

Now that you are awake, Gravelax gathers everyone together to discuss what is to be done. The mood is grim. "Before we elect a new Talotrix," he says, "we must find out if either of the female Ariax survived the battle."

"It would also be wise," says another birdman, "to properly survey our current surroundings. If we are going to make a home here, it would be nice to know we aren't sharing it with anything...nasty!"

"What about the Orphus Latix?" interjects Rical. "If there is any chance of growing it again, we must act immediately!"

A murmur passes around the assembly. All three matters need urgent attention. Some birdmen are clearly too badly hurt or fatigued to fly out today. Others stand and offer their help immediately. Though still recovering, you too put yourself forward. You alone with your magic have any chance of getting the Orphus Latix to grow. But that could wait until this evening, surely? Maybe you should fly out with one of the other parties? Will you:

    Concentrate your efforts on the magical herb?   Turn to **508**
    Join those returning to the ruins of your home?   Turn to **555**
    Or help scout the nearby mountains for danger? Turn to **631**

432

You concentrate on the ice and almost at once it begins to shift and break. Deep cracks flow outwards all around you, causing the nearest beasts to stamp about wildly. You have a second now in which to act, and if you are asked to roll the die in the next section you turn to, you may add one to the result. Now will you attack (turn to **484**) or flee (turn to **566**)?

433

Skyrll murmurs in your ear, "I don't like this Xanarel. I just get a bad feeling about these creatures. I certainly doubt any birdmen would have them as gatekeepers!"

If you want to follow his advice and fly away, you could head west (turn to **598**) or east (turn to **634**). If you disagree and want to go with them, turn to **485**.

434

You issue instructions to sweep the area and return to this place with all haste. Roll the die once separately for each birdman, deciding *before* each roll who you are rolling for. If the die roll for *you* comes up as a 6, turn to **468**. If it doesn't, but you roll a 6 for Ossen, turn to **689**. If the die roll for anyone else is a 6, turn to **649**. If none of the dice rolls a 6, turn to **558**.

435

The lightning bolt slams into your chest. You grimace but open your eyes in relief when you realise that your body has absorbed it and you are not hurt! Once again the power of the elemental crystal has saved your life! Will you now lead the way in through the window? (Turn to **674**) Or retreat from the tower at once? (Turn to **541**) (If you have the codeword KNOT, you *must* choose the first option.)

436

The Beotman raises an eyebrow. "We Beotmen are slow to involve ourselves in the affairs of orcs and men," he murmurs. He picks up his club and with a dismissive hand of farewell lumbers off in the opposite direction. When the others ask how it went, you admit you are not hopeful. Turn to **684**.

437

Ossen volunteers himself immediately to lead a party of men on the ground. He is clearly keen to prove himself to you, but his youth is a concern. Would he hold his nerve as a leader in the heat of battle? You reflect on the fact that this could have been you six months ago…return to **505**.

438

Your plan appeals to the Ariax sense of superiority over ground restricted species – but carries some risk. As one, you swoop towards the startled orcs! Roll the die. If you roll a 2 or less, turn to **587**. If you roll a 3 or more, turn to **513**.

439

Suddenly you feel the sickening sensation of being thrown backwards – followed by blackness. Pitted against the will of Nimax you have fallen short and your inexperience of mind-walking has proved disastrous; your mind is lost and even the Brilk cannot recall it to its body…

440

The yeti recovers quickly from the initial hit and flails out with a giant paw. The blow does not connect with you fully but it is enough to knock you sideways into the cave wall. As you gasp for breath, the monster bears down on you and the others are powerless to prevent the beast from savaging you with its razor sharp claws. You are torn limb from limb.

441

"There's something on the breeze this night," warns Skyrll sagely. "I think it prudent to set a watch, and volunteer myself to go first." If Gravelax is also with you, turn to **611**. Otherwise will you follow Skyrll's advice? (Turn to **648**) Or reassure him that you have found a safe place to sleep and set no watch? (Turn to **509**)

442

You float into the mind of the veteran and reveal his inner thoughts. As expected, Gravelax can be fully trusted. He truly admires you as he has previously stated and believes you are the prime candidate to be the next Talotrix! He is aware that he is probably the strongest surviving Ariax but is also comfortable as he is; it is not his nature to lead. Return to **501**.

443

There is a horrifying screech from over your shoulder as the lightning bolt slams into the chest of one of your followers, killing him instantly! Roll the die once for each of the other birdmen (re-roll any ties): the lowest scorer is the unfortunate casualty. Note down this loss (obviously you cannot follow any choices which refer to this birdman again).

Overwhelmed with grief and fury you launch yourself at the wizard and wrestle him to the ground. If you are alone, turn to **614**. If you still have at least one Ariax with you, turn to **568**.

444

The skies are rapidly darkening, filling the villagers with even more dread. You cannot be sure that the orcs will not attack at night so you volunteer the services of the dark-sighted Ariax as night watch-birds.

The men bed down for the night, weapons close at hand. You take first watch yourself and sit pondering events from the shelter of a tree with spreading branches. The Vzler would commend you for your noble actions, you are sure of that!

As the sun's rays stream across the village square next morning there has been no sign of the orcs. The rain has stopped and it is a beautiful morning, weather-wise at least! Turn to **666**.

445

The men show great courage in their running battle back to the Hieronaught but suffer many casualties. The disgusting gloats of the orcs as they hack apart fleeing victims are sickening to hear. If you have the codeword LOSS, turn to **497**. Otherwise, note down the codeword LOSS and turn to **562**.

446

You notice that Ossen has visibly grown in stature during the skirmish. There is a new glint of steel in his eye; he is relishing this! You reflect that it was a good choice to put responsibility on his shoulders. Note down the codeword MILE and return to **562**.

447

You seize the initiative, screeching for the tribe to fall back and regroup. Nimax appears frozen to the spot, looking about him in confusion and anger. The Ariax react to your cry but you see that one of the eagle-riders has picked Rical out as his next target and swoops down behind him! *React on instinct.* Will you shout a warning to your friend? (Turn to **660**) Or pick up a nearby spear and hurl it at the Scarfell? (Turn to **486**)

448

As soon as you act the others follow your lead. Almost as quickly however you feel a searing pain flash through your skull and contort your features in agony. You can see your comrades are suffering likewise and pull up with all speed. As you climb the pain recedes but just when you think you are safe there is an agonized cry from a birdman to your left. He blacks out and begins to fall. You dive down swiftly and catch him.

You are horrified to find that you are holding a corpse! Roll the die once for each of the other Ariax (re-roll any ties): the lowest scorer is the unfortunate casualty. Note down this loss (obviously you cannot follow any choices which refer to this birdman again).

There is a stunned, disbelieving silence. Yet another death. Following a mountain burial, you decide to continue your quest; there is nothing more you can do here. If you are now alone, turn to **609**. Otherwise turn to **566**.

449

The voice again drifts into your mind. "You have knowledge of elemental magic...but do not yet realise the full potential of your powers. But with the passing time ahead..."

The yaks seem to trust you and you understand that they are called Brilk, an ancient and mystical race. You then experience an extraordinary sensation; an energy coursing through your veins from your fingertips and toes to your very core. In fact, the Brilk have boosted your abilities and for the rest of the adventure you may add 1 to the die roll every time you make a magic roll.

"Now let me open your mind..." comes the voice again. It seems to be asking permission, though to do what you cannot be sure. Will you allow your mind to be 'opened' (turn to **606**) or refuse access (turn to **641**)?

450

You inform the group of your decision and they nod in agreement. Although the terrain is a little different to the icy mountains you are used to, Ariax are quite capable of surviving in the wilderness and you manage to find a shallow but dry cave to see out the storm in. A watch is set at the opening and the night passes without incident. Next morning you are relieved to find that the rain has stopped and you turn your attention to the journey south. Turn to **683**.

451

As you reach the open air above the forest you glance down. There at the uppermost window of the tower stands the wizard, calmly looking out at you with a self-assured smile on his face. He reaches out his hands and the air is suddenly filled with dagger-like shards of ice which arc through the sky at lightning speed. You cannot avoid them and your bodies fall crashing through the treetops below...

452

Gravelax glides in to land beside you as you walk across the village square. He estimates there are around fifty of the creatures, well-armed with swords, axes and the like, but one positive is that they have no missile weapons at all. Slit and the others listen intently. Gravelax then modestly tells you how he bombed the orc camp with a few boulders but that they began throwing debris at him and he couldn't do as much damage as he would have liked. You smile at your courageous and resourceful friend. Note down the codeword TEAR and turn to **444**.

453

You tell Slit that he needs to give these men the belief that they can win the day. He motions for silence and addresses them with admirable resolution considering he himself is terrified by the forthcoming battle, urging them to stand firm in the face of evil and trust that the Ariax will be able to swing the balance.

Despite the exaggeration of your influence, you can see that Slit's speech has had the desired effect on the men: they grip their makeshift weapons firmly and a grim determination seems to be creeping over them. The puffed out feathers beside you tell you that it hasn't hurt Ariax pride either! Note down the codeword FORTITUDE and turn to **505**.

454

You look around you; there are still many orcs rampaging through the village.

Roll the die. Subtract one from the roll if you have the codeword DEFEND. Subtract two if you have the codeword LOSS. Add one to the roll if you have the codeword FORTIFY or BONE. Add two if you have the codeword FORTITUDE. If the total is 3 or less, turn to **686**. If the total is 4 or more, turn to **667**.

455

You close your eyes and once again feel the supernatural sensation of the Brilk pervading your mind. This time you hear more than one voice and feel a rush of energy which swirls around your brain.

You have been granted the power to mind-blast (note down the codeword BLAST). Mind-blasting involves subjecting a single target to an excruciating burst of mental power, leaving them unable to think clearly or act normally for a few seconds. You may only use this power *once*, so choose wisely! The text will give you the option to use this power by asking if you have the codeword BLAST; you may ignore this option and save your power for later if you so choose.

You have no idea of how long you were in a trance but when you open your eyes you find the sun has climbed noticeably higher into the sky. You mentally thank the Brilk for their help and set off on the final leg of your journey home. Turn to **654**.

456

Ritsbrik is amusingly eager to take you on this expedition! If you want some of the other Ariax to accompany you on this search, turn to **670**. If you would rather go with Ritsbrik alone, turn to **655**.

457

You circle the mountain but can see no sign of any other living being apart from the yaks. You exchange confused looks with the others. If you want to land, turn to **525**. To hunt a yak, turn to **640**. If you'd rather just leave the area and continue south, turn to **566**.

458

"We discern little of life beyond our realm…" comes the reply, "You are the only bird-creatures we know…" Not very useful! Turn to **494**.

459

Your sudden appearance in the midst of the villagers causes great alarm! Many flee immediately into their houses but a few grasp farming tools and stand eyeing you warily.

"We mean you no harm," you say gently, remembering how physically imposing Ariax appear to normal humans.

Eventually one man steps forwards and addresses you. He has messy brown hair with a moustache to match and like the others wears grubby looking working-clothes. "Hail!" he says, trying to appear friendly but with a note of caution in his voice. "My name is Slit and I am the farm superior here in Dunstad. To what honour do we owe another visit by the feathered race?"

Your ears prick up immediately! "*Another* visit? You mean you have news of others like us?"

The man pauses. He senses your eagerness and clearly possesses a calculating brain as he answers with a certain confidence. "Well, you could say that, yes. And I will tell all…in return for a small favour."

You enquire as to the nature of this favour and Slit asks you to fly to the next village (Burbruk) with a message for their chief-herbalist. It is only a few miles to the west. Note down the codeword SLIT.

If you agree to take this message, turn to **504**. If you are suspicious of these humans and do not want to get involved in their affairs, turn to **683**.

460

You find it a simple enough task to command the tarpaulin to lift and there below you see the man's cart is full of bones! He quickly tries to strap it back down, chuckling nervously to himself and clearly hoping that you did not see!

Even though he lied to you about his wares, you could still head for the tower (turn to **599**). Otherwise you could continue on your way south (turn to **541**).

461

When you tell Slit what you have seen the colour drains from his face and he gasps one word: "Orcs!" Several other men in earshot run over and demand you confirm what you said.

"Please stay and help us," says Slit in desperation. "Dunstad was ransacked by orcs five winters back - dozens were killed and it took years to rebuild our lives! We are weaker now than then!" You do not have the heart to force the information you want out of him at this urgent moment and have a decision to make. Will you tell the other Ariax that you intend to help the humans defend their village (turn to **666**) or decide it is their problem and lead the way south (turn to **600**)?

462

The savage onslaught of the orcs is swiftly overrunning Dunstad! You fell two of the brutes with savage talon strikes but there are more and more of them and you are forced to take to the air, blood streaming from a leg wound. You are joined by the others and watch hopelessly as the door to the Hieronaught is kicked in and the men inside are massacred.

It is a swift and crushing victory for the green-skinned invaders. With a heavy heart you signal that you should fly south. It is a while before anyone breaks the sombre silence. Turn to **650**.

463

You grimace as your magic comes to nothing but there is no time to dwell on it; the Scarfell mounts his steed and spurs it in your direction! The eagle bears down on you with outstretched talons! *React on instinct*. Will you fling yourself sideways (turn to **668**) or leap directly upwards and hope to attack the rider with your feet as you do (turn to **563**)?

464

The adrenalin of the battle is wearing off the humans and they begin to count the cost of the victory. Slit takes you into a hut and sits down on a wooden bench. He thanks you for your help and, after addressing the survivors and organising the immediate recovery, says that he intends to honour his word.

"It must have been about four weeks ago," begins Slit, "when he came – a birdman like you."

"Just one?" you ask. Slit nods.

"Yes, and he was in a bad way. He collapsed out there on the road and some of the younger 'uns brought him in. Strange, but he couldn't speak to us or understand us like you can. Anyway our village healer managed to give him something which seemed to revitalise him over the next couple of days."

This is all well and good but you begin to wonder how it will help you to locate the rest of his tribe. You ask Slit if he noticed which direction he took when he left Dunstad.

"I do remember actually," replies the man. "He went that way," He points northwards, in the direction of your home. Puzzling indeed - have you missed something? Perhaps this was the very same messenger found by Ritsbrik?

This is disappointing; have you gone through all that just for this news? You rise and thank Slit anyway, wishing him well for the recovery of his village. "Actually," he says, "We have something of his! Maybe you could return it to him?" He leads the way to another hut and pulls out a long steel sword. "We took it and hid it when we found him," explains Slit. "We were going to give it back when we knew we could trust him – honestly – but he left rather suddenly!"

Your beak drops open at the sight of the sword. You have seen it before…in the hands of your treacherous mentor Nimax! Turn to **663**.

465

You speed off to the west with Rical, combing the mountain sides for anything of interest. You spot a large cave mouth far below and swoop down to investigate. Rical offers to stand guard while you enter. Inside, you find a high-roofed tunnel leading to an enormous cave littered with animal bones. You shudder to think what kind of beast could call this home! Then you hear Rical's voice calling your name urgently down the tunnel.

You run to meet him and see the reason for his warning: a huge shaggy yeti clambering up the cliff face towards you! It must be twice your height and possesses claws capable of killing an Ariax with one blow! Fortunately Rical has given you time to escape and you fly home, knowing that the yeti is unlikely to be able to scale the almost sheer rock face leading to your caves on the next mountain. Turn to **679**.

466

You feel you have neither the inclination nor the authority to pardon this birdman and bid him farewell, in the knowledge that you can always look for him again in the weeks to come if things change. If you are travelling alone, turn to **524**. If you brought others with you, turn to **532**.

467

You find that Skyrll has a complex personality. He is not that much older than you and certainly does not see himself in any kind of leadership role. However his mind is sharp and he is perceptive; in fact even now he is assessing escape options in his mind! Return to **501**.

468

Your search for shelter turns up something quite different! You find a few dozen humans huddled below you in a copse of trees. They appear to be a wide range of ages. What are they doing out here in the wild you wonder? You have met humans who are not Scarfells before in your trip to Iro and they were largely mistrusting and suspicious of you. But these people look almost frightened; by the weather…or something worse? If you want to fly down to them and make contact, turn to **502**. If you'd rather continue looking elsewhere, turn to **558**.

469

Someone in that tower could know something and you tell the others you are going to find out. If Ossen is with you, turn to **635**. If he is not, turn to **599**.

470

You take to the skies to the jeers of the men below you. Maybe not the most honourable action, but you owe these humans nothing. Note down the codeword SNUB.

Although the terrain is a little different to the icy mountains you are used to, Ariax are quite capable of surviving in the wilderness and you manage to find a shallow but dry cave to see out the storm in. A watch is set at the opening and the night passes without incident. Next morning you are relieved to find that the rain has stopped and you turn your attention to the journey south. Turn to **683**.

471

As the first orcs reach the outlying dwellings of Dunstad they get a nasty surprise! The plough spins up from the ground, cutting two almost in half and wounding several others. The nearby orcs holler in fear at the sight and hastily change direction. The front-runners are suddenly in among those charging in behind them and there is some in-fighting. You have blunted the initial attack but the effort was great and the plough drops back into the mud; you cannot do any more magic for the moment. If you have the codeword ATTACK, turn to **685**. If you do not have this codeword, turn to **562**.

472

You are pleasantly surprised to note that Scancaro is fighting as well as any in this battle! As he deftly avoids the sweep of a sword and fells another orc with a well placed punch you remember how nervous he was before the battle! He glides over to you and you join him in attacking another target. Note down the codeword WING and turn to **580**.

473

The snow whips directly into the Scarfell's eyes; he cries out in annoyance and staggers back, dangerously close to the cliff edge. A nearby Ariax gives him the shove he needed and he topples headlong to his doom.

If you have the codeword WING, turn to **687**. If you have the codeword HEIGHT, turn to **514**. If you have the codeword MILE, turn to **621**. If you have the codeword EYE, turn to **572**. (If you have more than one of these codewords you may choose which section to turn to.) If you have none of these codewords, turn to **595**.

474

You begin the solemn task. It is decided to place them all in one of the caves which you will then seal with your magic. You work in pairs but there just seems to be more and more of them. Rical it is who discovers Darfak, and with heavy hearts you carry him to his final resting place.

You hear your name called across the valley. It is a young Ariax named Ossen, one of those younger even than you. He tells you excitedly that one of the females is alive and being brought out now! A rare reason for celebration amidst the recent woe.

Eventually your task is complete; Astraphet's body being the last to be placed. As the others hover nearby you crack the rocks above the cave entrance, bringing down a mini-avalanche and sealing its inhabitants. It is now time to return to New Arian. Turn to **531**.

475

"Come on, what are we waiting for? We've been flying for hours! Let's hunt!" says Xoroan impatiently at your side. He begins to swoop down. *React on instinct*. Will you let him go (turn to **671**) or order him back (turn to **605**)?

476

"Liar!" The single word flares fiercely in your mind flowed by a short stab of pain into the deepest part of your brain. There is no doubt you have antagonised the yaks now and you decide to withdraw peacefully from the powerful beasts. Turn to **566**.

477

Just as you are beginning to get fed up, you see in the distance a collection of wooden huts and larger stone buildings that you recognise as human dwellings.

As you get closer you see it is overrun with ugly, green-skinned humanoids! They are almost Scarfell in size but clearly undisciplined; they are stamping about in the mud hacking randomly at trees and buildings with their swords and axes or brawling with each other and generally destroying everything in sight! Note down the codeword GREEN.
It goes without saying that you want to avoid *this* area! Will you:

    Continue south?   Turn to **450**
    Or follow the road leading east from the village
    (which may lead to another settlement)?   Turn to **526**

478

As the strange being glides closer you hail him courteously. He looks you up and down and you notice that his crossbow, held lazily in his lap, is pointing straight at you. Whether deliberate or not you will never know, but there is a sudden twang and the bolt is loosed, plunging straight into your chest and through your heart! You are killed instantly.

479

You try desperately to call the men's attention to this new threat, but even as you do the battering ram slams into the wall of the Hieronaught with a thud that resounds around the village. As well as cracking the stonework, it galvanises the orcs with the promise of further destruction and strikes a visible blow to the morale of the defenders. You must act quickly: will you attack the orc ramming party (turn to **688**) or use your magic to break the battering ram (now needing a 4 or more to succeed). If you make this magic roll, turn to **508**. If you fail it, turn to **490**.

480

"I don't like the idea of being cooped up in that building," says Xoroan directly, "Far better to fight out in the open – a strong initial strike that the orcs aren't expecting while we've got numbers on our side." Return to **505**.

481

The orcs fleeing south do not seem to have any kind of plan past self-preservation! Having made doubly sure, you bank sharply in the sky and swoop back to Dunstad. If you have the codeword FORTITUDE, turn to **571**. If you do not have this codeword, turn to **553**.

482

You relax your whole body and close your eyes as directed by the Brilk, entering a kind of dream state where you still retain consciousness. Ghost-like you leave your body and drift rather than fly towards home. The snow is tinged with purple in your vision and you feel no breeze or sensation of temperature at all. You've experienced many strange things recently but this beats them all!

In the mouth of the cave you left days before your fears are confirmed: Nimax stands alone with his thoughts, gazing out across the mountains! It is all you can do to quell your rising anger, something the Brilk warned you could be very dangerous while mind-walking. If you've seen enough and want to return to your own body, turn to **603**. If you want to try and enter Nimax's mind, turn to **581**.

483

You launch yourself towards the traitor but he sees you coming and pushes the other birdman at you. As you disentangle yourself, Nimax coldly thrusts the spear under your wing and into your side, unsighted. You fall backwards, mortally wounded, looking up into the face of your murderer who is already feigning sorrow at your fall...

484

Time to show these beasts who is king of the mountains! Roll the die, adding one to the roll if you have the codeword OUT. If the total is 1 or 2, turn to **538**. If you get a 3 or 4, turn to **448**. If the total is 5 or more, turn to **632**.

485

"We'll see where they take us, but keep your eyes open," you say. The little creatures lead you down a well-trodden path which winds through the trees. The inclement weather makes for a gloomy half-light but this forest is still far more airy than Arcendak back home.

You walk for ten minutes or so, the little men chattering away to themselves for most of the time. You follow them straight through some thick bushes and when you look up you notice that the little creatures have gone! No-one saw where they went! Before you can make another move though, you find that a thick root has encircled your ankle and further tendrils of vegetation are tightening around your body. The more you struggle, the more they constrict – and the same is happening to the others!

Then you become aware of a disturbance in the undergrowth some way off, accompanied by the snarling of a large beast! Did your guides deliberately lead you into a trap? You cannot get free and decide to use you magic on the plants. Roll the die. If you roll a 1 or 2, turn to **612**. If you roll a 3 or 4, turn to **565**. If you roll a 5 or more, turn to **681**.

486

You quickly grab the spear but when you look up you see Rical falling forwards with a spear in the back! In blind fury you fling your weapon and score a direct hit on the Scarfell, who throws up his arms as he is unseated. You run to your dying friend but blinded by grief you fail to see the spear coming which ultimately kills you...

487

A stone wall is all that stands in the way of freedom – and you have time to concentrate and summon your magic! You run your hands over the smooth surface and feel the power coursing down your arms and through your palms. Cracks appear soon enough, spreading in all directions as your comrades look on open beaked!

But you are not safe yet! As the stone crumbles and splits and blocks tumble outwards onto the forest floor, you are aware that the noise could easily alert your captor. You signal for caution as you climb through the gap in the wall to freedom. Roll the die. If you roll a 1 or 2, turn to **451**. If you roll a 3, 4, 5 or 6, turn to **682**.

488

You collect as big a rock as you can carry and swoop low over the orcs, letting it fall over the largest group. Two of the brutes are crushed and the others look up into the evening skies to see you swooping overhead, like a spectre. They begin hurling smaller rocks and bits of broken wood skywards, and shouting language you are unfortunate to be able to understand! Having seen enough, you turn in the air and fly as fast as you can back to Dunstad. Note down the codeword TEAR and turn to **444**.

489

As the orcs pour in, multiple ambush groups spring out hurling pitchforks and other assorted makeshift projectiles. The furious orcs howl and curse but the men of Dunstad are gone, sensibly refusing to go toe-to-toe with the charging orcs. But it has been enough; the initial orc attack has been blunted.

If you have the codeword ATTACK, turn to **685**. If you do not have this codeword, turn to **562**.

490

The power flows into the trunk and cracks stream down it towards the gnarled hands of the orcs. But you cannot muster enough to do any more and as you redouble your efforts an orc behind you throws a hand-axe into your back from close range. The orcs heedlessly trample your dying body in their eagerness for more blood…

491

As modestly as possible you remind the assembly of the Scarfell attack on Egratar and your part in its defence. Rical springs up. "It is safe to say that if it wasn't for Xanarel, we would all be dead!" cries your friend.

"Ah yes, I have heard an account of this!" retorts Nimax. "We are fortunate indeed that Xanarel possesses such…*talents* shall we say? And is it true that their acquirement coincides not only with the death of the Vzler but an excursion to Musk? Do we *know* that it is not by Xanarel's doing that the

Scarfells were able to tame the Moogoll?" He casts his gaze around the circle, to some nods. Others avert their eyes and look down at the ground.

You struggle to contain your emotions in the face of such twisted reasoning, but getting angry will only play into Nimax's hands. Turn to **588**.

492

You speed off to the west, combing the mountainsides for anything of interest. You spot a large cave mouth far below and lead the way down to investigate. Scancaro offers to stand guard while the rest of you go in. A high-roofed tunnel leads to an enormous cave littered with animal bones.

"What manner of beast..?" wonders Rical aloud. It is fated that you should find out! Scancaro races into the cavern, looking scared.

"It's coming!" he splutters, and you follow him, wondering why he didn't call to you from the cave entrance!

Too late: blocking your escape is a huge shaggy yeti! It must be twice your height and possesses claws capable of killing an Ariax with one blow! As it lumbers forwards you have the presence of mind to use your magic to freeze the moisture on the tunnel floor, hoping to make the charging monster lose its footing. Roll the die. If you roll a 1 or 2, turn to **647**. If you roll a 3, 4, 5 or 6, turn to **573**.

493

It seems that your words lift a weight from Eyrax's shoulders. "I will not let you down Xanarel," he says. "If I can contribute to the success of this mission, I will." Note down the codeword OUT and turn to **532**.

494

Just then, three other Brilk trot across the snow, tossing their heads and snorting. The others seem disturbed by this, as if receiving bad news. You appear to have been forgotten, and the mental connection has been broken. There's nothing for it but to depart. Turn to **566**.

495

The description of the 'orcs' fits those creatures you saw earlier, back the way you came. If you want to head north to find them, turn to **544**. If you don't believe this is a worthwhile lead and want to continue south, turn to **650**.

496

Slit grabs you by the hand and starts pumping it up and down as he thanks you, a custom that reminds you of Vashta the wizard's behaviour. You begin by looking over what you have to fight the orcs with. Dunstad is home to over two-hundred people, but many of them are women and children and none of them are trained warriors.

"We can muster about eighty fighting men," says Slit, "though they will have only their farming tools as weapons I'm afraid. The only other aid we could seek would be the Beotmen; the solitary half-giants who live in the lands to the east. But only you could possibly reach them in time."

You hope the men have the stomach for the fight! The sun will set in just a few hours, so you must decide how best to use that time. If (despite the weather) you want to fly to where the orcs are camped to see what you're facing, turn to **578**. If you'd rather give another Ariax this mission, note down who you send). You could fly into the Beotlands and seek the aid of the Beotmen? (Turn to **636**) Or you could stay in Dunstad and see if you can organise and strengthen their defences? (Turn to **551**)

497

Very few ever reach their destination; overrun by orcs they are slaughtered in droves. You are joined by the others and watch hopelessly as the door to the Hieronaught is kicked in and the remaining defenders are massacred.

The battle has been lost and with a heavy heart you signal that you should fly south. It is a while before anyone breaks the sombre silence. Turn to **650**.

498

You have noted a subtle change in Skyrll. His experiences in the southern lands have changed him and he returns to the tribe with his beak held high. He tells you that he hopes you become the next Talotrix, and will back you all the way if Nimax has indeed returned. Note down the codeword HEIGHT. If you have the codeword OPEN, turn to **554**. If you do not have this codeword, turn to **654**.

499

Rical is first to volunteer, but much as you would like to have him with you he is clearly not sufficiently recovered from Crackbeak for such a journey and the hardships it may bring. Similarly drained is Ritsbrik and he announces quickly that he is not fit for selection.

This leaves five others. The general consensus is that to take all five would leave the rest of you vulnerable (the Scarfells may return) so you decide to take just one or two Ariax with you.

Gravelax you already know. The veteran warrior is keen to accompany you, but would also make a good stand in leader here.

The second volunteer is called Xoroan, another of the Vzler's protégés and a capable warrior. You are told he was outstanding during the battle of Egratar.

Next up is one of the youngest Ariax left alive, Ossen. He is enthusiastic but a little overeager in his desire to be chosen!

Skyrll is a quiet, reflective birdman. His background is as a craftsbird and he simply offers his service without show.

The final option is Scancaro, another birdman from Arguttax's ranks. You met him in passing during the battle with the Scarfells and feel he is volunteering primarily because he feels guilt at coming through the battle unscathed. But how would he cope with the outside world?

You mull over the options. If you decide to take one or two of these birdmen with you on your search, note down their names and turn to **661**. If you announce that you will travel alone, turn to **582**.

500

Nothing comes of your magic this time. It seems the yaks are aware of what you were attempting to do because they begin to advance on you. You have a strange feeling they have blocked your attack…but how could they? Will you attack them? (Turn to **484**) Try to show friendship? (Turn to **662**) Or flee the area? (Turn to **582**)

501

A slightly different voice continues in your head. "We can allow you into their minds if you wish…just enough to discover a little of their true character…" If you wish to take the Brilk up on their offer (they reassure you it is quite safe) turn to the sections indicated below, which will return you to this one afterwards.

For Gravelax, turn to **442**. For Ossen, turn to **539**. For Scancaro, turn to **633**. For Xoroan, turn to **619**. For Skyrll, turn to **467**. In addition, if you have the codeword OUT you may turn to **575**. Once you have read all of the minds that you wish to, or if you choose not to do this in the first place, turn to **494**.

502

You glide down to land a short distance from the humans so as not to frighten them, and ask what they are doing out here in the wilds. The bedraggled group seem less wary of you than you had imagined and you are approached by an elderly man with wispy grey hair plastered to his head with the rain.

"Orcs!" he spits. Several of the female humans begin weeping at the very mention of the word. The old man tells you how dozens of these orcs, 'green-skinned humanoid creatures who delight in wanton destruction' rampaged through his village of Burbruk earlier today, killing most of the inhabitants! He and any others who could fled for the hills.

A short man with a shaven head and his arm in a sling steps forwards. "The orcs will feast tonight but tomorrow I fear they will set a course for Dunstad, the next village along from us! It is quite a way on foot or we would warn them…"

If you offer to carry the news of the orcs to Dunstad, turn to **518** if you are alone or **673** if the other Ariax are with you. If you would sooner leave the humans to sort out their own business, turn to **540**.

503

You sprint down the spiral stairs of the tower, screeching to Ossen. You hear his answering call from the very depths of the building and find him locked in a dingy stone cell. You take your time to concentrate and use your magic to split the door in two down the middle. Ossen shakes his head in wonder as he steps through the wreckage and you explain what has happened. You notice that he has visibly grown in stature during his adventure. There is a new glint of steel in his eye; he is relishing the danger!

You hurry back to the summit of the tower and are relieved to get out into the open air. Note down the codeword MILE and turn to **541**.

504

Slit gives you the message (something about trade that is of no interest to you) and you speed westwards, following the road that leads from Dunstad to Burbruk. You have flown some distance when you see what must be Burbruk on the horizon. As you get closer however you see that all is not well; in fact around fifty ugly, green-skinned humanoids, well-armed with swords, axes and the like are stamping their way down the road from the village in the direction of Dunstad! A quick check over Burbruk reveals it to have been devastated – there are no living beings in sight!

If you want to return to Dunstad and warn the villagers, turn to **461**. If you'd rather leave the humans to their fate, turn to **683**.

505

As the villagers organise themselves you call an Ariax council of war on the roof of the Hieronaught. There is still no sign of the orcs. To listen to what each of your followers has to say about the forthcoming battle, turn to the sections indicated below, which will return you to this one afterwards.

For Gravelax, turn to **601**. For Ossen, turn to **437**. For Scancaro, turn to **535**. For Xoroan, turn to **480**. For Skyrll, turn to **561**. In addition, if you have the codeword OUT you may turn to **645**. Once you have heard all you wish to hear, turn to **570**.

506

The men of Dunstad answer your call, sallying forth from the Hieronaught and the orcs suddenly find themselves faced with club, talon and pitchfork! The Beotman has forged his way through to the biggest orc, a snarling brute in crimson armour who swings his blade at his head. The Beotman blocks the blow with his club and smashes the orc senseless with a mighty left hook!

As the orcs fall back you keep up the momentum by using your magic to shake the ground under their feet; fear has become your number one weapon.

The stragglers are being overrun and slain by groups of bold villagers. Within minutes, the orcs have gone: the battle has been won and you are joined on the ground by your fellow Ariax. The Beotman is the hero of the hour but has suffered some nasty looking wounds and is led away to have them seen to. If you have the codeword SNUB, turn to **585**. If you do not have this codeword, turn to **464**.

507

It is an intense, draining effort to stay in Nimax's mind but within the few seconds that you can stand it you experience the jealousy and hatred that your former mentor feels towards you, coupled with his burning desire to be the new Talotrix.

You drift back to your body as quickly as you can and open your eyes, knowing that there is another battle yet to come. Bidding the Brilk farewell, you take to the skies for the final leg of your return journey. Turn to **654**.

508

You take the now familiar herb, wilted and brown around its dark green edges, and fly to a plateau at the summit of the mountain. In the Forest of Arcendak the Orphus Latix grew on quite rocky ground so you locate a similar area.

You kneel and reverently place the plant in the ground, willing the earth, rock and vegetation to take it and grant it a second lease of life. The power channelling through your hands is reassuring...but only time will tell how successful you have been. If it doesn't grow now, then that's it.

Some time later, the other groups return, bringing with them one of the female Ariax, alive! There is rejoicing at this rare bit of good news! Turn to **622**.

509

You feel as safe as you ever have as you bed down for the night. Roll the die and add the number of Ariax with you to the result. If the total is 5 or more, turn to **556**. If it is 4 or less, turn to **623**.

510

You fly for over an hour but every forest yields only disappointment. If you want to steer your course more south-west, turn to **634**. To continue searching in this direction, turn to **548**.

511

The lightning bolt slams into the chest of the unfortunate, who is killed immediately. His body drops like a stone out of the sky, crashing through the forest canopy below and out of sight. Note down this loss (obviously you cannot follow any choices which refer to this birdman again).

If you are now alone, turn to **628**. If you still have at least one Ariax with you *react on instinct*. Will you flee (turn to **541**) or push on for the tower, and revenge (turn to **674**)? (If you have the codeword KNOT, you *must* choose the final option.)

512

It is hard to tell from the Beotman's expression whether this matters to him or not. Roll the die. If you roll an odd number, turn to **528**. If you roll an even number, turn to **569**.

513

Two orcs are successfully plucked from the ground and howl in terror at their plight! They are dropped right into the midst of the others, causing comparatively few casualties but striking fear into the remainder as you continue to swoop menacingly overhead! If you have the codeword BONE, turn to **629**. If you do not have this codeword, turn to **454**.

514

Amidst the commotion you hear Skyrll's raised voice shouting your name and turn to see him locked in combat with Nimax, who wields a Scarfell spear! What is going on?

React on instinct. If you have the codeword BLAST, turn to **537**. If you do not have this codeword you could either attack Nimax (turn to **483**) or demand he releases Skyrll (turn to **610**)?

515

Although you sweep the area thoroughly, you find nothing. Ritsbrik seems perplexed and you overhear one of the others suggesting that maybe the messenger wasn't dead after all! The good-natured bickering which breaks out is amusing, but suddenly you have the strange feeling of being watched... You scan the mountains all around you but see nothing. Not very reassuring! You shudder involuntarily and hastily suggest a return home. If you want to assess the offers to travel with you before you set off in search of the forest-birdmen, turn to **499**. To go alone, turn to **582**.

516

You are suddenly racked with intense mental pain – it feels as if your skull will split! After a few seconds it subsides just as abruptly as it started but your head is still pounding and you must deduct one from the die roll if asked to make one in the next section you turn to. After that you will have recovered. You hear the mysterious yak repeat its message inside your head. If you now kneel, turn to **557**. If you want to lead the retreat, turn to **583**.

517

In the silence your feathers prickle with anticipation. Then you are somehow aware of being asked a question: "Are you a magic user..?" Will you mentally reply that you are? (Turn to **449**) Or deny this? (Turn to **476**)

518

You first return to your appointed meeting place and tell the others what you have discovered. They listen with interest about these humans, their only previous experience of men being the Scarfells! Turn to **673**.

519

As you leap forwards, the wizard points his index finger and another bolt of lightning bursts forth! Roll the die. If you roll a 1 or 2, turn to **534**. If you roll a 3 or 4, turn to **443**. If you roll a 5 or 6, turn to **591**.

520

You fly for a good long while but the landscape below is depressingly bare. There is nothing but the odd trundling wagon or wild animal roaming about and the gathering storm is making flying extremely unpleasant. Maybe the Beotmen are all sheltering from the rain. If you want to keep searching anyway, turn to **592**. If you think you should return to the village, turn to **684**.

521

The men seem to draw courage from your presence. On your signal they surge from their hiding place, slaying two orcs and immediately running for cover. Another band of men cuts across as you retreat, and you gather in hiding once more unscathed.

Roll the die, adding two if you have the codeword ATTACK. Add a further one to the roll if Gravelax, Xoroan or Ossen are also leading ambushes. If the total is 2 or less, turn to **462**. If it is 3 or 4, turn to **593**. If it is 5 or more, turn to **659**.

522

Two orcs saw you land and charge towards you, howling for your blood. But before they can get close enough, you pour your elemental power into the barrel, causing the water to gush out at them like a fist and knock them backwards! Most of the other orcs are easily able to avoid this torrent – it has not hindered them as much as you had hoped – but you have gained a small advantage. If you are asked to roll the die in the next section you turn to you may add one to the roll. Will you now join the hand-to-hand fighting on the ground? (Turn to **677**) Or try the idea of using the orcs as bombs? (Turn to **438**)

523

Once more you engage your hated enemies in bitter air-to-air combat! Nimax appears frozen to the spot, looking about him in confusion and anger. The Ariax react to your cry but you see that ahead of you a Scarfell has dismounted, drawn his axe and begun preying on wounded birdmen that are not as agile as others. If you have the codeword BLAST, turn to **678**. If you do not have this codeword, you decide to use you magic to blind the Scarfell with a cloud of mountain snow. Roll the die. If you roll a 1 or 2, turn to **463**. If you roll a 3 or more, turn to **473**.

524

That night you find a high up hidden crag and settle down as you have on your other expeditions away from home. But soon after you fall asleep you are specifically targeted by a lurking figure nearby who sees to it that you never wake up. The identity of your murderer remains a mystery…

525

As soon as you land, the nearest yaks turn their heads and slowly walk towards you. As you look this way and that you realise that they are moving to encircle you!

If Xoroan is with you, turn to **680**. If he is not, but Skyrll is, turn to **618**. If neither of these two Ariax is present will you hold up your hands in friendship? (Turn to **662**) Attack the yaks? (Turn to **484**) Or if you sense danger, you could use your magic to crack the ice beneath the yak's feet to demonstrate your power (needing a 3 or more to succeed)? If you succeed with this magic roll, turn to **432**. If you fail it, turn to **500**.

526

The rain is intensifying and there are only isolated bushes and trees out here on the road. Finally you do indeed make out another village through the downpour, similar in size to the first one. You have met humans (who are not Scarfells) before in your trip to Iro and they were largely mistrusting and suspicious of you. If you want to make contact and warn them of their danger, turn to **625**. If you would rather not get involved and seek shelter elsewhere in the surrounding countryside, turn to **450**.

527

Ossen makes it to the tower safely and enters through the window. You wait in anticipation for his return. After ten minutes you are concerned – what could be taking him so long? Another five minutes pass and you decide that you must go in after him...Note down the codeword KNOT and turn to **599**.

528

The Beotman gazes thoughtfully into the distance. "I will think about it," he says, "But I have other things to attend to..." You take this as a no and know that to pursue the issue would be pointless. Turn to **684**.

529

When nothing comes of your magic you are forced to fall back. You pick up a group of men and lead them in a rapid strike on two orcs who seem distracted by hacking apart a wagon. The orcs are quickly slain and you take the chance to look about you. If you have the codeword TEAR, turn to **489**. If you do not have this codeword, but you have the codeword DEFEND, turn to **462**. Otherwise, roll the die, adding two if you have the codeword ATTACK. Add a further one to the roll if Gravelax, Xoroan or Ossen are leading ambushes. If the total is 3 or less, turn to **462**. If it is 4 or 5, turn to **593**. If it is 6 or more, turn to **659**.

530

For the remainder of the morning, there is a buzz of anticipation in the air and only one topic of conversation! You spend the time in contemplation with Rical out in the open. A few hours later, the entire tribe (apart from the female) assembles around the edge of the appointed bowl of rock, which commands a panoramic view in three directions.

"Before we take a vote, we must assess the strengths and weaknesses of each candidate," says an Ariax whose disfigured beak displays the lasting legacy of Crackbeak. There is general agreement to his suggestion. You see Nimax glancing round the circle. He then makes eye contact with you for a second before looking away. You know that if Nimax is elected Talotrix you could not bear to stay and serve him. The same is certainly true in reverse.

The key issue is who do the Ariax believe is telling the truth about what happened? At the moment the audience is divided.

As the younger of the two, you are offered the chance to speak first. Will you concentrate on your recent achievements? (Turn to **491**) Or on Nimax's treacherous nature and murderous intentions? (Turn to **669**)

531

Leaving the others to relate your news, you collect the Orphus Latix, wilted and brown around its dark green edges, and fly to a plateau at the summit of the mountain. In the Forest of Arcendak the herb grew on quite rocky ground so you locate a similar area.

You kneel and reverently place the plant in the ground, willing the earth, rock and vegetation to take it and grant it a second lease of life. The power channelling through your hands is reassuring...but only time will tell how successful you have been. If it doesn't grow now, then that's it. Turn to **622**.

532

You fly onwards for the rest of the day, keeping a moderate pace to allow the non-magically enhanced birdmen a chance to keep up with you! As darkness falls you find a high up hidden crag and prepare to settle down for the night as you have on your other expeditions away from home. You have never before set a watch in Arian. If Skyrll is with you, turn to **441**. If he is not but Gravelax is present, turn to **611**. If you chose neither of these birdmen to accompany you, will you set a watch (turn to **648**) or not (turn to **509**)?

533

"We discern little of life beyond our realm..." comes the reply, "You are the only bird-creatures we know..."

There is a pause before you hear the voice again: "Now let me open your mind..." It seems to be asking permission, though to do what you cannot be sure. Will you allow your mind to be 'opened'? (Turn to **606**) Or refuse access? (Turn to **641**)?

534

The lightning bolt slams into your chest. You are dead before you hit the ground.

535

Scancaro is clearly uneasy about the coming conflict; his suggestion that you use you magic to frighten the orcs into fleeing reveals a certain reluctance to do battle and you remember that healing rather than fighting is his speciality. Return to **505**.

536

A man with messy brown hair and a moustache to match runs over to you puffing with exhaustion. "Thank you, thank you strangers!" he pants, "My name is Slit and I am the farm superior here in Dunstad. You have arrived in the nick of time - we undoubtedly owe you our lives! To what honour do we owe another visit by the feathered race?"

Your ears prick up immediately! "*Another* visit? You mean you have news of others like us?"

"Why yes!" replies Slit, a little surprised. Seeing your eagerness to hear more, he takes you into a hut and sits down on a wooden bench.
"It must have been about four weeks ago," begins the man, "when he came – a birdman like you."

"Just one?" you ask. Slit nods.

"Yes, and he was in a bad way. He collapsed out there on the road and some of the younger 'uns brought him in. Strange, but he couldn't speak to us or understand us like you can. Anyway our village healer managed to give him something which seemed to revitalise him over the next couple of days."

This is all well and good but you begin to wonder how it will help you to locate the rest of his tribe. You ask Slit if he noticed which direction he took when he left Dunstad.

"I do remember actually," replies the man. "He went that way," He points northwards, in the direction of your home. Puzzling indeed - have you missed something? Perhaps this was the very same messenger found by Ritsbrik?

This is disappointing; not the lead it appeared to be. You rise and thank Slit anyway, wishing him well for the recovery of his village. "Actually," he says, "We have something of his! Maybe you could return it to him?" He leads the way to another hut and pulls out a long steel sword. "We took it and hid it when we found him," explains Slit. "We were going to give it back when we knew we could trust him – honestly – but he left rather suddenly!"

Your beak drops open at the sight of the sword. You have seen it before…in the hands of your treacherous mentor Nimax! Turn to **663**.

537

You had resolved not to waste your power on Nimax, but the urgency of the situation justifies your actions. You step towards him and unleash the mental-blast! Nimax immediately releases his victim and staggers backwards, hands to his head. As you rush to aid your fallen comrade you see a Scarfell swoop down behind Nimax and even as he regains his senses and glowers at you with savage fury in his eyes, a spear bursts through his chest!

You duck as the Scarfell swoops overhead. Nimax drops to his knees gurgling blood before falling face down in the snow, dead. Turn to **690**.

538

The yaks have been angered and unleash the devastating force of their psychic powers upon you. An intense pain builds rapidly in your head until it becomes unbearable and you black out, never to regain consciousness…

539

Inside Ossen's mind you discover the young Ariax's burning desire to prove himself to his elders like you have done. He looks up to you with something approaching hero worship and is desperate for you to be the new Talotrix. You feel rather embarrassed to be privy to these private thoughts, but no doubt flattered too! Return to **501**.

540

You are fortunate to soon find a shallow but dry cave to see out the storm in. A watch is set at the cave mouth and the night passes without incident. Next morning, you are relieved to find that the rain has stopped and you turn your attention back to the journey south (turn to **683**).

541

A few miles further south you come across a huge, ogre-like man with a protruding jaw sitting slumped up against a tree by the side of a road. If you have the codeword CLUB, turn to **620**. If you do not have this codeword, you land and rush over to him, finding him to be sorely wounded. He looks up through half closed eyes in a face caked with dried blood.

You ask what happened to him. He can manage few words but you find out that yesterday he was attacked by a band of green-skinned orcs. His wounds are mortal, but before he dies he leaves you with a cryptic message. He mumbles something about the orcs and birdmen. You dearly wish you could ask if anyone else can confirm what he said, but you are the only one who can understand. Did he mean what you thought he did: that the orcs had a birdman prisoner? If you have either the codeword GREEN or SNUB, turn to **495**. If you have neither of these codewords, you have little idea where to search for the orcs (turn to **650**).

542

Slit gives you the message and you speed westwards, following the road that leads from Dunstad to Burbruk. As promised you see Burbruk on the horizon after a few miles. But as you get closer you see that all is not well; in fact the village is overrun with ugly, green-skinned humanoids! They are almost Scarfell in size but clearly lack discipline; they are stamping about in the mud hacking at things with their swords and axes or brawling with each other and generally destroying everything in sight! A quick check over Burbruk reveals it to have been devastated – there are no living beings in sight! Note down the codeword GREEN.

If you want to return to warn Slit and the other villagers, turn to **644**. If you'd rather leave nature to run its course and seek shelter elsewhere, turn to **450**.

543

You motion for silence before delivering a rousing speech about courage in the face of the enemy and solidity in the defence of their home. You pledge your full support to the village and talk up the fighting prowess of the Ariax, saying that you have come through harder battles than this before (which is true)! The men listen in silence, their faces grim. It is difficult to tell what kind of effect your speech has had. Turn to **505**.

544

You fly north, yet another diversion on your seemingly never-ending quest to find the forest-birdmen. You soon pick up a distinctive trail of devastation through the countryside and follow it eastwards along a dirt track that snakes over the horizon.

A broken signpost to 'Dunstad' informs you of the name of the village you see in the distance. When you get there you find a pitch battle raging between the orcs and the inhabitants of the village, rugged looking men but poorly armed with pitchforks and other assorted farming equipment. The orcs are outnumbered but their strength and ferocity more than makes up for this and it is only a matter of time before the humans succumb. There is no sign of any birdmen. Will you:

Join the battle on the side of the humans?	Turn to **638**
Join the battle on the side of the orcs?	Turn to **594**
Or leave things to run their natural course and go elsewhere?	Turn to **650**

545

You close your eyes and once again feel the supernatural sensation of the Brilk pervading your mind. This time you hear more than one voice and feel a surge of energy which swirls around your brain.

You have been granted the power of truth-speak (note down the codeword TRUTH). When you direct this power at a chosen target, they will be compelled to answer any question you put to them truthfully. You may only use this power *once*, so choose wisely! The text will give you the option to use this power by asking if you have the codeword TRUTH; you may ignore this option and save your power for later if you so choose.

You have no idea of how long you were in a trance but when you open your eyes you find the sun has climbed noticeably higher into the sky. You mentally thank the Brilk for their help and set off on the final leg of your journey home. Turn to **654**.

546

Although you sweep the area thoroughly, you find nothing. Ritsbrik seems perplexed and you overhear one of the others suggesting that maybe the messenger wasn't dead after all! You smile at the good-natured bickering which breaks out and suggest that you return home. If you want to assess the offers to travel with you before you set off in search of the forest-birdmen, turn to **499**. To go alone, turn to **582**.

547

Eyrax is intrigued rather than horrified to hear the news. His kinship with the tribe that made him an outcast has understandably diminished over time. "Does this change my...situation?" he asks hesitantly. Under the circumstances, will you grant him a full pardon and direct him back to Rical and the others? (Turn to **656**) Say that you will accept him back into the tribe if he accompanies you on your search for the forest-birdmen and proves himself worthy? (Turn to **493**) Or despite recent events, uphold the long traditions of the Ariax and disappoint him? (Turn to **466**)

548

In the distance you see another large forest. You swoop over the treetops, again screeching for other birdmen. After a couple of wide sweeps of the area you land and are joined by the others. There has been no activity whatsoever.

You exchange disappointed looks but then something does emerge from the trees, at ground level. It is two small creatures, who resemble half-grown humans. They wear very grubby clothes made of a patchwork of materials and while one has a shock of brown hair which appears uncontrollable, the other is bald.

"Come, come!" squeaks the hairless one and they both begin beckoning you into the forest with them. If Skyrll is with you, turn to **433**. If he is not will you go with the little men? (Turn to **485**) Or fly away; heading either west (turn to **598**) or east (turn to **634**)?

549

"We should stay and fight!" urges Xoroan, forcefully. "This could be our best lead yet about the whereabouts of the forest-birdmen," he adds, seeing your bemused reaction to his initial outburst. Will you agree to help the men of Dunstad? (Turn to **496**) Or stay out of it and seek shelter elsewhere? (Turn to **470**)

550

Apart from a flock of crows that you disturb, you see no evidence of birdlife at all. You keep one eye on the tower, but there is no activity there either. Then you notice a horse and cart being driven around the edge of the trees by a human in a blue weather-beaten travelling cloak. The cart is covered so you cannot see what is in it. Will you land so you can speak to the man? (Turn to **584**) Head for the tower? (Turn to **469**) Try screeching to attract the attention of any forest-birdmen about? (Turn to **626**) Or leave this forest completely and continue south? (Turn to **541**)

551

Dunstad is an out of the way agricultural settlement surrounded by farmland for miles around: hardly a fortress! Apart from one large building in the centre of the village made of stone, the dwellings are little more than mud huts and cannot be defended. There is no wall around the perimeter and the river is narrow enough to leap over in many places.

Nevertheless you enlist a dozen willing volunteers to help and they strategically place obstacles such as barrels and sharpened stakes in the path the orcs will take. Others begin boarding up windows and stockpiling anything that can be thrown in the main building. Note down the codeword FORTIFY.

If you sent Gravelax out on the scouting mission, turn to **452**. If you sent out any scouts but not Gravelax, turn to **675**. If you did not send any scouts, turn to **444**.

552

You land in the thick of the fighting, calling the offensive. A handful of brave villagers respond to your cry but they cannot match the ferocity and power of the orcs. The casualties continue to mount until it becomes obvious that the battle is lost. You join the other birdmen who have already withdrawn from combat.

It is a swift and crushing victory for the green-skinned invaders. With a heavy heart you signal that you should fly south. It is a while before anyone breaks the sombre silence. Turn to **650**.

553

On your return to Dunstad you are dismayed to see that in just a few minutes the battle has swung against the defenders. Most of the surviving men are fleeing in disarray from the scene and the muddy ground is strewn with human casualties. You are joined by the others and watch hopelessly as the door to the Hieronaught is kicked in and the few remaining men inside are massacred.

The battle has been lost and there is nothing to be gained by staying. With a heavy heart you signal that you should fly south. It is a while before anyone breaks the sombre silence. Turn to **650**.

554

You are passing near to the mountain home of the Brilk and wonder whether it would be worthwhile visiting the mysterious beasts to seek their help. If you decide to do this, turn to **630**. If you just want to get home as quickly as possible, turn to **654**.

555

You join Rical and three other birdmen and fly swiftly off into the morning sun. As you reach the familiar landmarks which tell you that home is near, the haunting absence of the Tower of Egratar is as terrible a monument to Scarfell supremacy as there could be. Scores of corpses lie where they fell, some half buried in drifts of powdery snow.

Will you lead the way directly to the caves where the females resided? (Turn to **604**) Or leave that to the others and begin the job of collecting bodies? (Turn to **474**)

556

The night passes without incident and the snow is soon flashing past beneath you again as you speed through the crisp morning air.

Below you a herd of yaks roam here and there at the base of a mountain. Perfectly common, but what is unusual is that there are wooden fences (like pens) built on a slope nearby. Does this indicate that these yaks belong to a being of higher intelligence? This is certainly too far out to be Scarfells, but you know of no other race likely to keep yaks in Arian. Will you:

Descend and investigate on foot?	Turn to **525**
Hide and observe the yaks from a distance?	Turn to **574**
Or ignore what you see and fly onwards?	Turn to **566**

557

The others follow your lead and kneel also. More of the yaks trudge over to see what is going on. You hear the voice in your head again, "The leader may stand..." which you do. Then there is a pause. Are the yaks communicating with each other psychically you wonder? Will you:

Appeal to them that you mean no harm?	Turn to **672**
Ask what they are?	Turn to **624**
Or be silent and wait for them to 'speak' again?	Turn to **517**

558

As no-one has found anything suitable, you continue to plough through the driving rain together until you find a shallow cave in which to see out the storm and try to dry your feathers. A watch is set at the cave mouth and the night passes without incident.

Next morning, you are relieved to find that the rain has stopped and the outlook for the day is much brighter. You soon come across a road leading from south to east and decide to follow it. Will you head south (turn to **683**) or follow the road east (turn to **613**)?

559

At the sight of the approaching rider, Gravelax flies to your side, a look of terror on his face. "Xanarel!" he gasps, "I have seen this creature before, in a dream - a nightmare - two nights ago! It brings only death!" These are extraordinary and uncharacteristic words to hear from the usually level headed Gravelax! Based on this extraordinary tale will you:

Flee immediately?	Turn to **642**
Attack the rider?	Turn to **576**
Or dismiss the dream and greet him?	Turn to **478**

560

You are keen to find out how Eyrax has been treated on his return to the tribe. You find that he and Rical have become good friends and most of the other birdmen feel that you made the right decision: a new era is dawning with new rules. Roll the die. If you roll a 1 or 2, turn to **530**. If you roll a 3 or more, turn to **639**.

561

"The important thing is to keep one of us flying high at all times as a lookout," says Skyrll. "If these orcs are cunning they will encircle the village and attack from all sides." Return to **505**.

562

Orcs are everywhere! You see the other Ariax are gathering in the sky above and join them. If Ossen is involved in the battle, turn to **446**. If you left him in Arian or he has been killed, read on.

The orcs are relentless in their attack and so eager for destruction that they spend time gleefully hacking at walls, trees and dead bodies as they pass. You look for a leader of some kind but there is no obvious candidate! You can think of several ways that you can help turn the tide. Will you pluck a few orcs from the ground and drop them on the others from above? (Turn to **438**) Join the hand-to-hand fighting on the ground where you are most needed? (Turn to **677**) Land in a tree and use you magic to bring it to life and attack the orcs (needing a 5 or 6 to succeed)? (Turn to **653** if you make this roll.) Or land by a rainwater barrel and use your magic to turn this into a weapon (needing a 3 or more to succeed)? (Turn to **522** if you make this roll.) If you fail either of these magic rolls, turn to **616**.

563

You are fast, but whether intentional or not the eagle pulls up sharply at the same time and your wings become entangled. Before you know it the Scarfell is on top of you and you both fall from the sky. As you hit the ground, your head strikes a rock and the weight of the Scarfell winds you. This leaves you unable to properly defend yourself as the man hacks at you with his axe…

564

The yeti flails out with a giant paw but you all manage to avoid it and gratefully take to the air in safety. Xoroan berates Scancaro for not giving you an earlier warning and although you feel the same you can see that Scancaro is genuinely devastated by his mistake. Turn to **679**.

565

The roots and branches wrapped around you withdraw rapidly at your mental command, but try as you might you cannot will the same freedom for the others - and the thing making the roaring noises is getting nearer! Will you try to free your friends manually (turn to **597**) or face the beast (turn to **657**)?

566

You leave the strange beasts far behind you and stop for no other reason than to eat for the rest of the day. Early next morning, you come to the rolling brown foothills of the lands beyond the mountains. This is the third time you have ventured this far south but a new experience for the others and you chuckle to yourself at their awe and wonder.

There are many small woods dotted around. You screech as you fly over them but there is no answering cry. It is also starting to rain!

To the east you know there is woodland as you have been that way before; equally you saw no sign of birdmen. A wide river runs south-west from the mountains. To follow the river, turn to **598**. To go east, turn to **510**.

567

The rain shows no sign of abating so you urge everyone to keep their eyes peeled. Roll the die. If you roll a 6, turn to **468**. If you roll anything else, turn to **558**.

568

The wizard is far more agile than you imagined and manages to roll you off him immediately. As he staggers to his feet however he is cut down from behind by a savage talon strike.

You are helped to your feet. Although unhappy with the slaying of an enemy who had his back turned, the wizard undoubtedly intended kill you. If you have the codeword KNOT, turn to **503**. If you do not have this codeword, you hurriedly leave the tower (turn to **541**).

569

The Beotman gazes into the distance in thought. "I will think about it," he says, "I have seen orcs in the Beotlands lately…" You are unsure if this means he will come or not but know that to pursue the issue would be pointless. Note down the codeword BONE and turn to **684**.

570

You return to ground level and Slit looks to you to organise the men. One suggestion is to gather all the humans into the Hieronaught and make a stand there. If you decide on this note down the codeword DEFEND. You could instead station all the men outside in groups, ready to mount hit and run attacks on the orcs and fight them in the open (note down the codeword ATTACK if you decide on this strategy). Otherwise you could do a mixture of the above; some defending the Hieronaught with others laying ambushes before falling back to the main building (do not note down any codeword if you choose this plan).

Next you need to give your fellow Ariax their instructions. For each one you can either assign them to lead a human ambush group, defend the Hieronaught or fly high above the village to get an overall view of how the battle is going. Note down your decisions as you will be asked about them later. (If you chose the codeword DEFEND, you will have no birdmen leading ambushes.)

All of a sudden, an Ariax voice cries "Listen!" You do so and immediately pick up the sounds of the orcs approaching from the west. Soon enough you see them; brutal, ugly-looking greenskins, chanting and shouting their terrible war-cries as they come.

"To your positions!" you cry, "The Battle of Dunstad is upon us!" Some echo your defiant shouts and all around you the humans mobilise, preparing themselves as best they can. There is a dreadful lull as they then have to wait in anticipation for the orcs to reach the outskirts of the village. It is time for you to act! Will you:
    Fly ahead and use your magic to hold them up? Turn to **652**
    Lead one of the ambushes personally? Turn to **521**
    Or fly high to get a more strategic view yourself? Turn to **676**

571

As you glide to another area where the defenders are hard pressed, you see six orcs running through the melee carrying a tree they have felled to use as a battering ram! They stomp straight for the Hieronaught and you doubt whether the building will be able to stand up to their battering for long! Will you respond by attacking the orcs while their hands are full? (Turn to **688**) Trying to rally the men round to fend off this attack? (Turn to **479**) Or using your magic to break the battering ram (needing a 3 or more to succeed)? If you make this magic roll, turn to **608**. If you fail it, turn to **490**.

572

Amidst the commotion you hear Eyrax's raised voice shouting: "I was watching you!" and turn to see him locked in combat with Nimax, who wields a Scarfell spear! Blood is streaming from a wound in Eyrax's side. What is going on?

React on instinct. If you have the codeword BLAST, turn to **537**. If you do not have this codeword you could either attack Nimax (turn to **483**) or demand he releases Eyrax (turn to **610**)?

573

You are getting better at this! Almost as soon as you will it, the rock around your feet ices over and you retreat backwards as the shaggy creature does indeed slip and falls face first on the floor! Needing no further invitation, the Ariax swoop over the prostrate yeti, all avoiding injury. Turn to **679**.

574

The yaks are minding their own business, wandering about picking at any scraps of vegetation they can find growing in the rocky ground. It must be *someone's* herd though. If Xoroan is with you, turn to **475**. If he is not, will you hunt a yak for a meal (turn to **640**) or search for the 'someone' first (turn to **457**)?

575

Eyrax genuinely intends to follow you loyally. Years of living in the wild have hardened him to danger and he will make a useful follower. Having been out of contact with any other birdmen for so long however, he feels apprehensive about eventually returning home. Return to **501**.

576

You nod to your comrades and together swoop towards the incoming rider. The bemused expression on his strangely hued face does not change. Then there is a sudden blinding flash as if from nowhere! You clutch your face in your hands but it is too late – and the enemy fulfils Gravelax's vision with his sword…

577

In a split second you realise that the bolt is coming directly at you! Roll the die. If you roll a 1, 2 or 3, turn to **534**. If you roll a 4, 5 or 6, turn to **435**.

578

You go as swiftly as you can to the other village, arriving soaked to the last feather. You find the orcs apparently untroubled by the weather, ransacking every hut and currently in the process of toppling a weather-beaten stone statue that stands in the village square. As you watch, it falls headlong into a thick morass of mud, splattering those nearby to the delight of the topplers.

What will you do to give the orcs an early taste of your power? You could drop a rock or two on them from above? (Turn to **488**) Or you could use your magic to blow up some of the rainwater barrels around (needing a 2 or more to succeed). If you make this magic roll, turn to **651**. If you fail it, turn to **643**.

579

The men show great skill and courage in their running battle back to the Hieronaught, suffering only light casualties. The disgusting gloats of the orcs as they hack apart their fleeing victims are sickening to hear. Turn to **562**.

580

The arrival of your Ariax is vital to this particular skirmish. As the orcs are whittled down, numbers gradually begin to count in your favour and they are slain. It is testament to your inspiration that the men you supported immediately rush off to help out somewhere else! If you have the codeword BONE, turn to **629**. If you do not have this codeword, turn to **454**.

581

You float towards Nimax until you stand almost on his shoulder. He seems to sense something, turning his head slowly in your direction...but he cannot see you. You continue directly into his mind. Roll the die. If you roll a 1 or 2, turn to **439**. If you roll a 3 or 4, turn to **507**. If your roll a 5 or 6, turn to **617**.

582

The others respect your decision; you have after all always delivered in the past working alone. With your elemental powers, no other Ariax can keep up with your speed anyway! Next morning, you bid farewell to Rical and the others, charging Gravelax with stewardship of the tribe until your return.

This is the first time you have really been able to stretch your wings and go full pelt for hours at a time at your new top speed and it is exhilarating indeed! You had expected to feel drained of magic power afterwards, but when you stop and rest it does not seem too bad.

You are many miles from home when your sharp eyesight suddenly picks out the unexpected: that looked like the figure of a birdman you saw in the distance, observing you from behind some rocks on an outlying mountainside! Could it be another forest-birdman? You look again and see nothing. If you want to investigate, turn to **596**. To ignore it and continue with your mission, turn to **524**.

583

You take to the sky, enough with these yaks! Roll the die. If you roll a 1, turn to **538**. If you roll a 2 or 3, turn to **448**. If your roll a 4, 5 or 6, turn to **566**.

584

The man gapes in fear as you dramatically swoop towards him. He fumbles about for something to defend himself with, coming up with a twisted wooden staff. You attempt to calm him and explain that you only seek information.

"I heard of none like you!" he exclaims, regaining his composure as he sees you mean him no harm. He begins babbling about himself: "I'm one of the foremost tradesmen in northern Faltak! Mostly wizards I deals with – the finest exotic ingredients! Aah – and you's looking for wizards so as to ask about your others? Well look no further than that there tower," he points to the protrusion in the forest. "Home to a customer of mine and a fine friendly wizard is 'ee. I'd try him if I were you and fly up there to his window!"

A strange human-creature indeed, but could he be giving you useful advice? If Scancaro is with you, turn to **658**. If he is not will you investigate the tower as the man suggests? (Turn to **599**) Or will you continue on your way south? (Turn to **541**) If you are feeling nosy it occurs to you to use your magic to channel the breeze and lift up the corner of the canvas covering of the cart to look underneath (needing a 2 or more to succeed)? If you make this magic roll, turn to **460**. If you fail, choose one of the other options above (you may only try this roll once).

585

You detect a certain coldness from the surviving villagers. "You left us to be butchered by those things!" cries one angry man and it is clear that despite your efforts your presence here is unwelcome. You cannot find Slit anywhere; perhaps he is dead. With guilt replacing the euphoria of victory, you lead the Ariax south in search of your forest kin. Turn to **650**.

586

You plant your feet in the squelchy mud as the full orc force charges towards you! Fortunately (despite the sludge) you do manage to call up your earth-breaking magic and the orcs at the front are forced to leap aside or hurdle the rapidly spreading cracks that snake towards them, filling up with mud as they do! More than one orc loses his balance and falls into a newly formed bog!

You have blunted the initial attack but the effort was great and you cannot do any more magic for the moment. If you have the codeword ATTACK, turn to **685**. If you do not have this codeword, turn to **562**.

587

One comparatively quick witted orc sees the danger coming. As you grasp the warty arms of one of his kinsfolk, he leaps onto his back and uses him as a platform to hack at you with his sword. The filthy blade bites deep into your shoulder and you are dragged down into the mud. By the time the other Ariax have fought the orcs off it is too late to save you…

588

There is a sudden cry from the far side of the circle of "Scarfells!" and an Ariax in that area topples backwards over the precipice with a wooden spear through the neck!

You turn in disbelief to witness six spear-carrying Scarfell eagle-riders swooping around the blind side of the mountain behind you! They must have been searching for the remnants of your tribe and now intend to finish you off! *React on instinct*. Will you lead an immediate counter attack (turn to **523**) or signal for an ordered retreat (turn to **447**)?

589

Once you are at a safe distance, the pain is gone almost as quickly as it came. Was it the yaks doing that? If so, they are clearly dangerous! If you nevertheless want to land and try to make contact with them, turn to **538**. If you'd rather leave well alone now, turn to **566**.

590

"Yes…we know. We are not yak though…" comes the reply. "We are the Brilk…"

There is a pause before you hear the voice again: "Now let me open your mind…" It seems to be asking permission, though to do what you cannot be sure. Will you allow your mind to be 'opened' (turn to **606**) or refuse access (turn to **641**)?

591

The full force of the bolt hits you square in the chest and you immediately feel energised with a massive surge of electrical power! Seeing the wizard waving his arms and already beginning another incantation, you instinctively send it back to him! The force of the new lightning bolt smashes the wizard into the stone wall. He crumples dead to the ground, a victim of his own evil magic. If you have the codeword KNOT, turn to **503**. If you do not have this codeword, you hurriedly leave the tower (turn to **541**).

592

Finally, you find what must be a Beotman trudging across the plains below. You swoop down to land and greet him courteously. He parts the long straggly hair that is plastered to his face in order to look at you. (If you have encountered Beotmen in a previous book, this is not one you have met before.)

The Beotman would clearly make a powerful ally in combat. Since only you can talk to and understand him though, you decide to keep it brief. As you outline your need for his aid against the orcs, will you try to appeal to him by:

Telling him that you are a friend of the Beotmen (whether this is true or not)?	Turn to **512**
Warning him that the orcs could be coming this way next?	Turn to **627**
Or saying that the humans will probably look to reward him if he helps them?	Turn to **436**

593

Many of the other ambushes have been less successful than yours and the human casualties have begun to mount. You have blunted the initial orc attack but it has come at a price. Note down the codeword LOSS. If you have the codeword ATTACK, turn to **685**. If you do not have this codeword, turn to **562**.

594

You swoop into the fray, easily dispatching two startled men before shouting to the nearest orcs that you fight on their side. The ugly green-skins chortle with horrific glee at your words but you soon learn your mistake: as you turn your back to defend yourself against a determined looking farmer you are chopped down from behind by the filthy black blade of one of the treacherous orcs…

595

You turn your attention to another opponent, and out of the corner of your eye see that Nimax has picked up one of the used spears. As you launch yourself forward to aid a stricken comrade, you feel the self-same spear plunge into your neck and fall to the ground gurgling blood. Nimax has finished your long running feud decisively in his own treacherous manner and is now destined to be the new Talotrix…

596

Intrigued, you fly to where you last saw the figure. As you get nearer, a head pokes up from behind the rock and you see that it is indeed an Ariax and one of your tribe by the looks of it! When he sees that he has been spotted he stands and waits for you to land. You do not recognise him at all!

"Who are you?" you ask. The birdman tells you that his name is Eyrax. He is an outcast from your tribe, having failed to complete the Fygrinnd coming of age trial more than twenty years ago. He has lived alone in the mountains ever since.

If you want to update him on what has recently befallen the Ariax, turn to **547**. If you'd sooner leave him alone and continue on your journey, turn to **524** if you are travelling alone and **532** if you are not.

597

You slash and tug at the strangling vines and with a little help from your magic manage to drag the others free. You run from the scene, not even stopping to look back when you hear the ravenous beast behind you burst through the foliage where you were so recently trapped.

Back out in the open air, you could head generally westwards (turn to **598**) or east (turn to **634**).

598

For miles and miles the river winds its way through pleasant countryside. The rain which has persisted for most of the day is getting heavier and you begin to think of looking for shelter. A flash of lightning illuminates the sky. You hold a quick conference: this kind of weather is very unusual in Arian and flying is becoming uncomfortable and difficult. Even if your elemental powers protect you from lightning (which you are not certain of) it could be very dangerous to your companions.

It is decided to seek shelter. A wood, a cave or something similar is all you seek but visibility is reduced by the rain. Will you stay together in a pack to search the hills you are in (turn to **567**), split up to search (turn to **434**) or push further south (turn to **477**)?

599

The tower is an ominous sight as it looms closer, an ancient moss covered structure. Suddenly a lightning bolt flashes from the small window at the summit! Assign a different number between 1 and 6 to each Ariax in your group (including yourself) and roll the die until one of these numbers comes up. If your number comes up first, turn to **577**. If a different birdman, note down who it is and turn to **511**.

600

You take to the skies to the jeers of the men below you. Maybe not the most honourable action, but you owe these humans nothing. Note down the codeword SNUB and turn to **683**.

601

Gravelax makes his point directly and concisely. "These men are not warriors; they cannot defeat the orcs in open battle. We must use them to defend the Hieronaught while any who dare should mount hit and run attacks on the orcs with us until their numbers are low enough for us to overwhelm them." Return to **505**.

602

The battle on the ground is bloody and brutal. But it takes two men to fell each orc and they just seem to keep coming! You are gradually being surrounded and decide to lead the way through a back alley to the Hieronaught.

You are in sight of the main entrance when a man at the window shouts, "Look out!" At that moment you feel the weight of a huge orc leaping down upon you from the roof of a hut you were passing – it is an ambush! The orc slices you open with his sword and stomps off looking for more blood as you lie dying in the mud…

603

You hurriedly float back to your body and open your eyes, knowing that there is another battle yet to come. The Brilk seem to know something of what you have seen. "You face more danger yet, young one…" they say, "we can extend your power if you so wish…teach you how to mind-blast or truth-speak…"

If you don't fully trust the Brilk you can bid them farewell and head for home (turn to **654**). On the other hand, if you'd like to learn how to 'mind-blast', turn to **455**. If you'd like to learn how to 'truth-speak', turn to **545**.

604

Inside the tunnel you smell the musty odour of death. You find yourself accompanied by a craftsbird named Skyrll who warns you that the ceiling here shows signs of damage and could collapse. You take his advice and use your magic to seal the rock before progressing to the deeper caverns that house the females.

When you reach your destination you receive mixed tidings; one of the females is dead…but the other still clings to life! With reverence and care, Rical and Skyrll help her down the tunnel and out into the open air.

Soon both tasks are complete, Astraphet's body being the last to be laid to rest in a cave chosen to be a tomb. As the others hover nearby you crack the rocks above the cave entrance, bringing down a mini-avalanche and sealing it forever. Each is left to his own thoughts for a few minutes. It is then time to return to New Arian. Turn to **531**.

605

Xoroan initially ignores your command but as you follow him down he does stop, an impassive look on his face. As soon as you land, the nearest yaks turn their heads and slowly walk towards you. As you look this way and that you realise that they are moving to encircle you!

If Skyrll is with you, turn to **618**. If he is not, will you hold up your hands in friendship? (Turn to **662**) Attack the yaks? (Turn to **484**) Or if you sense danger, you could use your magic to crack the ice beneath the yak's feet to demonstrate your power (needing a 3 or more to succeed)? If you succeed with this magic roll, turn to **432**. If you fail it, turn to **500**.

606

You relax and close your eyes. You hear nothing this time but feel your mind being stimulated and refreshed. Recent events are stirred up in your memory: Vashta and Erim pulling you from the quicksand...the giant grabbing Rical...on trial in Iro...Nimax and the firebrand...swallowing the elemental crystal...facing the King of the Scarfells...the fire of the Moogoll...

You are interrupted by the Brilk. "Though you have seen much, you have not yet fulfilled your ultimate destiny...but this knowledge is not for you as yet..." Note down the codeword OPEN.

There comes another pause. Will you take the opportunity to ask the Brilk about forest-birdmen (if you haven't already)? (Turn to **458**) Or you could ask them about your travelling companions? (Turn to **501**) If you'd rather remain silent, turn to **494**.

607

You follow the wizard's instruction, keeping an eye out for a means of escape. "Good!" he says. "Of high intelligence I see! Now this way if you please?" He points you down a set of spiral steps which take you to the very bottom of the tower. Finally you come to an unlit tunnel which leads to a stone cell. The wizard magically locks the door behind you, but he has not tied your hands.

If you have the codeword KNOT, turn to **664**. If you do not have this codeword, turn to **487**.

608

You swoop down and grasp the trunk, screeching for effect as the power flows down your arms and splinters the battering ram into fragments. The orcs cry out in fright and flee, unable to comprehend what they have seen. Nearby orcs who witnessed what you did look around uncertainly, some joining the retreat.

As the orcs fall back you keep up the momentum by using your magic to shake the ground under their feet; fear has become your number one weapon.

Assign each Ariax with you a different number between 1 and 6 (not including yourself) and roll the die once. If you roll the number of one of the Ariax, that Ariax was unfortunately killed during the fighting. Note down this loss (obviously you cannot follow any choices which refer to this birdman again). If Ossen is killed, remove the codeword MILE if you had it. If Scancaro is killed, remove the codeword HEIGHT if you had it. If you roll an unassigned number, all of your followers have survived.

The stragglers are being overrun and slain by groups of bold villagers. Within minutes, the orcs have gone: the battle has been won and you are joined on the ground by your fellow Ariax. If you have the codeword SNUB, turn to **585**. If you do not have this codeword, turn to **464**.

609

When night falls, you settle down to a sleep troubled by the day's events. But things are about to get worse! Soon after you fall asleep you are specifically targeted by a lurking figure nearby who sees to it that you never wake up…

610

Nimax looks at you incredulously, seemingly unaware of the fighting going on all around him. His response is to slaughter his poor captive by driving his spear through his back!

You furiously launch yourself towards your hated enemy! But fate is on Nimax's side this day and even as you draw first blood with your talons a Scarfell does his dirty work for him: hurling his spear into your back with savage force. You slump to the ground and die in a pool of your own blood at the feet of your deadliest enemy…

611

At the first mention of setting a watch, Gravelax shakes his head. "What could possibly reach us up here Xanarel?" he asks. "Do we set watch at home, even in these troubled times?" If you want to set a watch anyway, turn to **648**. If not, turn to **509**.

612

It is slow work to remove the offending creepers; they just don't seem to be responding to your magic. As you continue to struggle, a huge black creature with scaly skin, burning red eyes and massive jaws crashes through the undergrowth with a deafening roar. Pinned by the vines, you have no chance against this thing…

613

The road meanders through hills and dales. You then come across farmland, suggesting a human settlement. Minutes later you find that you are right; a small village is nestled in a shallow valley. Would they welcome the Ariax? If you want to make contact with the villagers, turn to **459**. If you would rather turn your search south, turn to **683**.

614

The wizard is far more agile than you imagined and manages to roll you off him immediately. As he staggers to his feet long shining strands shimmer from his fingernails and wrap themselves around you. You try to fight back using your own magic, but these ropes are anything but natural and you find yourself powerless in the wizard's grip. Unfortunately he has decided that having a living specimen of your race is unnecessary…

615

Gravelax sidles over to offer some private advice. "Xanarel, although you are clearly of greater natural authority, I think it would be wiser for this man to deliver a rallying cry; do not forget that our appearance is as strange to them as they to us…" If you want to take Gravelax's advice, turn to **453**. If you want to speak to the men yourself, turn to **543**.

616

As you concentrate, an orc axe suddenly appears quivering in the wood mere inches from your head! You quickly decide to abandon your attempt at magic in order to save your own skin! Because of your hesitation, the next time you are asked to roll the die you must subtract 1 from the roll.

Now will you try picking a few orcs from the ground and dropping them on others from above? (Turn to **438**) Or join the hand-to-hand fighting on the ground? (Turn to **677**)

617

It is an intense, draining effort to stay in Nimax's mind but within the few seconds that you can stand it you experience the jealousy and hatred that your former mentor feels towards you, coupled with his burning desire to be the new Talotrix. Nimax had been a precocious talent of the Vzler, tipped for greatness in almost exactly the same way as you before your coming of age. He feels no remorse about his previous behaviour towards you.

You hurriedly float back to your body and open your eyes, knowing that there is another battle yet to come. The Brilk seem to know something of what you have seen. "You face more danger yet, young one…" they say mentally, "we can extend your power if you so wish…teach you how to mind-blast or truth-speak…"

If you don't fully trust the Brilk you can bid them farewell and head for home (turn to **654**). On the other hand, if you'd like to learn how to 'mind-blast', turn to **455**. If you'd like to learn how to 'truth-speak', turn to **545**.

618

"I sense no malice here Xanarel," says Skyrll quietly. His eyes flick about watchfully. Will you now hold up your hands in friendship as Skyrll advises? (Turn to **662**) Attack the yaks? (Turn to **484**) Or use your magic to crumble the ice beneath the yak's feet (needing a 3 or more to succeed)? If you succeed with this magic roll, turn to **432**. If you fail it, turn to **500**.

619

While reading Xoroan's mind you find that, unusually for an Ariax, he has a naturally aggressive personality and sees things very much in black and white. For example, while respecting you for your achievements, he also thinks you far too young to be considered as the next Talotrix. He does not want the position himself however and will loyally support you in your current quest. Return to **501**.

620

A Beotman at last, but sorely wounded. He looks up through half closed eyes in a face caked with dried blood.

You ask what happened to him. He can manage few words but you find out that yesterday he was attacked by a band of green-skinned orcs. His wounds are mortal, but before he dies he leaves you with a cryptic message. He mumbles something about the orcs and birdmen. You dearly wish you could ask if anyone else can confirm what he said, but you are the only one who can understand. Did he mean what you thought he did: that the orcs had a birdman prisoner? You think back to the village of Dunstad. More crucial than you may have thought! You decide to end your search and return as fast as the others can manage! Turn to **444**.

621

Amidst the commotion you recognise Ossen's raised voice and turn to see him wrestling with Nimax for possession of a Scarfell spear! What is going on?

React on instinct. If you have the codeword BLAST, turn to **537**. If you do not have this codeword you could either attack Nimax (turn to **483**) or demand he releases Ossen (turn to **610**)?

622

Later that afternoon you hear a commotion outside. A birdman named Ritsbrik hurtles into the cave with what he describes as an amazing story to tell! All present crowd round to listen to his tale. He is out of breath and has evidently flown hard to get here as quickly as possible.

"I was scouting to the east," he begins, "when I met…another birdman!" This prompts a cascade of questions and comments but Gravelax silences them.

"Who was this birdman?" he asks, a note of suspicion in his voice.

"Not one of us!" replies Ritsbrik excitedly. "He had come from a far off land – there must be another tribe out there similar to us but different too,"

"Different how?" someone shouts.

"Well, thinner feathers for one thing," Ritsbrik explains. "Warmer down there it must be. Taller than us too I'd say, or at least this one was. He wore a strange covering of leaves over his body and a necklace made of forest flora."

"A forest dwelling tribe?" muses Gravelax.

"So where is this birdman now?" you ask.

Ritsbrik hangs his head. "Dead…he was badly wounded when I found him. Something got him in the mountains…"

"And did he say where he came from?" enquires Gravelax.

"No, he didn't speak our language. Just pointed south. He must have been sent to look for us."

You debate what is to be done in response to this news. You have not come across any evidence of other birdmen during your adventures in the southern lands, though this doesn't mean it's not true of course!

"If there *is* another tribe of birdmen out there, now would be a good time to make contact!" says Rical.

"If anyone is to go searching for them I must go," you point out, "I may be able to communicate with them."

"Can we spare you or any others right now?" asks an older birdman.

It is agreed that an ambassadorial mission would be well worth the risk. If nothing is found, nothing will have been lost! Once again the other Ariax seem to look to you for leadership and you announce that you will undertake this task as you have the greatest knowledge of the southern lands and the power of languages. You will leave at first light tomorrow. Others begin staking their claim to travel with you. Will you:

Look over the volunteers?	Turn to **499**
State that you intend to go alone?	Turn to **582**
Or ask Ritsbrik to take you to see the body of the birdman before making any other decisions?	Turn to **456**

623

Although you feel safe, there is a hidden danger that you had not counted on. Soon after you fall asleep you are specifically targeted by a lurking figure nearby who sees to it that you in particular never wake up…

624

The voice appears willing to tell you. "We are the Brilk…" it says, again in your mind. Then you are aware of being asked a question: "You seek something, feathered-one; what is it you are searching for..?" Will you mentally reply that you seek forest-birdmen? (Turn to **533**) Or deny that you are searching for anything in particular? (Turn to **476**)

625

Your sudden appearance in the midst of the villagers causes great alarm! Many flee immediately into their houses but a few grasp farming tools and stand eyeing you warily.

"We mean you no harm," you say gently, remembering how physically imposing Ariax appear to normal humans.

Eventually one man steps forwards and addresses you. He has messy brown hair with a moustache to match and like the others wears grubby looking working-clothes. "Hail!" he says, trying to appear friendly but with a note of caution in his voice. "My name is Slit and I am the farm superior here in Dunstad.

When you tell him what you have seen the colour drains from his face and he gasps one word: "Orcs!" Several other men in earshot run over and demand you confirm what you said.

"Please stay and help us," says Slit in desperation. "Dunstad was ransacked by orcs five winters back - dozens were killed and it took years to rebuild our lives! With your might we may prevail! We know of the power of your race!"

Your ears prick up immediately! "You mean you have seen others like us?"

"Why yes, recently we were visited by..." then he shrewdly breaks off and changes tack. "I will tell all...if we get through this alive..." Note down the codeword SLIT.

You do not have the heart to force the information out of him at this moment and have a decision to make. If Xoroan is with you, turn to **549**. If he is not, will you tell the other Ariax that you intend to help the humans defend their village (turn to **496**) or decide it is their problem and look for shelter elsewhere (turn to **470**)?

626

You skim the surface of the trees, screeching to alert any bird-life of your presence. Although none of the hoped for birdmen appear, you have summoned a single raven which breaks the treetops and flaps towards you, cawing. You cannot speak to birds, but it is clear that it intends you to follow it...to the tower.

Could the raven be leading you to birdmen in that tower? If you want to find out, turn to **469**. If you'd rather ignore the raven and continue south, turn to **541**.

627

The Beotman looks at you thoughtfully. "I will think about it," he says, "The orcs are indeed a hated enemy..." You are unsure if this means he will come or not but know that to pursue the issue would be pointless. Note down the codeword BONE and turn to **684**.

628

As you dwell for just the merest of seconds on this latest tragedy, you miss the second lightning bolt, directed unerringly at your head. You are killed instantly.

629

The casualties continue to mount on both sides. As further options tumble through your mind, the body of an orc suddenly flies past you and crashes through the wall of a nearby hut! You turn in wonder to the sight of the Beotman from yesterday striding into the village wielding an uprooted tree as a club!

The orcs do not even come up to the Beotman's shoulder and cannot hope to match his strength. As you watch, he brings down his club on another orc's head, crunching him senseless to the ground. Though some of them attempt to take on this giant enemy, many others have seen enough and flee before him.

Is this time to call out the rest of the men and make a concerted push to rout the orcs? If you decide that it is, turn to **506**. If you'd rather be more cautious and hold your position, turn to **454**.

630

You remember roughly where you encountered the Brilk and soon spot them from the air. As you swoop down to land they move to encircle you as they did before.

You mentally greet them and find that you are able to communicate quite easily in this way. You tell them of your fears that Nimax has returned to the tribe. A single Brilk voice drifts into your mind, "We know not of whom you speak...but if you wish, we can help you to mind-walk for him..."

You ask what 'mind-walking' is and the voice explains. "We can allow you to leave your physical body...and travel through the non-physical world to find your enemy...but be warned it may not be attempted by the novice without risk..."

If you want to take the Brilk up on their offer, turn to **482**. If you decline and decide to head for home and confront Nimax face to face, turn to **654**.

631

The surrounding mountains appear as white and featureless as ever; this should not take long. You and Rical are joined by two others and you renew your acquaintance with Scancaro, a birdman you came across during the Scarfell attack. He seems keen to stay together in a pack but you could cover more ground if you split up. If you decide to go along with Scancaro as one single group, turn to **492**. To split into pairs, turn to **465**.

632

The yaks have been angered and you are suddenly racked with intense mental pain! You just manage to pull away and as you surge upwards you feel the pain subside. You are greatly relieved to find that you all managed to reach safety. These yaks are clearly dangerous and no-one is keen to tangle with them again! Knowing when you are beaten, you decide to get on with your mission (turn to **566**).

633

Inside Scancaro's mind you find an insecure and nervous character. Being physically the weakest of the group as well he worries about letting you down. You are unable to tell how he would fare in the kind of dangerous situation you have found yourself in so regularly in the past months but his loyalty and good intentions cannot be doubted. Return to **501**.

634

You fly over the pleasant countryside. The rain which has persisted for most of the day is getting heavier and you begin to think of looking for shelter. Then in the distance you see a collection of wooden huts and larger stone buildings that you recognise as human dwellings.

A flash of lightning illuminates the sky. You hold a quick conference: this kind of weather is very unusual in Arian and flying is becoming uncomfortable and difficult. Even if your elemental powers protect you from lightning (which you are not certain of) it could be very dangerous to your companions.

It is decided to seek shelter. If you want to try the village, turn to **665**. If you'd rather avoid humans, turn to **450**.

635

Just then Ossen grabs your arm. "Let me go ahead Xanarel!" he says, "I'll scout out any danger and report back!" He clearly wants the opportunity to impress. Will you tell him to be careful but give him the chance (turn to **527**) or say that you think it wiser to stick together (turn to **599**)?

636

You set off through the deluge. Some of the villagers misunderstand and shout for you not to desert them! You do not know how far the Beotlands extends – how long will it be worth searching for? Note down the codeword CLUB. If you want to head due east, turn to **520**. To fly more south, turn to **683**.

637

You stand atop a hut out of sword-strike and screech to the men of Dunstad. Roll the die, adding two to the roll for each of the codewords FORTIFY and FORTITUDE that you have. If the total is 3 or less, turn to **497**. If the total is 4 or 5, turn to **445**. If it is 6 or more, turn to **579**.

638

Most of the surviving humans are making a last stand in a large stone building in the middle of the village though a few still fight hit and run battles with the orcs in the open. Some of the stronger looking villagers shout for a withdrawal to 'the Hieronaught' (which you reason must be the stone building).

The orcs are relentless in their attack and so eager for destruction that they spend time gleefully hacking at walls, trees and dead bodies as they pass. You note with interest that they carry no missile weapons at all but when you look for a leader you see no obvious suspects.

There are several ways that you could try to help turn the tide. Will you pluck a few orcs from the ground and drop them on the others from above? (Turn to **438**) Join the hand-to-hand fighting where you are most needed? (Turn to **677**) Land in a tree and use you magic to bring it to life and attack the orcs (needing a 5 or 6 to succeed)? (Turn to **653** if you make this roll.) Or land by a rainwater barrel and use your magic to turn this into a weapon (needing a 3 or more to succeed)? (Turn to **522** if you make this roll.) If you fail either of these magic rolls, turn to **616**.

639

Eyrax finds a quiet minute to talk to you about Nimax. When Eyrax left the tribe, Nimax was a juvenile Ariax and he did not know him. Eyrax's opinion since meeting him here has been that there is something shady about your former mentor and he does not trust him. Note down the codeword EYE and turn to **530**.

640

You swoop down as you have many times before, looking for a clean kill. But as you descend, you are suddenly racked with intense mental pain – it feels as if your skull will split! You attempt to pull up immediately! Roll the die. If you roll a 1, 2, or 3, turn to **538**. If you roll a 4, 5 or 6, turn to **589**.

641

You mentally thank the Brilk but politely decline, still wary of the strange creatures and their supernatural abilities. It is time to go (turn to **566**).

642

As you turn to heed Gravelax's premonition you hear a malicious chuckling from the rider. From a saddlebag he pulls out a crystal ball containing swirling purplish-black smoke. This he throws in your direction; there is a splintering sound and you are all engulfed in choking black clouds! When you attempt to fly out of them, the clouds follow you! You try to use your magic to clear them away but nothing happens: this is no natural smoke! An Ariax voice cries out in anguish but you are powerless to do anything. You do not see the sword-strike which eventually kills you coming either…

643

Ironically, it could be the deluge of rain itself which hampers your efforts; nothing comes of your magic this time! The orcs notice you perched atop the barrel and grab their weapons immediately. You beat a hasty retreat from the village and wing your way back to Dunstad, bedraggled but alive! Turn to **444**.

644

You swiftly return to Dunstad. Slit emerges from a hut to greet you but when you tell him what you have seen the colour drains from his face and he gasps one word: "Orcs!" Several other men in earshot run over and demand you confirm what you said.

"Please stay and help us," says Slit in desperation. "Dunstad was ransacked by orcs five winters back - dozens were killed and it took years to rebuild our lives! We are weaker now than then!" You do not have the heart to force the information you want out of him at this urgent moment and have a decision to make. Will you tell the other Ariax that you intend to help the humans defend their village (turn to **496**) or decide it is their problem and lead the way south (turn to **470**)?

645

Eyrax admits he knows little of warfare but reckons that the quickest way to get rid of the orcs would be to look for their leader and kill him. The rest would then surely flee in disarray. You hope it will indeed be that easy! Return to **505**.

646

"Tell us the truth Nimax!" you cry, pointing dramatically towards your foe and mentally calling up your truth-speak powers as you do. "It was I alone who found the firebrand snake and you tried to murder me for it while I slept!"

"Yes, I did!" retorts Nimax to the amazement of all, and none more so than himself! "It is right that *I* should be heir apparent of Astraphet, not you! You who win your victories through circumstance and fortune rather than long years of dedication as I have done!"

There is a stunned silence around the dell. Then Nimax stands and takes the offensive, pointing aggressively towards you. "More wretched trickery!" he rages, "Those words you heard were not mine!" Turn to **588**.

647

Your magic fails you under the intense pressure of the onrushing yeti and you are forced to flee back into the cave. The other Ariax, whose name is Xoroan, has gathered a selection of the larger bones from the floor and flings one with all his might at the monster. It smacks it square in the face, causing it to roar out in pain and momentarily close its eyes. "Run!" shouts Xoroan. Roll the die. If you roll a 1 or 2, turn to **440**. If you roll a 3 or more, turn to **564**.

648

The night passes without incident although at certain times during your shift you had the uneasy feeling of being watched. You rebuke yourself for having an overactive imagination! The snow is soon flashing past beneath you again as you cut through the crisp morning air.

Below you a herd of yaks roam here and there at the base of a mountain. Perfectly common, but what is unusual is that there are wooden fences (like pens) built on a slope nearby. Does this indicate that these yaks belong to a being of higher intelligence? This is certainly too far out to be Scarfells, but you know of no other race likely to keep yaks in Arian. Will you:

    Descend and investigate on foot?   Turn to **525**
    Hide and observe the yaks from a distance?   Turn to **574**
    Or ignore what you see and fly onwards?   Turn to **566**

649

When you arrive back at the meeting place, one of your followers has some interesting news. You bid him tell you quickly before you are washed away in the rain!

He came across a few dozen humans sheltering in a copse of trees – though of course he couldn't communicate with them. Apparently they looked frightened; surely not just because of the rain? You wonder what they are doing out in the wild. When you have met humans who are not Scarfells before they were largely mistrusting and suspicious of you.

If you want to go to them and make contact, turn to **502**. If you'd rather stay away from humans and want to continue looking elsewhere, turn to **558**.

650

You set off south once more. After about an hour you see, beginning as a small speck on the horizon, a figure approaching speedily from the west. It appears to be a man riding a small dragon-like mount. When he gets a bit closer you see that it is not a human at all as he has a purplish tinge to his skin and pointed ears. He is armed with a long sword strapped to his side and a crossbow. He wheels his steed around to halt in the air before you. If Gravelax is with you, turn to **559**. If he is not, turn to **478**.

651

You land unseen behind the barrels and begin working your magic on the wood. The power warms your palms and the planks of the barrel begin to creak as they expand. Suddenly there is an almighty crack and the barrels explode outwards, showering the nearby orcs with torrents of muddy water!

The orcs are already soaked, but you make sure they see that this was your elemental power at work. They begin pelting you with smaller rocks and bits of broken wood, and shouting language you are unfortunate to be able to understand! Having seen enough, you turn in the air and fly as fast as you can back to Dunstad. Note down the codeword TEAR and turn to **444**.

652

The orcs look as bloodthirsty and savage as any Scarfell you have ever met! You fly before them wondering how best to use your magic. You could land and rupture the earth below their feet (needing a 4 or more to succeed). Otherwise you could take a large metal plough that stands idle nearby and send it spinning towards the orcs (needing a 3 or more to succeed). If you successfully crack the earth, turn to **586**. If you animate the plough, turn to **471**. If you fail either magic roll, turn to **529**.

653

Rarely is your magic as spectacular as this! As you sit very still, channelling all your power into the wood you feel a shudder that runs all the way through the trunk. Two orcs running past gets the surprise of their life as the thick branches of the tree suddenly whip out like arms, breaking through armour and bone with ease!

It is a great drain on your power and you cannot make the tree lift up its roots and walk. Nevertheless it accounts for two more orcs with its deadly lashing branches before you can control it no more. If you have the codeword BONE, turn to **629**. If you do not have this codeword, turn to **454**.

654

Eventually, you recognise before you the mountains of New Arian. The sun is shining brightly in the sky; it is the kind of morning that makes the snow appear blindingly white. You take a deep breath before descending to the cave entrance where you are greeted by a sentry who tells you that he has important news.

"I know," you reply softly. When you enter the main cave Nimax is there, recognisable even with his back to you.

"Xanarel!" cries Rical. There is an awkward silence. Nimax turns to face you.

"Xanarel!" he exclaims. "I welcome you back, even though it seems in my absence the story of our last meeting has been somewhat...*twisted*, shall we say?"

When you last saw Nimax, he was trying to murder you so that he could return home with the life-saving firebrand snake and claim hero status for himself! Thinking him dead, you had done the decent thing and merely said (to all but Rical) that Nimax had been bitten by the snake (which was true).

At this point Rical bravely interjects. "Nimax has told everyone that *he* found the firebrand snake and you set upon him, left him for dead and took it for yourself! I have told them the truth!"

You fix the conniving Nimax with an icy stare and he returns your gaze unemotionally. He is aware of his audience!

Another Ariax steps in to break the uncomfortable atmosphere. "Nimax has declared his interest in being our new Talotrix," he says, and a slight smile creeps around Nimax's beak. "Do you, Xanarel, also wish to be considered?"

The number of nodding heads gives you the confidence to assert that you do. Nimax frowns. "Aside from Nimax and Xanarel, does anyone else wish to put themselves forward for the position?" continues the birdman. Silence.

"Then I suggest we convene in the hollow at the top of the mountain this afternoon to discuss the appointment of our new leader."

If you have the codeword IN, turn to **560**. If you do not have this codeword, turn to **530**.

655

You set off immediately. After an hour or so, Ritsbrik begins circling a particular area, telling you that the corpse is somewhere close by. You suggest that the snow may have covered the body and swoop down lower to see. It is a fruitless job and Ritsbrik sits on an outcrop of rock to rest.

You join him, but you have been specifically targeted by a lurking figure nearby. He approaches silently from behind and dashes out your brains with a large chuck of rock…

656

Your decision clearly means a lot to Eyrax. After all these years he can finally go home. You tell him your name and also Rical's to help him integrate with the tribe. Note down the codeword IN. Now it is time to resume your quest. If you are travelling alone, turn to **524**. If you brought others with you, turn to **532**.

657

You prepare for battle. Just then, a huge black creature with scaly skin, burning red eyes and massive jaws crashes through the undergrowth almost on top of you! It is far larger, more hideous and more powerful than you could ever have imagined and you are crushed under its bulk, bones breaking with the impact! Then it turns its jaws on you…

658

You hear Scancaro's voice behind you, speaking quietly. "I can't understand a word he says Xanarel, but I don't like the look of him, even for a human! What's he say?"

You briefly fill him in. "Then personally I'd stay *away* from the tower!" he says.

Will you investigate the tower anyway? (Turn to **599**) Continue on your way south? (Turn to **541**) Or use your magic to channel the breeze and lift up the canvas of the cart (now needing a 3 or more to succeed)? If you make this magic roll, turn to **460**. If you fail, choose one of the other options above (you may only try this roll once).

659

The orc juggernaut has been slowed by the courageous efforts of the men of Dunstad and casualties have been surprisingly light so far. But the battle is far from won! If you have the codeword ATTACK, turn to **685**. If you do not have this codeword, turn to **562**.

660

"Rical!" The note of urgency in your voice is enough to alert your friend and he dives prone just as the eagle-rider swoops past. The spear is thrown but it clatters harmlessly onto rock.

If you have the codeword WING, turn to **687**. If you have the codeword HEIGHT, turn to **514**. If you have the codeword MILE, turn to **621**. If you have the codeword EYE, turn to **572**. (If you have more than one of these codewords determine randomly which section to turn to.) If you have none of these codewords, turn to **595**.

661

You announce your selection and the chosen ones prepare for departure. Next morning, you say your farewells to Rical and the others and take to the sky in a generally southerly direction. You make a swift start, eating up the miles over the featureless snow-carpeted mountains, each wondering what the discovery of another tribe will mean for your own.

You are many miles from home when your sharp eyesight suddenly picks out the unexpected: that looked like the figure of a birdman you saw in the distance, observing you from behind some rocks on an outlying mountainside! Could it be another forest-birdman? You look again and see nothing. If you want to investigate, turn to **596**. To ignore it and continue with your mission, turn to **532**.

662

You are unsure what to make of these beasts! But what you were definitely not expecting was to suddenly hear a voice in your head; a soft melodic voice that comes from nowhere! Reading the surprised expressions of the other Ariax it is clear that they hear it too!

"Kneel..." the voice is saying. It is certainly a command but delivered coolly and calmly. Will you:

Kneel as it bids?	Turn to **557**
Refuse to kneel?	Turn to **516**
Or try to flee?	Turn to **583**

663

"In a 'bad way' you said...?" you repeat to Slit. "It couldn't have been a *snake bite*, could it..?"

"Why yes it was!" replies the man.

So Nimax survived the bite of the firebrand and found refuge in the very village you now stand in! And if Nimax was to return to the tribe in your absence...you decide to leave for home immediately and find out what's been happening.

The journey north is uneventful, but a feeling of unease grows stronger within you the closer you get to home.

If Skyrll is with you and is your *only* surviving companion, turn to **498**. If this is not the case but you have the codeword OPEN, turn to **554**. If you do not have this codeword, turn to **654**.

664

A stone wall is all that stands in the way of freedom – but you can't leave without Ossen! The door may have been magically locked, but the interior *wall* has not and you have time to concentrate and summon your magic! You run your hands over the smooth surface of the wall and feel the power coursing down your arms and through your palms. Cracks appear around the bricks soon enough, spreading in all directions until you can carefully and quietly remove enough of them to clamber through!

The feeling of entrapment and fear of discovery reminds you of the tunnels and caverns of Musk! Fortunately this tower is nowhere near the size of the city of the Scarfells and you quickly find Ossen in a similar cell to your own on the next level up. The wall of his cell yields as easily as your own.

But you are not safe yet! You get to work once again, this time on the exterior wall of Ossen's cell. As the stone crumbles and splits, and blocks tumble outwards onto the forest floor, you are aware that the noise could easily alert your captor. You signal for caution as you climb through the gap in the wall that leads to freedom. Roll the die. If you roll a 4 or less, turn to **451**. If you roll a 5 or 6, turn to **682**.

665

Your sudden appearance in the midst of the villagers causes great alarm! Many flee immediately into their houses but a few grasp farming tools and stand eyeing you warily.

"We mean you no harm," you say gently, remembering how physically imposing Ariax appear to normal humans.

Eventually one man steps forwards and addresses you. He has messy brown hair with a moustache to match and like the others wears grubby looking working-clothes. "Hail!" he says, trying to appear friendly but with a note of caution in his voice. "My name is Slit and I am the farm superior here in Dunstad. To what honour do we owe another visit by the feathered race?"

Your ears prick up immediately! "*Another* visit? You mean you have news of others like us?"

The man pauses. He senses your eagerness and clearly possesses a calculating brain as he answers with a certain confidence. "Well, you could say that, yes. And I will tell all…in return for a small favour."

You enquire as to the nature of this favour and Slit asks you to fly to the next village (Burbruk) with a message for their chief-herbalist. It is only a few miles to the west. Note down the codeword SLIT.

If you agree to take this message, despite the weather, turn to **542**. If you are suspicious of these humans and do not want to get involved in their affairs, you seek shelter elsewhere (turn to **450**).

666

You check on your companions, who are all rested and ready for action. Slit is busy organising the evacuation of the women and children of Dunstad and the men make their final preparations for battle. Then everyone gathers in the village square, periodically casting nervous glances westwards.

You stand with Slit and the other Ariax on the steps of the main building, the Hieronaught. With the orc attack surely imminent, the time is right for a speech that will give heart to the men of Dunstad in this, their darkest hour. If Gravelax is with you, turn to **615**. If he is not, will you speak to the men yourself (turn to **543**) or delegate the task to Slit (turn to **453**)?

667

You see in the distance that a group of around a dozen men have gathered in hiding, clearly mustering for a decisive strike. The orcs lack of leadership is beginning to show and they have become spread, having encountered more resistance than they anticipated. The men have gained heart now they have seen that the orcs can be killed.

You split the Ariax force at this pivotal moment as there are many areas that their support could prove vital. The group of men you were just watching charges into a group of four orcs, slaying one and routing the other three! You smile to yourself but then wonder if this is part of a ruse; are these orcs really fleeing or will they double back and mount a surprise attack of their own? If you want to follow them to make sure, turn to **481**. If you want to concentrate on the fighting in Dunstad, turn to **571**.

668

You land with a bone-jarring thud on the icy rock. You hear the screech of the eagle and the curse of the rider as it swoops over you, talons missing your back by inches.

If you have the codeword WING, turn to **687**. If you have the codeword HEIGHT, turn to **514**. If you have the codeword MILE, turn to **621**. If you have the codeword EYE, turn to **572**. (If you have more than one of these codewords, determine randomly which section to turn to.) If you have none of these codewords, turn to **595**.

669

The full tale unfolds publicly for the first time. Nimax stands stock still for the entire duration, arms folded. When you have finished, he smirks.

"And you believe this of me, one of the Vzler's most trusted Ariax?" he asks the crowd, throwing his arms open. "This rogue not only commits the heinous act, he then tries to put the blame on *me*, his intended victim!" If you have the codeword TRUTH, turn to **646**. If you do not have this codeword, turn to **588**.

670

Two other birdmen quickly volunteer to accompany you. "Not necessary!" blusters Ritsbrik, confusingly, but the decision is made and the four of you set off immediately. After an hour or so, Ritsbrik begins circling a particular area, telling you that it is somewhere close by. You suggest that the snow may have covered the body and swoop down lower to see. Roll the die. If you roll a 4 or less, turn to **546**. If you roll a 5 or 6, turn to **515**.

671

Xoroan swoops down as he has done many times before, looking for a clean kill. You descend in his wake, but he suddenly pulls sharply up, clutching his head as if in agony! You stop in alarm! Roll the die. If you roll a 1 or 2, turn to **538**. If you roll a 3, 4, 5 or 6, turn to **589**.

672

Your plea is not acknowledged but is met with a question: "But does your race not hunt yak for meat..?" Will you mentally admit that you do? (Turn to **590**) Or deny this? (Turn to **476**)

673

You follow the directions the villagers gave you and soon see Dunstad appearing through the downpour. Your sudden appearance in the midst of the stunned villagers causes great alarm! Many flee immediately into their houses but a few grasp farming tools and stand eyeing you warily.

"We mean you no harm," you say gently, remembering how physically imposing Ariax appear to normal humans.

Eventually one man steps forwards and addresses you. He has messy brown hair with a moustache to match and like the others wears grubby looking working-clothes. "Hail!" he says, trying to appear friendly but with a note of caution in his voice. "My name is Slit and I am the farm superior here in Dunstad."

When you tell Slit what you have seen and been told by the survivors of Burbruk the colour drains from his face. Several other men in earshot run over and demand you confirm what you said.

"Please stay and help us," says Slit in desperation. "Dunstad was ransacked by orcs five winters back - dozens were killed and it took years to rebuild our lives! With your might we may prevail! We know of the power of your race!"

You ears prick up immediately! "You mean you have seen others like us?"

"Why yes, recently we were visited by…" then he shrewdly breaks off and changes tack. "I will tell all…if we get through this alive…" Note down the codeword SLIT.

You do not have the heart to force the information out of him at this moment. If Xoroan is with you, turn to **549**. Otherwise, there is a decision to make. Will you tell the other Ariax that you intend to help the humans defend their village (turn to **496**) or decide it is their problem and lead the way south (turn to **600**)?

674

You swoop in through the window, senses straining for danger. You enter a gloomy, circular chamber crammed full of scrolls, books and other wizarding paraphernalia. The wizard who attacked you stands facing the window, wearing heavy crimson robes with gold trim. He stares malevolently at you from under bushy black eyebrows.

"Stay right where you are!" he commands. "Make no move! Now, whatever manner of creatures you are, kneel in deference!" You can see that coming here was a mistake; it's all about getting out alive now! Will you do as he asks? (Turn to **607**) Or risk his wrath and attack? (Turn to **519**)

675

The Ariax glides in to land beside you as you walk across the village square. You are told that there are around fifty of the orc-creatures, well-armed with swords, axes and the like, but one positive is that they have no missile weapons at all. Unfortunately the orcs then spotted the Ariax and began hurling debris into the sky, forcing his withdrawal. Turn to **444**.

676

From your vantage point you see the green tide sweeping away everything in its path as it surges through the outskirts of the village. It doesn't take long to confirm what you had suspected: the orcs subtlety does not extend beyond all-out attack!

Roll the die, adding 2 if you have the codeword ATTACK or subtracting 1 if you have the codeword DEFEND. Add a further 1 to the roll if Gravelax, Xoroan or Ossen are leading ambushes. If the total is 4 or less, turn to **462**. If it is 5 or more, turn to **659**.

677

This is the way of the warrior; the speed and skill of the Ariax more than able to match the strength and brutality of the orcs!

If Scancaro is involved in the battle, turn to **472**. If you left him in New Arian or he has been killed, roll the die, adding 1 to the roll if you have the codeword FORTIFY. If you roll 3 or less, turn to **602**. If you roll 4 or more, turn to **580**.

678

You step towards the Scarfell and unleash the full force of the mental-blast! He immediately releases his victim and staggers forwards, hands to his head, dangerously close to a cliff edge. A nearby Ariax gives him the shove he needed and he topples headlong over the precipice to his doom.

If you have the codeword WING, turn to **687**. If you have the codeword HEIGHT, turn to **514**. If you have the codeword MILE, turn to **621**. If you have the codeword EYE, turn to **572**. (If you have more than one of these codewords you may choose which section to turn to.) If you have none of these codewords, turn to **595**.

679

Leaving the others to relate the news, you take the now familiar Orphus Latix, wilted and brown around its dark green edges, and fly to a plateau at the summit of the mountain. In the Forest of Arcendak it grew on quite rocky ground so you locate a similar area.

You kneel and reverently place the plant in the ground, willing the earth, rock and vegetation to take it and grant it a second lease of life. The power channelling through your hands is reassuring...but only time will tell how successful you have been. If it doesn't grow now, then that's it.

Some time later, the other group returns, bringing with them one of the female Ariax, alive! There is rejoicing at this rare bit of good news! Turn to **622**.

680

Xoroan suddenly launches himself impetuously at the yaks, eager for blood! Roll the die, adding one to the roll if you have the codeword OUT. If the total is 4 or less, turn to **538**. If the total is 5 or more, turn to **632**.

681

You channel your fear and desperation into your magic and command the hostile plants to withdraw. To your relief (and the amazement of the other Ariax) they do, slithering from your bodies as quickly as they had come!

Just at that moment a huge black creature with scaly skin, burning red eyes and massive jaws bursts through the bushes, but you are already gone and adrenalin carries you all to safety, the last Ariax scrambling skywards without the loss of so much as a feather!

High in the sky, the others cannot thank you enough – you have undoubtedly saved everyone's lives! But now it is time to refocus on your task. You could head generally westwards? (Turn to **598**) Or east? (Turn to **634**).

682

As you reach the open air above the forest you glance down. There at the uppermost window of the tower stands the wizard, a look of anger on his face. He reaches out his hands and the air is suddenly filled with dagger-like shards of ice which arc through the sky towards you at lightning speed! But you are out of range; the ice-daggers dissolve into thin air before they can reach you. You have escaped, but it is clearly not a good idea to linger here any longer than you have to! Turn to **541**.

683

You fly on for a couple of hours over hills and valleys, fields and scrubland. You find that the weather is much better further south! When you see a huge forest spread across the horizon, you quicken your pace to explore more closely!

As you approach, you notice a circular tower projecting skywards amid the sea of green. It is reminiscent of the Tower of Egratar, though much smaller and built of dark-grey stone. The roof is conical and of maroon slate. A single black opening serves as a window in its uppermost region. Do you want to:

Investigate this tower?	Turn to **469**
Screech for birdmen as you did before?	Turn to **626**
Or fly around the forest, searching silently?	Turn to **550**

684

Your sense of direction is (as always) impeccable and you soon arrive safely back in Dunstad. If you sent Gravelax out to scout and disrupt the orcs, turn to **452**. If you sent anyone else but not Gravelax, turn to **675**. If you chose not to send anyone, turn to **444**.

685

Out in the open, the orcs are cutting swathes through the defenders. Unless you act swiftly, this will turn into a bloodbath. Will you try and organise a counter charge? (Turn to **552**) Or an organised retreat to the Hieronaught? (Turn to **637**)

686

You have to reflect that the men of Dunstad are even less hardy than you had guessed: they are being pushed back everywhere and very few remain alive out in the open. You fell two more orcs with savage talon strikes but there are more and more of them and you are forced to take to the air, blood streaming from an arm wound. You are joined by the others and watch hopelessly as the door to the Hieronaught is kicked in and the men inside are massacred.

The battle for Dunstad has been lost and there are tragically few survivors. With a heavy heart you signal that you should fly south. It is a while before anyone breaks the sombre silence. Turn to **650**.

687

You turn round, looking for new danger behind you but instead see Scancaro locked in combat with Nimax, who wields a Scarfell spear! As he sees you from the corner of his eye, Scancaro calls for your help! What is going on?

React on instinct. If you have the codeword BLAST, turn to **537**. If you do not have this codeword you could either attack Nimax (turn to **483**) or demand he releases Scancaro (turn to **610**)?

688

You swoop down towards the ramming party, slashing out with your talons and pulling sharply up again. Your targets howl in pain, but four more burly orcs move in to defend the rammers, brandishing long spars of wood torn from a demolished hut.

The battering ram thuds into the wall once again. You must act quickly and use your magic to break the battering ram (now needing a 5 or more to succeed). If you make this magic roll, turn to **608**. If you fail it, turn to **490**.

689

Ossen returns to the group buzzing with excitement! He trips over his words in his haste to explain what he has seen. While searching for shelter he happened across a group of humans, and despite the language barrier, "made friends" with them! You are apprehensive; you have met humans (who are not Scarfells) before in Iro and they were largely mistrusting and suspicious of you. But Ossen's enthusiasm is hard to dampen and you find yourself agreeing to go with him.

You glide down to land a short distance from the humans so as not to frighten them and ask what they are doing out here in the wilds. The bedraggled group seem less wary of you than you had imagined and you are approached by an elderly man with wispy grey hair plastered to his head with the rain.

"Orcs!" he spits. Several of the female humans begin weeping at the very mention of the word. The old man tells you how dozens of these orcs, 'green-skinned humanoid creatures who delight in wanton destruction' rampaged through his village of Burbruk earlier today, killing most of the inhabitants! He and any others who could fled for the hills.

A short man with a shaven head and his arm in a sling steps forwards. "The orcs will feast tonight but tomorrow I fear they will set a course for Dunstad, the next village along from us! It is quite a way on foot or we would warn them…"

If you offer to carry the news of the orcs to Dunstad, turn to **673**. If you would sooner leave the humans to sort out their own business, turn to **540**.

690

You are relieved to see the outlines of three of the Scarfells diminishing into the distance, winging their way back to Musk. The other three lie dead amongst five Ariax bodies.

There were plenty of witnesses to Nimax's final act of treachery. Ritsbrik, whose report led to your search for the forest-birdmen, steps up before you. "We have all been taken in by that crafty bird, Nimax," he says. "He intended to murder you with a Scarfell spear just now – and we'd have all counted you as just another casualty." It is true that your life has been again saved by a fellow Ariax.

Ritsbrik continues. "I came across Nimax in the mountains. He tricked me into telling you the lie about the dead birdman: he wanted to get rid of you so that he could become Talotrix in your absence. I went along with it because I believed his tale about you and the firebrand snake. I am truly sorry."

Those others who were taken in by Nimax's lies concur. When the motion is put forward for you to be the new Talotrix, there are no dissenters; the decision is unanimous.

Over the next few days, life begins to return to a new definition of normal. You use your magic to extend the cave system you are living in and create concealed look out posts in case the Scarfells return. With your appointment has come a feeling of moving on and a renewed air of optimism. This feel-good factor is increased by two more wonderful pieces of news over the next few weeks. Firstly, the Orphus Latix is showing signs of rejuvenation in its new environment; secondly there are three new hatchlings…one of which is female!

As you stand alone on the summit of the mountain one morning, looking west over the beautiful panorama of New Arian, you reflect on the extraordinary hand that fate has dealt you. A chance meeting with Vashta in the Forest of Arcendak led you to Iro where you learnt of the legend of Nevsaron (and also avoided catching Crackbeak). Because of this you gained your elemental powers and were able to prevent the total annihilation of your tribe by the Scarfells.

Rical glides in to land beside you. You smile at your friend. There is still much work to be done but the future of the tribe, with you at its head, is looking brighter than it has done for some time…

Printed in Great Britain
by Amazon